ASH AND GOLD

LYDIA R. OUTLAND

The author grants the final approval for this literary material.

First printing

This is a work of fiction. Names, characters, places, and events are the product of the author's imagination or are used fictitiously. Any resemblance to actual events, locales, or persons, living or dead, is entirely coincidental.

Print ISBN: 978-1-68433-886-3
PUBLISHED BY BLACK ROSE WRITING
www.blackrosewriting.com

Black Rose Writing | Texas

ISBN: 978-1-68433-886-3
PUBLISHED BY BLACK ROSE WRITING
www.blackrosewriting.com

Printed in the United States of America
Suggested Retail Price (SRP) $24.95

Ash and Gold is printed in Calluna

ACKNOWLEDGMENTS

Endless thanks to my family and friends who have supported and encouraged me throughout everything. I am so truly blessed.

Special thanks to Tessa, Emma, Luke, Aaron, my uncle Chris, my father and my wonderful mother for giving up their time, efforts, and advice to help bring about this little novel of mine.

I also wanted to thank the members of the WriteOrWrong Virtual Book Club and the Black Rose Writing community for their kindness and overwhelming support.

And of course, thanks to Reagan Rothe and the Black Rose Writing team, because without them this novel would never have seen the light of day.

ASH AND GOLD

"TRUE—nervous—very, very dreadfully nervous I had been and am; but why will you say that I am mad? The disease had sharpened my senses— not destroyed—not dulled them. Above all was the sense of hearing acute. I heard all things in the heaven and in the earth. I heard many things in hell. How then am I mad?"

—Edgar Allan Poe, *The Tell-Tale Heart*

PROLOGUE:

1997

The woman stumbled, almost falling to her knees in her haste. She managed to catch herself against a brick wall and took a few seconds to rest, pulling in jagged gasps around the chilly air. Her breathing gradually slowed as she squinted into the darkness. It was a gloomy evening. Dim, cold, with a sharp wind that threatened rainstorms soon to come. The woman barely noticed. She was oblivious to the breeze that tugged against her hair and nightgown, or the bits of glass that had lodged themselves in her bare feet as she ran down the vacant alley. No, her attention was enveloped solely in the great swell of her belly, the weight of which had caused her many imbalanced stumbles during her impromptu stroll through the darkening city.

She had encountered few people that night, which was good. The ones she did see were homeless huddled around their trash can fires, looking the very picture of classic poverty. Something worthy of Dorothea Lange's camera. Their eyes had followed her, yellowed mouths opened wide as they watched the pregnant woman stumble by, wearing little more than a white shawl, her brown hair sweaty and flying behind her like some long, dripping train.

She took two deep breaths before continuing, throwing all her strength into putting one foot in front of the other. Time was running out. Her little girl was on the way. As if in response to this thought, a shock of pain racked up the woman's abdomen. She bit back a scream and leaned against the wall, eyes squeezing closed.

"Hold on, hun," she panted under her breath, biting her lip hard as another contraction broke inside her, sending out an intense flood of pain.

Everyone always said it would hurt. No one ever made any secret that childbirth would be painful, but you could never quite understand the earth-shattering nature of such all-consuming agony until you were experiencing it. Loretta decided she could have lived a long and happy life never having to suffer such an experience firsthand. But it was a bit late for that, and time was running short.

"Hang in there, honey," she gasped, bare feet padding against the cold pavement as she continued. "Just a bit longer. Almost there." She was close, so very close. Just a few dark alleys away from the hospital. But as she turned down the first, another contraction sent her to her knees. She groaned, and tears began to flood down her face. The bag she had been carrying dropped heavily to her side, the contents clattering angrily within.

What sick bastard thought this up, anyway? she wondered bitterly. Who had decided, "let's take one of the most natural things in the world, literally *bringing life* to the Earth—giving *birth*—and why don't we make that shit as painful as possible? Sound good?"

Loretta Ambrose didn't think it "sounded good." In fact, she had long ago decided that the entire female makeup was a giant cosmic joke. One big middle finger from nature to womankind. Hmmm, how about, every month you bleed like a stuck pig? How about every month you have horrible cramps, headaches, acne, and bloat up like a disgusting sweaty balloon? How about mood swings that toss you from one side to the other on a rickety ship of emotion in a hurricane of hormonal turmoil? All of this being the body's punishment for **not** being pregnant. Then, when you finally **do** get pregnant, you still swell up like a sweaty balloon, emotionally tossed about, and oh yes, that's right, have some of the most excruciating hours of your life. This being followed by the entire weight of the world landing on your shoulders as you realize this beautiful little human you just created is now wholly, utterly, and helplessly depending upon you not fucking up as a mom.

Well, Loretta thought bitterly, *at least I don't have to worry about that part, do I?*

A sharp, rasping laugh escaped her. It was a shaky thing that turned into a hollow sob deep down in her chest. Her contraction, thankfully, had abated, but instead of getting back to her feet, she plopped herself down on her butt and leaned her back against the large green garbage bin that stood at the mouth of the alley. A little break, yes, that was all she needed. Just a brief rest, and she would be up and on her way to the hospital again.

As she eased her aching... well, *everything*, she stretched her legs out on the dark and dirty concrete. Loretta tried to ignore the sneaking suspicion that this rest wouldn't be brief. Fate knew for a *fact*, it wouldn't be. It knew Loretta was done long before she closed her eyes and slipped from this world and into whatever comes after. It watched her final moments, not with satisfaction, but with inevitable assurance. The calm demeanor of someone, or something, that knows things could go no other way.

Loretta breathed in and out, slow and steady, just as all those books said to do. They had read so many by this point. She remembered last Tuesday, when Cam had sat on the edge of the tub, book open on his lap, and read out loud in that deep and ever so gruff voice of his. The type of voice that was low enough to soothe, but with just enough edge to excite. Loretta had listened, ensconced in a vanilla-scented bubble bath with her stomach poking defiantly above the frothing surface, letting his voice coax her into a calm doze. Oh, how she wished she could hear his voice right now.

"Oh, shit," she said to no one but herself, for the alley was empty save for the few rats that scuttled along the edge of the opposite wall. Their thin, prickly tails whipped behind them in the moonlight that cast everything in an eerie, silver glow. Loretta reached for the discarded bag with much grunting effort and pulled it to her side. She unbuckled the top and pulled out her new Nokia 3110. Cam had bought the cell phones about two months back, one for himself and one for her. They had been expensive to say the least. Loretta nearly choked to death on a spoonful of cereal when Cam had presented them as a surprise. She didn't understand why he would have spent so much on something that they would probably never use. But Cam had insisted, saying that they still had plenty of money left from his mother's inheritance. Besides: "When we need em, we'll **really** need em," and oh, boy, did she need it now.

She dialed and waited as it rang cheerily in her ear, but she wasn't met by Cam's soothing voice. An answering machine's dull, monotone instructions greeted her. She cursed under her breath as his cell went to voicemail.

"Damn it, Cam. The **one** time you don't answer your damn phone." But that wasn't the message she wanted to leave him. Those were not the last words she wanted him to hear coming from her mouth, because they would be the last. She was sure of it now. The baby wasn't waiting. So, as his voice grumbled, "This is Cameron. Leave a message," and the phone gave a loud beep in her ear, she forced a smile onto trembling lips. "Hey babe. It's happening. She's coming. She's coming quick, so please, please call back."

Loretta paused as another contraction flooded her. She squeezed her eyes closed, gritted her teeth, and rode out the storm. She gasped as it passed and went on. "Whoa, that *sucked.* Anyway, I'm not at the hotel. *She* found it. I was dozing when I heard her trying to come in, so I just grabbed the bag and ran out the back. You took the car, so I just ran. Got away. Think I lost her, but I went into labor," Loretta's water had broken barely a block away from her hotel room, sending warm and slick liquid streaming down the inside of her thighs towards her ankles "... guess baby wasn't a fan of all the jiggling," Loretta laughed. "I'm near the hospital now, in an alley just a block or so down the road." She gave him the street name. "Honestly not sure what to do next Babe... should I stay put so you can pick me up here, or should I try to make it to the hospital?" she knew as she said the words that there was no chance of that. She wasn't leaving this alley. She was exhausted, every muscle in her body hurt, and she didn't think her legs would support her *standing,* let alone *moving.* No. This was it. This was her spot. She could call 911, have an ambulance pick her up and take her the rest of the way to the hospital, but therein lay the same issues. Cam wasn't there. But others would be. People that didn't understand. People that wouldn't believe what was happening. Hell, they themselves barely knew what was happening, or what was *going* to happen. But whatever did happen, Cam *needed* to be there. Be there to fix it. To make things right. If he wasn't there when their baby came into the world, so much could go wrong. What would happen to their child? No, he had to be there. He said he would fucking *be there.* He promised her.

"This can't start yet, Babe. You *have* to *be **here*** when she comes or..." her breath rattled in her throat, "Babe, they'll take her away. They'll take her away and you won't be able to—" Another contraction. She breathed through it. "This wasn't the plan at all. I don't know what to do. Cam... I'm scared. What do I do?" her voice broke. "I really need you *here*. We *had* a *plan*... Call me back." She winced as she felt another contraction. "***Now*** would be great." She ended the call, bent down to wrap her arms around her stomach, clenching against the pain. When it passed, she leaned back against the trash bin, panting, and began to cry.

This was ***not*** how it was supposed to go.

Cam was going to go out and pick up the tacos she had been craving for the past hour. Hot tacos, covered in guacamole, absolutely drenched in it. He was supposed to come back, and they would curl up on the bed with some shitty comedy TV show on (*I Love Lucy* probably) and wait for her to go into labor which wasn't supposed to be for a while yet. She was supposed to be cooking a few more weeks at least, but all this sudden running around and jostling had kicked that timeline up and her baby girl was ready to see what all the fuss was about.

It wasn't supposed to be like this.

Cam was supposed to be dancing around her in a new father panic. He was supposed to grab their "baby bag" and bring her to the hospital. In a car. Not on foot. They were *supposed* to go to the hospital together. They were *supposed* to make sure the doctors knew *Cam* was the father, make sure he had custody. To be sure that no one else could claim their baby, to make sure *she* didn't come for their little girl. They were *supposed* to go through all of this ***together***. Loretta was *not* supposed to be alone, in the freezing night, feet full of glass, dragging her pregnant belly to the hospital. This. Was not. The ***plan***. They were supposed to have a chance to say goodbye. They were supposed to have a last kiss. Of course, they *had* a last kiss, they just hadn't known it at the time. Cam had flipped his keys in his hands and leaned down to where she lounged on the bed, surrounded by pillows.

"Don't forget extra guacamole," she reminded him, tugging at his collar, drawing him closer.

"Of course," he said with a grin and a wink. "I'm not an idiot." He had kissed her then. A slight thing, quick but soft, sweet, and to be honest, not the worst last kiss that Loretta could have hoped for. Although, she had hoped for so many more. She had hoped for so many things that she would never have. She ran a trembling hand over her stomach and sighed. Loretta rubbed the tears angrily from her eyes and grabbed the phone from the spot she had dropped it. She redialed Cam's number and forced her voice to be steady.

"Hey, Babe, it's me again. I just thought... I thought I... I wanted to leave our baby girl one more message. Just one more time," Loretta took a ragged breath, running a hand over her belly which was, for the time being, restful. Her little girl had taken a break from kicking around, and she had a brief bout of calm between contractions. That was nice. But it wouldn't last long. It was all about to start...and it was all about to end. "God, babe, I wish you were here," Loretta said, her voice breaking softly around the words, like a hand full of snow, hitting and scattering into flakes of white fluff soon to melt. "But she'll be waiting for you if you can't make it in time. I know you'll figure it out. You will find a way to protect her. So... this is for her. Play it for her someday, will you? When she's ready to hear it. When she really needs it." She took another jagged breath, tears sliding hard and fast down her face, but she did her best to keep her voice clear. "In case we were right, in case things go wrong... Cam, I love you. I love you so much. Always have, always will." She cleared her throat and wiped her eyes, running her hand over her stomach once more. She closed her eyes and smiled. Her heart was breaking and coming together all at once. She was filled with the overwhelming joy of creating this new little life, and the pain of knowing she would never meet it. She cleared the lump from her throat before speaking to her unborn daughter — one last time.

"Hey there, honey. It's me. Your mama. It's been a long ride, huh? Well, you're almost here... and I just have one last thing I need to tell you..."

PART 1:

Twenty-Four Years Later

A girl lay quiet and comfortable in the back seat of the gray, two-door Jeep Wrangler. Her hair spread across the back seat like a brown halo that dripped down and piled into a muddy puddle on the floor below. Her long, pale lashes rested gently on her cheeks, one arm curled as a makeshift pillow under her head while the other dangled off the edge of the seat, fingers lost in her own hair. The seat belts sat forgotten by her head and feet as the car rumbled along the dark road, slowly jostling her awake. She could hear the engine grumbling through the seat against her ear and the sound of a classic rock station playing over a staticky radio system.

Through her muddled, sleep fogged thoughts, she tried to place the sound. She had nothing against the classics, but they were never her go-to. To her friends frequently verbalized dismay, she leaned more towards country. Not that new shit. That fake rapping, pop-infected, nausea-inducing, fallacious mimicry of country that tended to play on the popular stations these days. No. No, she liked older country. Real country. The country music that still said something, still told a story, a *real* story. Dolly Parton, Willie Nelson, Merle Haggard, and of course, Johnny Cash, those were her idols. Her friends Cooper, Linny, and Andrew had grown so tired of their biggest hits (which she frequently had on re-play) that they cursed their names and whined whenever it was her turn to take charge of the playlist.

No, classic rock was Cooper's wheelhouse. He was the type of guy who knew when every AC/DC album came out and where it was the biggest hit. He could name the bass players of every band from Led Zeppelin to CCR and knew every lyric to every song by heart. When it came to country, however, she was the master. Country was all hers.

So, she couldn't for the life of her remember why there would be classic rock on the radio. Not that classic rock in the car was utterly uncommon. Cooper was the only one out of their little group that had a working vehicle at the moment, and that gave him almost ultimate power over the playlist. Cooper, however, had left town the night before to visit his sister three cities over and would be away for at least a week.

So, that left just two questions. Who was playing classic rock? And more importantly, whose car was she in?

The girl scrunched her eyes tighter together before finally, regretfully, opening them. She had been teased ruthlessly in elementary school and junior high for those eyes. Not because of the rather mediocre, muddy brown pigment that had bored her every time she looked in the mirror, or the thick but almost translucent array of lashes that were invisible without mascara. No, it was the sheer size of her eyes that caused her so much grief as a child. Her eyes were so large that she had earned the terribly clever nicknames of "buggy," "bugs," and "fly face." One time in elementary school, a little girl with brown braids, pink ribbons, and an already fully developed resting bitch face named Candy Finberge had run up to her on the playground and called her "souzer eyes." When she had slowly blinked at Candy and asked if she had meant "saucer eyes," the little bitch-faced girl had given an indignant, and quite loud, hissy fit. She had then stormed off with a final shriek of "Stupid bug eyes!" over her shoulder.

As the years passed, and junior high shifted to high school, the calls of "bug eyes," and "fly face," quickly dissipated. Although her eyes didn't shrink, the rest of her began to grow and fill out, making her eyes less awkward when set in an older face and taller frame. Suddenly, her large eyes were not so much a punch line as they were an excuse for boys to lean on her desk with cocky smiles and a "my, my, what large eyes you have." She would then respond with the expected "the better to see you with, my dear." Giggling would ensue, oddly enough from the guy's side, not from her, and then usually by that point the teacher would walk in and make everyone take their seats. "Saucer eyes" and "fly face" had been completely forgotten. Unfortunately, one nickname had stuck and stuck tight.

Buggy blinked in that slow way she had, giving her lids plenty of time to travel the vast distance from opposite sides of her irises and back again. As her vision cleared, so did her mind. When the clouds of sleep were finally fanned away from the surface of her consciousness, her heart began thudding wildly in her chest.

What the hell was going on?

She was in the back seat of some two-door Jeep she didn't recognize with two guys, two utter strangers, in the front. Buggy couldn't make out much about them in the darkness, only the vague glimpses caught through passing headlights or taillights that briefly illuminated their faces in a blinding white or ominous red. The driver was a man in his late forties or early fifties. Streaks of gray decorated a full head of coarse, brown hair that traveled down the side of his face to a short, scruffy beard. He wore a dark blue or black button-down shirt with the sleeves rolled up, revealing a large watch and what looked like a circular tattoo on the inside of his wrist. His companion looked to be in his mid to late twenties, not much older than Buggy herself. She couldn't tell if that red in his brown hair was actually there or if it was merely a trick of the taillights. His silhouette suggested a long nose, high cheekbones, and sharp, clean-cut jawline. Buggy would have easily found him handsome under any other circumstance, but she was a little distracted by the terror bubbling inside her gut to give much notice. The younger man was fiddling with the staticky radio as the other complained in a low, irritated grumble.

"Theo. Pick. A. Station. You're driving me crazy."

"You need a better radio," the other answered, ignoring his friend's complaint and continuing to shift through the fuzzy channels, skipping a rap station Buggy didn't recognize and a country one she did. She heard a chorus of "Mama Tried" by Merle Haggard before the channel shifted again. Buggy almost asked them to turn it back, but the sound of her own heart thudding in her throat and ears would have made it hard to hear anyway.

"Yeah, I know, I know, bitch about it one more time, why don't you," the older man grumbled in a gravely tone that suggested his lungs were extremely familiar with nicotine and smoke.

Buggy didn't move. She didn't sit up. She barely breathed. She just lay there completely still, listening to these strangers bickering like an old married couple over a broken radio, and tried to remember how she got there.

She had been at work.

Being a dental hygienist wasn't the most glamorous of professions, but it had suited her just fine for the past few years. The environment was nice and bright, and her coworkers were friendly. Most of them even liked country music, so they got along just fine. In fact, Elwin Family Dentistry was where Buggy first met Linny. Linny had already been working at Elwin's for a year and a half before Buggy stepped in fresh out of Sacramento City College with an Associate's Degree in one hand, a Certificate of Achievement in another, and two extremely large eyes wide with excitement.

Lin Luan Williams had been coming out of a particularly plaque-filled appointment and her ninth, "Do you floss? No? Well, get on that," comment of the day. Her nerves were frayed to the breaking point when Buggy dinged the little bell on the table. Linny had looked up, ready to paste on an all too fake smile that instead dropped into a glittery, lip gloss-smeared "O."

"Hello," Buggy had said, "My name's Briar Pierce. I'm... well, it's my first day." Linny had simply sat there, mouth open, before saying very loudly:

"Holy shit sticks, girl. How do those eyes fit in there?"

Buggy had laughed out loud. Linny had grinned and instantly claimed the girl as her own. She had taken care of Buggy like a big-eyed puppy dog, showed her the ropes, and had been her best friend ever since.

It had been a long Monday, and Buggy had been worn out. Erratic sleep, bad dreams, and a particularly rough weekend had made the walk to the bus station more a show of dragging feet. She had been headed home for dinner with her sister, Sandra, who she hadn't seen for a few days. Buggy wasn't exactly excited about it. There was going to be a loaded discussion that Buggy had been dreading ever since Sandra found her little secret stashed in her top left dresser drawer, but Buggy knew she couldn't avoid it forever. She really did need to talk to someone, and not just about *that*. About everything. All the dreams, the weird things that had been happening to her recently. Keeping it bottled up was killing her. She needed to tell someone. It was time. So, she was headed home.

Linny had left early that day, and Buggy had been one of the last out the door. She remembered waving goodbye to Candice, the receptionist, and heading towards the station a few blocks down the road. She had been taking the bus ever since her car decided to up and die on her without warning a little over a week prior, but she didn't mind so much. The buses were well-kept around her hometown of Marshall County California. Besides, she had always liked a pleasant walk.

That was where her memory ended. Walking. A rather exhausted walk, but beautiful all the same. A cold December winter had taken over the city which meant two things: it started growing dark around five-thirty when she got off, and Christmas lights. They all began turning on one by one as she made her way down the street. Red, green, and bright white lights blinked, flickered, and winked warmly at her as her boots clicked against the cold pavement, gleaming with hours-old rain and reflecting twinkle lights. The roads were busy, full of people in their cars heading home from a long day's work, eager to be inside and out of the cold. Ready to be curled up by the fire with a cup of something hot and strong clasped between thawing fingers. One car zoomed by with its windows slightly rolled down and "I'll Be Home for Christmas" trickling into the sky. The streets were busy, but the sidewalks were bare. Nobody wanted to be out in the frosty air.

Buggy remembered tugging her long, wool coat tighter around her, a puff of breath fluttering from her mouth as she picked up the pace and turned the corner towards the bus station. Then someone had called her name. Not her nickname. Not even her first name, Briar, or even her surname, Pierce. They called her by a name that was just as much her own, but which she had never used a day in her life.

"Bennu." It had been spoken extremely near, in a voice unfamiliar. Buggy had turned and then... there was nothing. She didn't remember what happened next. She didn't remember seeing anyone, she didn't remember everything going dark, or the hands that caught her before she could fall. She was on the street, and then she was in the car. Buggy took a mental inventory of her condition. She felt no pain. Her hands were not tied, her legs were not bound, and her head had not been hit. She had hit her head before, tripped like the ungainly klutz that she was, and knocked herself out. Her head had throbbed for days. No, if they had knocked her out, it wasn't by brute force.

How she got here was an interesting question. However, the more important question was: what the hell was she going to do now? By the speed at which the other car lights, lamp posts, and street signs were zipping past, they couldn't be going any slower than fifty-five, and there was no way she could leap out of the car without likely killing herself or being hit by another vehicle on the freeway. If she waited until they reached their destination... well, she really didn't want to do that either. She *was* curious why they had not tied her up. The first rule of kidnapping someone, right? Make sure they can't get away? And why in hell was she being kidnapped in the first place? It wasn't like she was part of some wealthy family that would pay for her safe return with a stack of unmarked bills in a black suitcase. She had family, but they made moderate incomes. Nobody was going to bed on sheets made of money, which is the usual go-to for kidnappings, at least as far as her extensive knowledge of TV crime shows was concerned. Buggy also had friends, but they barely had enough money to scrape together rent every month, so it couldn't be that either. No, if they wanted her, it wasn't for money. That didn't soothe her. In fact, it only terrified her more, because if they were not after money, what the hell *did* they want? She didn't want to find that out.

"I gotta use the John," the younger man said, having given up on the static-free radio search and left it on an almost audible Christmas station.

"Again?" the older man chuckled. "You're worse than a woman."

"Shut up and pull over," the younger man snipped. "There's a rest stop at that next off-ramp." Buggy remained very still as she felt the car pulling off to the right and beginning to slow down.

"She still asleep back there?" the gruff voice asked, and Buggy slammed her eyelids closed, praying to God that it was in time as the younger man turned in his seat.

"Like a baby," he said, and then paused. "You really think this was the best plan? I mean, couldn't we have tried talking to her first?"

"Trust me," the gruff voice answered as the car slowed to a stop and the parking brake gave a little creak as he pulled it into place. "She wouldn't have listened. This is the only way. If she is anything like... I know her. We didn't have time, and she won't trust easy."

I know her? Buggy wondered, mind whirling, trying to place his face, but quite sure she had never met the man before in her life.

"And this is supposed to help that, how?" the young man asked. Buggy could almost hear the auburn eyebrow cocking on his forehead.

"Just hurry up and get back, will ya?" the gruff voice answered. "We got to put as much space between us and that town as possible before sunrise."

"Alright, alright, I'm goin', I'm goin'." There was the sound of shifting, the sweet creak of an old hinge-door being opened, and the thud and shake of the door being closed.

Buggy waited, breathless, trying to stop her hands from trembling. She wanted to give the younger man time to be far enough away before she made her move. On the radio, John Lennon was singing "Happy Xmas (War Is Over)," and Buggy slowly opened her eyes. The older man was leaning back in his seat, one hand resting on the wheel, the other on his lap. He was humming along with the song, head turned towards the driver side window, looking out at something Buggy couldn't see, as John Lennon sang on.

Buggy launched forward. She shoved the empty passenger seat down, threw open the door with an indignant whine of hinges, and bolted out. Her captor had been so surprised by her sudden movement that it took him a few seconds to react. She slammed the door closed behind her just as he lunged. He hit the door hard, and she was already running.

"Help!" she screamed with every ounce of air in her lungs. "Somebody, help me!" She screamed and ran, for who, or towards where, she didn't know. Lights shone brightly by the bathroom showing, to her terror, a nearly empty parking lot. She caught sight of one lonely semi-truck parked off at the far end of the rest stop, and she ran for it. No, running up to strangers in a truck isn't really a good idea, but it seemed better than the alternative. But she never got the chance. Before she could make it even a few steps farther, a strong pair of arms folded around her, and she toppled onto the pavement. She hissed in pain as her knee tore open under her jeans.

"Get off of me!" she yelled, trying to shake off the man who was now holding her down. "Get off of me, you son of a bitch!"

"Aida please, calm down," the man said in that same gruff voice, now out of breath.

"Who's Aida? Get the fuck off me." Buggy twisted under the man's grip, found one of his hands, and bit down hard. He yelped in a most unmanly high-pitch fashion and instinctively pulled away. Buggy took the opportunity to wriggle out of his grip, stagger to her feet, and start running again.

"Stop!" the man had gotten up and started off after her. "Please, just wait!"

She did not wait. She ran and ran until....

"Bennu!"

Buggy's steps slowed to a walk. She stared down at her feet as they stuttered even further from a walk to a sludgy scrapping against the cold pavement, and finally stopped altogether. She watched them with utter amazement and horror. Why the hell was she stopping? She didn't want to stop. She wanted to run to whatever corner of the Earth was farthest away from those two nut jobs, but her legs, her damn legs, were betraying her before her eyes.

"Bennu..." the voice spoke again, closer this time, almost soothing. Buggy began to feel lightheaded. Despite every fiber of her soul screaming at her to do the opposite, she turned back around. They were both there. The older man cradling his wounded hand and his companion who had caught up to them from the bathrooms. He was the one who said the name, and he was the one who spoke again. When the final syllable was out of the young man's mouth, Buggy's knees buckled. The world swirled around her as she tipped in slow motion towards the ground. From far off, she could still hear John Lennon's voice gently singing of hopes and fears, but even that was fading into a dampened white noise, muffled by the curtain drawing closed over her mind. Everything grew dark around the edges, as the two strangers stepped towards her.

"Wha...." Buggy stumbled but caught herself, blinking long and slow. "What's happening?" she mumbled, tongue stiff and heavy in her mouth. The strangers cautiously made their way to her side.

"Don't be afraid," the older man said, reaching out towards her, blood dripping slowly down his wrist from her teeth marks.

"Fuukk... youuu..." the words slurred from her lips as the world grew darker.

"And this is supposed to be good how, exactly?" the younger man asked, glancing up at his companion with a scowl.

Buggy's head spun fast, her arms began to tremble, and she tipped forward. "Oh shit!" The young man was able to catch her before her head hit the pavement, but by that time, Buggy was asleep.

PART 2:

10 Days Previously

I

Briar Rose Pierce (or "Buggy" as she was more affectionately known) was named because of how she was found. Her parents loved to tell and retell the tale. Every birthday morning, they would crawl into her bed, snuggling up as much as they could, her dad's long legs still hanging off the edge anyhow. Her mom would plant a kiss on her cheek, and they would paint the picture of a little newborn baby girl found fast asleep. She had been woken by the kiss of a handsome prince who brought her, joyously, into her parents' arms. As she grew older, the birthday story continued, but it slowly morphed into the real events, which were a little less fairytale. Little newborn Buggy had been asleep when she was found, but not because of some witch's spell. She had been an inch from death, abandoned in an alley beside a big, green trashcan. It had been dumb luck that she was found at all. She was chilled to the bone, sprinkled with rain, on a cold, fall evening covered in dirt, ash, dust, trash, and a tattered white nightgown, which was the only thing her birth mother had left to protect her from the cold. Well, that, and the bag, of course.

The "prince" that woke her with a kiss had actually been a paramedic named Jerry Keller. He had given her CPR to restart her little heart. Jerry still checked in every couple of years. The experience had been fairly traumatic for him. At the time, he had a newborn at home tucked in safe and sound with his wife. As he watched Buggy's little limp body slumping against his efforts, all he could think was, "she could be mine." When she finally drew her first breath and began to cry wildly, he joined her without hesitation. He kept an eye on her ever since, through her hospital stay and even through the process of adoption when the Pierces officially welcomed her into their little family.

So, Briar Rose became her name, but even her parents didn't call her by it anymore. Just as everyone else in her life had done, they had adopted

"Buggy" with ease. It had been so long since Buggy had actually heard her real name that she didn't even recognize it when it was called to her across the counter at the dentist's office.

"Briar! Is that you? Little Briar Rose?" Buggy looked up to see a man smiling at her with a wide, bleach-toothed grin. He had a slightly pudgy build that spoke of many nights in front of the TV with a beer in one hand and a bag of cheesy Doritos in the other. His hair was graying, and a little messy in the back, as if he had forgotten to brush it before leaving the house and resorted to using his fingers as a makeshift comb. Although the rest of him, down to his slightly rumpled white button-down shirt, was a bit haphazardly put together, his teeth were obviously immaculately cared for. Perhaps even a bit obsessively. Recognizing him, Buggy remembered seeing several little tubes of toothpaste, dental floss, and a travel toothbrush in his desk when he opened it briefly to get a pen or calculator to explain an equation.

Buggy smiled. "Hello, Mr. Harrison. How are you doing today?" Her high school AP calculus teacher leaned against the counter, flashing another proud white smile her way, gray flyaway hair swaying comically above his head.

"Well, gee, I'm doing just fine! Just come in for a cleaning. What have you been up to, my most diligent student?" Another nickname of hers, but one explicitly reserved for Mr. Harrison. She had been a decent student all through high school. Buggy was never an honor roll, most likely to succeed, or valedictorian type of girl, but she got decent grades and worked hard for them. Harrison, and several other of her teachers, seemed to appreciate that in her. Unlike many of the other students who were either skating through with half rolled eyes and "don't really give a shit" attitudes, or even those few brainiacs who found everything so easy and nearly pinned their straight A's to their shirt like some sort of medal of honor, her teachers tended to like Buggy. They appreciated that she actually *tried* and took her under their wing on more than one occasion when she found herself struggling. Harrison was one of her frequent helpers. Buggy and mathematics had never been friends. They had a mutual distaste of each other at best, and straight-up hostilities at worst. Mr. Harrison had been more than happy to lend a hand.

"Oh, a little of this, a little of that," Buggy said with a warm smile that lit up her large eyes in a way that proved nearly hypnotizing to the lucky viewer, although she was usually unaware of this fact. She wasn't exactly a shockingly beautiful girl. In most ways, she was rather plain, to be honest. Average height, a little lean on the weight, with a long torso, arms, and legs. Her skin was a lovely, tanned honey color (which she liked), but she also had plain and almost lank brown hair that tumbled in uneven waves down to her hips (which she did not like). Buggy usually tied it back in a low ponytail or braid to keep it out of her way. She had rather thick brows that she never tamed to her satisfaction, but also a sweet button nose that gave her face a young quality. She was a young woman, but that button nose and the liberal spattering of freckles on her sharp cheeks and shoulders, not to mention the large doe eyes, gave the impression that she would be turning sixteen in the upcoming month, not having turned twenty-four a few months back. She also had a severe resting expression that usually made her appear unapproachable and in a constant state of mild irritation. But it was those eyes, those shining eyes that glittered with light when she was happy and when her resting expression broke into a genuine smile. The eyes that had caused her so much grief as a child were the same feature that revealed a warmth in her, a light that made her attractive in ways that were not initially striking but ultimately cast a stronger hold.

"Still in school?" Harrison asked. Buggy nodded.

"I've got one AA under my belt and taking a few classes here and there."

"Ever consider a four-year?"

Buggy shrugged and nodded. "Just saving up a little before I do."

"Good," Harrison smacked a ringed hand on the counter. He had been divorced long since Buggy had known him, but he had never taken off the ring. It was one of those things that everyone noticed, but no one dared speak of. "And you enjoy working here, I take it?"

"Oh, she loves it," Linny said, coming to lean heavily against Buggy's shoulder, flashing a smile at the man standing on the other side of the counter. Her red hair was twisted into a messy bun at the top of her head, and her lips had the same bright lip gloss sheen that seemed permanently fixed to her smile. "Too much actually. We have to kick her out the door when her shift is over."

"Okay, I'm not that bad," Buggy frowned over her shoulder.

"Eleven times," Linny said, ignoring Buggy and speaking to Mr. Harrison as if he was the only person in the room. "Eleven times, she's stayed hours after she should have gone home."

It was true. Along with freakishly large, and expressive, eyes Buggy was also born a bit OCD. She couldn't leave work until all her equipment had been sanitized and wiped down at least twice and lined up by systematic size and use. She had a method, and she couldn't leave until every bit of the method was completed. She knew this about herself and was good about getting a head start on the cleanup. She was usually very successful, finishing in plenty of time before her shift had ended. However, every so often, the end of the day would sneak up on her. Someone arrived late to their appointment, or someone else was squeezed in at the last minute, cutting into precious "cleanup" time. Everyone else simply cleaned up in a hurry and ducked out when their time was up like normal human beings. But Buggy had a method, and she couldn't go home until it was finished. Just like she couldn't go to the bathroom without washing her hands before and after to the tune of "ABC," or walk out her front door without checking the lock three times or fall asleep without first turning on and off her bedroom light (also three times) and tapping the dream catcher that always—always—hovered above her bed. Did any of that really make sense? Not even to Buggy. But she couldn't seem to stop it either.

"I have never put in for overtime or anything like that," Buggy reassured Mr. Harrison as if he would judge her for something that he didn't even know she had. Or at least, she thought he didn't know. Mr. Harrison might be in permanent denial about his marital status, but that didn't make him unobservant. He had always seen the way Buggy had lined up every pen, pencil, and eraser beside her immaculately cared for notebooks. Other kids put their stickers, their logos, their "Danny loves Mary" scribbles across the front of their books, even their textbooks, but not Buggy. Her things were clean, clear of any personalization, which was sort of a personalization in of itself. He also remembered when a passing student had bumped her desk, casting a cursory apology over his shoulder as he made his way to the back of the room, not noticing the look of utter horror on the girls face as her pens were sent cascading from their perfect place, bouncing against the floor. He had watched her eyes widen so far that, for a split second, he wondered if they would fall out of her head and bounce in pursuit of her pens. Her little mouth had begun to open, and for another terrible moment, he thought she may start to scream or burst into tears. She had done neither. She had simply closed her mouth, took three deep breaths in her nose, and out her mouth, then reached over to retrieve her runaway writing equipment, and lined them slowly and carefully back into position on her desk.

"I'm sure you didn't, dear," Mr. Harrison smiled. She wasn't the type to make her troubles anyone else's. She tucked them deep into her pockets and kept them all for herself. "Welp," he said, tapping that ringed hand on the counter one last time before pushing away and straightening up with a groan and a rather loud snap from a particularly distressed section of his spine, "I better get out of your hair."

"It was nice to see you, Mr. Harrison," Buggy said, giving him another one of those smiles that would be tugging the corner of his mouth up for the rest of the day.

"Nice to see you to, Briar Rose." Harrison waved to Linny, who returned it with a little lazy wiggle of her fingers, and stepped out the door, bumping the bell that hung above it and sending a cheerful jingling sound to mix with a gust of chilly November air.

"Nice guy," Linny said, leaning against the counter, "Your old high school teacher?"

"Yes, he is, and yes, he was," Buggy answered, turning her attention down to the paperwork she had been doing before Mr. Harrison's more than welcome interruption. This was partly because she *did* need to review the schedule before the end of the day, but also because she knew by Linny's tone what was about to come out of her mouth next. Sure enough.

"Were you guys doin' it?" Linny asked as matter-of-fact as if she had been wondering which class he taught. Buggy let out a sigh as her head dropped hard in good-natured exasperation, her chin hitting her chest.

"No, Linny, we were never 'doin' it.'"

"Just asking, you never know," Linny said, holding up her hands in the universal sign of 'whoa chill bro, it's all good.' "It would just explain a few things is all."

"What do you mean?" Buggy asked, not sure if she actually wanted the answer. She didn't, by the way.

"Like, why he was so *super-duper* excited to see you again," Linny said, adding a ditsy, teen girl lilt to her words. "No teacher of mine ever lit up like that when I walked into a room."

"Well, that's probably just because you gave them too much shit during class time."

Linny thought, shrugged, but wouldn't be cowed. "And it would also explain why you never date anyone... you know... like ever." Buggy laughed out loud.

"Because I'm pining after Mr. Harrison?" she chortled.

"Yeah, I guess not," Linny said, eyes narrowing at Mr. Harrisons retreating back as he made his way across the parking lot. "You could have done better. Unless he was a real looker back then and just... took a wrong, *wrong,* turn somewhere down the road," She looked down at Buggy with wisdom in her green eyes. "Not all men are like fine wine."

Buggy laughed but reached out and smacked Linny's arm. "Shush, he's a really nice person!"

"Oh, I'm sure he's got a **greeeeat personality.**" Linny nodded and dodged as Buggy moved to smack her again, "Well, enough girl talk, we got work to do," Linny ducked out of the entry room and into the back office out of sight. Buggy turned back to her paperwork but looked up as a tutting noise disturbed her focus. "Not that work, *Briar Rose,*" Linny held up the box in her hands and jiggled it. The contents trilled and ruffled with an unmistakable sound. Buggy frowned, thick brows scrunching together to form a disapproving line over her doe eyes.

"Christmas decorations?" she asked, "Now? Really? It's not even December yet."

"Oh, pish posh," Linny said, waving one hand dramatically in the air, temporarily dropping the box, only to snatch the edge again before the contents tipped and spilled out all over the floor, "It'll be December in like, four days. Besides," She looked around the empty waiting room, which had been vacant most of the day apart from Mr. Harrison, and that little girl who cried every time she came in for a cleaning. Other than those two, the day had been unusually quiet. "When are we going to have another day this mellow, huh? Might as well take advantage." Buggy thought, shrugged, and got to her feet, tossing her pen on the paperwork that could honestly wait an hour or two.

"Why not?" she said, lighting her face with a smile, "Let Christmas begin!"

2

Buggy slipped into the seat of her car, slamming the door behind her. She wasn't generally the "slam a door" type of person, but the hinges on her old, blue Toyota Corolla had been growing consistently stickier over the past year, to the point where she needed to give it a strong tug or the door wouldn't close at all. The slamming was just an unfortunate side effect. Her stepdad, Simon, had been trying to convince her to let him buy her a new car (or at least pay for some repairs) for the better part of two years. It was a lovely offer, but she always turned him down. Buggy didn't really like taking any kind of help from Simon, no matter how well intentioned his efforts. It was probably unfair how against his help she was. Buggy could tell how much he wanted to do *something* for her. She knew he was hoping it would turn into some bonding moment between them. The time when she *finally* accepted one of the many offers of assistance he had given over the years after marrying Buggy's mom. Cars, new clothes, trips out of town, flights to visit old pen pals in other states. She turned them all down with a smile and a "thank you," but a "no" all the same. The only time she had been tempted was when she had been accepted into Claremont McKenna College, a very prestigious four-year university that her high school friend Stella Bellson (one of her only real friends at the time, other than Cooper) was also, astonishingly, planning to attend. It had been dumb luck that they both had gotten in, and they spent an entire week celebrating. Buggy played along, not wanting to rain on Stella's parade, but also knowing she would probably not go with her.

Claremont was expensive. Extremely expensive, and because both her parents had solid incomes, she didn't qualify for financial aid. She had held onto hope for a scholarship or two, but the few she qualified for ended up going to other students, leaving Buggy to break the bad news to Stella. Stella had cried and said they would Skype all the time and text every day.

Every day turned into every week, then to every month, until finally it had stopped altogether. Sure, they sent "Happy Birthday!" messages, and liked Instagram updates, but other than that their friendship had frankly fizzled out. Buggy had not been surprised. That was the way of things, wasn't it? Some people moved on. Some people got left behind. Buggy wondered from time to time what it would have been like if she had taken her stepfather up on his offer.

Hearing the news of her acceptance letter and financial situation, Simon had instantly offered to pay for all four years, along with any train or plane rides back and forth for visits with family. That had been the only time she had hesitated. Buggy had seen the gleam in his eye when he thought he finally had her. But she only smiled and shook her head.

After all, Simon liked to offer all these things, but he and Buggy's mom weren't exactly independently wealthy. They were reasonably well-to-do, he being a fairly successful defense attorney, and she holding down a respectable state position. Still, they were not in a place to be throwing money around either. Not at the levels of a costly four-year university. Especially after her mother had surprised Buggy with the news that she would be a big sister soon. Well, half-sister, and *soon* was a few years back now. Little Jasmine (or Jaz as she was more commonly called) had celebrated her fifth birthday last August. But money had never been the main reason Buggy's answer was always in the negative.

Buggy simply didn't **want** to accept her stepfather's help. It wasn't a cruel thing or even a power thing. She liked Simon well enough. He was a nice guy and good to her mom, but she could never bring herself to take him up on his offers because it felt too much like betraying her dad. Brandon Pierce was not a wealthy lawyer, but a middle-class divorcee working a full-time state job that paid quite well but didn't afford him much to throw around after bills were paid and taxes were taken care of. He had plenty to live a comfortable life, but not enough on his own to buy Buggy a car at random or pay for tuition. Although she knew he would in a heartbeat if he could. Taking Simon up on *anything* felt too much like spitting at her father's feet, and she would never do that. She liked Simon, but he would always be "the guy that's not my dad." He couldn't help that, and she never blamed him, not for her parents' divorce, not for anything. After all, that had nothing to do with him.

Buggy's parents had been discussing divorce behind closed doors for at least a year before Simon was even a blip on the radar screen of their lives. They had only met because discussions turned to actions shortly before Buggy's seventeenth birthday. Her parents had started consulting with divorce lawyers, and Simon happened to be an old friend of her mother's current lawyer, who just happened to stop by for a visit while Buggy's mom was finishing up a meeting. Despite the awkward, and some would say (including Buggy herself, although she never mentioned this to her mother) inappropriate circumstances of their meeting, their affair began. As soon as things were settled between her parents, Simon did his very best to endear himself to Buggy and her older sister Sandra. Not in a desperate, "I want you to like me because I love your mom" way, but with a genuine desire to be liked. Sandra, being the open-hearted person that she was, had welcomed Simon without hesitation. Buggy was grateful for this, seeing as it allowed her to keep Simon at arm's length without feeling too guilty, but Simon never gave up on trying to connect with her. It was an insistent wish that started small at first but which grew over the years to an almost piteous pitch. However, Buggy's dad would always be her dad, and Simon would always be "that nice guy that sits next to her mom at the dinner table." The one who called her daughter but was not her father. Nothing personal. It was just how it had to work.

Buggy sighed, releasing every stress of the day in one long, slow breath. Most people liked lazy days, able to lounge around with little to do but twiddle your thumbs and hum your favorite theme songs under your breath, straightening up only when your boss turns a corner, to create the pretense of business. Buggy hated it. For her, it made the day feel like 1 t would never end. After she and Linny had finished decorating the waiting room, the back office, and left little cheery Christmas knickknacks, and little statutes of a prancing, red-nosed Rudolph's in every room, she buckled down for three and a half more tedious hours with little to do. She tried to keep herself busy. She finished all her paperwork, proofread everyone's schedule, completed her equipment clean up routine twice, cleaned the back office from top to bottom, and was just about to get started in the waiting room when Linny kicked her out the door with a half-hour to spare in her time.

"Seriously, leaving early for once isn't going to kill you," Linny said, frowning at Buggy's protest. "But *I will* if you don't stop climbing the walls and get your ass out of here. Seriously. Go. I'll catch up with you at The Lookout." Buggy, too exhausted from the mental strain of having so little to do, finally relented, and stepped out into the light drizzle that had started a few minutes before.

She dropped her bag on the passenger seat, slipped the key into the ignition and started up the car with a hesitant stutter and sputter from the engine. As the car rumbled to life, Buggy reached for the gear shift, but her hand hesitated, flowing over its grip. She felt the engine heating up, the air beginning to blow warmth against her legs, fingers, and face, but her hands trembled as if it was a frosty breeze.

Maybe one more time....

Buggy reached over the gear shift and opened the glove compartment instead. She rifled around, fingers running across the various papers, knickknacks, and discarded chopsticks until she found what she was looking for. It wasn't discarded exactly. As a matter of fact, it had been placed quite carefully within the compartment beneath pens, wrappers, and notebooks which she tossed on top, not in any actual indifference, but a failed attempt at such. She did this often, pretended not to care. Pretended that she didn't think about the little stack of cassette tapes split between her glove compartment and the old and fraying bag in her trunk. But she thought about them all the same. She found her mind drifting to them often, so often that her friends would sometimes joke with her about her daydreams and the curious blank expression that would cross her face without warning.

It was a hard thing not to think about, really. The white nightgown and that bag were the only two things her birth mother had left her. Or abandoned alongside her, more like. After the charming prince paramedic had carefully bundled a newly squalling Buggy into the back of his ambulance, he ducked back outside. He grabbed the nightgown and bag from the homeless woman who had found her in the alley, tossing them quickly inside before racing for the hospital. After the officers tasked with finding her family were unable to glean any useful information from the nightgown and the contents of the bag, they were returned to her. As much as anything can be returned to a newborn. They were packed around wherever she went, from the hospital to the social service agency, and finally to her parents who kept them a secret until she was thirteen years old. Everyone agreed, from the nurses, social workers, and her parents, that she had a right to that bag and the cassettes it contained. But they waited until she was old enough to handle it. Since that day, her life had never quite been the same. The daydreams began. It was inevitable. No matter how often she tried to pull herself away, the cassettes always drew her back. They called to her, like a voice whispering her name, soft and slow. She turned to it, because she had no choice but to follow.

Buggy turned off the car, pulled out the cassette player and small stack of tapes from the compartment and laid them out on the passenger seat beside her. There were three of them, each carefully hand decorated. Each with their own color and labeled in bright ink with an unmistakably talented hand.

The first case was lined with powder blue parchment. A bright green label said: *22nd birthday*. A little curly heart was drawn at the end, which always made Buggy smile.

The second cassette had a soft green background with black font titled: *New Years 2019*. This one had multicolored fireworks exploding around the words. There were many others in the bag, but it was the third, which was lined in rather abrupt pink paper, that Buggy had kept in the glove compartment since she first learned how to drive. Its label was written in a bright orange script that said: *Open When You're Feeling Lonely*.

Buggy lifted this one off the seat, opened it with the flip of her thumb, and pulled it from its protective casing. She pushed it into her old silver cassette player (another item left to her), flipped it closed, and turned up the volume. She pressed play. She waited. After a few seconds and a short cackling sound, a voice began to speak.

"Hi there, honey," the voice was soft and sweet, the exact twin to hers in almost every way, "it's me..." the voice hesitated, as if debating the very words she was about to say. "Your mom."

Buggy closed her eyes. She had heard this all before. Heard it time and time again. Listened until she had the entire message memorized. She knew it by heart. She knew them *all* by heart. Every breath, every tone, every word, every hesitation, and heartbeat, yet she couldn't stop replaying them. Those tapes were all she had of her birth mother, after all. The mother who had given her life. Then left her behind.

A familiar hollowness opened in her chest. That voided feeling that always followed her, no matter where she went or what she was doing. That empty space which blossomed wide beneath her ribcage like some malformed flower, born wilting. The one that tells her she is missing something, something important. Suddenly, Buggy really wanted a drink. Or two. Or five.

"I guess you're not feeling too good right now," her mother's voice continued so low that Buggy turned up the volume even more. "That's okay. I get that way sometimes too. Guess it runs in the family." The soft, unsure laugh echoed throughout the car, and the corners of Buggy's mouth turned up in a smile.

"But I'm guessing that's more my fault than anyone else's, isn't it, hun?" the woman Buggy had never known sighed. "I'm sorry, dear. I really am. Believe me, I wish I was there. I wish I was there with you now... and I wish I could convince you that I am. Because I am, you know. I'm there with you now... more than you could possibly know." A little breath and another crackling sound told Buggy that her mother had shifted in whatever seat she was sitting in while recording. She could almost see her, with her feet folded underneath her, the same way that Buggy herself liked to do. Same hair being brushed quickly away from large eyes, but perhaps her eyes had been a prettier color than Buggy's own. Blue or green or something like that.

"Anyway," her mother continued, "I want you to know you're not alone. Even when you feel like you are. Even if you feel like there is no one or nothing... you're not alone. You have... so many... so many people that love you. And I love you, little one. I really, really, do. Until the end of my days and after. Always have, always will." Buggy squeezed her eyes against the tears that welled there, denying them exit, refusing to let them fall.

"Well, anyway, hun, I'm sure you're busy doing important and great things, but before you get back to them, I just wanted to say—" But Buggy didn't get a chance to hear what her mother was going to say, because a sharp tap jerked her from her quiet state. Her eyes opened to see Cooper watching her curiously through the window. A light rain trickled down his face and nose. His hair—a mixture of chocolate brown and deep sangria, purple highlights—was glittering with water droplets. The color highlights were a style he had been sporting for so long now, it looked quite natural on him. Cooper had been around sixteen when he had tried them out on a whim, but—in Buggy's opinion—it was his father's adamant disapproval that solidified it as part of his signature look. Her friend had never been the antagonistic type, but he did have a stubborn streak when it came to people telling him what he could and could not do.

Buggy lurched for the cassette player, switching it off, cutting her mother off mid-sentence. She turned back and rolled down her window.

"Cooper! Whatcha doing here?"

"I was just passing by. Thought I'd stop in and bug you guys till you got off," he said, leaning in a little, one arm on the upper part of the window and jerking his head towards the closed door of the dental office. "Leaving early?"

"Linny kicked me out."

Cooper grinned, a drop of rain detaching from the crease at the corner of his eye and slipping down his cheek. "Too slow a day for you, huh?" It sometimes worried Buggy how well Cooper knew her. She tried extremely hard to hide her little eccentricities, but it was a difficult thing to keep from the people you spent a lot of time with. And it wasn't exactly a problem for Cooper to see that side of her. She really liked Cooper and normally wouldn't mind such a close friend knowing everything about her, but things had been a bit... different recently. They were both home-grown in Marshall County, had gone to the same schools and hung around the same places. They had been friends on and off through middle school and high school, friendly with one another but never really running in the same crowd. Cooper was more of the outgoing, football-playing, classic jock type, minus the classic dickishness associated with the position. Actually, he had always been an insanely nice guy. Eagle Scout, volunteer at the local animal shelter, getting between bullies and new freshman kind of nice guy. But he still hung with the "in" crowd, and Buggy was never inclined. To be perfectly honest, she didn't really enjoy groups or crowds at all. She was more of the "eat lunch alone with music in her ears and not feel awkward or left out," kind of girl. It wasn't that she was confident. Buggy was plagued by the same insecurities and anxieties as every other teenage girl. Far more than most, in fact. She didn't think herself too good for everyone else. That thought never even crossed her mind. She had just always had a way of doing things. A method of laying out her utensils by her plate, her napkin in her lap, her diet Coke to the left of her tray, and her water bottle to the right. She had a method, one that was very difficult for her to deviate from, and she found it a little easier to accomplish without the curious sideways glances she always got from her fellow students. Everyone noticed her curious nature. And kids can be cruel.

Cooper, on the other hand, had never been cruel and had, on several occasions, slapped down his own friends who tried weakly to make fun of the girl with her organized tray. This had drawn them closer for a while. He spent time with her, pretending he wasn't keeping an eye on her. She enjoyed the company enough not to care. Come sophomore year in high school, she had grown into her eyes, her body had begun to fill out, and there was no longer any need for Cooper to defend her from his buddies. None of them were laughing at her anymore.

Oh, what big eyes you have! The better to see you with, my dear.

Buggy and Cooper grew distant the last years of high school, only sharing a "hello" or a smile as they passed each other in the crowded halls. Their friendship came back with a vengeance when they ended up at the same junior college and found themselves taking multiple classes together. They had been close ever since, and Buggy loved spending time with him... but when he was able to simply "know" things like this—about her and how she was—it made her a little uneasy. He had never made a move on her, never asked her out or anything of that sort. However, over the past few months, she had noticed him looking at her. Not in a creepy fashion, just in a *soft* way. Like when their little group hung out and watched *Friends*, she would be intent on an episode and just happen to glance over and see Cooper's eyes sliding away from her, a smile still on his lips. She had never considered Cooper having feelings for her before, not *really*. She wasn't stupid, she knew that most friendships between a man and a woman had some sort of sexual undertones. It was almost unavoidable, even if neither really wanted to make anything of it. It just always hung there. That unspoken possibility. That ever-frequent daydream, brushed aside with haste and ease. But Buggy had never really considered it **that** much of a possibility. Since the day they had become friends, Cooper had always been dating various cutie pies. He religiously made time for *Friends*

Marathon Fridays, but the rest of his weekends were occupied by long drives with new "special" friends. Over the past few months, however, Buggy had noticed his weekend dance card becoming suspiciously empty, and those sideways smiles a lot more frequent. She tried to push the thought away, thinking that she was just being self-absorbed or reading too much into things... and yet she couldn't stop that small tickling sensation from flitting through her chest every time she caught him looking.

"So slow," Buggy said, head dropping down to her chest, large eyes rolling dramatically. Cooper grinned.

"Well, it's Friday. The workday is done, and so is the boredom. Come on, since you're free early, let's hit The Lookout." Buggy's smile faltered. Linny had another hour in her shift, and Andrew mentioned that he'd be getting off of work late and might have to meet them at his house for the marathon. Which would leave just her and Cooper in their favorite dive bar. Alone with alcohol. Normally she would be thrilled to have some one-on-one time with Cooper, they had not gotten much of that since their little group formed... but those glancing half-smiles.

Stop it. She thought viciously to herself. *You're overreacting. It's nothing. You're probably just making it up anyhow. I mean, it's Cooper. That's just his face.* She found herself scrambling for an excuse in any case.

"Oh, I dunno," she stuttered slightly, searching vigorously for a truth. She never liked to lie. Those stupid, large, "window to the soul" eyes made it difficult. So, when she *did* need to lie, she would take a truth and bend it until it fit the shape she needed. It didn't always work. Especially since truths were not always so flexible. To her great relief, she found one willing to bend.

"My car!" she said, a little too excited. It was her ritual on Fridays to drive home from work, drop off her car, and Uber over to The Lookout, which was only a few blocks away from Andrew's house. "I really should take my car back first..." She looked at her button-down white blouse, black jeans and black flats. She had left the pink uniform coat in the office, and the clothes she had worn underneath still looked in pretty decent array, but not exactly The Lookout attire. "Maybe change."

"Oh, just leave your car here. Nobody will mind, and I'll bring you back to pick it up tomorrow," Cooper waved his hand dismissively, "And you don't need to change. You look nice."

Buggy smiled but reached for her keys in the ignition. "Thank you, but I would really feel better if—" She turned the key. The engine gave a grumble, a stutter, an odd clunking noise that didn't belong in any engine. Finally, it shuddered itself to silence. Buggy just stared at her dashboard, as if waiting for all the dials and gauges to light back up. *Surprise! Just kidding! Your car didn't just die at the most inopportune moment possible! It wouldn't do that to you, no way!* She turned the key again. This time it gave another little clicking stutter start, a loud knocking sound followed by a puff of white smoke which began seeping silkily up around the edges of the hood. "Oh no, no, no..." Buggy groaned, "That isn't just a dead battery, is it?"

"Ah, with that knocking sound?" Cooper shook his head. "'Fraid not."

"Shit."

"Plus side," Cooper grinned, "Now you get to go to the bar." Buggy looked up at him, a little exasperated, but Cooper persisted, "Come on! Leave it here. No one's gonna steal it if it can't even idle, and I'll help you get it towed tomorrow morning. I've got AAA. I mean, I guess you could just sit in your car all night if you'd rather," he looked up to the sky. Another few rain drops broke and scattered down his cheek like tears. "But I'm getting a little cold out here so..."

Buggy sighed and shrugged. Oh well, she really did want a drink. She opened her door, pulling the key out of the ignition as she did so. Cooper, delighted, stepped back so she could exit, but Buggy hesitated again. Her eyes swept back to the cassettes, still waiting patiently on the passenger seat.

"Umm, do you mind if I store a few things in your trunk until we get back to my house tomorrow?" She knew, even if someone broke in her car to steal the random change she might have hidden around, they would probably leave the cassettes (really what use were they these days), but she didn't like the idea of leaving them all alone in a broken Corolla in the dead of night. It just felt wrong.

"Sure thing," Cooper said. Buggy snagged up the tapes and player, then ran around the back to pop open her trunk. It was mostly empty except of a wool blanket, a spare tire, a flashlight, an extra can of pepper spray (the first always being on her person) and last but never least, the small shoulder bag. It was a gray leather thing, with a flap over the top and a two large silver buckles in the front. The soft gray material was worn almost completely through in a few places. It was a bag that her birth mother had obviously used for a long time and often. Buggy quickly unbuckled it and placed the remaining tapes and player in with the others before clasping it closed again and pulling it over her shoulder.

"Those what I think they are?" Cooper asked, a little lower and quieter than his usual peppy, cheerful lilt. Buggy looked up at him as she snapped her trunk closed, water flying off from the quick, jarring motion.

"Uh, yeah," she said, watching him. She waited for him to say something else, to finally ask her about them. He had caught her listening to the tapes a time or two and had been curious. She had given in and told him the gist of the truth, about them being recorded messages from her birth mother, but he had never pushed the subject. He had never asked what they said, or if they explained why she had left Buggy half dead in a dark alley and not at the hospital or a fire station like a rational human being would do in desperate times. She could see the questions arise in his mind, an almost perceptible wave of curiosity crashing to his lips, but he had yet to let any of them free. Buggy was always waiting for the moment when the questions would surge too high and escape that damn smile. To Buggy's relief, today was not the day. Cooper only nodded, walked over to his car, popped the trunk, and motioned for her to follow.

Buggy smiled and went to him. She could feel her braid growing heavy as the light rain grew thicker and tumbled faster from the sky. Inside, Cooper's trunk was safe and dry. Buggy even found an empty box among the random assortment of scattered papers, crumpled fast food bags, and books. It held her bag perfectly. Buggy closed the trunk with another splash of water, securing the precious cargo.

"And now," Cooper said, pointing his keys out in front of him like a sword and he some king, leading great men to battle. "Let us drink!"

3

"Concentrate."

"I'm trying."

"Obviously not hard enough."

"Well, you're kinda being distracting."

"If I'm able to distract you, then you are not concentrating hard enough."

"Oh, for the love of God—"

It was a warm room they were in. Warm and spacious. The cabin was two stories high and had that classic log cabin look about it. No antlers decorated the walls, but there was plenty of carved wooden furniture, home-woven rugs, and plaid blankets draping the soft and fraying couches. The only thing out of place were the stain glass windows high up the wall. They depicted various scenes of nature—roses growing, a sun setting, horses dancing in a meadow. They all cast moonlight onto the cabin floor in various green, red, and blue shapes that stretched and twisted as the moon moved across the sky.

On one side of the large, open living room was a wooden staircase that led to the upper floor. To the other side stood a wide open-mouthed fireplace lined with charred red brick. Inside the fireplace, several stacks of sturdy oak crackled and burned. They sent flickering red and orange flames to lick up the chimney, forever ravenous for more.

In front of the fire sat a boy in his twenties. He sat cross-legged on the rug, bathed in the fire's hot, orange glow. His hands rested open-palmed against his legs, fingers curling gently inward. His eyes watched the flame intently, trying to concentrate on every flicker, every sway of the fire. He tried to block everything else out of his mind... and yet....

"Anything?"

The boy glared over at his companion.

"For shit's sake, Styger, could you leave me alone for ten minutes? Just ten minutes, that's all I ask." Styger, a tall and scruffy faced man of forty-seven years, glowered down at the boy.

"We are running short on time, Theo."

"I know that," Theo snapped. "But guess what, you pestering me every five seconds is not helping."

"It's not that difficult, just concentrate."

"Not that difficult?" Theo gaped. "Seriously? You think this shit is easy?"

"Always was for me," Styger answered.

"Oh well, goodie for you," Theo grumbled, turning back to the fire. "You had years of training and practice. Not to mention an element of personal connection, *none* of which I have had, by the way." It had been six short months since Styger had found him. Six short months since Theo started this nightmare of a roller coaster ride. Six months of him questioning his own sanity, sitting in front of various fires, candles, and lit matches, trying to meditate and think. Trying to do something that he had no idea *how* to do.

Styger sighed. "You're right. I'm sorry. Can we just get back to it, please?"

"Sure," Theo turned. "As soon as you leave."

"Theo..."

"I mean it, Styger. Go. Get out. Get a beer. Take a smoke. Go to town. Jump feet first off a cliff. I don't give a damn what you do, but you need to give me a chance to do this *alone*."

"Fine!" Styger threw his hands into the air in frustration. "Fine!" With that, the man turned and huffed his way out the front door. "You call me if you get anything."

"Sounds fair." Theo heard the door slam and then the deep rumble of an engine turning over. The Jeep revved, and soon its sounds faded into the distance. Theo sighed with relief and turned his attention back to the flames. He breathed slowly, in through his nose and out his mouth. He watched the fire rise and twist and lick around the wood, slowly but surely devouring it. Turning it to ash.

Theo had no idea how to make this work. Styger kept telling him that it was natural. A second nature that he just needed to tap into once. After that, he would have access to it forever. Although, seeing as Theo didn't know what that "second nature" felt like or how he could be sure he accomplished accessing it, the whole process was a proverbial pain in the ass. When he had first sat down before the flame, Theo had turned and had asked Styger how he would know when it happened. How he would know when he succeeded. Styger had only shrugged.

"It's like porn," he answered, "You'll know it when you see it."

Theo carefully watched the flames flit and flutter but still experienced *nothing*. He sighed, breathing in through his nose and out his mouth, trying to block out everything but the fire. Only the flames. An hour passed as he sat there, although he refused to look at the clock. He refused to give time the satisfaction of knowing that he felt its passing. He had spent so many nights like this. So many nights just sitting, thinking, and trying to put the mental middle finger to time itself. He just watched the flames as they ate away at the oak, slowly crumbling the wood to splinters, and further into gleaming coals. He watched closely, watched it all, breathing in and out. He breathed and wondered: how had his life come to this place?

He had a good job. Granted, working as a car mechanic in Temecula California wasn't the most lucrative of professions, but he made a solid living, and someday he would own the shop. His mom ran the place and taught him everything she knew, which turned out to be quite a lot. About cars, at least. There was a whole other story, one about her past, that she conveniently neglected to tell him a single thing about while growing up. Not until a strange, scruffy-faced man showed up at the shop one day. His mom's eyes nearly fell out of her head when she saw Styger standing there in the doorway. She had ushered him into the private office without a word and closed the door behind them. Lots of hushed and hurried words were exchanged, none of which Theo could hear. He got the whole story eventually, however. Oh, boy, did he ever.

"Theo..." his mother had started. They were sitting at the kitchen counter later that evening when she slid a drink across the table towards him. The last time she had handed him a drink before sitting down for a "talk" had been when he was seventeen and his mother had to explain why his newest stepdad, Bill, had not been home in a few days. And why he wouldn't be coming back again.

"Theo... you remember all those dreams you had when you were little? All those funny feelings you got before Maggie went to the doctors?"

"Yeah," Theo had answered. Maggie had been their neighbor back when he was eight. She was a sweet, friendly lady of thirty-five, and by all accounts in perfect health. She would come over and have dinner with him and his mom from time to time, just to shoot the breeze. One evening, Theo started having this funny feeling. She would walk through the door and Theo felt like there was something off... something wrong. He felt a pressure in his chest every time he got near her. Like someone or something was pushing against him. It made him nervous and fidgety. It grew worse and worse over the next few dinners until his mother asked him what was wrong. He had told her, truthfully, that he had that funny feeling in his chest. He had expected his mother to brush it off, smile, and say "oh you" in that way she always did, but this time she didn't. She had watched him for a long while, searching him with her eyes, seeming to peer into his very thoughts. She had then stood up without a word and went to talk to Maggie. Maggie went in for a checkup two days later.

Stage three breast cancer.

Maggie had fought hard. She went through multiple surgeries, chemo, and had lived to make it out the other side. At least, as far as Theo and his mother knew. Maggie had moved out of state to be closer to her cousins in Utah while she was healing, and they had not heard from her for years. Theo's mother had always insisted that Theo had saved the woman's life.

"You remember those 'funny feelings' you had with her?" his mother had asked, scooting the glass across the tile, a little closer to his hand.

"Yeah, Mom, but what does that have to do with the dude from this morning?"

"Well... that *dude*, his name is Styger. He's, uh, an old friend of mine. And you two have something in common."

"Which is?" Theo had swallowed. Was this it? Was this the time, his mother would finally tell him. Tell him that the strange guy who showed up at their auto shop with his scruffy beard and his gravelly voice wasn't just some friend from way back when. He thought he was going to finally know who his real father was. That didn't happen. Not one little bit.

"You are both psychic."

"What?" Theo laughed out loud, but his mother didn't even crack a smile. Her face remained stony and grave. "Mom?"

"You're a psychic, Theo. Well, kind of. You're a special kind of psychic. All those funny dreams you had growing up—all those funny *feelings*—they weren't for nothing. Each of them meant something... I just... I didn't want that life for you so I..."

"Mom?" Theo leaned on the table, still smiling. "Mom, you're kidding, right?"

"No, Theo," she said, looking up. "I'm deathly serious. You saved Maggie... now you may need to save someone else."

And oh boy, the story just got better from there.

Theo watched the flames. They licked and danced and did all those things that flames liked to do. Except, apparently, open whatever third eye was supposed to be hidden in his head. No, they just danced there, mocking him, fluttering, and taunting. Theo ignored their jeering and simply watched. Watched and thought about a girl he had never met. He breathed. In the nose and out the mouth. In the nose and out the mouth... in the nose... and out the—

An image flitted through his mind. A strange, semi translucent image, one that came and went, leaving only a faint trace of... gold? It was barely there. It was gossamer paper skimming back and forth through his thoughts, so brief that Theo thought he might have drifted into a doze. Thought it was just a dream image playing through his semi-conscious imagination, but then....

Theo blinked.

"Oh," was the sound that escaped him after three and a half hours of silence. He got to his feet slowly, unsure that the ground still existed. As if it might just drift away when he pressed against it and he would start falling and never stop. The ground held steady, and he walked over to the small coffee table in front of the long, gray couch where he had left his cell. He picked up his phone and dialed Styger's number.

"Hey, kid," Styger said, sounding a lot calmer than he had before leaving. Must have had a few smokes. Taken a walk. That usually chilled him out.

"Hey," Theo answered. He was glad, but also a little surprised, to hear his voice was steady. He still felt like the ground might just give out beneath him. It wouldn't be the weirdest thing to happen in the last five minutes.

"Anything new?" Styger asked.

"Well," Theo started, then hesitated. "It wasn't porn, but...." There was a long pause on the other end of the line.

"On my way," Styger said, and the call ended.

4

Buggy cursed herself for being so neurotic. She and Cooper had a wonderful time from the instant they stepped inside The Lookout. It was just as smooth and easy as ever, hanging with Cooper. There was no awkwardness, no profession of affections beyond friendship. They just sat at the bar, chatting up the bartender and swapping old stories and new updates of their lives. She felt a bit ashamed of her earlier hesitation, and for reading too much into a simple smile. Buggy had a habit of doing that, reading *too much* into things. Going over things in your mind is alright, but Buggy had a tendency to obsess over a singular event in a way that she didn't think her friends did. She would take an idea and put it on a little table in her mind. She would then shine various multicolored lights on it. She would walk around it, lift it, let it down again, scrutinizing it from every possible angle and for every possible meaning. She poked and prodded until she, and the idea itself, was utterly spent. All this to, generally, find that it was precisely what she had expected in the first place. Buggy had wasted many perfectly good hours overthinking. She didn't like this about herself and did her damnedest to keep it *to* herself...but she also couldn't seem to stop. It was just another one of her methods. It was lining up her dental equipment in the proper order. It was her soda can on the left and her water bottle on the right. It was just the way she worked. Buggy had come to accept that fact, but it didn't mean she had to like it.

"Another one?" Cooper asked, noticing her drink was, by this time, mostly ice.

Buggy grinned. "Obviously."

"Hey," Cooper leaned towards the bartender who, tonight, was a woman in her late twenties. She had a wide smile painted in bright barbie-pink lipstick and sported a corset and plunging neckline that left little to the imagination. "Could I have another whiskey sour, please?"

"Sure thing, Sweetie," she smiled, and leaned against the counter, straining her already strained corset. "Another rum and Coke for you?"

"Please." The bartender flashed him another broad smile, ignoring Buggy altogether, and sauntered off to make their drinks. Buggy watched Cooper watching the bartender walking away and chuckled to herself.

"So, how's Megan?" Buggy asked, reminding him, just in case he had forgotten about his latest "special friend" somewhere within the folds of the bartender's skirt.

"Megan?" Cooper asked, sitting back and frowning for a second. "Oh! Megan! Yeah, no, she dumped me weeks ago."

"Oh damn, I'm sorry," Buggy's smile melted.

"Eh, it's alright," Cooper shrugged. "No big deal."

"Did she say why?"

"Something about me not focusing enough on our relationship," he said, eyes involuntarily drifting back to the bartender's skirt as she leaned over to grab a fresh bottle of rum from under the bar.

"Can't imagine why," Buggy mumbled, shaking her head.

"But how about you?" Cooper asked, turning back to her. "Anyone new on your horizon?" Buggy was saved the awkwardness of answering when she was nearly knocked off her chair by the tackling hug that was Andrew.

"Dude, you scared the shit out of me!" Buggy scolded, but hugged him back, nevertheless.

"Sorry," Andrew said, giving her shoulders another tight squeeze before taking the stool at her other side, "Couldn't resist. Got off work sooner than I thought I would. How are things, Buggy Bear?" Buggy scowled up at him, nearly cricking her neck with the effort. Andrew Elbre was tall, even while sitting down. He stood over six feet and was as skinny as a preverbal bean pole. There were genuine concerns while he was growing up. Whispers of anorexia and bulimia were tossed around his school and the Elbre house itself. These whispers grew to full-blown conversations as his growth spirt hit hard in the height department but never seemed to influence his waistline. After much protesting from Andrew, a few tests from various doctors, and four infamous weeks in therapy, Andrew's family was forced to conclude that this was just how Andrew was. What he lacked in weight, however, he made up for in an enthusiastic and slightly flamboyant nature which endeared him instantly to anyone who spent two seconds in his company. Even if, from time to time, he could be a bit of a pain.

"I swear," Buggy groaned, "Andrew, you are the only person on the face of this Earth that can make the world's worst nickname just, *so much worse.*"

"Oh, yeah?" Cooper grinned, paying for the drinks and sliding over Buggy's whiskey sour with barely a glance at the bartender this time. "How about... Buggypuss?"

"Buggypants?" Andrew added.

"Buggyboo."

"Bugster?"

"For the love of God," Buggy grumbled, taking a sip of her drink, which turned out to be more whiskey than sour, thank the Lord.

"What's God doing now?" Linny asked, pulling up a stool on Andrew's other side. She had changed out of her work clothes and into a brown leather jacket, black pants, and a matching t-shirt. She always kept a change of clothes in the back of her car, particularly for *Friends* Marathon Fridays.

"Not saving Buggy from us fast enough," Andrew answered, motioning to the bartender.

"Oh, well, what else is new?" Linny flashed a grin.

They spent a couple hours at the bar, chatting, laughing, and making fun of Buggy's nickname—the usual—before deciding it was time to start the main event. Andrew placed a call to the nearest (and dearest) pizza joint in town as they closed their tabs and started out the door into the chilly November air. The walk wasn't long, but they had barely made it outside before Linny was groaning about frost bite and frozen fingers. They made it to the pizza place (all fingers and toes attached) and picked up their order. They traversed the last block and a half to Andrew's, where they set up their usual circle of couches, bean bag chairs, and blankets. They placed the pizzas in a place of honor between them and Cooper passed out another round of beers as Andrew fired up his beloved flat screen.

They had run through the entire *Friends* series four times by this point and had come back around to the second season, picking up where they left off last Friday. It happened to be the episode when the group watched their old prom video and Rachel and Ross finally got together. As Andrew,

Linny, and Cooper all sighed with happy satisfaction, Buggy groaned and gagged.

"How dare you!" Andrew tossed a pillow in Buggy's direction.

"I'm sorry I just... I don't get the appeal!" Buggy said, catching the pillow and throwing it back at him.

"It's Ross and Rachel!" Andrew protested, hands spread in exasperation.

"Rachel and Ross!" Linny agreed, waving around her already half empty beer bottle for emphasis.

"Eh," Buggy shrugged, "I prefer Rachel and Joey to be honest."

"Are... are you INSANE?!" Cooper asked from beside her.

"It's Ross and Rachel! They were made for each other!" Linny insisted.

"Made to irritate the shit out of me," Buggy laughed.

"It's official," Cooper said. "I have always suspected, but now, I am *sure*. You have no soul."

"No, you just have no taste," Buggy jabbed him in the arm, and he splayed himself back as if she had dealt him a mortal wound. She rolled her eyes.

"You disgust me," Andrew said, shaking his head and taking another sip from his own beer.

"Fine with me," Buggy shrugged. "Pass me another piece, would you?"

"No!" Andrew grabbed the pizza box, jerking it out of her reach. "Pizza is for the sane!"

"Fine, fine, Rachel and Ross, Ross and Rachel, bla-bla-bla, can I have pizza now?" Andrew eyed her cautiously, but slid the box back on the table. Buggy slid another slice of steaming pepperoni on her plate.

"You have no sense of romance."

"Accurate," Buggy answered around a mouthful of pizza, utterly unfazed.

"Yeah, seriously, what's up with that?" Cooper asked, going for another piece himself.

"What do you mean?" Buggy asked.

"I..." Cooper glanced in Buggy's direction and then shrugged. "Never mind."

"He means," Andrew said, leaning closer and pointing a piece of pizza in her direction. The end flopped downward, and a bit of pepperoni escaped onto the table. "Well, you're like, what, a twenty-four-year-old girl who instantly puts up an emotional blast shield when it comes to romance or dating."

"What? No, I—well—I mean," Buggy stuttered, frowning a little.

"You do!" Linny interjected, loud enough to make Buggy wince.

"You're getting this just because I don't like 'Ross and Rachel'?" Buggy grinned and cocked her left brow. "You're drunk."

"True, but what does that have to do with anything? So are you!" Linny laughed and shook her head. "But no, I'm talking real life to. Like, when we go out, do you know what your face looks like when someone even comes up to *talk* to you? Well, let me tell you," Linny widened her own, slightly red, eyes and drew her brows down to a mockery of Buggy's severe expression, *"daggers*. And God forbid they *hit on* you."

"In my defense, drunk guys at bars... not nearly as hot as they think they are," Buggy rolled her eyes and reached for her drink. "Negative hotness, in fact."

"Okay, fair, but that's not it. I mean, do you *ever* date? I know you've never taken me up on the offer to set you up with anyone. Which has bummed me out to no end, by the way."

"Like I've told you before... our taste in guys... very different," Buggy said.

"But you don't even give me a chance to *tell* you about the guy before you say no!" Linny whined. "You seem averse to the idea of romance just on principle. Do you even watch rom-coms?" Linny narrowed her eyes at her as if suspicious of some terrible lie. "I bet you hate weddings, don't you?"

"That's ridiculous. I love weddings!" Buggy laughed. "And why is everyone suddenly so concerned with my love life?"

"Probably because there is such a glaring lack of it," Andrew piped in cheerily, dabbing at his pizza with a paper napkin to wipe away the excess grease.

"Okay, starting to actually feel attacked now," Buggy scowled. "How did this conversation divulge into my life choices getting picked on?"

"Yeah, guys, maybe we should drop—" Cooper started, eyeing Buggy's shift in expression, but Linny interrupted.

"But it's very true!" Linny sat up, Ross and Rachels make out session completely forgotten. "Seriously, Buggy, I don't think I've ever heard of you going out on a date... ever. Cooper," Linny turned to him. "You've known her longest. You ever seen her date someone? How about a little middle school crush?"

"I'd really rather not—" Cooper started, casting another glance at Buggy.

"That's a 'no.'" Andrew laughed.

"I guess I'm just not that into dating," Buggy shrugged.

"Why not?!" Linny protested. "Free food, free booze, free make outs. What's the downside?"

"Have you ever *paid* for a make out?" Buggy grinned. "Cuz, if so, we should talk."

"Shuddup, I'm seriously curious."

"Well..." Buggy took another bite, chewed, swallowed. "I just... I don't know. I'm just not a fan. I'm not against it in general or anything, it's just—for myself—not a fan."

"And whhhhhyyy's thaaaaat?" Andrew propped his elbows against his knees, resting his chin on top of laced fingers, waiting for her answer. Buggy noticed that his eyes were also a little glazed.

"Well..." Buggy thought a moment. She was several drinks and half a beer in by this point, so she was riding a decent buzz, causing her honesty to come easily. Andrew and Linny's eyes were on her, and she could even feel Cooper leaning in, despite himself. "Frankly, because feelings are gross."

"Excuse me," Cooper barked a laugh. "Feelings are 'gross'? That's your answer?"

"Yep." Buggy took another large bite of pizza.

"I don't... I don't even know how to answer that," Linny said, flabbergasted.

"Cool, then can we get back to watching Ross and Rachel being a disaster waiting to happen?" Buggy asked, turning back for the TV screen.

"We absolutely may not!" Linny protested with another dramatic wave of her bottle. To Buggy's relief, she heard her phone ringing from the kitchen. She slid her plate on the table, stepped over Cooper's legs, and went for it.

"This is so not over!" Linny called after her. Buggy shot her tongue out in response and closed the door behind her. The kitchen itself was small with a hardwood floor and stained gray tile counter tops on which her phone chirped, angry at being ignored for so long. It vibrated against the tile, clattering slightly in its insistence on being heard. She picked it up and drew her finger across the screen to accept the call without bothering to check the ID. At this time of night it would be one of two people—her dad or Sandra. Buggy's money was on Sandra. Her older sister worked as an editor for the local newspaper, and the way she drove to and from work always took her past Elwin Family Dentistry. Sandra knew she wouldn't be home tonight—the group tended to stay over at Andrew's after filling themselves to bursting with beer and pizza—so she wouldn't expect Buggy at the apartment they shared. However, she probably saw Buggy's car still out in front of the office and wanted to make sure she actually was at Andrew's as expected. She always kept tabs on her little sister. Sandra was only a few years older than Buggy herself, but she had taken up the "big sister" mantle with great gusto ever since the Pierces brought little Buggy home. She never hovered or got into Buggy's business as much as Buggy knew Sandra would *really* like to do, but Sandra knew that Buggy had many little methods. An outline for how things should go during any given day. Every Friday she was supposed to leave her car at home and Uber to Andrew's or the bar. Buggy's car being left at the office was an anomaly in the method, and Sandra knew how Buggy handled anomalies in her methodology.

"Hyello!" Buggy said, pressing the phone to her ear. Instead of her big sister's lyrical voice as was expected, Buggy was greeted by silence.

"Hello?" Buggy said, again. "Sandra? That you?" Silence. Buggy pulled the phone away from her face to look at the ID of the caller.

Unknown Number.

Buggy frowned and put the phone back to her ear.

"Hellooo? Anybody there?" Silence. "No? Okay." Buggy hung up and slipped the phone into her pocket. Probably another one of those scammers that call a million different numbers just to see who picked up. Later, maybe in a few days, she would start getting scam recordings meant to frighten her. "Important" calls from the office of Social Security, or the good news of having won a contest worth a million dollars! And *all* you have to do is give them your social!

Great. Buggy rolled her eyes. She snagged another beer out of the fridge and made her way back to the living room where Ross and Rachel still nauseated, and Linny continued to poke fun at her love life. Buggy forgot the call as soon as she sank back into her space on the couch next to Cooper. It was probably nothing anyway.

5

Styger lowered the phone from his ear without a word. He had forgotten how to breathe. She had sounded just like her. *Exactly* like her. He had forgotten just how sweet, how lovely that voice truly was. How it filled him with memories that once brought him so much joy, but now cut him so deeply that he wanted to cry. He didn't, though. Instead, he turned, slowly, towards the younger man who watched him carefully, curiously, face creased with worry.

"Well?" Theo asked. They had spent a short time searching the web. Theo had been able to see flashes, images of a town in his mind, and even got the name of the county. They looked up Marshall County, and after sifting through several articles about James W. Marshall and his discovery of gold, they found the location of a small county about two hours out of the Sacramento area. Although small, it was highly populated, packed with people, any of who could be the one they were after. Theo had gone back to his place in front of the fire, and it came easier this time. Just as Styger said it would. This time he had seen an office, with the words "Elwin Family Dentistry" written in large letters on the glass door. They had looked it up online and found the office number and a list of employees, but they didn't provide their numbers specifically. Instead, they went down the list of names and looked up each person in the phone book, which was fully available online to Styger's surprise. They only had to search five names, all the others were obviously male names, and the girl they were looking for was a *girl* after all. They called, listened to each voice mail and had several 'oops' sorry wrong number conversations before Styger suddenly stopped pacing, face going stony, phone pressed to his ear.

"It's her," he said, mouth going completely dry. God, he could use a cigarette right about now. Maybe a whole pack.

"Are you sure?" Theo asked, scrutinizing Styger's wan face.

"Yes. No question," he nodded. "She sounds... it's her."

"Alright. Well, hello there..." Theo grinned, looking down at the name next to the number Styger had just called, "Briar Pierce. It worked! Whoa, okay, that's insane!" Styger turned away from Theo's excited expression and walked to the wooden bar at the side of the living room. He had built it himself two years ago. Carved every inch, sanded every corner, and stained it a deep and glossy brown. He pulled open the double doors on the bottom and grabbed one of the many bottles of bourbon. He opened the smaller drawer on top and grabbed a couple glasses from within and began to pour.

"So," Theo asked, watching Styger's back with caution. "What now?"

"Now," Styger said, turning around with two glasses in his hand. He handed one to Theo. "I am going to have a smoke. A long smoke." Styger clinked his glass against Theo's, before walking past him. He stepped out the front door and to the porch outside, making a beeline for the bench swing that hung down from the roof. He sat with a little grunt and pulled the pack from his pocket.

It was a lovely night. The cool day had shifted into a chilly evening, and the stars peppered the sky around a crescent moon. The shadows and silhouettes of hills and trees were all that could be seen for miles around. Styger always loved his place. It was quiet. Calm. You could think here in ways that were impossible in the city down the road. *She* had loved it too. Maybe even more than him.

Styger slipped the cigarette between his lips and rifled around in his pocket for his lighter. When he found it, he flipped it open and lit the cigarette. It burned bright red before dimming into a smoky ashen tip. He closed the lighter with a sharp click and pulled. The smoke filled him, and he relaxed a little, letting it flow back out of his nose like some old dragon.

She had not liked his smoking. She had always crinkled that little button nose of hers whenever he slipped.

Really, Cam? Really? She would ask, scowling at him, but not without love. She didn't like the smell, that was for sure, but she mostly hated the things because of what they did to the human lung. What horrible damage they could cause. She hated them because of what they might do to *him*. He had done his best to cut it out after they had gotten together. He had been good most days, but he was only human. The only time he had managed to stop altogether was when she told him she was pregnant. After she was gone, however, he found fewer and fewer reasons not to pop open a new box and light it.

Really, Cam? Really? He remembered every lilt of that voice, every emphasis, ever curve. He knew that voice better than he knew his own.

Hyello! Hello? Sandra? That you?

He would know that voice anywhere. It was imprinted in his mind, as it would be until the day he died. He thought he would never hear it again. Thought it was lost to him forever.

Cameron Styger put out his cigarette, downed the last of his bourbon, and placed the empty glass on the bench beside him. The swing gave a protesting creak of old hinges as he leaned forward. He covered his face with his hands and began to cry.

6

Deep within the abyss, the hollow space shifted. It twitched, surface shivering like a breeze being blown across a calm lake. It rippled, fluttered, vibrated with newly discovered life, newly discovered being. The stillness broke, the calm melted away. The thing churned in on itself, reorienting, resonating, *becoming*. The first coherent thought was formed.

Finally.

The word bristled out from the dark, filling the hollowness with something just as empty, just as much itself as it had always been. It had taken a long time... but now, it was awake.

7

"Briar... Briar dear..."

Buggy groaned, blinking slowly awake at a quarter to four in the morning. Another nightmare. Another damn nightmare. It was getting ridiculous how many times she closed her eyes and found herself in some deep, evil dream where everything went terribly wrong. Dr. Hernandez, her old therapist, used to tell her that dreams were a way for the mind to process events in one's life while unconscious. A method of dealing with them, organize them into memory and filing them away. At the time, this made sense to Buggy. Back when she had still been seeing Dr. Hernandez, she had been having a lot of nightmares, but they all had to do with the classics. The "sleeping through the exam" dream. The "showing up to a presentation with no pants on and being laughed at" dream. The dreams of failure and rejection that naturally plagued those with perfectionist tendencies and social anxiety, which Buggy had learned, she had in spades. But these dreams... these recent dreams, they had nothing to do with grades, or public ridicule. They had to do with death.

Buggy had heard many times, from such reputable sources as high school classrooms, topical internet articles, and friends chatting around campfires, that you cannot die in dreams. That you would always wake up just before whatever was killing you could finish the job.

Buggy knew that was bullshit. You could die in dreams. She had done it quite often by now. These new nightmares, they always ended the same way. Her deaths came in different forms. Sometimes she could see it coming, sometimes she couldn't. Sometimes it was quick. Someone unseen shot her in the head, or she flung herself off a cliff, or she took a sip of tea, knowing it was poisoned, but unable to stop her hand from bringing the cup to her lips. The latter dream she liked the most. The poison was calm, quiet, and she just drifted off to sleep. Other times her mind wasn't so kind. Sometimes a man, whose features were too blurred by the dream to make out, choked her slowly to death. A few times she was tied to a stake like some witch, screaming as she watched the faceless hoard throwing even more torches on the pyre. Dreams of being in darkness, being torn to pieces by people or things she couldn't see. There was also the dream of the woman in the black gown... the one with the red stone around her neck and the straight edge razer in her hand... Buggy didn't like to think about that one. But the worst one of all, and the one that came to her more often than the rest, was that strange house.

That burning house.

On the floor, facing up, Buggy would watch as the thatched roof caught fire. She watched as the flames licked up the walls, undulating from red to orange to a demon blue. In the dream she would lay there, unable to move, tied down by horrible, horrible pain. The type of pain that nailed you into place. The type of pain you begged to end. The type of pain that made you pray for death, and in that dream death always came.

It all felt so real. So damn real.

Unsurprisingly, Buggy's sleep had been erratic at best over the past few months, and she had grown used to waking at random times and odd hours. She could usually fall back to sleep again, but she always gave herself a little time to make sure the dream had gone far enough way before slinking back into bed.

This dream, the one she had just woken from, she'd had before. One of a darkness so deep she could see nothing. Nothing at all. Not even her own fingers and hands, and all she knew was that she was drowning. She was falling deeper and deeper into the abyss, hands and arms flailing, trying to swim back up to the surface, knowing that oxygen and salvation was just a few breast strokes away, but also knowing with certainty that she would never make it in time. The pull was too strong, and so she fell, down, down, down. It had been one of those rare occasions when she had woken before death had its way with her, and Buggy wasn't eager to go back and let her dream finish what it started. No, thank you very much. So instead, she sat up.

"Briar..."

Buggy blinked, looking around at the room. She thought she might have heard something, maybe someone calling her name, but everyone else was still asleep. It was dark except for the TV, which cast the room in the mild, blue-green light of the DVD home screen. They had clicked "play all" and let the disc run until the end, by which time they had all fallen asleep, splayed on couches, the floor, wrapped in blankets, all still surrounding the coffee table and the remnants of the demolished pizza. Buggy grunted and pushed herself up further on the couch. Cooper lay fast asleep next to her, head leaned against the opposite armrest like a pillow. His mouth hung slightly open as his form rose and fell with the rhythmic breath of someone in the deepest corners of dreamlands unknown. Buggy smiled. He looked so dopey. It was actually quite cute. A bit of hair fell across his closed eyes, tangling with his lashes. Buggy reached out, about to brush the hair aside... then she stopped and dropped her hand away.

She slid off the couch as smoothly as possible, trying not to wake him. She stepped over Andrews's long legs and went for the kitchen. Her head was still swimming from alcohol, and she felt a nasty headache coming on. She could feel it starting to pound on the edge of her temples, working its way slowly but diligently deeper, taking root, growing fast. Lucky for Buggy, Andrew always kept a bottle of aspirin in the cabinet above the sink. She tiptoed in the dark across the cool floor and reached up to the cabinet. She was about to shake a pill or two into her hand when she noticed a dark figure standing in the doorway. Buggy squeaked and nearly dropped the bottle, which would have scattered pills all over the floor. She caught it just in time and scrambled for the light switch on the wall next to the sink. She flipped it on, and a half-blinding light filled the little room. She raised a hand to shield her eyes.

"Cooper?" Buggy squinted at him. He was leaning against the door frame in a rather "un-Coopery" kind of way. His arms were crossed, head tilted down with a half-smile playing his face, as if amused by what he saw, but not enough to afford his usual full-faced grin.

"Hello, Briar," he said, still in that half-smile. "What on Earth are you doing up at this time of morning?"

"Aspirin," Buggy said. She shook the little bottle, rattling the contents. "What's your excuse?"

"Just woke up," Cooper shrugged. "Finally." He pushed off the door frame and came into the room. "Thought I would say good morning, while I can."

"...Okay," Buggy frowned a little as Cooper stepped towards the fridge and pulled it open, casting himself in its white-blue light. He was acting weird. "Hey, are you feeling alright?"

"Me?" Cooper glanced up at her and smiled, but it still looked wrong. It wasn't his cheery grin. It was thin and amounted to more of a smirk than anything, as if a mockery of his usual happy expression. He pulled back from the fridge, two beers in hand. "I am doing just fine, Briar." He popped both lids open with the bottle opener on his key chain, the one that was shaped like a beer bottle and sported a colorful "Welcome to Las Vegas" inscription. He had bought it on Linny's twenty-sixth birthday, when the four of them had made the last-minute decision to throw all their things in the car and drive. When they finally made it there, they realized they had forgotten to pack one very crucial thing.

"Seriously, that one?" Buggy laughed when Cooper made it to the cash register. "Little tacky, no?"

"It's Vegas!" he had replied with a grin. "Of course, it's tacky. That's what makes it timeless!"

Back in the kitchen, Cooper slipped the keys into his pocket. They jingled a little as they hit bottom and rested there.

"Briar?" Buggy frowned but took the beer when he offered it to her. Hell, maybe it would help her sleep. Keep that dream at bay. She shook out an aspirin and downed it with a sip of beer. She set the rest of the pills aside on the counter and turned back to Cooper. "Since when do you call me Briar?"

"You prefer your actual name, do you not? Even if you do not really fight your nickname anymore... you do not really fight much of anything anymore, do you? Well, except 'feelings,' of course," Cooper's smirk widened, "those are 'gross' right?"

Buggy laughed, a little nervously now as Cooper leaned against the opposite counter, watching her intently. An odd feeling was bubbling up in her stomach. Not the same one Buggy got when she caught him glancing at her... no... this was something colder. It spread, tingling to her arms and down to her toes. She was nervous. She wasn't quite sure why she was nervous. No, that was bullshit, she knew exactly why. It was the way Cooper was looking at her with that strange expression. That very, "un-

Cooper" way. He sounded odd to, although Buggy couldn't place her finger on how. "I was kinda joking when I said that."

"No, you were not." Cooper shook his head, but his eyes never left her. To distract herself, try to break the awkwardness she was feeling, Buggy pushed on the counter with her hands, sliding up to sit on the tiles next to the sink. She shook out another of the aspirin and swallowed it with a second sip of beer.

"Yeah?" she asked, "You can read my mind now?"

"Close enough," Cooper answered. He pushed off the counter. "Enough to know that you were not joking. Never have about that kind of stuff. You have a problem, you see. A problem with *feeling.*"

"Okay, dude," Buggy rolled her eyes and moved to slide off her perch, but Cooper had other plans. He stepped forward, leaning against the counter, one hand on either side of her seat, trapping her in her place.

"Cooper what—" Buggy blanched.

"You see," Cooper continued, ignoring her protest. "When you *feel...* when you get that sensation in your belly, or those butterflies in your chest. When you feel the shock of fear or even that soft warmth in your heart that says you care about someone or something... oh, you *do not like any of that,* do you?"

"Co—"

"Do you know why you hate to *feel,* Briar?" Cooper interrupted, as if she had never started speaking. "Why, you run from it. Because you do run from it, do you not? You mediate it through your 'methods,' or you separate yourself from it through booze." Cooper clinked his bottle against hers, which was still clutched tight in her fingers. "Why else are you up at nearly four in the morning with a drink in your hand?"

"You handed this to me, remember?" Buggy tried to laugh, but it came out gargled, like it slipped and fell on something slimy. He was leaning in so close now, that weird half-smirk lifting to show a small section of white teeth.

"And you know why you hide and run and avoid those gross, gross feelings?"

"Cooper could you just—" Buggy raised her free hand, ready to push him away. But she hesitated. She realized she was afraid to touch him.

Cooper kept on, purring in that strange, mocking tone. His head was tilted down, casting his usually bright eyes into shadow.

"Because feelings like that, they pop up without your permission. That feeling you get when your heart is telling you something your head does not want to admit. That you are not in control. You cannot stand it. Because you like to be in *control*. Right, Briar dear? And when you cannot be in control, you shut it down. You run, run, run away." He nearly giggled this last, and wiggled his fingers in the air between them, as if demonstrating a mosquito taking flight.

Buggy's eyes were wide. *What the shit...?*

"Are you high?" Buggy asked, a part of her hoping that he was. Hoping that this weird, mocking grin that spread ever wider on his face was due to some sort of drug. Because this wasn't like him at all. Not one bit like him to be—Then all thoughts derailed as he leaned in a little more. Buggy tried to lean away, but her head met the cabinet door with a hard thud. She winced in pain but said nothing. She couldn't open her mouth, and Cooper wasn't finished yet.

"You run, or you hide because when you do not have control over your feelings, that means *someone else does*. And you know better than anyone," Cooper leaned in even closer, lips brushing against her ear, making her shiver, "people sometimes just *leave*, do they not? People sometimes get divorced. Move away. Sometimes the ones that are supposed to love you the most, they just disappear without a trace, without explanation. One way or another, you always seem to *lose*. Lose and get left behind over and over. Left with nothing but emptiness. A little hollow space in your chest." Buggy's eyes darted to his, so close now. She had never told him about that. The strange void in her heart. She wanted to ask him how he knew, but her voice had evaporated from her throat. "It is a reminder of everything you have lost... all those things remembered and forgotten... and how much you could still lose. But guess what? I can make those nasty feelings all *go away*. Just wait and see. Because, I promise you one thing, Briar dear," he said pulling back slowly, letting his nose trail lightly against her cheekbone until she could feel his warm breath against her lips. She could almost taste that half-smirk as it spread a little wider. She shivered again but didn't dare move. "I am awake now. And I? I am not going anywhere."

Buggy let out a breath as Cooper pulled back. He took a drink of his beer as he moved to the other side of the kitchen, nearly downing half the bottle in one. He placed it on the counter with a little click and looked back at Buggy, who sat stunned. He smiled, winked, and disappeared back into the living room, leaving his bottle on the counter.

Buggy slid from her perch, heart thudding, hands shaking a little. She hesitated there, unsure of what to do, or how to feel about the insane scene that just took place. *What the actual fuck?* How the hell could he have used her birth mom's abandonment like that? She got that he was trying to make some sort of point, but that was downright cruel. Him bringing up her parents' divorce in that manner was bad enough, but she had not told him about her birth mom so that he could throw it in her face when it was convenient for him. No, that was too far. He'd had a lot to drink that night, they all had. She could smell it on his breath when he leaned in. But that was no excuse. She didn't care if he was drunk or high or both. Shock had faded, and now she was pissed. She dropped her beer on the counter with a hard click and followed Cooper into the living room, ready to give him a piece of her mind. Better late than never. She went over to where he seemed to have returned on the couch and paused. He was there, laying in the exact same position he had been when she had gotten up. His hand lolling in the open air between the couch and the ground, his mouth half-open, and his chest rising and falling in that same slow rhythmic manner. He indeed looked asleep. His hair was even back to being scattered over his closed eyes.

Buggy frowned. Had he seriously fallen asleep in the two minutes it took her to clear her head and walk out of the kitchen? That seemed quick, but there he was, fast asleep. She scowled and made her way back towards the kitchen. She would talk to him about it tomorrow then. Buggy stepped into the yellow light of the old kitchen bulb and paused. She looked at the spot where Cooper had placed his beer only a few short minutes ago. The counter was empty. Her beer bottle sat precisely where she left it by the sink, but Cooper's seemed to have vanished. Buggy looked around the floor, wondering if it had toppled off for some reason, but there was nothing. No broken glass, no spilled beer.

What the hell?

She made her way towards her beer bottle and picked it up. As she did so, she heard a light jingling sound. A chill ran up Buggy's spine, and her throat closed tight. She reached down and patted the pocket of her cartoon coffee cup pajamas. She had accidently left the pair at Andrew's last weekend, which had turned out to be a lucky thing. The cheery little cups had wafts of steam rising from their lips, and little yawning faces with eyes scrunched closed. The phrase: "Not a morning person" was scrawled in messy calligraphy between the cups. She loved those pajamas, mainly because they had pockets. Now, as she reached down and checked the pocket of her right leg, she wished she had never even seen them before. There was a heaviness there, one she had not noticed until now. She reached in and pulled out a set of keys. Hanging beside the long and cumbersome row of car and apartment keys was an opener in the shape of a beer bottle with "Welcome to Las Vegas" written across its face.

Of course, it's tacky! That's what makes it timeless!

Buggy swallowed, but her throat had closed so tight it made the action nearly impossible. Cooper had put this in his pocket. She had heard it fall and jingle there. She had watched him do it... hadn't she? And he had never touched her. He had leaned in close on the counter, but she would have noticed if he slipped them into her pants. No, they had been in his pocket when he walked back into the living room.

Or had that actually happened? She thought about the way Cooper had looked on the couch, fast asleep, like he had never gotten up in the first place. She thought about the vanishing bottle, and how none this made logical sense. It had *just* happened, but none of it made *any sense*. Was it possible... could she have imagined...? No, that's ridiculous. She couldn't have imagined all that. But the bottle... the keys....

Buggy hastily tossed the keys onto the table as if they had transformed into hot coals. They skidded and clattered against the wall before finally coming to a halt. She tipped her beer bottle up and drank till it was gone. She tossed the empty into the recycle bin beneath the sink and flipped the light switch off, casting herself into eerie darkness.

She had a lot to drink, and her head was still fuzzy. She needed sleep. That is what she needed. This would all make sense as soon as she got some shuteye. She made her way back into the living room, but rest didn't come for a long time. Instead, she clicked play on the controller and watched as Ross and Rachel started their affair all over again, doing her best not to think about a little bottle opener hanging on a key chain.

8

"Lucy! I'm home!" Buggy called as she stepped through the door to her apartment later that afternoon. At some point, Buggy must have drifted back off to sleep, because she was shaken awake by Linny around nine-thirty that morning. They made the traditional Saturday morning pancakes and eggs and bid their goodbyes for the weekend. Since Buggy's car was still toast, Cooper had dropped her off outside her apartment.

"You sure you don't want me to get it towed to the shop today?" he asked, frowning as she pulled her shoulder bag from his trunk.

"No, it's alright," she said, "Tomorrow will be soon enough." Buggy hesitated. "Hey, Cooper."

"Yeah?"

"Umm..." she paused and geared herself up for this possibly very unpleasant conversation. Buggy hated uncomfortable discussions. She usually avoided them at all costs. She had once before literally stopped mid-argument with a co-worker, turned, and walked out of the room. That is how much she hated emotionally charged discussions. This, however, wasn't a random co-worker at a part-time job back when she had just graduated high school. No, this was one of her oldest and closest friends. And she needed to know. She had woken that morning to several points in the previous evening having been blurred by alcohol. She needed to know if the conversation in the kitchen had been one of them. And if it wasn't, Buggy needed to talk to him about it. "I need to ask you something."

He blinked—obviously taken aback by the serious tone she had adopted. His eyes looked confused, but his smile didn't waver. "Okay. Shoot."

"We, uh, we talked last night, ya?"

"You mean about how much you hate Ross and Rachel?"

"No... I mean when we were alone in the kitchen." He looked more confused. "You brought up my mom?"

"When was this?" Cooper frowned.

"Last night." Buggy was getting a little frustrated. Was he just pretending not to remember? "At four in the morning... I sat on the counter. You started talking about feelings, and you mentioned my mom...." Cooper was shaking his head.

"Buggy, I didn't wake up last night."

"Cooper," Buggy sighed. "Please don't screw with me. I'm way too tired—"

"I'm serious," Cooper protested, eyes wide and innocent. "Here, hold on, look." Cooper pulled out his phone and tapped on his Fitbit app. He had gotten his first Fitbit as a Christmas present from his sister about two years ago. Since then, he had been glued to the thing. Even tracked his diet, steps, and water intake. Mostly for fun (he had always been a fairly fit kind of guy) but that didn't stop Andrew, Linny, and even Buggy herself from teasing him about it. However, his Fitbit didn't only track calories and step counts. It also tracked sleep patterns. He pulled up his sleep record, which depicted little blue lines running horizontally across the screen with little red lines breaking up the sections of sleep. He tapped on last night's entry and held it out for her to see. The long blue line was broken only by a few short red lines which told precisely when he had woken up the night before. None of them appeared around four o'clock. No, from two until seven-thirty AM, there was just a solid section of blue. Deep, deep sleep. Buggy stared at it, confused.

"Seriously?" Buggy took the phone in her hands for a better look, scanning the entry closely.

"Four slices of pizza, four beers, and there is no waking me," Cooper said, smiling again.

What the hell? But...? Buggy frowned. God, maybe she *had* imagined it. All her dreams had been rather vivid recently. The first extremely vivid dream had come the morning of her twenty-fourth birthday. Well, not so much a dream as a nightmare. One full of fear and fire, as that strange house burned down around her. She had woken up screaming, but Sandra had been there, reminding her what was reality. Buggy had quickly reoriented. She had known it was a dream after she woke, although the thought of it still made her cringe. Last night's dream (if that is what it was) seemed like a whole other level of realism. She could still remember exactly how it had felt when he leaned in, had felt his breath against her ear. Then again, she usually thought dreams were real at the time they were happening. Buggy had thought the other dreams had been real—had *felt* her flesh sloughing off as she burned alive in the house—had believed she was falling through the darkness, drowning in nothing—that had all felt real. If last night was a dream, if she hadn't *actually* woken up from the drowning dream, but only *thought* she had woken up... well, it would explain a lot. The way Cooper acted, so unlike himself. Cooper's non-existent beer bottle. The keys that magically transported from his pocket to hers. Suddenly, the idea of it all being an illusion was the only answer that made sense.

"Oh shit. I'm sorry, Cooper, I must have dreamed it."

"That's okay," Cooper laughed, putting his phone back in his pocket. "Just out of curiosity, what did dream-us talk about?" Buggy looked up at him. He seemed totally normal today. His usual wide smile was back on, and all traces of the half-smirk were gone. His gaze was bright, and the little smile lines creased the edges of his eyes once more.

Buggy opened her mouth, hesitated, then changed her mind. "We talked about the weird co-dependent relationship you have with that Fitbit of yours," she grinned. Cooper rolled his eyes. "Nah, it's not important. It was just..." Buggy shrugged "Well, frankly, you were a bit of an ass."

"Oh? Well, I apologize for dream-me," he said, smiling wider. "Want me to kick his ass?"

"Nah," Buggy shook her head, relief flooding her. All tension evaporated with one easy explanation. Just a nightmare. Thank God. "He gets a pass this time."

"Well, if he ever bugs you again, let me know."

"I'll be sure to do that. Thanks for the ride." She turned to go inside.

"Of course.... Hey, Buggy?" Buggy turned back around to meet a rather serious looking Cooper. "Is something wrong?"

Buggy did her best to keep her smile in place. She could see the concern in Coopers eyes. It was a strange thing to see in his usually carefree expression. Buggy decided it wasn't a good look on him, so she widened her smile.

"Just a weird ass dream," she said.

At least I didn't die in this one, Buggy thought to herself. *That's something.* It was all just a silly dream after all. No big deal, right? She was fine. Totally fine.

You keep telling yourself that, Briar dear.

Buggy shook the thought away and said cheerily: "I just need some solid sleep and I'll be good."

Cooper had shrugged, nodded, and smoothed away his worry lines with a classic Cooper grin. They said their goodbyes, and Buggy went inside. She stepped into her apartment, closing the door behind her with a little snap.

"Sandra! You home?" Buggy looked around the empty apartment. It wasn't a very large place that they shared, but it was big enough. Two bedroom, one bath with light blue wallpaper and dark blue trim. The first time Buggy followed Sandra into the place, she felt like she was walking into a cloud. One of those soft and puffy white fluffs that drift lazily across a blue sky. That feeling faded after a few months had gone by and she had grown used to the sight. But every so often she would remember that first time, that first look, and she would smile. She had been so excited when she moved in. Her first apartment. Granted, it had technically been Sandra's apartment first. Being the older sister, Sandra did *everything* first. The perfect apartment, the ideal girlfriend, the dream job that she always wanted, she got it all first. Buggy wondered, not infrequently, if she should feel jealous of her big sister. But she knew she never would, not really. She couldn't bring herself to resent Sandra even if she tried.

Buggy took a glance around the place, calling out, but Sandra didn't answer. Buggy stepped into her room and flipped on the light. Her room was the same soft blue as the rest of the apartment and organized to perfection. She had a desk to one side with all of her schoolbooks, notebooks, pens, and laptop all arranged. She had her makeup lined up and ready on the counter in front of the mirror attached to her dresser. They were placed in descending order of use, going from most frequently used on the left, to least often used on the right. That, however, was mostly it for things out in the open, except of course, for her pictures. Pictures of her and Sandra, and her and her parents (separately of course) hung inline on the walls. A picture of her, Cooper, Andrew, and Linny, arm in arm outside some concert hall she no longer remembered the name of, sat by her bedside table.

Buggy went to her bed and sat down, setting her shoulder bag beside her. She picked up the picture of her and her friends, mid-guffaws of laughter. Cooper had been wearing a cowboy hat for some reason. It was pulled down low over his face, sunglasses covering his eyes. Buggy stared at the picture, a frown pulling her lips.

You know why you hide and run and avoid those gross, gross feelings? You know better than anyone... people sometimes just leave, do they not?

Buggy turned to the bag at her side. She unlatched the little buckle and flipped it open. She riffled through the dozens of cassette tapes until she found the one she wanted. It was in a little case with silver paper and written on the cover in pink lettering were the words: *When You Miss Me.* Buggy pulled it and the cassette player out of the bag. She pressed the little button that popped open the recorder and slid in the tape. The play button clicked. The cassette started playing with a little initial whine, and there was a rustle from the recording. Her mother must have been shifting in her seat.

"Hey, honey," the soft and familiar voice broke the silence. Buggy closed her eyes to listen. "To start off, I miss you too."

"Oh, yeah?" Buggy asked the empty room. "Then why the hell did you leave me?" The recording ignored her and continued.

"I know this all must be hard to understand. I know you must have many questions... but I need you to know that this wasn't my choice. I don't *want* to leave you behind." She heard a ragged breath, and Buggy squeezed her eyes tighter, willing her heart not to beat faster as the voice on the other end of the recording began to cry. "I never wanted you to have to grow up without me. I want to be there for all of it. Your first steps. Your first words. *All* of it. I want to be there when you go to high school. When you fall in love for the first time. I want to be there for you when your heart is broken for the first time. I want to hold you, and I want to tell you that everything will be okay. I want to be there as you achieve all your dreams because I *know* you will," the voice laughed on the other end of time. A time long gone and passed far behind. Buggy swallowed hard. "You're a fighter, little one. I can tell. You'll fight for what you want, and I wish I could be there to fight right alongside you. Please, please believe me when

I say this isn't what I want. If I could have, I would have stayed with you. All I ever wanted was to watch you grow up into the wonderful girl I am sure that you have become. But fate has other plans for us... but please know that I love you. I always have. Always will. I lov—" Buggy pressed the stop button, eyes still closed. She opened them, and got to her feet, leaving the recorder on the bed next to the bag. She went to the little kitchen that she and Sandra shared and walked directly to the cabinet next to their small white fridge and opened it.

Inside, several unopened wine bottles were laying on their side. Behind those were a mostly full bottle of vodka—Sandra's—and a half-empty bottle of whiskey—Buggy's. She pulled it down and poured herself a few fingers. She topped that off with some diet Coke from the fridge and sipped at it while contemplating the chasm in her chest. That oh-so-familiar emptiness that told her something was missing. Something was lost. Buggy wondered how long it could last. That void. That hollow area just beside her heart. That dragging feeling that tore through her chest and down to her stomach where it hung, heavy in its emptiness. She wondered, but not for long. She already knew.

This feeling... it wasn't the type of thing to disappear or go away. It was born inside her, and there it would stay. It was there long before she ever pressed play on the little tape recorder, and it would live long after she finally destroyed the things, because she did plan to destroy them someday. And why? Perhaps a way of moving on? As a way of childishly getting back at the mother who had left her? She wasn't sure when, or why, she had first contemplated destroying them, but she planned on destroying them eventually all the same. Or, at least, that is what she kept telling herself, despite the years that ticked by without a single tape out of place in her care. She still held onto the possibility like a shield, a way to make the tapes have less power over her, less control... but only a little less.

She had told this plan to Sandra, who had been uncertain about the idea. Sandra wasn't certain about any of it, and why should she be? Sandra could never understand, although she tried awfully hard to do just that. She had not been born with this empty space in her heart. She had been born and raised by her parents, her actual parents, and had always had her rightful home. Her parents had not even split up until several years after she had moved out and become entirely self-sufficient. Sandra had always been whole. Buggy had always felt a little broken, and not just because her birth mother abandoned her to die in a dark alley. No, it went deeper than that... like she was actually missing a section of her soul. A piece forgotten. A hollowness that grew over the months until it felt like it might swallow her whole.

Sandra couldn't understand, but that didn't mean she was unsympathetic. The few people who Buggy had told about these feelings had grown a little weary of Buggy's struggles. Not out of any malice, or even indifference. They simply had no control over it. They could do nothing but listen to the same issues, bemoaning the same emptiness, the same loss, over and over, until finally, quite unknown to themselves, they lost interest. They no longer wanted to hear that Buggy was hurting. They didn't want to hear about how she sometimes felt empty, confused, or *wrong* on the inside. They didn't know *what to do* with that information. They could *do nothing* with it, and it made them hate themselves a little. So, they avoided it, and Buggy was more than happy to oblige. She had never wanted to talk about it in the first place. It had been her parents who had dragged it out of her when they found her, fourteen years old and crying, the tape recorder playing in her lap. They were the first to comfort her. They were the first to push her to go to therapy. They were also the first to put up that wall. That wall people seem to grow after a few years of hearing about that same old empty space in a person's heart. Those same old pains that should have long ago been healed over, long ago *fixed*. It came, invisible, into being, becoming more solid each time they asked how Buggy was doing and she answered, "not great." Buggy wondered why they kept asking if the answer disappointed them so much, but she figured that out as well. They asked because that was *their job*. Her parents may not have given birth to her, but they were her parents and (to them) her happiness was their responsibility. Her feeling *whole* was their responsibility. Every time she said: "not great," it was like they had failed her. Everything they tried had fallen short. They were not her birth mother, and they couldn't bring the voice on the other end of the line into reality. That wasn't their fault, of course. None of this was their fault, but it didn't stop them from blaming themselves, and unintentionally, maybe blaming Buggy a little as well. They tried so hard, were truly wonderful parents. Buggy appreciated them, loved them, and could meet them partway, right?

Besides, it wasn't always that bad. That "void" feeling had come and gone over the years, some years worse than others, some much better. Sometimes it faded so far into the background that it was almost completely ignorable, but eventually it would appear again, never to fully go away. It was only the past few months that things had really started hurting again. But she had been doing so well for so long, and they had gotten so comfortable with the idea that her therapy was over, that she had been *fixed*. Buggy would feel bad bringing this new flair-up to her family. So, she started lying. She wasn't very good at it of course, doe eyes and all, but she was getting better. It was all about twisting that truth.

Sandra had never bought it though. Buggy's sister still *really* wanted to know and know *everything*. Good with the bad. Buggy had tried to lie to her once. She had smiled in what she had thought was a convincing manner.

"I'm doing good actually," she had nodded her head, trying to make her body language match her words. "I think I'm over the worst of it. I really do." Sandra had watched her for three long seconds, sharp brown eyes narrowing with every passing moment until they were dark slits.

"Lie to me again," she spoke sweetly and with a smile, but her eyes meant business. "And I'll kick your little five-four ass, do you understand me?" Sandra had never needed to follow through on that threat. That had been the first and only time Buggy had tried an out-and-out lie to Sandra. Ever. No, she never lied outright to Sandra... but Buggy had her own secrets all the same. Like the little secret in her sock drawer.

Buggy heard a key rattling in the door lock. She checked her watch, which told her it was only two in the afternoon. Shit. She quickly downed the rest of her drink and put the glass in the dishwasher before Sandra could walk in. She knew her older sister wouldn't appreciate Buggy with a drink in her hand at that hour of the day. The door opened.

"Lucy, I'm home!" Sandra called. Buggy heard the clatter of keys dropping onto a table.

"Oh, hey you!" Buggy called back, stepping out of the kitchen to greet her.

Sandra was, well, frankly, *beautiful.* She had deep mocha skin with long dark brown hair that always seemed perfectly placed. Currently, it was tied back in a long braid that fell all the way down past her hips, with just a few loose strands falling around her warm eyes, framing her face.

"Hello, beautiful!" she called, closing the door and dropping her purse on the coffee table. "How was your Friday? Also, is there something wrong with your car? I saw it parked outside your office last night."

"Yeah, something's up with it, I don't know," Buggy shrugged. "I'm getting it towed to Jimmy's tomorrow."

"Oh, I'm sorry, that sucks. Do you need a ride to work on Monday?" Sandra asked, hands resting on her hips, a habit that she picked up from their mom.

"Nah, it's alright. The bus is right down the street. But thanks.... What?" Sandra was watching her with narrowed eyes.

"You okay?"

"What?" Buggy asked again, trying to smile with confusion.

"You were listening to *her* again, weren't you?" How the hell did she always know?

"Lil bit, yeah." Buggy shrugged and plopped down on their couch, not bothering to pretend she didn't know what Sandra was talking about. The cushions let out a sigh of air from its various broken seams.

"How are you?" Sandra asked, sitting down next to her, elegantly crossing her long legs.

"Eh," Buggy shrugged, leaning her side against the couch, one arm hanging off the back. "Not the best, but not the worst."

Sandra nodded. "Well, better than shitty."

"Yeah," Buggy smiled, looking over at her, "much better than shitty."

Sandra smiled, satisfied, and changed the subject. "You've got a big presentation tomorrow, right?"

Buggy shrugged. She had been taking evening and weekend classes for the past semester, slowly building up a transferable unit base for an English degree. Then she would finally transfer over to a four year, probably Sacramento State. She would only have to spend a quick two years at most. In and out. Much cheaper.

"Yep, I do," Buggy answered. Sandra raised an unsatisfied brow, and Buggy shrugged. Buggy hated public speaking and had been dreading this presentation since the class had begun. Public speaking was, unfortunately, a requirement to transfer, so she decided to get it out of the way. She had been working on the assignment for over a month now, having had to pick out a hot button issue in politics and develop a PowerPoint presentation summing up the issue and then presenting her own views and possible solutions. Buggy had glared daily at the assignment in her syllabus, loathing it long before she had to work on it, and loathing it even more when she finally did.

"Wanna practice some more?" Sandra offered, leaning forward, already in "study mode." Like Buggy, Sandra had never been an honor roll, salutatorian-type of student. However, again like Buggy, she was a hard worker. She refused to put in less than one hundred percent effort, no matter what the subject matter or topic. She and Buggy had spent many a late night quizzing each other during middle school, high school, and college. They would make it an event and end up sitting cross-legged on the carpet surrounded by scattered papers, stacks of worn note cards, and a bottle of half-drunk wine.

"Nah," Buggy said after a brief hesitation. She had been practicing her speech every day, in the mirror, in front of Sandra, even a few times in front of Linny. They had all been helpful, but unfortunately it did nothing to soothe her nerves. "I just... ulg, I don't even wanna talk about it."

"Fair enough," Sandra said, leaning against the couch, resting her head in her hand. "And how was *Friends* Friday?"

"Great as always."

"And how is Cooper?"

"Why do you say it like that?" Buggy scowled, unaware of the pink sheen creeping up under her freckles.

"Like what?" Sandra blinked.

"Coooooooper," Buggy mimicked, exaggerating the emphasis her sister had added. "Why do you say it like that?"

"I didn't say it like that," Sandra twirled her braid between her fingers, grinning wickedly. Although Sandra was always invited to *Friends* Marathon Fridays, she rarely had the opportunity to join in the festivities. The few times that she *had* joined, she had watched Cooper and Buggy talking with a little too much attention. Later, when Buggy had started noticing Cooper's sideways smiles, Sandra had not mirrored Buggy's concerns. She had been delighted.

"Yes, you did. You always do," Buggy accused, frown deepening.

"No, I don't."

"Yes you—you know what, I'm not getting into it with you." Buggy shook her head in defeat. "No, Sandra, you're perfectly innocent and fooling absolutely everyone with your sly ways."

"I thought so, thank you very much." Sandra's wide smile fell a little as Buggy gave a great yawn. "But... you're sure you're okay? You do look tired."

Buggy hesitated, "Just some shitty sleep again. But I'm definitely not bad. Promise."

"I'll take it!" Sandra laughed, clapping her hands together.

Buggy smiled. She loved Sandra and her "take the small blessings as they come" attitude towards life. She was an inspiration that Buggy was always trying to meet. A daydream she was always trying to catch and bring into reality. Sandra made it look easy. Simple as breathing. For Buggy, it was her guiding light that she turned to when she herself didn't know how to think or act.

What would Sandra say? How would Sandra think?

"How'd your day go yesterday?" Buggy asked, flipping herself over, legs sprawling the back of the couch, hair falling down the front where her legs should be, and piling on the floor. "You meet up with Christina this morning?"

"The paper is good. And yes, I met up with Christina. Oh, Buggy, it's all going so damn well!" Sandra clapped her hands together once more. Buggy doubted she even meant to do it. It was just another one of those things that was so purely... Sandra.

Buggy rested on the couch, ready to listen to her sister prattle on about her day. All the monotonous things she had done. All the day-to-day routines that Sandra made sound like magical events all on their own. She always made everything sound wonderful. Not in a "look how wonderful life is, don't you feel guilty for not appreciating every God-blessed moment of it" kind of way, But just in a "Hi, I'm Sandra, and I love everything" kind of way. It wasn't naive when she spoke, it wasn't silly... it was beautiful. It was *light*. And God in heaven forgive her, but Buggy ***did*** envy her sister one thing. Her point of view. She envied the eyes that Sandra saw the world through. She wished for the love that seemed to bloom through Sandra to the world around her. She bathed herself in it at every opportunity. She envied her sister that, but she loved her more. She loved her with every fiber of her being. To every inch of her core, she loved her. And she would sooner burn the world than watch that little light fade from her sister's eyes.

"Well then tell me all about it," Buggy said, a smile spreading wide across her face, legs lolling in the air above them.

9

Theo sat in front of the fire, hands resting gentle on his knees. He watched the flames bristle and writhe in the hearth, dancing its harsh dance, and thought about how it was so much easier now. Easier to connect. Connect to that person he had never actually met. After the first time, the first connection, the first *touch*, it was easier to make it happen again. Easier to reach out to her, gently *see*. He couldn't read her thoughts. No, that would be **really** creepy, and this was creepy enough as it was. But he could see things, *feel* things. Things that weren't *his* to feel. Things that belonged to a girl he had never known and yet had begun to know. Slowly but surely. With every reach, with every connection, with every glimpse. They were images mostly. Images of things she saw often, things that she felt strongly about. The Elwin Dentistry sign, the image of a tanned girl with long, dark, braided hair. A worn gray bag full of cassette tapes with labels Theo couldn't read. They were too fuzzy in his mind and only lasted half a second in their imagery. These appeared more often than all the rest, frequently flickering across Theo's mind as he sat in front of the fire, breathing in his nose and out his mouth. Connecting. Reaching out.

Theo tried not to think too hard about it. Tried not to think too hard about what a horrifying violation this was. He wasn't reading her diary. He wasn't leaning down over a computer with spider fast fingers, taping a keyboard and searching through her inner most thoughts. They were just wisps. Feelings. Flashes. Brief—and yet—they were **not his**. They didn't belong to him, and the guilt that boiled hot in his belly threatened to suffocate any sort of productivity of the action. He knew why he was doing this. He knew he was trying to help—and yet—It still felt horribly wrong.

Theo continued to breath in his nose, out his mouth, and reached. Reached for her. Reached and found....

Theo frowned. There was something wrong. There was something *else*. When Theo had felt the wisps before they had been bright. Shining. Lovely really, even if there was no gleam of joy, there was a bitter sweetness in the feelings he had. Bittersweet, soft with a sharp edge around the clouds of gentle golden light. But this, what he had just touched... it was different. It was gray. Slimy. It was *wrong*.

"Styger!" he called loudly.

"Yeah, kid?" Cam Styger responded from the other room. The sizzle of breakfast was audible from the living room, sending the wafting smell of burnt eggs and bacon grease Theo's direction.

"Something's wrong." There was a light clicking sound as Cam turned off the stove. Theo heard his loud footfalls as he came to stand in the doorway.

"What do you mean? You lose track of her?"

"No..." Theo said, eyes squinting at the fire. "I still feel her... but... not *just* her..."

"What do you mean?" Cam stepped into the room, and Theo could almost feel the anxiety wafting off of him in thick waves. And then he realized, he **was** feeling his anxiety. It swept out from Cam as a strange warm pressure that seemed to be almost— Theo shook the thought away. That wasn't important.

"I mean, I feel something else. Some sort of... **else**... I don't know how to explain it."

"Shit," Cam growled, apparently not needing an explanation. "It's happening."

"What's happening?" Theo turned, watching Cam grab his coat off the rack by the door. Cam threw it at him, and Theo caught it, mouth going dry. "Oh, shit. You mean, *it's* happening?"

"We need to go."

"Where?" Theo asked, slipping on the coat, and staring at the older man with bemusement.

"To her."

"To-wha-her? Now?!" Theo squeaked, jerking the coat over his shoulders. "Seriously?"

"We are out of time," Cam said, snagging the Jeep's keys off the coffee table. "Now, Theo. Let's go." Theo stared at him for a long while, and Cam just stood glaring at him until he finally spoke.

"Well, okay, fuck, I guess." He caught the keys when Cam tossed them.

IO

There was truly little Buggy could do about it now. It was already over. Her presentation had come and gone, and if Buggy thought she felt crappy before stepping up to the front of the class and opening her mouth then—holy shit—she had another thing coming. All their questions, comments, jokes, and jabs rolled around her mind like some sort of torturous hamster wheel. Each question had a clear answer, but as always, she found them far too late. Buggy could never answer when she was stressed out. Never. She would always think of the right answer, the true, coherent, beautiful, and somehow elusive answer, ten minutes after the question was asked. Always too late.

Her presentation had not ended well. It had started decently, but as the minutes ticked by, and the longer those watchful eyes were on her, Buggy's already minimal confidence waned. By the time they reached the Q and A section after the presentation, her mind was completely frayed, edges blurring into nonexistence. She couldn't gather her thoughts fast enough to answer as the anxiety dragged her coherent mind deeper and deeper into panicked darkness. All she could do was stand there under the flood of questions as they turned to snickers, with nothing to say. All she could do was wonder. Wonder why these children masquerading as adults thought that this was a fair thing to do? Why did they think that attacking her was a good idea? Because they had. They had seen her fumbling around their follow-up questions, had seen her drowning in her own fear. Instead of giving her a second to catch her breath, or throw her a lifeline, they pounced, claws wide, fangs bared. Weren't they all too old for this? It hadn't lasted long, just a few minutes at most. The professor looking up from his computer long enough to notice what was going on and quickly put an end to it, apparently as surprised at the rest of the class as Buggy herself. Because, why? What did they gain exactly?

Did it make them feel more powerful, Buggy wondered? Did they simply not like her? She could understand that. She wasn't the most social person at school. Just like in high school, she tended to keep to herself. Sandra always told her to be careful about such things. Warning her that keeping her walls up all the time made her seem distant, cold, mean even. Buggy could understand if people didn't like her, but to go as far as public shaming? As short as it was, such public ridicule could leave a person hollowed out, ugly even to themselves. It wasn't like they were insulting her looks. They were not insulting her large eyes, too big for her face. They didn't call her "bug face" or any of the juvenile insults meant to tear down her appearance. No. Their snickers were insulting her intelligence, which for Buggy, was *so much* worse. People could make fun of the way she looked all they liked. Her leggings, her hair, her style, her makeup. She didn't give a flying fuck what anyone thought about those things. Those things meant nothing to her. Even her eyes could be made to appear smaller with thick liner and makeup. Those things were easily changed if she felt the need, although she had never felt the need. They were things she could handle. Something she could build a method around. Her intelligence wasn't. Sure, she could study, go to school, work hard, and she did all of those things and more, but when it came right down to it, her mind worked the way that it worked, and she couldn't alter that. There was a baseline of intelligence and how information was processed. She couldn't change that. Insulting that which she could not change, not control... well, that was the problem now, wasn't it? Control.

Because you like to be in control, right, Briar dear?

Dream-Cooper's sneering voice whispered in her ear, and Buggy brushed it away as quickly as she could but was unable to deny the truth of those words. Because she *did* like control. She hated the alternative. So, she kept trying. Created patterns for herself, well-worn ways that had proven useful in the past. Well-worn patterns of how things must be done. Drink to the left, water to the right, napkin in her lap. Earbuds in, the rest of the world out. She had control over that. She had her methods, but she didn't have methods for everything.

Standing before a crowd of people that somehow decided that her intelligence was just such a funny, funny little joke for them to play with— she had no method for that. So, all Buggy could do was wait, nod, smile, and hope that it would be over soon. She knew it was a small thing. Knew that it was just a moment and would be left in the past. If she let it. But she had a method for those kinds of moments as well. A method for the moments with no methods. She would roll that memory around in her mind for hours, weeks, or even years.

She could only wait until it was over, sit down, and slowly drown in her shame and self-loathing. She wasn't even angry at the people that humiliated her. No, she had no real anger or hate towards them. All of those emotions were directed inward as if each were a hammer, and she beat her soul with it. It bled. As it always did. And that void, that ever-present hollow space in her chest seemed to shift, grunting in agreement.

It was later now, and Buggy was sitting at her kitchen counter back in her apartment. A glass of whiskey and Coke twirling listlessly between her fingers. She glared at it as if it had said something particularly nasty. This had been another routine that she had developed over the past few months. Something to accompany her vivid dreams since her twenty-fourth birthday. Every time before she took a drink, she would look at it, think about it, and decide if today was the day she poured it down the drain. Her anxiety—that hollow space in her heart—it had all been growing worse, and she wasn't handling it very well. She already knew that. She wasn't an alcoholic, but she had started a little bit of self-medication when things got bad and all she wanted was to get away from herself. She knew that it wasn't a great road to tiptoe down. She knew *that* best of all. And yet....

Buggy raised the cup to her lips and downed half the glass in one gulp.

"Not today, I guess," she said to no one in particular, seeing as there was no one else in the room besides herself. Sandra wouldn't be home from her dinner with Christina for at least another three hours. She spent most of her free time with Christina these days. Buggy didn't mind so much. Christina was a nice girl who treated her sister like the beautiful person that she was. Buggy was so glad for her and knew that it wouldn't be long before Sandra came home from one of those late Saturday night dates with a large ring on her finger. Then she would start a new chapter in her life. She would leave.

Now, **that** did make Buggy sad.

You know better than anyone... people sometimes just leave, do they not?

"Shut up," Buggy grumbled to her own thoughts. Thankfully, they listened.

Buggy checked the clock on the wall, watched its long hands ticking slowly around the daisy patterns against its back. She had three hours to get utterly shitfaced before Buggy's loving, but also annoyingly concerned, sister got home. Buggy downed the rest of the glass and made herself another. It had been perhaps a week, maybe a week and a half, after her birthday that she had started keeping two bottles of whiskey. The first was on display in the kitchen drawer for Sandra to see. That was the one she would check every time she got home, although she tried to be sneaky about it. That was the one that Buggy would take one, two shots from at the most. The other bottle, her second secret bottle, was the one she kept in her dresser cabinet stuffed between her underwear and socks. *That one* went down faster and was replaced a bit more frequently, but Sandra never saw it. Buggy thought this a kindness, really. If Sandra only watched the bottle in the kitchen drawer, then by God, she would have nothing to worry about.

Buggy poured herself another glass and walked it over to the TV. She switched it on and started scrolling through Netflix. Nothing better to distract her from a crappy day than to have a few drinks and watch a mindless TV series that was basically a carbon copy of every other TV series. The attractive main character with his goofy sidekick who just happens to be equally attractive. The beautiful love interest who is inevitably kidnapped or blackmailed at some point during the series. The drama. The action. The plotlines were so plastic, so predictable, it was hilarious. Buggy knew every step, knew every dramatic reveal before it happened. She frequently pissed Sandra off by blowing some "secret" plot element forty minutes before it was revealed.

"How the hell did you know that?" Sandra would ask, eyes wide with surprise and irritation.

"I can see it," Buggy would answer simply. "I can just see how it's going to end. I always do."

Buggy smiled to herself, chose a random TV cover that donned a beautiful man in a cop's uniform standing next to an equally beautiful woman in a power suit. She clicked the play button, and sank deeper into the couch, mournful only of the fact that her drink was growing low and she would soon have to get up to refill it. All thoughts of the day were quickly swept away by alcohol, beautiful faces, terrible writing, and predictable plot lines.

She still had two-and-a-half hours to go.

Her phone rang on the couch beside her to the tune of John Denver's "Take Me Home Country Road." Buggy frowned down at the screen over her glass. She reached for it, ice clinking in her drink.

Unknown Number.

Buggy frowned and accepted the call.

II

"Hello?" the voice on the other end of the line spoke, and it felt like a hand had grabbed ahold of Cam Styger's heart and squeezed. He could hardly breathe. "Helloooo?" Cam's mouth opened and closed a little. He had no intent to say anything, but he also didn't want her to hang up. He wanted to keep listening to the sound of her voice, just a little longer. "Anybody there?" He could hear a slight slur around the edges of her words, barely noticeable, but Cam could tell. He could always tell. "No? Ooookay." There was a small little beeping sound in Cam's ear.

Wait. Cam thought, but the line was dead. He pulled the phone away from his face.

"You alright?" Theo asked, glancing over to him from the driver's seat as headlights flashed briefly over his face. Cam ignored his question.

"How far out are we?"

Theo checked the GPS attached to the dashboard. "We're still about seven hours out of Marshall County... well, that is, if we plan on stopping to sleep at any point."

"Sure, but not yet," Cam said, leaning back into his seat. "Wake me when you need a break."

"Sure." Pause. "Hey, Styger?"

"Yeah, kid?"

"What are we gonna do when we get there?"

"I don't know yet," Cam answered honestly. This wasn't how things were supposed to go. They had a plan. This wasn't even close. How the hell was he supposed to explain? How the hell was he supposed to make this work? *Could* they make it work? More importantly, could they make it work in time? If Theo was right, if the girl was no longer "alone," then time was running out fast. It would be coming for her soon. The clock was ticking, and things were about to get rough. "I honestly don't know yet."

"But we'll figure it out, right? I mean, we got this, right?" Theo asked a little hesitantly.

"... Sure, kid. We got this."

"Once more *with feeling*," Theo laughed.

For the first time in months, Cam's lips broke into a grin, as his eyes slid closed.

12

12

"Briar... Briar... wake up..."

Buggy opened her eyes. She was still lying on the couch in her living room. The TV was paused on a dim screen with the words: "Are You Still Watching Netflix?" slowly judging her from across the room. She leaned up on her arm and looked around. Her glass sat empty on the coffee table next to her cell phone. Buggy looked down at the thick woolen blanket that had been draped over her side and tucked around her feet. Sandra must have come home at some point after Buggy had dozed off and tucked her in. Buggy groaned and leaned up a little higher. Her head was really throbbing, and her tongue tasted like stale whiskey and soda.

"Briar dear..."

Buggy looked around towards the voice. "Sandra?" It sounded like her sister was speaking from the darkened hallway. "Sandra? You up?" Buggy slid out from under the blanket, toes digging into the soft rug. She got up and walked in the dim light from the TV towards the hall. She blinked in the dark, hands dragging across the wall, feeling for the light switch.

"Sandra?" She flipped on the light. The hallway was empty except for the shoes lined up by the door, and the few jackets hanging on the coat rack waiting for the winter's first snow. They wouldn't have to wait long if all the weather reports could be believed. Still no Sandra. But Buggy had heard—or she thought she had heard—a voice. It had woken her up so she... obviously must have imagined it.

"Not unnerving at all," Buggy mumbled to herself, trying to force a little humor into her tone, a little levity to laugh off the churning feeling in her gut. But that feeling seemed to have developed a voice of its own and it whispered sweetly into her ear, sending a shiver down her spine.

Are you going a little crazy there, Briar dear?

Of course not. Buggy barked in her mind, trying to quiet that little train of thought before it could pick up speed and whisk her away to darker places. It was an easy thing to do in the still of night, with goosebumps prickling up her arm, mind still foggy with the trace wisps of whisky tumbling through her system.

Are you sure, Briar dear? the other voice soothed, as if inviting Buggy somewhere. Through a door, or down a road. Welcome aboard. Let's see where this train goes, shall we? The little voice continued. *Are you so sure? I mean, hearing things that are not there... that is never really a **good** sign now, is it?*

"I'm just tired," Buggy didn't notice that she had started speaking out loud. It was her body taking over, trying to gain power over the other voice in her head without her truly deciding to do it. "I'm just tired. Need some more sleep." Besides, hearing strange things in the night, wasn't really all *that* strange. Everyone did that. When it was late at night and you were all alone, it was only natural to imagine ghosts in the shadows or monsters under the bed. It was a survival technique developed over centuries of the human race living on this Earth. Imagine worst case scenarios and then you can be prepared for them, even if they do not actually happen. Hearing things when you are tired and alone, perfectly normal. A trick of the weary mind.

Oh, Briar... what an utter child you are.

"Oh, shut up," Buggy grumbled, growing irritated with her own thoughts now.

Little baby Briar, the voice pressed on, undeterred. It even sounded delighted at her annoyance. Reveling in it. *Cannot even admit to herself that she might be slipping. That she might be losing a little bit of that oh-so-precious **control**.*

"Shut up," Buggy snapped again. Her face scrunched into a twisted scowl, but a deep corner of her soul flinched, disquieted, by these thoughts spoken in her mind as if by some cruel, twisted version of her own heart. Again, the voice went on.

*Because it is all about **control**, is it not, Briar dear?*

"Just stop," Buggy hissed, heart starting to beat hard in her chest as her nerves sparked and tendons twitched involuntarily against bone. Her arms jerked at her sides, and the hair rose high on the back of her neck.

What? Going to stomp your feet, little girl? the voice leered in her mind, nearly panting with enjoyment. Slobbering like a dog over a bone. Dripping with anticipation. *Going to whimper and cry, little girl? Going to be a little bitch, little girl?*

"I said *shut up!*" Buggy barked. Her voice hit the wall, bouncing back to her like a verbal racket ball.

"Buggy?" an actual voice spoke from behind her.

Buggy nearly had a heart attack as she flipped around. Sandra was poking her messy-haired head out of her bedroom door from the other side of the living room. She rubbed her sleepy eyes as she looked over at Buggy. She laughed a little as Buggy sighed and leaned against the entrance to the hall.

"You okay?" she asked.

"Yeah," Buggy laughed. "Yeah, I'm totally fine. I just..." She looked back into the empty hall. "I just thought you were..." Buggy shook her head. "Never mind."

"Were you talking to yourself," Sandra frowned.

"What? No." Buggy answered automatically in the negative. But was that true? She honestly didn't know.

"You sure you're okay?" Sandra asked, taking a step out the door, brow furrowing.

God, I hope so. Buggy thought.

"Thought I heard something. Guess not though," Buggy smiled. "Dream, I guess. I'm going to head back to bed."

"Well... alright," Sandra yawned and slipping back into her room. "Goodnight."

"Goodnight!" Buggy called back as Sandra's door slid closed. Buggy looked around to the empty hallway, shook her head, flipped off the light, and turned off the TV. As the screen went dark, she felt the hair rise on the back of her arms and neck. As if there was someone in the dark... someone watching her.

Buggy hastily grabbed her phone off the table and flipped on the front light. The bright white beam flew out, and she turned with it, checking the surrounding room. Empty. By now Sandra would be curled up under her floral comforter, night-mask slipped down over her eyes. Buggy was, essentially, alone. Then why did she feel like someone was there? Why did it feel like there was someone skulking, unseen, but seeing *her* all to clearly? From where, Buggy didn't know. Perhaps the kitchen, the hall, or from some spot in one of the many dark, dark corners, she felt eyes watching her. They followed her movements. Followed her as she walked to the door next to Sandra's. She opened it and stepped into her organized room. It wasn't until she had shut the door behind her, enclosing herself in her little *controlled* environment, that she finally felt alone. Buggy flipped back the sheets, checked her lights, tapped the little blue dream catcher that hung above her bed three times (as was her method) and hoped that tonight it would do its job. She then snuggled down deep and pulled the covers up to her chin.

She must have just imagined it, Sandra's voice in the hall. She must have just been half asleep and dreamed it up. Just as she had dreamed up Cooper in Andrew's kitchen? Did that really seem likely? She had not been getting a great deal of sleep recently, and the sleep she had gotten had been sporadic and restless. Vivid dreams didn't make for restful nights... especially when those dreams tended to filter back to that same burning house. And the mind enjoyed playing tricks when it was sleep deprived.

Buggy turned over onto her side and checked her phone one last time. She checked her messages. Just a few encouragements from Cooper and Linny, received hours before her presentation had started. She checked her previous calls and particularly noted the calls from the Unknown Number. She frowned. They were from the same unknown caller. The same recorded scam probably, but it was a little unsettling all the same. Luckily, there was an easy fix for that problem. Buggy clicked on the number, pressed options, and then hit the "block" button, before turning off her phone and casting herself back into darkness. She laid there a few minutes, sleep beginning to seep in to dampen her conscious mind when she remembered she had not brushed her teeth.

"Damn it," she groaned and got out of bed. She went into the bathroom where she began another method of hers that she had perfected since she was a little girl. Dental floss. Brush. Water pick. Brush again. Rinse. Mouthwash. It was this little obsessive routine that had first made her father suggest she become a dental hygienist. It had started out as a joke but turned into a serious option as a four year went on the back burner and Buggy floundered for direction after graduation. How do you choose what you want to do with the rest of your life? How *can* you choose that?

"You don't have to decide for the rest of your life," her dad told her soothingly. "You just have to choose what you wanna do for now. You can always change your mind later. Just think of what to do for now." Well, "for now" turned into several years, but Buggy supposed it had been a good decision overall. It was a good job. Not her dream job, but what on earth counted as a dream job anyway? Buggy didn't know. She kept meaning to figuring out the answer to that question, but things always came up, or she got busy, and never could seem to get around to it. And so, here she was.

Buggy glared at her tired reflection in the mirror as toothpaste foam built up at the corner of her mouth. Her eyes were tinged red from drinking, and she noticed the skin around them looked thin and blue. God, all she wanted to do was sleep, and she would as soon as she was done. It took her over fifteen minutes to perform her little ritual. But it was her method and oh, how Buggy hated to deviate from her methods.

13

"Okay. Do you floss regularly?"

It was just another Tuesday afternoon at Elwin Family Dentistry, and Buggy was on her fifth cleaning of the day. The same five sessions of lighthearted but ultimately forgettable small talk. The same five mind-numbing thirty minutes of scraping coffee stains off back molars. The same five "notes to self" for Buggy to suggest a reminder is attached to a client's next appointment date, asking them to kindly *brush their teeth* before their next cleaning. Five half-hearted apologies for the states of their mouths. Five concerns about cavities, and what was about to be an equally half-hearted excuse for why, even though they are reminded at least twice a year, they have not been flossing.

"I always mean to," Mrs. Finlly said, eyebrows scrunching together in embarrassment and shame. "But I just keep forgetting. Besides, it hurts my gums."

Buggy had taken her scraping tool out of the woman's mouth so she could answer her question, but she quickly got back to work after she was finished.

"Mrs. Finlly, it only hurts because you never do it. If you get some gentle, soft floss, and just remember to use it, it will only be sore for the first few days. Your gums are strong suckers, they'll get used to it quickly. I'll tell you what, your mouth will be much happier for it. Gums too."

Mrs. Finlly smiled and nodded slightly around Buggy's fingers. She gargled some comment about Buggy being right and how she would try again tomorrow, while Buggy prepared herself to have this exact same conversation with Mrs. Finlly in six months. Buggy finished up her cleaning, gave her a polish, and sent Mrs. Finlly off with a smile and a wave of thanks. Linny was perched cross-legged on the break room counter when Buggy stepped in to grab a bottle of water from the fridge. She would have loved a cup of coffee. Unfortunately, Dennis Elwin, the head dentist and her boss, thought it bad form to have one of the most teeth-staining beverages in a dentist's office. It didn't set a very good example. Buggy thought that ridiculous, seeing as none of the clients could even see into the break room, let alone judge them for what they were drinking in there. However, he owned the office, so anything he said went. Besides, to make it up to all the women in his office, he kept the refrigerator stocked with sugar-free, flavored waters. Non-carbonated, of course.

"Mrs. Finlly?" Linny asked, looking up from her phone. She was wearing the same pink uniform scrubs jacket as Buggy, and her red hair was knotted into a loose bun at the nape of her neck.

"Yep," Buggy said, popping open the little fridge and snagging one of the cherry-flavored water bottles out of its neat row.

"Still not converted to our Lord and savior dental floss?"

"Afraid not."

"Poor soul," Linny shook her head as she turned back to her phone, glossed lips shining in the light from the screen. "I'll pray for her gums." Buggy laughed as she popped open the top of her water bottle and took a cherry flavored sip. "So, how'd your presentation go?" Buggy took a few extra seconds to swallow and turned a little away from Linny before answering.

"I definitely lived," Buggy said in a cheery voice, twisting the cap back on the bottle.

"Told you it would go alright!" Linny grinned. Buggy returned her grin and nodded, but kept her eyes averted. There was a light, jingling noise as someone came in the door and into the front office.

"Hello?" a male voice called out. Linny and Buggy glanced at each other.

"Isn't Candice out there?" Buggy asked.

"Guess not," Linny checked her watch. "She should have been back from lunch twenty minutes ago but—"

"Hello? Excuse me?" the voice called again.

"Shit," Linny started getting up.

"Nah, stay, you're still on lunch," Buggy waved her off.

"You sure?" Linny asked, already easing back down, phone rising.

"Yeah, it's probably my next cleaning, anyway." It wasn't. Instead of Mr. Linden, who Buggy was expecting, there was a man in his mid-twenties with red-brown hair. He had been looking around the empty waiting room at the various pictures of smiling people with perfect teeth when she found him. He looked up as she slid behind the counter. He had soft green eyes, which widened in surprise as they caught sight of her.

"Hello," Buggy grinned at him, "How can I help you?"

He didn't answer at first, just looked at her as if he was seeing something very strange. For a second, Buggy was sure she had a piece of spinach in her teeth or mascara smeared across her cheek. She was about to pull out her phone and check her reflection when the guy blinked, shaking himself out of his temporary reverie.

"Sorry," he said with a little nervous laugh. "Sorry, you just... you have very pretty eyes." He grimaced. "That's a weird thing to just say to a total stranger. I'm sorry."

Buggy laughed and waved a dismissive hand. "That's alright. I've heard worse... much worse. How can I help you today?"

"Oh, uh, I wanted to set an appointment for a cleaning. If that's okay?"

"Perfectly okay," Buggy said. He seemed very shy. He was extremely nervous, eyes darting around, and only meeting hers occasionally. Poor guy. Must be one of those with dentist office phobia. More common than most people liked to admit. "Are you a patient with us?"

"Uh, no,"

"That's alright, I'll just have you fill out some paperwork for me if you don't mind."

Buggy gathered a small stack of intake papers and handed them to him. He took them with a smile and a "thank you" and sat down in one of the waiting room couches to fill them out. While he did that, Buggy turned to see Linny leaning against the door frame to the waiting room office. She motioned Buggy to come over.

"Well, he's cute," Linny whispered, nodding in his direction.

"He is kinda cute," Buggy looked over and shrugged. "Cute nose."

"And eyes," Linny grinned. "You should ask him out."

"Excuse me?" Buggy scoffed.

"Why not?" Linny asked.

"On top of it being completely unprofessional? Cuz, no."

"Laaaame," Linny huffed.

"You ask him out then," Buggy countered.

"I'm already juggling three guys, thank you very much. I don't need more. Besides," Linny grinned, "I'm not the one that made his jaw drop and drool a minute ago."

"His jaw didn't drop," Buggy said, rolling her eyes.

"Close enough," Linny shrugged.

"Finished?" Buggy asked as the guy got to his feet and started making his way back to the counter.

"Uh, yes."

"Alright then," Buggy took the paperwork and started taping on the computer and scanned through the calendar. "Let's see... we have an appointment available for next week, actually. Friday at nine thirty. Does that work for you?"

"Sounds good," he said.

"Perfect. We'll see you then..." Buggy checked the paperwork, "Theodore."

"Theo," he corrected with a smile.

"Well, nice to meet you, Theo," Buggy said, returning his smile. "And we'll see you Friday."

"Great. Thanks." He waved to both Buggy and Linny before stepping out the door with another light jingle of the door's bell.

"C-u-t-e," Linny said, sliding up to sit on the counter facing Buggy. Buggy shook her head but gave Linny a grin.

"Linny. Give up on my love life already,"

"Never," Linny said flatly.

* * *

Cam was waiting in the Jeep, switching through the staticky channels trying to find something, *anything* that wasn't Christmas music. He had finally come across an oldies station, Johnny Cash was "Hurt"-ing all over the place when Theo opened the passenger door.

"Well?" Cam asked, as Theo slid into the seat and slammed the door behind him. Theo looked over, his expression a mixture of bemusement and wonder.

"Oh, it's definitely her," he said. "I mean... definitely her. It was creepy how definitely *her* she was." Cam nodded. "Well..." Theo paused, awkwardly. "What now?" Cam stared out of the windshield at the slowly graying sky. Dark clouds tumbled through the sharp breeze that had picked up over the previous evening. Snow was on its way.

"Tonight, we find a place, and we sleep up."

"And tomorrow?"

Styger looked over at him. Theo had never seen the man looking so tired.

"Tomorrow, we start planning our gamble. And pray to God that it pays off."

14

Sandra woke from a rather dull dream about reviewing a dreadful local play for The Marshall County Chronical when a noise from the other room gently pulled her to consciousness. She yawned and rubbed her eyes. Her room was nearly blacked out by the night. The only horizontal beam of light came from the crack under her closed door. Sandra frowned down at the light and checked the clock on her bedside table. The numbers gleamed a dim green and told her that it was two-forty-three in the morning. Sandra's frown deepened. She looked back to the crack under the door and heard feet shuffling from the other side. Sandra flipped the covers back and swung her legs around. She got up and opened her door with an eerie creak.

"Buggy?" Sandra squinted as the light from the living room broke across her face. She stepped out of her bedroom, leaving the door open behind her. "Buggy?"

Sandra found her in the kitchen. She was in her cartoon coffee cup pajamas, staring out the window over the sink. Her reflection was mirrored against the dark night outside. Her eyes were glazed, only half-open, staring at nothing. Sandra called her name again, but Buggy didn't respond. Sandra moved further into the room.

"Buggy?" Sandra tapped Buggy on the shoulder, but Buggy still didn't respond. Sandra stepped directly in front of her. Buggy made no move, and her large eyes remained glazed and unfocused. Her lips were moving ever so gently, as if she was trying to whisper something but made no sound. To Sandra's horror she saw the glaze of Buggy's eyes condense at the corners, and tears began to slide down her freckled cheeks. "Buggy!" Sandra raised her voice as a sickening nervousness rose, and a tinny taste clawed at the back of her tongue. She took her sister by both shoulders and began to shake her. Buggy's arms wobbled uselessly at her sides, but her eyes refused to focus, and the tears fell faster. "Buggy!" Sandra yelled in her face, giving her another hard shake. Buggy's eyes scrunched closed, paused for a second, and then flew open with the effort of shouldering open a jammed door. Buggy blinked rapidly, finding Sandra.

"Sandra?" Buggy asked, confused. "What are you doing?"

"I could ask you the same thing!" Sandra laughed, relief and nerves cracking her voice. "What are you doing out here? Late-night snack?"

"What..." Buggy looked around as if seeing their kitchen for the first time. Absentmindedly, she reached up to wipe her eyes. "How did I get here?"

"You don't remember?" Sandra frowned a little. "I think you were sleepwalking."

"Since when do I sleepwalk?" Buggy frowned back.

"I don't know," Sandra said with a shrug.

"First time for everything, I guess," Buggy laughed and rubbed the back of her neck. "And my sleep recently has been super..." Buggy shook her head. "Sorry I woke you."

"That's okay," Sandra shrugged. "I'm just glad you didn't sleepwalk your way out of the house." They both laughed.

"Well, goodnight. Again," Sandra smiled. "Get some good, non-walking rest."

"I'll try."

Sandra slid back into her room with one last look at her little sister. She was still in the kitchen, looking around, trying desperately to remember why she had walked into the room in the first place. Sandra had heard of people beginning to sleepwalk because of stress and weird sleeping patterns. Buggy definitely had both of those commonly throughout her life, but it had grown much more problematic over the past few months. Pretty much since her last birthday. Sandra remembered having to shake her awake that morning. Tears had been spilling down her face then as well. She woke up crying, slapping her arms to put out invisible flames, but she had stayed in bed. She had not gotten up and moved around. That was just a bad dream. This was a whole other level thing. Those empty whispers... those sightless eyes spilling over with tears. They had been glassy but filled with so much *pain*. Anguish. Whatever dream Buggy had been in, she had been suffering something terrible.

It all seemed to just be getting worse. Sandra would be lying if she said she had not started to grow concerned. Buggy had been acting more and more on edge, jumpy. She had been slowly isolating herself, spending more time alone in her room with those damn cassette tapes. She was pulling away from Sandra, she felt it, although Sandra wasn't sure Baggy was even aware she was doing it. She was pulling away, speaking less, sleeping less. She was still telling Sandra the truth... or at least, Sandra hoped she was. Although Sandra had started to wonder if her little sister was telling her everything. Her answers to Sandra's questions—they felt like there was something missing in them. Like a puzzle, mostly formed, but with a few edge pieces misplaced, little spots standing empty in the image. Something Buggy was leaving unsaid. Sandra knew this might just be in her imagination, and she hoped it was, but she was still finding herself spending a great deal of time concerned about her big-eyed baby sis and that concern was growing with every week that passed. Possibly concerned enough to do a little poking around.

Sandra snuggled down under her covers, but sleep didn't find her until long after the light under the door had gone dark.

15

As Sandra slipped slowly back into lands of calm dreams—and Buggy lay on her bed, eyes wide, terrified to fall back to sleep—a slender woman wearing a black, leather jacket pulled up outside the vacant Elwin Family Dentistry office. Her Harley Softail gave one last disgruntled snort before she cut the engine and kicked down the stand with one thick, lace-up, riding boot. She flipped up the visor on her helmet, resting back in her seat as she pulled out her phone to check the address. She nodded to herself. This was definitely the place, but definitely not the time. She needed to wait till the office opened, but her blood was already pumping fast in her veins. She was so close now, waiting felt impossible. However, there was nothing else for her to do—not with the shops closed and all their employees tucked snuggly in their beds.

She searched her phone, found the number she wanted, and pulled off her helmet. From underneath, a cascade of long, blond hair tumbled down to fall around her shoulder and back in thick waves of mixed gold. The blond pressed the call button and held the ringing phone to her ear as her cheeks were assaulted by the chilly December air.

"It's Waverly. I'm here," she said, looking up at the dark glass doors and the little "closed" sign hanging on the locked doorknob. "Yeah." she said, answering some question posed on the other end of the line. "Yes. I know. I'll scout things out... yes, I've got the picture. No, Mom, I understand. I know what needs to be done... love you too." The blond hung up the phone and slipped it into her jacket pocket. As she raised the helmet back to her head, the sleeve of her black jacket pulled back, momentarily revealing the small circular tattoo that stood dark against the skin of her wrist. Waverly secured her helmet and dropped her hand, sleeve sliding back into place, tattoo disappearing.

There was a hotel a few blocks back. She would rest there, catch a few hours of sleep, and come back in the afternoon, when all the employees were back at their work. Then she would see if the girl was here. Waverly was trying not to get her hopes up. There had been false starts before. She had been sent to many places, many small towns, and big cities, all with the hope that this would be the one. Hopes that this would be the right place, the right *girl*, but she was only ever met with disappointment. Not surprising, they were always thin leads. Thin and weak Hail Mary throws from a woman whose psychic abilities had atrophied from lack of use and lack of training. Waverly had begun to wonder if her mother had ever possessed the gift at all, or if she only *thought* that she had. She never told her mother this, of course. That would have earned her nothing but a sharp slap upside the ear, and she received enough of those as it was while growing up. No need to add to the list.

But no matter how many false starts, or weak leads that ended in nothing, Waverly couldn't help the small flicker of excitement in her belly as she cast one last glance at the Elwin Family Dentistry sign.

Maybe—just maybe—this would be the one. Maybe this time the flashes, the images her mother had been talking about (but which Waverly had never been able to understand) would finally pan out. Waverly had not been born with the gift, a fact that her mother never let her forget. Her mother had been hoping to have a child with the ability, the *talent,* to help reach out and find the girl that they had spent their lives trying to track down. It ran in their blood after all, but apparently not in Waverly's. So, Waverly had been tasked with following up on every wispy, smoke thin lead that her mother came up with. Always to a dead end, and yet... maybe this time it would be different. Maybe it could be over.

Waverly flipped the visor back down over her face and revved the engine, which rumbled to life between her legs.

Just maybe she could fix what others had broken.

Just maybe she could do what her mother had been unable to do for so many years.

Just maybe she could save everyone.

16

The rest of the week had passed in the same rhythmic routine as always. Cleanings, polishing, checking for cavities, and as ever, the ominous warnings to floss that everyone seemed determined not to heed. If dental hygienists were heralds of the apocalypse instead of heralds of inevitable tooth decay, the impending ruin of the world would be shrugged off with pure ease. Of course, everyone would be scrambling at their door, desperate for entry and advice after shit had hit the fan, and it was too late to turn back. Nobody likes to participate in prevention. But they also hate being told that they could have stopped it. Hate to admit that they had a hand in their own fate. Everyone always thinks it couldn't happen to them... until it does. Until it is too late to turn back.

The days had churned by, and to Buggy's utter relief, Friday had arrived. As glad as she was, it didn't make her any less exhausted. Her sleep had gotten worse, delving into entirely new realms of continuous waking and shattered dreams. Her nightmares had started happening every night now. Every time she closed her eyes, she was dropped into a world of pain and fear. Sometimes she couldn't breathe. Sometimes she felt like she was being crushed by some invisible weight. Other times it felt like hands clutched at her throat in the dark, cutting off her air. Many times, these took place in darkness, but the other dream, the one she feared most, that one was in blazing light.

It was so bad that Buggy was getting scared to let herself doze at all. That day she was running on a scattered two hours of sleep, caffeine, and wishful thinking. It was taking a toll. She was able to see just how much of a toll when her tray of cleaning equipment slipped out of her fingers. The tray and tools scattered, clattering loudly across the tiled floor.

"Buggy?" Linny leaned around the edge of the door, as Buggy stooped to clear up her mess. "You alright? Oh, good Lord," she stepped all the way through the door. "Buggy, you look..."

"Tired," Buggy smiled, placing every tool back on the tray with care, already creating a mental checklist of things she would need to clean them properly.

"I was gonna say, 'like shit,' but sure 'tired' also works. You still having nightmares?" Linny asked, frowning, leaning down to help.

"Yeah, I mean—wait—how do you know about my nightmares?" Buggy asked, looking over at her. Linny laughed a little, but it was low and short and didn't hold her usual good humor.

"You were talking in your sleep last Friday. Didn't get much detail, but it didn't sound pleasant."

"Oh..." Buggy gave a great yawn.

"Here," Linny slipped the tray out of her hands as Buggy placed the last tool on top of the pile. "Go take an early lunch. Catch a nap in the back room. Neither of the Elwin's are here, so make it a long one."

Buggy thought about protesting, saying she could push through it, but then her vision suddenly blurred Linny's face, making it fuzzy around the edges and turning her green eyes into wet brushstroke smudges.

"You sure that's okay?" Buggy asked, and Linny waved her hand, dismissing her concern.

"I'll take your next client. Nobody else should be in for a while. Slow day. We're all good. Seriously, go take a nap."

Buggy nodded gratefully and made her way to the patient room in the back. The room itself was pristine, all prepped, but had gone unused for the past three weeks because of an electrical issue that made it fairly useless when it came to powered tools, polishers, and X-ray machines. It usually stood empty, but still held one of the seven comfy patient chairs that leaned all the way back. Buggy slipped inside, closed the door behind her, only leaving a small crack open in case Linny called her. The room was dark, cool, and as Buggy crawled into the chair and pushed it manually back, she felt sleep already taking over her mind. It pulled her eagerly with both hands, securing its grip around her consciousness before she even finished closing her eyes.

She only had enough time to hope that there would be no dreams before she was enveloped by sleeps cool embrace.

The dreams came shortly after.

* * *

It was the house. A small little place made of logs, clay, and thatch. There were no pictures, no decorations, just wooden chairs, a table, and a few makeshift shelves filled with random ornaments, clay pots, and things that were too blurry to see, smudged out by the dream world. Unimportant. It was a simple house, more of a hut or cottage really. Small, spartan, and it burned like kindling in the fire that raged around her.

She dragged herself across the ground, fingernails digging into the dirt, breaking with the effort. She barely felt the pain of splintering fingernails. She was too consumed by the rest of the pain. The pain in her broken legs that reverberated up her spine and back. The pain of her bruises, her broken nose, and her torn skin. The pain in her lower body, that pain between her legs that belonged only to one source, but she pushed that pain aside. She couldn't think of that now. If she thought about it, if she accepted it into her mind as a reality, she would be consumed by it, and she needed to get away from the fire. That would consume her first. It was eager, crawling for her faster than she could crawl away. Its flaming teeth snapping at her toes, her ankles, her thighs, ready and waiting to gobble her up. No, not gobble. It would take its time. It would chew slowly, swallowing away her life with every savored taste of flesh. She needed to move faster, but her arms were already so tired, and the door seemed to pull further and further out of reach. It spread like a tunnel, miles away now, but she still dragged her broken and beaten body with every bit of strength she had left, leaving a jagged trail of blood in her wake as smoke and dirt filled her mouth.

The door grew a little closer and hope flitted tentatively in her soul, only to be painfully snuffed out as the ceiling gave a monstrous creak. The fire chewed away its supports and a wooden beam came crashing down in front of her, blocking the door. Her only exit, still so far away, was truly lost to her now.

She stopped dragging her body and pried her broken fingers out of the hot dirt. She turned to lay on her back, eyes on the thatched ceiling now alight in red and orange flames. She began to cry. She felt it was her right. Isn't it everyone's right in the end? Their right to mourn the life they never had? The missed opportunities? The mistakes they made? And she had made many mistakes. Many regrets. She couldn't have taken any of them back, but she might have had the chance to make up for them. But, no more. Redemption was lost, and she cried for it.

The flames didn't heed her tears. They didn't care for her pain. They only wanted her flesh, and they came for it with ravenous need. They licked her toes, just a taste, and the girl's tears turned to screams.

"Mama, help me!" she screamed to the sky of fire as it crackled on, deafening in the roar of its consuming sound. "Mama, save me! Please, it hurts!" The flames ate her words just as it consumed her body. Bit by bit, it swallowed her, screaming.

As screams turned to whimpers, and her vision went dark, she imagined she heard a voice. Her mother's voice calling to her from the darkness beyond the flames.

"Bennu!" it called.

Mama

The girl heard. The girl smiled. The girl died.

* * *

Buggy lurched forward in the chair. She moved with such force that she toppled off completely, landing hard on her knees. She knelt there in the dark, trembling, tears streaming down her face. *Why?* Why was this happening? This wasn't fair. All she wanted was some sleep. All she wanted was a little goddamn sleep. That wasn't too much to ask.

Buggy dragged her fingers across the ground, trying to feel where she had fallen in the unused dental room. She felt the base of the chair beside her and pulled herself towards it. She had a flash of memory, of doing a similar crawl in the burning house and jerked herself to her feet. In her haste, she slammed her head against one of the chair's armrests which sent her crashing back to the floor.

"Shit," Buggy hissed, rubbing the top of her head as it started to throb. "Shit. Shit. *Fuck.*" She felt for the armrest and used it to pull herself to her feet, tears still sliding down her cheeks. She moved in the dark, hands trailing over every countertop, every tray, looking for the door.

She needed to get something. Sleeping pills, perhaps. Buggy shook the thought away as quickly as it came. What if they worked too well? What if she fell asleep and couldn't wake up in time to get out of the dream? She was tired of burning.

Therapy? Must be something mental, right? She had not been to her therapist for over three years now. She had been doing really well, actually... until the past few months, she had been doing damn good, but maybe it was time to call up good old Dr. Hernandez.

Hello, Doc. I've been having dreams where I die and usually burn alive. Think there's a problem? Got a pill for that shit?

Buggy found the counter by the door and ran her hand up the wall. She found the doorknob and pulled it open. She sighed in relief as the light from the hallway broke across the room. She turned, rubbing her still throbbing head, then froze. Her already large eyes widened as she looked at the dental chair she had been sleeping in a moment ago. Its soft purple faux-leather lining was heavily dusted with what looked like gray and black powder. It covered the seat and spattered across the tile floor below. There were even long smudges that trailed across the tile where she had dragged her knees, looking for the chair.

Buggy stepped closer to it, reaching down with hesitant fingers, and ran her index over the seat. It wasn't wet like paint, but instead seemed to push away as she moved. She pulled her hand back and looked at it. She rubbed it between two fingers, and her heart began to sink. She held it up to her nose and sniffed.

"No," Buggy groaned, recognizing the smell. "No, no." No. Not paint at all.

Ash.

Black and gray ash spattered like blood at a forensic crime scene investigation. It sprayed across the seat, the floor, and was flung halfway up the walls. She was staring in open mouthed horror when she realized that the ash on her fingers was still warm. Buggy closed her mouth with a snaping of teeth and backed out of the room. Her heart was thudding hard in her chest, panic and adrenaline filling her veins, sending a buzzing to dampen all sound.

What the *hell* was going on?

Buggy looked down at her hand, continuing to rub the substance between her fingers, hoping it would vanish. It didn't. She needed to clean it. She needed to clean it all away. She needed to get rid of it. It needed to be gone, all gone, and *now*. Buggy looked around but saw no one. Candice must be out on break, and Buggy could hear Linny in a nearby room, chatting with a client as a polish machine whirred softly in the background. She darted quickly into a nearby bathroom. She started unwinding the white roll of paper towels propped on the sink, gathering as much as she could without taking the whole roll. She turned on the sink and let it heat up.

It needed to go away. All of it. Every last bit. She would get rid of it.

It was then that Buggy noticed her reflection in the mirror above the sink. Her face was deathly pale, her wide brown eyes were bloodshot and glassy, but that wasn't the problem. The problem was the ash. It smeared her face, broken only by the tracks where her tears had carved their path down her cheeks. It peppered her neck and pink scrub coat with dark gray smudges. Buggy stared at her reflection as the water turned hot in the sink and sent puffs of steam up before her reflection. For a terrifying moment, it looked like smoke. She instantly jammed the handles to the side, cutting off the stream with a small squeak.

Buggy leaned against the sink, breathing heavily, mind reeling. She waited till the panic calmed, and the sick feeling in her stomach subsided enough that she was pretty sure she wouldn't puke. She looked back up to her reflection and gave a little yelp.

The ash was gone. She was still pale, and her eyes were still red and bloodshot, but the ash was gone. She was clean, her coat pristine and crisp pink. Buggy moved like a hollow phantom, leaving the bathroom to stand in the doorway of the unused dental workroom. There was no ash there either. There was nothing. Nothing but clean tile and faux-leather seat covers.

Hallucinating. A small, humorless, sickening trill of laughter exploded out from her mouth and then died there as suddenly as it had started. *The dreams were not enough. I've started hallucinating.*

Buggy walked back to the bathroom in a daze. She closed the door behind her, locked it, then turned on the faucets, filling the room with the sound of water. She dropped the lid on the toilet, sat down, and buried her face in the crumpled handful of paper towels.

Buggy began to cry.

It was her right.

17

Buggy cleaned herself up, splashing cold water over her face to lessen the swelling around her eyes, plastered on a smile, and got back to work. The rest of the day had toppled by, like a stack of books falling off a shelf. Messy, sudden, and ending with a loud "bang" when she slammed her shoulder into the door while heading out for the night. She had walked to the station in a daze, caught the bus, and tried to keep herself from being lolled asleep by its gentle swaying as it trundled down the road. Finally, thankfully, she made it back home.

Buggy twisted the key in the apartment lock. She tried to push it open, but it didn't budge. For some reason, the door swelled when the weather grew colder, when it rained more often, and the air filled with chilly humidity. By Christmas, the thing was almost immovable. They had always been meaning to fix it, but never got around to it. And now wasn't the time. Now was the time to crash on the couch and perhaps just stay there forever.

Buggy gave the door a little shove and a kick, finally pushing it open. She stepped in, dropped her keys in the little broken coffee cup with "I'm not a morning person," written down the shattered and re-glued side. It had been a gift from her mom and Simon on the first Christmas both Buggy and Sandra shared in their apartment. Buggy had dropped it the next day and couldn't bring herself to just throw it away.

She flicked on the light and moved into the living room. She dropped her bag on the couch and then followed suit. She was asleep in seconds. For once, she had no nightmares. Her mind must have been too tired to dream up any new horrors to show her. There was just sleep, and she lost herself in a deep thirty-minute nap. She came out of it, not refreshed, but recharged. Ready to rally. She went to the kitchen, pouring herself a glass of water and popping open a can of Redbull from the fridge to wake herself the rest of the way up. She came home to pick up a few things, and then in an hour or so she was heading off to The Lookout. It was a Friday evening, and she didn't care if she was tired, the tradition must continue. And oh boy, did she need this. After today—after the ashes that weren't actually ashes, but most likely a sleep deprived hallucination—let's just say Buggy really needed to relax. She needed an escape from whatever bullshit was going on in her own head. Few drinks. A few laughs. That was what she needed. She needed to get away from herself. Away from everything. She would deal with whatever the hell was going on later.

Was that the best plan? Probably not. Okay, definitely not. It was an absolutely terrible idea, adding alcohol to the mix, but she didn't really care. She couldn't *deal* at the moment. She was too tired to deal. All she wanted to do now was get drunk. Drunk and argue with Cooper about why Ross and Rachel sucked as a couple. And, with any luck, she would party until she couldn't keep her eyes open a second longer, crash for a solid ten hours of dreamless sleep, and the entire issue would be resolved.

That was the only thing she was prepared to do that day. That was all she was ready to handle. That was it. She was not prepared for what she found.

Buggy frowned as she noticed the light was on in her room. That had definitely not been on when she left. She had double-checked the light. Okay, she had checked it precisely *three times* before she left the house that morning. It was part of her routine, her method. That oh-so-important method that she couldn't stray from or else she would spend the day obsessing over things that might go wrong. What if she left the light on and it jacked up their electricity bill and they went broke? What if the landlord complained and had them evicted? What if there was a fluke fault in the electrical line that started a fire and burned down the building with all their stuff inside? You know, all those absolutely reasonable things for a person to worry about when they don't check their bedroom light three times in a row.

That light had been off. Buggy was sure of it. She dropped the glass of water on the table with a clink and moved towards her room with caution.

"Sandra?" she asked, pushing the door open. Sandra shouldn't have been home for at least another hour or so, but perhaps she got off early and... what? Decided to hang out in Buggy's room for no good reason? "Sandra?"

Buggy stepped in and surveyed her room. Nope. No Sandra. There was nobody at all, but that didn't stop Buggy's heart from sinking down so low she felt it clatter against the bottom of her stomach.

She stared at her dresser, whose left drawer stood open to the world, underwear and socks revealed. The bottle of whiskey, however, wasn't there. No, that oh-so-secret second bottle was no longer nestled there like a patiently waiting mistress. It was placed on top of the dresser and reflected in the mirror propped behind it. The half-filled bottle shined, naked, exposed to the world. On the bottle, Buggy saw a little green sticky note. She stepped slowly forward as if into a den of lions, ready to be pounced on at any second. Buggy reached out, took the note, and read a short and ominous message written in Sandra's hand:

We'll talk about this when I get home?

Buggy stood for a time, reading and rereading the words as her heart rolled around in the empty pit of her gut. Anger and guilt vied for dominance in her chest, crashing like waves, spilling and sloshing over. What had Sandra been doing? Why was she going through her things? Was it because of the nightmares? The sleepwalking? Or did she have some sort of actual explanation for this blatant violation of privacy? This was absolutely ridiculous. Sandra had no right to do that. Still, the guilt raged just as hard. It had been a secret Buggy had kept from her sister. It was as good as lying without actually having to use words. And there it was, out in the open. There was going to be a fall out, and likely an emotionally driven conversation about it and why Buggy felt the need to hide it. Why did Buggy need it? How much, exactly, had she been drinking, and for how long? How was she doing? How was she *feeling?* How—why—what—when—liar—such a liar—does this seem like *control* to you? Hmm, Briar dear? Does it?

Buggy crumpled the piece of paper in her hand and turned to leave the room. She paused a few steps out the door, closed her eyes, cursed, and turned back. She went over and turned the nob on the lamp, and the light went out. She turned the nob again and light-filled the room. She repeated this two more times, then her method was complete. She closed her door on the darkness and left the apartment behind. In her haste to run away from her troubles, Buggy completely forgot the shoulder bag full of cassette tapes hidden under her bed.

* * *

Buggy had just knocked back her second shot and was on the way to a decent buzz when her phone vibrated in her pocket. She flipped her shot glass over onto the bar and reached for it. She checked the name of the caller.

Sandra

Buggy groaned a little.

"What's up?" Cooper asked, sliding into the seat next to her.

"Nothin," Buggy answered, but Cooper tipped her phone to see the name blinking there.

"Uh, oh." Cooper smiled. "You guys on the outs or something?"

"Not exactly," she said, signaling for the bartender.

"Well?"

"Well, I kinda messed up... and sort of lied."

"And she found out?"

"Yup," Buggy thanked the bartender who brought her another shot. She threw it back.

"And instead of waiting for her to come home or calling to discuss it like a grown-ass human being," Cooper said, watching Buggy drop the third shot to the table. "You ran away and came here early."

"Pretty much, yup. How did you know I was already here by the way?" Cooper flashed her a sideways glance. "She called you, didn't she?" Buggy said, eyes sliding closed.

"Yep."

"How does she even have your number?"

"So," Cooper leaned against the bar, head propped up by his hand, sangria highlights smushed between his fingers. "Remember your last birthday? When we got separated from Linny and Andrew?"

"Vaguely," Buggy shrugged. It had been one hell of a night. Buggy had been excited about her birthday coming around for months. She loved birthdays, who didn't? However, for some reason, she had woken up in a bad mood. Actually, that wasn't so surprising. She had woken up, jerking herself from the first nightmare. It had been the first night she burned in the house of her mind. She had been dragging most of that morning, and Linny mistook it for birthday blues. She had pushed them all to go drinking and dancing and Buggy couldn't turn around without finding Linny, pressing another drink into her hand. Buggy had been willing enough. Whatever blurred out that damn dream. She pushed it a bit too far that night, however, and good sections of the evening were missing. Although, Buggy could catch fluttering images, pieces of memory like crumpled leaves drifting in the breeze of her mind. She was able to snag one or two if she tried. She did so now, mentally catching one image in particular. Her eyes opened wide with embarrassment as the image drifted into sharper focus. "Oh no..."

"Oh yes," Cooper said seeming to know which memory she had chosen.

"I was... I was puking, wasn't I?"

"Yep! Right into the gutter."

"Like the classy bitch, I am." Buggy groaned and rubbed her eye.

"So much so, in fact, that the Uber driver saw us and drove right on past," he said, drawing a hand through the air in demonstration.

"Oh, God," Buggy covered her face with her hands. "Oh, God, oh, God. How did we get home?"

"Well, I wasn't much better than you at the time," Cooper said, "So there was no way *I* was driving. I asked to borrow your phone, and between all the puking, gagging, and whatnot," Buggy grimaced, "you were able to unlock it for me, and I called her. Like a wonderful big sister, she came and picked us up. That night we decided to exchange numbers just in case something like that happened again."

"So, she called you, and you knew where I would be, obviously." Buggy glanced up, "She didn't happen to mention...?"

"Why you're dodging her calls?" Cooper shook his head. "Nope."

Buggy turned back to the bar and signaled the bartender.

"But I could take a few wild guesses," he said, looking down at the shot glasses lined on the bar.

Buggy looked back up at Cooper, scowling in defiance. "Here to kill my buzz?"

"Nope." Cooper shrugged. The bartender handed Buggy another shot, which she took gratefully. The third shot had just started to kick in and her mind was growing fluffy, thoughts coming quicker to her lips then they might otherwise.

"Here to fix me?" Buggy's voice was meant to come out as a joke, but it ended up coming out far quieter, more vulnerable than she had intended. For a split second she thought that Cooper may not have heard her, but then he started chuckling. Cooper reached out and took the shot out of her hands. He smiled, downed it, turning it over and clicked it to the table, lining it next to the rest.

"Buggy," Cooper shook his head. "You don't need fixing. I don't think you're broken. Never have." Buggy watched him as he turned and asked the bartender for two whiskey sours and a couple glasses of water.

"What *do* you think then?" Buggy asked, tentatively, wanting to know the answer... but also a little scared to find out. Cooper frowned a little, thinking before he spoke.

"I think, on a good day, you're quirky. To say the least. And right now... well, I think you're going through some shit," he said, leaning against the counter. His eyes glinting in the lights behind the bar, discolored by the glow through the bottles of alcohol. "Right now, I think you're having a hard time over something. I don't know what exactly, but you've had a great deal of shit in your life that could make anyone stumble. But I also know you're a pretty private person, even with the people you care about and who care about you. I think you wouldn't tell me even if I asked. I know whatever it is, whatever's going on, you're smart enough to know that this," he pointed to the shot glasses on the table, "Is postponing the issue, and at some point you're going to have to face the problem head on. And I know you *will* face it head on when you're ready. And when you do, you're going to be okay. Because you are far stronger than you think. I know whatever is going on, whatever's got you twisting, you're gonna figure it out. You're going to be okay... because you're not broken."

Buggy opened her mouth, but nothing came out. She was stunned into silence, and the alcohol was making it hard to pick out the right words, but that was alright, Cooper wasn't done speaking.

"Let me guess, your parents are the ones who want to 'fix' you, right? They probably wanted to fix you ever since they caught you checking the locks three times." Buggy glanced up at him. She was constantly shocked at how much attention he paid. Or perhaps she was just not as good at hiding her eccentricities as she thought she was. "So, parents want to fix you. Sandra wants to help you, show you the *right* way to deal with whatever you're dealing with. And me?" He slid her drinks over after he paid the bartender. He carefully placed her whiskey sour to her left and slid her glass of water to a spot by her right hand. Buggy nearly cried. "I *know* I'm useless. I know I don't understand and can't really do anything for you. What I *can* do is be here with you. Be here *for* you. Just say the word, and I'm there. Wherever that may be." He lifted his glass and clinked it against hers. "So, I guess I'm just along for the ride." Buggy continued to watch him as he took a long drink. Her fingers chilled against the glass in her hands.

"I wanna kiss you now," she said conversationally, as if she had been thanking him for a compliment and not contemplating the implosion of their friendship. Cooper looked up, hair falling in his eyes, which were momentarily widened in surprise. He smiled again.

"Then, why don't you?" he asked, in an equally conversational tone.

"Because you're right," Buggy said, twirling her whiskey sour between her fingers, and drawing patterns in the condensation dripping down the side. "You're right. Right now I'm... twisting. It's just..." *It's so much worse than you think*, "I'm having trouble sleeping..." *I have dreams that I'm dying. Burning. It hurts so much.* "I'm... a bit of a catastrophe right now, and I'm not sure why." *Why is this happening to me?* "Right now, I'm just... so..." Her free hand moved, fingers curling into claws at her chest, just above the cavernous empty that gaped in her heart. Buggy searched for words, words to describe the sucking void in her chest that had been opened, dragging her down. The one that seemed to scream with unheard gray voices. But the words didn't come. Buggy thought about her dreams. Her weird restless nights. Waking up in the middle of her kitchen with Sandra standing there looking at her like she was crazy. She thought about the nap she took in the office. The ashes that had no explanation and vanished without reason. She thought about dream-Cooper with his head tilted down, smirk curling his lips into a snarl. How real he felt. How hot the ash had felt in her hands. *Oh, God, Cooper, I'm not quirky. Not anymore. I'm going crazy. I'm hallucinating. I'm losing my goddamn mind.*

"Right now, I'm just…" *I'm scared. I'm terrified.* "I need to work some stuff out. Till then, I'm scared it will make me ruin things." She thought about the green note stuck to her little secret that was a secret no longer. She thought about the expression on Sandra's face when she'd opened the drawer. The sheer disappointment that must have creased every beautiful feature.

Buggy looked up at Cooper, who was watching her intently. "And I really, *really* don't want to ruin this." Cooper considered, then nodded.

"Okay," he said, lifting his glass. "To not ruining things. Other than our livers, of course."

"Oh, those sons of bitches have no chance." Buggy grinned, clinking her glass to his.

18

Cooper and Buggy were soon joined by Linny, and Andrew and the *Friends* Marathon Friday had begun. They talked, they laughed, they drank, and to Buggy's great horror, they stayed for karaoke. She refused to go up when her turn was called, but that was perfectly alright with Linny. It meant she got to sing two songs in a row. Andrew and Cooper and Buggy mostly stayed on the sidelines by the bar, cheering her on as she bellowed "Sweet Home Alabama" like a lunatic, hands waving in the air. Buggy laughed and sang along and danced with Andrew when he jumped up and took her hand. They swung around, his outrageous height contrasting with her somewhat shorter frame made for a humorous spectacle, and several people laughed and clapped. After the song was over, and after Linny returned from the debut of her singing career, Buggy slipped back off the bar stool.

"Be back!" she called over the sound of the next singer, some twenty-one-year-old blond who thought herself a regular Taylor Swift, singing "I Knew You Were Trouble."

"Where you going?" Cooper asked.

"Bathroom," she called back. Cooper nodded and turned back to the bar. It wasn't a lie, she thought, pushing through the packed room towards the back where a green neon arrow pointed towards the co-ed restrooms. That was where she was headed, after all. No, she didn't actually need to use it, but she *did* need a minute alone. Just a break from all the sounds, all the crushing mass of people. For once, in perhaps ever, there was no line. She slipped in the door, closed it behind her, and pressed the little lock button with her elbow so she wouldn't have to touch it with her hands. People were notorious for leaving bathrooms without even pretending to run the faucets. Buggy went to the sink and turned the water on cold. She splashed her face, letting the cool water drip down her nose and off her eyelashes, trying to clear her mind, which was a muddle of emotions and alcohol.

Watching Linny singing "Sweet Home Alabama" had made Buggy think of her mother's cassettes. It was a song that played in the background of one in particular, the one meant for her to hear on her thirteenth birthday, if Buggy recalled correctly. That cassette held a fairly short message. The recordings usually ran until the end of the tape, and sometimes even over to the other side. This one had been a short "hello," and "happy birthday" that only lasted the length of a single song. And that song just happened to be "Sweet Home Alabama."

A knock interrupted Buggy's brooding.

"Just a second," Buggy called. She turned off the water and gripped either side of the sink. She looked up at her reflection in the mirror. Water still dripped down her face and away from her large, bloodshot brown eyes. She could still hear her mother's voice in her mind. She had listened to each and every cassette over a hundred times. Okay, *almost* every cassette. There were exactly two recordings she had not yet broken open, because each tape was meant for a specific moment in her life, and she had yet to live all of them. The cassettes marked "Dream Job," and "First Love," were the only tapes she had not played and replayed.

Every other cassette she knew by heart. She had memorized every word, every element, every sigh and pause. She could replay every one of them in her mind, as true and accurate as if she was hearing it. She had tattooed every word into her brain because it was all she had left of the woman she had never met. All she would ever have.

People sometimes just leave, do they not?

Buggy wiped the tears out of her eyes before they could fall, and her mother's voice came to her mind once more, drowning out dream-Cooper's sneer.

To start off, I miss you. I never wanted you to have to grow up without me. Buggy pressed a hand into her eyes, trying to stem the flow of tears that came hot and hard. *I wanted to be there for all of it. Your first steps. Your first words. All of it....* Buggy put her hand back down onto the sink, fingers going white as she gripped it hard.

All I ever wanted was to watch you grow up into the wonderful girl I am sure that you have become...please know....

"Shut up," Buggy growled against the sweet voice in her ear, the voice that sounded so much like her own. Her head swam with alcohol and the room shifted around her, spinning unpleasantly. She gripped the sink tighter to steady herself.

Know that I love you.

"Shut up. Shut up. Shut up."

"Hurry up in there!" called a voice from the other side of the door as the knocking continued. Buggy barely noticed.

That I always have. I love you.

"Get out, get out, shut up," Buggy's voice broke as her entire body shuddered. "Stop talking. Get *out*."

I love you with all of my heart.

"Shut up!" Her eyes scrunched closed as she yelled at the empty bathroom, voice ricocheting back at her from the walls.

Always have, always will.

"Then why did you leave me?!" Buggy screamed. There was a creak a great cracking shudder. All at once, Buggy felt the sink give way under her hands with the thundering sound of ceramic hitting hardwood. She opened her eyes and saw that the entire bowl of the sink had broken in half. The second half lay in odd, morphed shards on the bathroom floor. She noticed several of the pieces looked bent in irregular liquid forms as if melted, not broken. Buggy was jolted out of her shocked daze as she felt a small pain splinter up her hand. She looked down. One of the pale white shards had buried itself in her palm. She reached with her other trembling hand and pulled the sliver out. Blood bubbled to the surface and began to stream down her fingers. An ominous "plip—plip—plip" echoed against the tile as it dripped form her hand and broke against the floor. Buggy backed away from the mess of ceramic, horror washing away any pain. It flooded her, crashing against the spurt of adrenaline humming through her veins.

Did *she* do that? Of course, she did that. She had literally felt the sink give under her grip. Felt it fall away, heard it hit the floor. But how the hell *had* she done that? Another knock came to the door, a little gentler this time.

"Everything okay in there?" a voice asked, sounding concerned.

"Everything's fine!" Buggy called back, eyes still on the shattered and melted pieces of sink scattered around her feet. She waited—waited for the pieces to disappear, to simply vanish like the ash from the office. She closed her eyes, silently wishing, almost praying that they would be gone when she opened them. Wishing that this was just another strange illusion or hallucination brought on by a lack of sleep. Just a trick of the mind. Fake. False. Not real.

She opened her eyes. The sink was still broken into shards on the floor, and her hand was beginning to drip faster, sending large read drops, splashing in grisly red splatters. She didn't give herself time to think it over. She didn't give herself time to consider anything. Buggy pulled a few papers towels from the silver box screwed to the wall and wrapped her hand, fingers trembling. It didn't stop her bleeding, but it slowed it down a bit. She gathered the chunks of ceramic, mopped up the droplets of blood, and tossed them in the waste bin She then pulled the plastic bag out of the little bin, tied it closed, and moved to the door. She opened it slightly. The second bathroom must have opened up because, to Buggy's relief, there was no one waiting out there as she stepped into the hall. She cast one last glance towards the demolished sink which looked almost comical standing there half missing. She then closed the door behind her and slipped out the back door under another neon green light that said "exit." The door clicked closed, locking behind her. She trotted down the little alley between The Lookout and a Chinese restaurant that Buggy had never gone too but which had always smelled particularly greasy. She tossed the bag full of ceramic pieces into the restaurant's green trash bin and closed the lid. She made her way back inside the bar where the Taylor Swift-loving blond had just started up another song.

"Hey!" Cooper called to her, then frowned and looked back around where the bathrooms were. "Did you just—?" Buggy cut him off.

"Ready to go watch some *Friends*?" she asked him, trying to hide the desperation in her voice. She needed to leave here. She needed to leave now. It seemed to have worked.

"Sure!" Cooper said, completely forgetting his previous question.

"I'm ready," Linny agreed, downing the last of her drink and jumping off the stool. "I'm tired of T-Swizzle."

"Here, here," Andrew said, closing his tab.

"Let's roll!" Cooper pointed towards the door as they all made their way to into the crisp night air. "Another *Friends* marathon awaits!" Buggy smiled and laughed along with the rest of them, but she kept her right hand buried deep into her pocket as they walked. It still throbbed and it still bled, but she only smiled. Buggy didn't let her friends see she was hanging on by a thread. A dark, tenuous thread.

19

All four of them stayed up half the night, chomping on pizza and chatting as *Friends* played in the background. Around two o'clock in the morning, Andrew, Cooper, and Linny had fallen asleep, but Buggy couldn't follow them. She could only lie in the dark, watching the characters play out their various life troubles on-screen, bloodshot eyes continually darting down to her hand. She had found a few Band-Aides behind Andrew's bathroom mirror, which had helped stop the bleeding, but it was still throbbing. With every heartbeat, she could feel the pain pulse, strong and accusatory. She tried not to think of the sink, or about how much trouble the bar owner would have to go through to get a new one, or how much such a sink might cost. It wasn't anything fancy, just a standard ceramic bowl, but they weren't exactly free either. There was no fixing the one that they had. No, that was beyond repair. Even if they had all the pieces, they wouldn't have been able to glue them back together.

Buggy remembered the almost liquified shapes the shards had taken. They seemed to have oozed, melted, and then instantly solidified again. No, they wouldn't glue back in place, none of the pieces fit, and now all the pieces were going to be picked up by the garbage man and disappear forever. Buggy wondered why she had done that. Get rid of the evidence? Even if the owner had been inclined to find out who had broken it, and even if they took the shards to be print tested, it had so many prints by this point that hers would be indistinguishable from all the rest. And in what world would anyone believe that *she* had done it, anyway? Her—with her thin frame, distinct lack of muscles, and large innocent eyes—who on Earth would believe that she had done that. That she had destroyed it with just her hands. Because she barely believed it herself.

She tried to remember if the bowl had already had a crack, some weakness, anything that could explain how she had broken it with her fingertips. Even if there had been a weakness, a fissure in the ceramic, that wouldn't explain the odd melting look they had. No, nothing explained that.

So, Buggy laid there, confused, terrified, exhausted, until she finally dozed off for a few short and restless hours. The next morning, they broke from tradition. Usually, they went their separate ways by lunch, each having obligations elsewhere. Andrew, with his yoga classes, and Linny and Cooper with their various relationships of the week. However, after finding Sandra's little note stuck to a half-empty bottle on her dresser, Buggy really didn't feel like going home quite yet. She would talk to Sandra, she had decided that. Cooper had been right, she needed to face the issue head on... no matter how *insane* it all sounded. So, she would start by telling Sandra everything. Tell her why she had kept the second bottle. About the dreams, the nightmares, the dream-Cooper, the ashes, the sink. How it had shattered in her hands, *everything*. She would tell her big sister all of it. She doubted Sandra would have any better idea what to do than Buggy herself, but it was time to tell someone. She would tell her about all the crazy shit that had been happening to her and let the chips fall where they may. She would face it. She would deal with it... just not today. She couldn't do it today. She could barely keep it together, and if she tried to talk to Sandra now, said any of it out loud, then she could never take it back. It would be out. It would be *real*. And she would shatter. Buggy knew she would. She would shatter, and she wasn't sure she could pick up the pieces. She would need to throw them away, right beside the bloody paper towels and twisted ceramic.

She just needed one more day. One more day to figure out how she was going to say it all. So, Buggy suggested they blow off obligations for the rest of the afternoon, go bowling, see a movie, and then perhaps more pizza and *Friends* that evening. Why not double the fun for the weekend? Andrew and Linny were all for it. Andrew started looking up hours for nearby bowling alleys while Linny stepped outside to cancel her date night with some guy who's name she couldn't remember, but she was pretty sure began with a T.

"God, I hope it's Tony," Linny said, putting the phone to her ear, "Or this is about to get real awkward, real quick." Linny closed the door behind her, and Cooper and Buggy were left along.

"What?" Buggy asked as she noticed Cooper looking at her. He was watching her, with an irritatingly *knowing* look in his eyes.

"You can't avoid her forever, you know," he said.

"I know," Buggy sighed and rubbed her eyes. "I'm gonna talk to her. Really, I just... want a little more time." Cooper shrugged.

"Might wanna let her know, though."

Buggy nodded and pulled out her phone. She pulled up Sandra's number and started a new text message.

I'm staying over at Andrew's again tonight. I know you want to talk, and we will, I promise. I'll be home tomorrow.

Buggy pressed send on her phone and waited. A few minutes later, Sandra replied.

Okay. Thanks for telling me. I'm having dinner with Christina's family tomorrow night in Sac. Depending upon how late things go, we may be spending the night.

Buggy nodded. She knew that. She and Christina had been dating for several years now and had made it a tradition to once a month have dinner with her parents. Drinks and charades were usually involved and lasted late into the evening. Sandra was terrified of driving in the dark, and Christina's family was more than happy to fix up the guest room.

Okay, Buggy replied. *I will be home after work on Monday.*

Then we chat a little? Sandra asked.

Buggy sighed, already dreading everything. Feelings were gross. Shame and causing disappointment... that was the worst. But it was time. She had put it off long enough. It was time to ask for a little help and get someone else's perspective.

Then we chat a little. She replied.

How you doing?

Buggy looked at the message for a long while. She tried to think of a proper response.

Well, you know, I'm okay, except that I think I am losing my goddamn mind, keep hearing voices that aren't there, sleepwalking, waking up covered in ashes for no reason, and breaking things I have no business being able to break. But other than that, peachy-keen!

Instead, she wrote:

Not great, but not the worst. Technically not a lie. It could get far worse than this. That was precisely what Buggy was terrified of.

Okay, Sandra replied. *See you Monday at the latest. Have fun! Be safe!*

Will do! Buggy replied. She looked back up at Cooper, who was smiling.

"Good girl," he said.

"And what about you?" Buggy asked him, "No plans to cancel? No new girl to update?"

"Nah, been taking a break from the whole dating scene."

"Oh?" Buggy asked, "Why's that?"

Cooper smiled, and Buggy saw that same sideways look in his eye. Not the one she had dreamed up in the kitchen, but the one that she had begun to grow familiar with. The one that elicited that little fluttering sensation in her stomach. The small smile that made her wonder. That made her sure.

"Oh, come on Buggy," he said, shrugging. "You know why."

Buggy was saved the trouble of thinking up a response as Linny burst back through the door, waving her phone in the air.

"Trevor! Damn it all, his name was Trevor! Fuck!"

Cooper and Buggy began to laugh.

* * *

It was Saturday afternoon, and Buggy was tired. They had gone bowling for a few hours, then jumped over to the movie theater and caught a showing of the latest action-adventure flick. Buggy entertained herself by whispering predictions to Linny and Cooper on either side of her, all of which came true. Predictable a plot as ever there was one, but entertaining, nonetheless. They had then snagged another pizza, some beers, and retreated back to Andrews's house for another round of *Friends*. Again, everyone had fallen asleep by two. Again, Buggy was left staring at the ceiling, terrified to close her eyes. What would she see? Cooper, with his head tilted down in that odd and off-putting way? The look of a predator watching its prey. Ready to pounce. Enjoying the prowl. Or would she hear her mother's voice, whispering sweet lies into her ears? Wishes never fulfilled. Or perhaps she would wake up in another pile of ashes. Or maybe a house of fire.

She dozed in and out of sleep for a few hours but woke early. She waited until the sun deigned to flood the day with its light, before finally climbing off the couch. Everyone else woke, had waffles this time instead of pancakes, then Cooper had driven her home. Buggy noticed that Sandra's car was gone from the driveway, and she checked her watch. She must have left a little early to pick up Christina and head down to Sacramento. She really did hate driving in the dark, and it had started getting dark extremely early as winter enveloped the season. Buggy was sure they would be spending the night in Sac. She had one last night to herself, and to plan out what she was going to say. That was good. She could even draw up a few note cards to refer back to if she felt like it.

A cold breeze cut at Buggy's face as she stepped out of Cooper's car.

"Hey, you alright?" Cooper asked, stepping out to walk her to her door. He always did that. It was one of those unnecessary, but utterly nice things he did. Very sweet. Very Cooper.

"Yeah, I'm okay, just tired," Buggy lied, flashing him a quick smile as she pulled out her keys. She was getting better at that all the time. It was a half-truth after all. She *was* exhausted.

"Hey... Briar."

Buggy jerked her head up, certain that she would see that tilting smirk that the dream had worn on Cooper's face. All she saw was the same warm smile she had known for years. She relaxed.

"Yeah?"

Cooper took a little breath, ran a hand through his sangria tinted hair, then began. "I don't care if you're a little messed up."

"What?" Buggy asked, confused.

"I mean, no, I mean I *do* care if you're messed up. If you're not in the best place right now, I *do* care. I want everything to be okay, and I want you to be happy. But I know my wishing that isn't going to make it magically happen... it's just... you said you didn't want to mess this up. I just wanted to let you know that you wouldn't."

Realization flooded Buggy with the nauseating speed of someone stomping on their breaks. She felt herself shift forward, but jerked to a stop by an invisible seatbelt—the fluttering sensation that darted through her chest and struck down towards her fingers. Oh, no. She wasn't drunk at all, let alone drunk enough for *this* conversation. She was hungover, her body was drained, and her brain was running at half speed. It was so *not* the time for this. Not at all. "Cooper..." Buggy closed her eyes, willing him to stop talking. Willing the feelings in her stomach, the anticipation, the fear, the curiosity, to all dry up and melt like those shards of ceramic sink. But feelings were not so easily tossed away, and Cooper continued.

"Nah just, hang on a sec," Cooper held up his hands. "You can run away once I'm done. Look, I know you pretty well by now. I know that you are a little eccentric and OCD. I know you like your drink to the left and your water to the right, and I know you're not a huge fan of feelings. I get that and—not gonna lie—I find it cute as hell. And even if you are a little *twisty* right now... I like you. Have for a while now. I don't mind if you're a bit of a mess at the moment, and I know you have to work through some stuff, and I'll give you space and time if that is what you want. I will never press you. I won't push you. But I really like you, and I think you like me... please correct me if I'm wrong." Buggy opened her mouth, closed it, opened it again, closed it again, like some beached fish searching for water. The sensations threatened to flood up her throat, and she pressed her lips together tight. Her eyes darted to the ground as a fluttering warmth rippled up her stomach and she rocked back a little on her heels. Cooper smiled, taking her silence as an answer. "Look. I think you're amazing. Twisty or not. And I think we could have something really good. If you feel the same way... well... I'll be gone for a little over a week." Buggy looked up, confused. Cooper explained. "Going to see my sister. She and Brian are moving, and they fell behind on the packing. They asked for my help. I'm going to head up tonight. So, I'll be out of your hair for a week or so, and you'll have a little time. You think about it. If I come back and you say nothing, then we go back to being just friends. Which is truly okay with me if that is what you would prefer." Cooper held up his hands again, as if showing her that he had nothing up his sleeves. "We have been friends for a long time now, and I never want to lose that, no matter what. If I come back and you say nothing, we forget this conversation ever happened, we stay friends, and I won't ever bring this up again." Cooper lowered his hands. "If, on the other hand, you'd like to take a try at being something more...."

"Then, you'll be back in a little over a week," Buggy said, eyes still on the ground.

"Yep," Cooper said. "Sound fair?" Buggy tried to speak, but nothing came out. Instead, she gave a nod. Cooper laughed, then his face grew a little more serious.

"Either way you choose, I want you to know that I'm here for you, okay? I may not know what's going on with you, but if I can be there for you in anyway, I want to be."

Buggy's throat had swollen closed. She tried to clear it, to force words up to her lips, but they were trapped down deep in her chest. She looked up at him, trying to convey her gratitude without words. It seemed to have worked because Cooper smiled and nodded.

"Alright then," he said, his smile widening into his signature grin. "See you soon... Buggybear." Buggy scowled and found her voice.

"Oh, for the love of God!"

20

It had been a lazy, rainy day, leading to a rather beautiful afternoon. Darkness had already started taking over the streets, and all the Christmas lights switched on in one swift glittering explosion of color. Every house, every building, every lamp post lining the rain-slick street gleamed and twinkled. Waverly had always loved the Christmas season. A time of joy, of light, of laughter and of giving. It was the time of white magic, love conquering all, and the endurance of hope in a world that continually tried to rip itself apart at the seams. A world made of scars, usually stitched together by dark, ugly thread, but come December, it was sewn with Christmas lights, and "Ode to Joy's" sung through the streets. For at least one month out of the year, the world could be beautiful.

Waverly sat in a cozy little coffee shop across the street from Elwin Family Dentistry. She sipped at her cappuccino, watching as the brunette behind the glass doors flipped the little sign over from "open" to "closed," and reminisced over the many hours she had spent decorating Christmas trees with her mother. They had spent long afternoons walking through the rows and rows of trees, needing to find the perfect one. Which they always did. Then they would take it home, clear a corner of the living room, and set the tree in a place of honor. They would throw on "White Christmas" and listen to Bing Crosby and Danny Kaye's playful banter as they strung light after light, decoration after decoration. They would then end the evening curled up on the couch, hot chocolate in hand. It was peaceful. It was soft. It was the brief, precious time when Waverly wasn't afraid of her mother, or of the manic flash in her eyes. It was the only time they took a pause from their searching. A brief opportunity for the fear to fade, and the anxiety to drift away with the steam wafting from their mugs, only to return as December ended and the lights came down. When the lights were wound up, and stowed back in their boxes, it all started again.

The search. The anger. The drinking. The dark flashes. The hitting. The stories of blood and death and darkness. The rest of the year was made up of scars and dark threads. Waverly had followed those dark threads. Her mother had described them as ugly, and jagged, but Waverly had never felt them herself. She didn't have the gift to *see*, but she went where her mother told her to go. She followed the threads with her, then followed them alone after her mother's accident had left her unable to travel. It was around that time—as her mother's pain meds increased and her sober days nose-dived—that December even lost its peace. So, Waverly continued to search for dark threads by Christmas light, until she was finally led to a quaint coffee shop on a Monday afternoon, watching the brunette slip on a white coat and step out of the dentist's office.

The search usually came to a dead end. It had never been the right girl before, but this time was different. This time... this time her mother had been *right.* Waverly had watched the girl for a time, watched her from that very coffee shop for hours. She hadn't needed to. She had known Briar Rose Pierce was *the one* the instant she laid eyes on her. It was unmistakably the right girl. She looked exactly like the photo. Exactly like the photo her mother had waved under her nose for nearly twenty-seven years.

"Memorize it!" her mother had barked in her ear, shaking her shoulder with one hand and cramming the photo against Waverly's face with the other. The strong stench of mixed whiskey and rum blew across her face with every word uttered, stinging Waverly's nose until her eyes watered. "Memorize that face, Waverly. Memorize the face of evil! You must know her when you see her. Memorize it!" Waverly had, and she had known it when she saw it.

Waverly got to her feet, dropped a tip next to her half-drunk coffee, and started for the door. She allowed the girl to walk a short distance down the street before she slipped out of the coffee house, exchanging its soft instrumental music for the chilly wind outside. She followed the girl at a distance on silent feet, eyes never leaving the figure ahead. Cars drove buy, spraying little spurts of fallen rainwater back up into the air beside her, but not close enough to touch either her or the girl that she followed. The owner of the dark threads, unseen.

The streets were empty except for Waverly and the girl. It seemed that no one else appreciated the beautiful lights of the city enough to excuse the nip in the air. That was good. That made things easy. Waverly picked up her pace as the girl turned a corner heading, she knew, towards the bus station nearby. She had watched the girl for days, learned her patterns, and saw her take this trip several times before making her plans. Plans for this moment, *the* moment. What she had been born to do.

Waverly reached into the inside of her jacket and felt the cold handle of the .38 Smith & Wesson. It hung, ready and waiting, in the holster under her arm.

Waverly had just started around the corner when she heard it.

"Bennu."

Waverly froze for half a second, then darted back around the building and out of sight. She peeked around just in time to see the girl stumble. A boy in his twenties with red-brown hair caught her as she started to fall.

"Crap!" the younger man said to himself, trying to hoist the now seemingly lifeless body of the girl in his arms. "Oh, crap. Oh, shit." The headlights of a car flashed a short distance away and an engine came to life. A gray Jeep wrangler came skidding up to the sidewalk where the young man and the unconscious girl waited. A man stepped out of the driver's side. Waverly recognized him and hissed under her breath, retreating a little further behind the building, but still watching.

The older man came up and lifted the girl out of the younger man's awkward grip.

"She's not a sack of grain, Theo," the older man said sharply.

"She's not exactly a pile of feathers either, Styger," Theo answered, but his voice was shaky. "She okay?"

"She's fine," Styger assured him. "Just asleep. Pop open the door, will you?" Theo did and laid Briar Rose Pierce gently across the back seat.

"Why the hell did that work again?" Theo asked, moving quickly for the passenger door and hopping in.

"I'll explain later," Cam Styger answered, sliding back behind the steering wheel. "Right now, we just gotta get the hell—" his words were cut short as he pulled the driver's door closed. The engine revved, and the car pulled away from the sidewalk. Picking up speed, it passed the corner where Waverly crouched in shadow. It took off down the road, took a left, passed the dentist's office, and disappeared. Waverly straightened up, cursing. They had gotten to her first. Stupid fuckers got her first. This was unacceptable. They wouldn't do what needed to be done.

She jogged back to where she left her Softail and straddled it. She slipped on her thick gloves, grabbed her helmet off the handlebars, and jammed it on her head. She glared in the direction that Cameron Styger and his little companion had taken her target. She imagined the dark threads spreading further and further away from her. She snapped the helmet's eye shield down, covering the striking blue eyes that glared from within.

She wouldn't let them get away. No. Cameron Styger would not fuck this all up. Not again.

Waverly turned the key in the ignition. The engine rumbled obediently to life. She peeled out of the parking space by the coffee shop. The Christmas lights streaked in her peripheral vision as she followed the dark threads wherever they may lead.

PART 3:

For The Love of A Daughter

I

Buggy shifted slowly, sleep begrudgingly giving way to consciousness. She groaned, opened her eyes and blinked a few times, trying to see clearly through the migraine pounding her head like a hammer with every heartbeat. She sat up, pulse rising from a tumbling trot to a full-throttled sprint as memories came flooding back to her. She remembered leaving Elwin's. She remembered turning the corner, and heading for the bus station. She had been wrapped in her thoughts. Turning them over and over in her mind as she tended to do. She built the script in her head, the words to tell Sandra exactly what the hell was going on with her. Whatever the hell that might be. She knew she was going crazy, at least a little, but that wasn't all. It wasn't only *mental.* If it had just been about the ashes, she would have chalked it up to hallucinations and nightmares and her brain on the fritz. But no, it wasn't all in her head. She had the scar on her palm as proof of that. There was something more going on, something Buggy didn't understand. She doubted Sandra would either, but Buggy couldn't keep it to herself anymore. It was getting worse, Buggy knew it. It would continue to get worse, and if she waited too long, it may become too late. Next time she may break more than a bathroom sink.

She had been rolling her newly formed script in her mind, changing a word here and there, as the bus station came into view. But then...

Bennu

Everything had gone dark. The type of inky blackness where you forget that things, objects, even people, exist. Perhaps she should have been grateful that it hadn't been dreams, but it was the type of dark where you float alone, formless ... until you forget even yourself. From this forgetting place, she had woken in the backseat of a Jeep with two strange men. Buggy had tried to escape. She had bitten one of the men's hands when he tried to pull her back into the Jeep. She had sprinted across an empty parking lot, screaming for help, until once more she heard that unknown word.

Bennu

Darkness again. Now what?

Buggy shoved herself to a sitting position, closing her eyes against the sudden nausea caused by the movement. She blinked again, and a room came into focus. It was large with wooden walls that made Buggy think of the Lincoln Logs she played with as a child. There were deer shaped lamps on a coffee table which confirmed it was a cabin of sorts. Buggy was lying on a large couch, half covered in a thick plaid blanket. The room was tall as well as wide, a spacious living room with the warm and cozy air that belonged only to well used cabins like this. The type of cabins that were frequently visited and made up of memories. It breathed with life around her, filling the air with a soft cinnamon scent, but Buggy noticed something weird about it. The light that flooded the room wasn't the pure clear light that usually accompanied normal windowpanes. It was tinted with red, blue, green, and orange, casting the room in mystical shades. Buggy looked up and saw the source. Stain glass windows lined the tall walls, circling her in images of flying birds, frolicking horses, and vibrant light.

Buggy moved to get up but was pulled back down by a fierce tug at her wrist. She looked down to see a handcuff locking her wrist to the wooden handle of the couch. She tugged at, trying to snap the handle. But it was thick, sturdy, and wouldn't budge. Not by simple tugging, at least. Buggy looked around for something, anything sharp. A saw or serrated knife would be ideal, but she would take anything that might cut through wood. Instead, she started violently, and bit back a yelp of fear, as she caught sight of someone sitting in front of the fireplace. She recognized him as the younger of the two men in the Jeep. The men that had taken her... wherever the hell she was now.

He had been sitting so quietly, not making a single sound or movement, that Buggy had initially missed him. She saw him now, and watched him as he sat, legs crossed, hands resting on his knees, palms up and open. He was staring into the fireplace where coals glowed dimly. His green eyes were glazed, not noticing her. Not seeing anything at all.

Is he meditating? Buggy wondered, irritation flooding her, intense and unexpected. *He and his friend kidnap me, turn my life upside down—even more upside down than it already was, which I didn't think was even possible—as crazy as it was getting. And he is. Fucking. Meditating?*

"Hey," Buggy barked before she thought about the consequences. Before her common sense could catch up to the rage that was billowing like some great flag in her heart, signaling the call to war. "Hey, dick head!"

He started, blinking rapidly. He turned, eyes unfocused until he finally saw her. They widened in surprise and Buggy was pleased to see panic dancing inside them.

"Oh shit," he whispered, more to himself than for her benefit. Buggy narrowed her gaze as his eyes darted away and then back again.

"Wait a second," Buggy scowled, looking closer at the man. "I know you... how do I know you?" She thought long and hard, watching him squirm uncomfortably under her gaze. Then realization struck her with the force of a car crashing through a store window, or a bolt of lightning severing an ancient oak into two blackened, smoldering husks. "Oh, you mother *fucker*," she growled, leaning towards him, the hand cuff digging deeper into her wrist, but she ignored the pain. "Theodore, right?" She remembered those eyes, that nose. That "cute nose" of his, and how Linny had encouraged her to ask him out. If Linny only knew. If only *she* had known. But how the hell could either of them have seen this coming?

"Um, 'Theo' actually," Theo said, turning fully towards her. His smile flickered unsure against his lips, twitching on and off again like a faulty electrical circuit.

"Guess you're not going to make your appointment," Buggy said, voice hollow, emotionless, which was a stark contrast to the ocean of feelings crashing in her stomach and pumping adrenaline hot through her veins.

"Yeah, uh," Theo stuttered, running a hand over the back of his neck. For being the kidnapper and not the kidnaped, Theo seemed terrified. "Nice to meet you?" The would-be statement came out as a question and Buggy barked a laugh that was fueled by flying sparks of fear and fury.

"Nice to meet you? You abducted me, you *ass*."

"Eh, okay, technically yes, but that was *not* my idea," Theo said, raising his palms in the air, half shrugging, half showing his empty, innocent hands. "I wasn't **at all** down for that."

"Oh, well then, if you're not 'down for that' then how about you uncuff me and I'll be on my merry way," Buggy said, eyes narrowing again.

"I..." Theo hesitated. "I can't." Buggy wasn't surprised, but her heart was beating faster now. It thudded against his ribs, trying to break out and get as far away from this place as she herself wanted to be.

"Aaaaand why not?"

"Uh," his eyes darted towards a large wooden door set into the wall to Buggy's left. It was a heavy door decorated with yet another stain glass window that stood in a bright oval at its center. Theo's eyes yearned for it, as if willing someone to walk through.

"Hey," Buggy snapped her fingers in the air, bringing his light green eyes back to her. "I'm over here, twitchy." Buggy was surprised. She had not thought about how she might act if something this terrible was ever to happen. Sure, she carried around pepper-spray, always checked the back seat of her car before driving off, all those basic preventative measures, but she had never really considered what she would do if something like this actually happened. If she was actually taken. She had no plan, no method for this. She thought she should be screaming, freaking out, panicking, and she wanted to, but there was another emotion that flowed to the top of the ocean in her chest. One that took hold, controlling all the rest, keeping the rest at bay with its sheer size. Rage. It dampened the panic just enough so she could breathe. She rode that rage like a surfboard, letting it guide her words, guide her voice, her actions across the seething waters of panic below. She knew she couldn't stay afloat for long. She had never been good at surfing, and she would soon slip up and fall headfirst into the water where she would drown in the emotions she was holding back. Till then, she would keep her head above water in any way that she could. Apparently, *her* way was to get pissed.

"So, fuck face, what's your plan here?" Buggy asked in a conversational tone.

"Fuck face?" Theo's eyebrows scrunched into a confused frown.

"Oh, no, no, no," Buggy barked, waving her one free hand in the air, jabbing an accusing finger at his face. "You don't get to act all hurt. You're the one who threw me in a back of a Jeep and drove me," Buggy looked around, trying to see anything out the stained-glass windows, but it was impossible, "to God knows where. Pretty sure that gives me the right to call you whatever the hell I want."

Theo stared in surprised silence. Then he shrugged. "That's fair."

Buggy frowned. What was this guy's deal?

"I'm really sorry about this," Theo said after another few awkward seconds of silence.

"I'm pretty sure I don't give a shit," Buggy answered, giving her handcuff a hard yank, and only succeeding in cutting into her skin once more with the cold metal. "Where am I?"

"In a cabin," Theo said simply.

"No shit," Buggy answered, glaring at him and ignoring the small trickle of blood that blossomed and ran down her wrist. "I meant where on the planet?"

"Somewhere safe," Theo said. Buggy just glared. Theo's eyes darted away. "Okay, I know it does not *at all* seem like it, but this *is* a safe place."

"Safe place, hmm?" Buggy asked, watching as Theo uncurled his legs and got to his feet. "Will we be handing around a talking stick? Chat about our feelings? Because I've got a few words on that front I'd just *love* to share."

"I'm sure you do," Theo said, disappearing through a second wooden door behind the couch, and into another room of the cabin that she couldn't see. Buggy craned her neck around, keeping an eye on the door until he came back out with a little white box in his hands. "And you have every right." Theo came nearer to Buggy and knelt by the coffee table in front of her. He opened the little box, which turned out to be a first aid kit. He pulled out a bottle of alcohol and some cleansing pads.

"What are you doing?" Buggy asked, although she already knew the answer. She just wanted to keep her mouth moving, keep the words coming. The longer she kept herself distracted, kept the anger up, the longer she would be able to keep herself from drowning.

"You mind?" he asked, motioning to the little stream of blood that was now threatening to drip off her index finger.

"You touching me?" Buggy said, scowling. "Damn straight, I mind." A nasty thought suddenly struck her, and she teetered on the edge of the board. She had heard of that kind of thing before. Sickos kidnaping young girls to fulfill all of their disgusting, depraved desires. Buggy felt the fear splashing over her feet and ankles, calling her to dive straight in. Luckily, rage was there to stabilize her. "And if you ever *do* try to touch me... If that is your plan here, if that is the point of this, I swear to God, I'll kill you."

Theo looked up, and Buggy thought she saw a flash of disgust cross his face.

"That's not why you are here, Briar," he said, holding out the alcohol and prep pads. "We aren't here to hurt you." Buggy glared at the items in his hand before slowly reaching out and taking them.

"Then why **am** I here?" Buggy asked, popping open the lid on the alcohol and tipping it to soak the pad. Theo moved away but scooted the first aid kit closer so she could reach the other items inside. Buggy pressed the alcohol-soaked pad to the broken skin on her wrist and hissed as it stung.

"That... is hard to explain." Theo's eyes glanced back to the heavy door.

"Oh yeah? So, you're going to let your companion explain instead?" Buggy asked. "The older guy with the scruff and circle tattoo, right? Save you the trouble?"

"Uh, frankly, yes," Theo answered with a half grin, as if they were old friends sharing a goddamn inside joke. Buggy felt like vomiting, or maybe spitting in his face. "This is more... his thing, not mine. I mean it is *my* thing now also, but it's more his *right* to explain it to you."

"I have no idea what you're saying to me right now," Buggy said, reaching over and riffling through the contents of the kit, looking for some gauze, and maybe some antacids if she was lucky. "How about you give me a ballpark of what is going on here then? If you don't want to get bogged down in specifics." Theo thought about it and must have decided that wouldn't be out of line for him to explain.

"We are trying to save you... you and others."

Buggy looked up from the kit, eyes widening a little. "Oh, God. This is a cult thing, isn't it? This is some hippy-dippy apocalyptic cult thing. Your gonna try to brain wash me into drinking the poisoned Kool-Aid. Well, I'm telling you one thing straight up, I am not gonna be anyone's sister wife, that's for damn sure."

Theo burst out laughing. It would have been a nice sound except for the petrifying situation in which it was uttered. It was hardy and belly deep, making him close his eyes and throw back his head with the force of it. "No," he said, when he finally caught his breath. "No, I promise no Kool-Aid or sister wives."

"Then what is it?" Buggy asked, finding, and snatching out a roll of gauze, unraveling a short length. She slid the hand cuff down as low as she could on her arm and started wrapping the cloth around the raw section of skin as a protective barrier between her and the metal.

"I really think Styger should explain," Theo said, watching her struggle with the one-handed work. "You want some help?"

"Nope," Buggy said, still wrapping a rather intelligent circle of white around her wrist. She tore it with her teeth, dropped the remaining gauze in the box and grabbed some medical tape.

"No, really, I could—"

"Go fuck yourself?" Buggy finished for him, stripping off a few pieces of tape with her teeth as well. "Yeah, I agree." Theo held up his hands in surrender as Buggy finished her work and dropped the tape back into the box alongside the gauze.

"Can I get you anything?" Theo asked awkwardly. He was obviously very new to this whole kidnapping thing.

"A phone would be nice," Buggy said. Theo grimaced.

"Is there anything not escape related that I can get you?"

"Nope," Buggy answered.

"You sure?" Theo asked, fingers fidgeting where they hung against his thigh. "I'd love pretty much anything to do at this point."

"Oh, I'm terribly sorry," Buggy said, trying to make her glare piercing. "Am I making you *uncomfortable*? Is this *awkward* for you?" Theo opened his mouth to speak, but the sound of a car engine made him look up.

"Oh, thank God," he said, darting for the large door with stained-glass. Buggy craned around to watch him slip through it, allowing a glimpse of sunlight and the short musical tinkle of chittering birds to flutter inside before he closed the door behind him. After he had disappeared, she turned back to the medical kit. Buggy had noticed *it* in there but had not wanted to grab it while Theo was still in the room. Tucked between the gauze she had found and a Ziplock bundle of Band-Aids, there had been a small scalpel. Not very long, nor very sharp, but it could do some serious damage to an eye or someone's carotid artery if given half an opportunity. And seeing as both her purse and pepper-spray were nowhere to be seen, her options were limited. She snagged it now, sliding the scalpel into the gap between the couch cushion and arm rest. She closed the lid of the kit and slid it further away on the table just in time for the door to open again. Theo stepped back inside, followed by the older man Buggy had seen driving the Jeep. His scruffy face looked at her with a strange expression that Buggy couldn't read. It looked like a mixture of amazement and pain. Buggy hoped she would be able to enhance the latter emotion as soon as possible.

Styger closed the door behind him and stepped up to a spot on the other side of the coffee table, facing Buggy. His sleeves were rolled halfway up, showing off the simple, circular tattoo on the inside of his wrist. It had originally been an inky black, Buggy suspected, but age and sunlight had faded it to a dark, graying blue. They faced each other in silence for a long time, Buggy not hesitating to meet the man's eyes. Knowing her glare came off as hostile, which was maybe not the best move for a captive. But, she didn't give a damn.

"Hello, Briar," Styger spoke in that same deep gravelly voice. Fear began to lap up inside her, and once more, Buggy suppressed it with anger and answered with bristling contempt.

"Hi, dipshit."

2

Theo met Cam at the door, nearly pushing him back out as he closed the door behind him, hard enough to make the windowpane rattle.

"She's awake," he said in answer to Cam's curious expression.

"For how long?" Cam asked, heart jumping into his throat. He would hear that voice again. He would hear *her* again.

"Just a few minutes," Theo answered, and grabbed Cam's shoulder as he made to push past him. "Cam she's not in a great place. Not surprising giving the situation but... take it slow."

"Do not tell me what to do with her, Theo," Cam growled. "This is none of your business."

"Like hell it isn't," Theo snapped, fingers digging into the older man's shoulder. "You're the one who dragged me along on this trip, remember? *You* are the one who made it *my business*. You were the one that had me find her, connect with her. And you were right about that whole psychic connection thing getting stronger. It has, ever since the first time. I can *feel* her. I can feel how she is feeling now, better than ever. I am telling you, Cam, if you turn over the whole bucket, dump all the information on her at once, it's going to destroy her. She is hanging on by a thread, and it's about to snap. Don't break her. Take it slow, or I swear to God there will be no saving her."

Cam glared at him, but after a moment, he nodded. Theo nodded back and let go of his shoulder. He turned and opened the door, casting one last warning glance over his shoulder before going inside. Cam took a long and deep breath before following him. Briar looked up as he entered, and Cam felt his entire universe go still. Nothing breathed, nothing moved, except for her. For a second, as her face tilted his way, it was all that existed. When her large eyes found him, there was nothing else to see. The world was silent as she saw him, and Cam felt like he was floating in those disk-sized, brown irises. He wanted to break the stillness. He wanted to throw himself at her feet. He wanted to weep like a child while kissing her little fingers. He wanted to hold her, hold her like he should have been holding her for the past twenty-four years. He wanted to toss Theo's warnings to the wind and tell her everything. Confess every sin, every mistake, every failure that had led them to this moment. This wonderful and terrible moment where the person he loved most in this world looked at him as if he was a stranger. Because he *was* a stranger. He wanted to tell her who he was. He wanted to lay it all out. He wanted. He wanted. He *wanted*.

But this wasn't about him or what he wanted. It was about what she *needed*. Theo was right. He needed to take things slow.

"Hello, Briar," he said, breaking the frozen world with his words. She blinked, lids traveling the long distance in a slow, methodic motion of pale lashes.

"Hi, dipshit," she answered coolly.

Cam blinked. It wasn't exactly what he had been expecting to come out of her mouth. Not exactly the form he expected that voice would take. It was the same voice, every bit the same, wrapped around those words. And her face, her eyes, they were so similar... and yet not the same. Because she was her own person. As similar Briar was to the woman that Cam knew, they were *not* the same person. There was more anger behind those brown eyes than had ever been in Loretta's. There was a sharpness in her movements, a harshness that he had never seen before. A twitchy edge that was unfamiliar on her familiar features. Cam supposed that could be due to the less-than-ideal circumstances, causing her to be more feral than was common... but he doubted it. They seemed too fluid, too natural to be anything other than well used mannerisms. She was in pain. Deep down somewhere, not just from the fear of the moment, she was in pain. Probably for a long time. It was just as much a part of her as the hate he saw in her eyes.

Cam swallowed back the lump in his throat. He walked forward, sliding the little first aid kit aside and taking a seat on the coffee table facing her. She leaned back into the couch, as far away from him as she could while still trapped to her seat. Her eyes watching his every movement with disgusted wariness.

"I know you have no reason to believe me," Cam spoke low and soft. Taking it slow. "But you are perfectly safe here." She said nothing, but Cam watched her fingers curl into fists by her legs. "We are not going to hurt you. We are not going to hurt anyone. You are not here to be ransomed. You are not here as some sort of elaborate scam or cultish fetish. You are here for one reason and one reason only."

"And what would that be?" she asked.

"So that we can save your life," Cam answered simply. Briar glanced up at Theo, who was standing off to the side of the room, arms crossed, eyes on the ground.

"As far as I can tell," she said, turning back to Cam. "You are the only threat to me."

Cam nodded. "Yes. I'm sorry for this... impromptu introduction. I would have preferred a different way of going about meeting you, but I'm afraid time wasn't on our side."

"What are you talking about?" she asked, scowling. There was another twitch at the corner of her eye. She was so afraid. It made Cam feel ill.

Take it slow. Cam could almost feel the warning wafting off Theo in palpable waves of anxiety.

"First, I should introduce myself," Cam held out his hand. "My name is Cam. Cam Styger." Buggy's eyes dragged themselves from his fingers and back up to his face, as effortful and forced as dragging a rake through a thick puddle of mud, or sludge.

"You're kidding, right?" Buggy sneered. Cam lowered his hand slowly, trying to ignore a twinge of disappointment curling like sharp claws in his belly.

"I get it," he said, nodding. "I do. You have no reason to trust me. But I promise you, I will prove it to you. I will prove that I mean you no harm, and that I am on your side. One bit at a time." Buggy remained silent, just continuing to glare. She pulled her feet up on the couch. Her legs pressed against her chest in an almost seated fetal position, putting an extra barrier between her and him.

"And why on God's green Earth would I ever believe you?" she asked after a few minutes of loaded silence.

Cam hesitated, running a hand down his scruffy face. That desperate wanting—wanting her to know—flung itself up from the deepest part of his gut, thundering to his lips. The truth battered desperately against his teeth for release.

"Because I'm—" he started hastily.

"Cam," Theo warned, cutting him off. Cam glanced over at Theo, who was watching him with disapproval. Cam stood and motioned for Theo to follow him into the kitchen. Briar watched them go like a cat locked in a cage, glowering over her knees. If she had any range on the cuffs, she would have started to prowl back and forth.

"Okay," Theo whispered, closing the kitchen door behind them for privacy. "Okay, taking it slow."

"We have to tell her *something*, Theo," Cam answered, irritated. "Right now, we are just two lunatics who plucked her out of her life and handcuffed her to a couch. We have to give her ***something***."

"I know... it's just..." Theo frowned at the closed door. "It's just... Cam, she's..."

"Hanging on by the skin of her teeth," Cam agreed. "I can see that even without your 'connection.'" Cam winced a little at the petulant and envious tone in his voice. He hoped Theo had not heard it. If he had, he made no indication as he went on.

"And even if you just blurted everything out all at once, why would she believe any of it? Our words mean nothing. We need something substantial. We need something that will be proof to her. Something solid. Undeniable."

"You know what's going to be really undeniable?" Cam asked, the petulant tone tiptoeing its way back into his voice. "When she burns this place down around our ears."

"Come on, Cam," Theo grimaced. "Something. There has got to be something."

"Well, we got the photo," Cam shrugged. "We could start there."

"Sure," Theo nodded, "but that won't be enough."

"I have what will be enough," Cam assured him without hesitation. "I have what will prove to her who I am. Who *we* are."

"You sure?" Theo frowned. "I'm talking *foolproof.* I'm talking there is no way she can—"

"Theo, trust me, I've got it," Cam interrupted. "When she's ready for it... I've got it." Theo ground his teeth, doubt flashing in his eyes, but passing by quickly enough.

"Okay... good. But we should still take it—"

"Slow, yes. I get it," Cam said. He heaved a sigh and his eyes trailed to the closed door. He could picture the girl on the other side, sitting there, sweet face twisted into a scowl, anger in her eyes.

"Hey, Styger. You okay, man?" Theo asked.

"Hell no," Cam answered with a bark of laughter.

"I keep forgetting," Theo's voice had dropped low and solemn, making Cam glance up with a frown.

"Forgetting what?" Cam asked.

"That this isn't only a lot for *her*."

Cam didn't answer, just continued to watch the closed door as Theo passed him, giving him a clap on the shoulder as he did so. "I'm going to go get some food. I saw a taco joint not far back. Give you a few. Just..."

"I know, I know," Cam said, waiving off his concerns. "Not too much information too fast. Slow." Theo turned to leave but looked around as Cam called him back. "Hey, Theo?"

"Yeah?"

"Get extra guacamole, would you?"

3

Sandra drummed her fingers against the table as the phone rang against her ear. The ringing went on and on until Buggy's cheery voice cut it short.

"Hello, you've reached Briar's phone. I'm obviously not available right now, but please leave your name and number. I'll get right back to you. Thanks!" The message was followed by a harsh beep. Sandra cursed and ended the call.

When Buggy had not come home on Monday evening, Sandra had assumed she had chickened out of their conversation. It was what she tended to do when things got too serious, or emotionally loaded. Sandra guessed Buggy had crashed at Andrew's, Linny's or, fingers crossed, Cooper's. This last was unlikely, but a big sister could dream.

She had grown irritated as Buggy dodged her calls into the night and into the following morning. However, her irritation slowly shifted into concern as Tuesday began to pass and heightened into near panic as the sun began going down without a single text or call. Night took the streets and Buggy had still not come home.

Sandra pulled up her text messages. She had sent Buggy six messages already today and had been keeping a close eye on their status. She saw that they had been read, but there had been no reply. Sandra knew Buggy hated confrontation, but this was a whole new level of bitching out avoidance, and Sandra was over it. With every passing minute, it became harder to stop her mind from nose diving into the worst-case scenario possibilities. Was she really ignoring her messages? Had someone stolen her phone? Could she not reply? Was something stopping her? Sandra shook her head, trying to disperse the useless train of thought, and typed out another message.

Briar Rose Pierce, I swear to God, if you don't at least give me a heads up on where you are and if you're okay, I'm going to call up Mom and Dad and you'll have to deal with them instead. You know dad will send out a search party. And retroactively ground you for life.

Answer. Me. Back. Now. Please. She considered the message, a glass of wine waiting untouched by her hand. She hesitated and then continued typing. *You promised you wouldn't lie to me.* She pressed send.

She waited. And waited. Suddenly, the little window under her text bubble changed from "delivered" to "read." Sandra leaned over her phone, eagerly. She was about to press the "call" button by Buggy's name and catch her when she knew Buggy was on the other end. Before she could dial, a little blue text box with three dots appeared to the left of her screen. Sandra let out a little breath as Buggy finally replied.

Yes. I did. And I promise I'm okay.

Sandra covered her mouth, letting out a great sigh as she leaned back in her seat. She had not realized how much tension she had been holding until it began to melt. Her back, which had been hunched up and prickling like a porcupine, smoothed out, and the weight in her shoulders fell away. She pulled her phone back off the table.

Where are you? You safe? You good?

Yep, I'm good. Buggy replied. *I'm hanging with Linny tonight.*

Now that the fear was dissipating from Sandra's system, the irritation was back.

*Okay girl, I know you don't wanna talk about the whisky bottle, but you can't just disappear and not tell me! That's just **not** okay.* Three little dots appeared as Buggy's phone replied.

I know. I'm sorry… I just can't deal right now.

Well tough shit, Sandra thought, but kept it to herself. Instead, she typed: *Just come home, okay? I'm not mad or anything.*

The three little dots appeared in the blue text bubble.

I will, just not tonight.

Sandra sighed irritably. Although Sandra had to admit, Buggy had a right to be pissy with her. She began typing again.

*Are **you** mad at **me**? Look, I'm really sorry I went through your stuff. That was very "mom" of me.*

Yeah, not exactly the coolest thing you've done, sis. Buggy replied, quicker this time.

I know, Sandra answered, *but you were acting weird, and it was kinda freaking me out a little. I was worried you might be trying something a little, uh, harder than whiskey.*

Three dots again. *What do you mean? Weird how exactly?*

Sandra frowned at Buggy's question but tapped out a response.

All the nightmares. Not sleeping. The sleepwalking. The talking to yourself... you know. The first time Sandra had caught Buggy talking to herself was when she had been standing in the hallway staring at the coats with confused eyes. She had been mumbling something and had stopped as soon as Sandra called to her. But that had not been the only time. Sandra started hearing Buggy mumbling to herself through the bathroom door in the mornings. She could never quite catch what she was saying, and it never lasted very long, but it had started happening more often than not.

Right, Buggy answered, *I guess that is kinda weird.*

Kinda? Sandra thought sarcastically, but instead replied: *Come home?*

I will. Later.

You know you're acting like a baby, right? Sandra pointed out.

I'm fully aware of that fact, yep.

Sandra couldn't help a small chuckle and shook her head.

Okay, okay, fine. Just give me some heads up, alright? And answer me back when I text or I'm gonna be worried you got abducted by aliens or something.

The little text bubbles popped up again as Buggy typed on the other end.

Ha-Ha, okay, will do. Will be home soon. Promise.

Sandra shook her head and tapped the screen.

Okay, Sandra paused. *You doing okay?*

The three little dots took a few minutes to appear.

Yep, I'm doing fine. Just needed to cool off a bit, but I'm doing good.

Sandra frowned at the message. Had Buggy just lied to her? She knew it had been risky going through her things. She knew there would definitely be blow back, but she had to know. Something was throwing her baby sister into a spiral, and she didn't believe it was all due to those damn cassette recordings. Drugs? Self-harm? Something even more terrible? She had almost been relived to find the bottle of whiskey. Not that she was at all happy about her sister drinking more, and was especially not happy about Buggy hiding that fact from her, but Sandra guessed it could have been worse. She still needed to talk with Buggy about it. She knew Buggy would be pissed that she had violated her privacy. She had been prepared for that. She had not been prepared for Buggy to start lying to her.

Had Sandra broken it? That bond, that promise, that always open door of communication between them? Had Sandra broken it by stepping over that line? Then again, maybe it had not been such an open door in the first place, since Buggy had been hiding that second bottle from Sandra for who knew how long. Maybe the door had only appeared open to Sandra. Maybe Buggy had lied about that too. This thought made Sandra's heart squeeze painfully in her chest.

It was never easy to realize you may not be as close to someone you love as you once believed you were, and Sandra had believed it. Had never been surer of anything else in her life as she was about that open door between her and her Buggy. Being forced to recognize the unstable nature of this structure in her life, once so unshakable, was truly heartbreaking.

"I'll fix it," Sandra said to the empty apartment around her. Her voice was determined. That was good. She would talk to Buggy, they would work it out, and they would fix the fissures. They would be okay. Buggy just needed to cool down a little. Just a little time. Sandra could give her that.

Sandra sat back in her seat, picked up her glass of wine with her eyes still on the cell phone now dark on the table, and took her first sip.

* * *

Theo dropped the phone back on the kitchen table next to the still warm bag of takeout tacos, feeling utterly disgusted with himself. It needed to be done. Sandra, Briar's sister (or so Theo had gathered), called multiple times a day. The damn thing wouldn't stop ringing, and if anyone on the other end (Sandra, or Cooper or anyone of the names that had texted Briar over the last evening) if they had reported Briar as missing, Theo and Cam would be in a world of trouble. This whole situation wasn't exactly ideal or even planned much at all. Pretty much the only "plan" was to throw off suspicion for as long as possible. Try to buy some time to explain things to Briar. Enough time to get her on board.

It wasn't hard really. All Theo had to do was press Briar's right thumb against the keypad on her cell while she was still asleep. He then went into the settings and changed the password to something he could remember, giving him full access to her phone. Theo had then scrolled through several recent messages from someone named Linny, apparently a close friend of Briar's if the copious amounts of texts were any indication. He gathered that Linny was a co-worker of Briar's after seeing a few messages regarding Elwin Family Dentistry. So, Theo sent her a text as Briar, saying that she didn't feel well and asked whether Linny could let their boss know, or even cover her shift for a day or two until she felt better.

Linny had answered "Of course!" and "Hope you feel better girl!"

That would buy them a few days, but not much longer. This was all a giant mess. Theo kicked himself for not fighting Cam on it—for not pushing for a better plan—but Cam couldn't be swayed. Theo knew the man had been so desperate to get started. Too desperate to find the girl and have her safe, that he wasn't thinking straight. Heavy handed, Cam had tripped and stumbled into this shit pile, dragging Theo down right with him. And Theo had let him.

"We are running out of time," Cam had insisted, and perhaps he was right. Briar's sister had said as much.

All the nightmares. Not sleeping. The sleepwalking. The talking to yourself...

If it was true, well, they had even less time than they thought. A lot less. They still should have done this better. It could have been more artful, but Cam wasn't in a careful mood. He was a full steam ahead kind of guy. Break first, explain later, sort of person. Especially in regard to Briar Rose Pierce. Speaking of which...

Theo closed his eyes and let his mind go. He was getting better at this. With every time he practiced, every time he tried, it was becoming faster. Especially now, with the girl so nearby. He didn't even need the flames to focus on anymore. He was what he was, and he was growing stronger. He only needed to close his eyes and let his mind go. And because Briar was what *she* was, his mind found her easily. He could feel the emotions wafting off her, even through the walls. They came in warm waves, splashing through the air and crashing against him. He felt her frustration, anger, and below it all, a desperate, flailing fear.

Theo sighed. They needed to explain all of it and soon, but he was scared. How were they going to make her believe? And if they could somehow get her to understand, what might it do to her? Theo was worried that it might break her. If it broke her, there was no getting her back. Her problems were deeper than she could possibly know, and if Briar broke, it would open up the opportunity for the *other* one. If that happened....

"Theo?" Theo opened his eyes and looked around. Cam had walked into the kitchen and stood watching him. Theo saw the question in the man's eyes and answered.

"Bought us a little time," Theo said, gesturing to the phone that had now gone dark. "But not much."

"Okay," Cam said. "Anything else?"

"Yeah," Theo answered. "Her sister—"

"Sister?" Cam frowned.

"I assume adopted," Theo answered, but quickly moved on. "She said that Buggy's been—"

"Buggy?" Cam interrupted again.

Theo sighed. "It's a nickname of hers, apparently."

"Why the hell would people call her that?"

"I donno, but it probably has something to do with the flying saucers she has as irises."

"What?" Cam still looked confused.

"Never mind," Theo shook his head. "It's just a nickname."

Cam's eyes cast down as he mumbled the name to himself. "Buggy...? I've missed," Cam took a breath, "... everything."

Theo hesitated. "Maybe, but you haven't missed the chance to save her. Not yet at least... but we really need to get on that."

"What do you mean?" Cam asked, focus returning as concern flooded his features.

"The sister said Briar has recently started sleep walking. Having nightmares. Talking to herself."

"Damn." Cam ran a hand down his face.

"We have to tell her," Theo said. "All of it."

"But you just said we shouldn't do that," Cam said, frown deepening. "That she couldn't handle it yet."

"I don't think she can," Theo admitted. "We *should* take it slow. We *should* take our time...but it is already started. The Daughter is awake. We are officially *out* of time." Theo could see the leeriness in Cam's eyes, but he also saw the relieved smile. He had been waiting for this for so long that it was hard for him to see the danger through the anticipation. It was hard for him to see how things could so easily go wrong. Full steam ahead. He didn't yet believe in the consequences.

That was why Theo was there. It was why his mother had told him to go with this strange man and believe his strange stories of psychics and seers and their mission to prevent a great evil. That he, Theo, was key for it all to work, and that he was also the last resort if it everything went wrong. Theo would have to do what was right because, if things *did* go sideways, Cam wouldn't stop the girl. He couldn't. He was too close to this. She meant too much to him.

So, Theo would have to do it. Theo would have to prevent the unspeakable from happening. If the evil inside Briar, if it took control, he was the only one who could prevent her from hurting others. If they failed to save Briar, Theo would have to be the one to stop her. By any means necessary.

But could he? Theo had never been a violent man, but this wasn't about violence. This had nothing to do with what *he* wanted to do. It was about what he *had* to do.

Still... could he?

Theo watched Cam nod in understanding and hoped, and prayed to God, that he wouldn't have to find out.

4

Buggy looked up as Theo stepped back into the room. He came around the couch and slid a plate of food onto the coffee table. She looked at the three steaming, soft tacos next to a little bowl of guacamole, then back up at Theo. He sat down on the floor on the other side of the table with his own plate and started eating. She watched him in silence, letting the tacos go cold in front of her. They didn't speak until he had scooped the last bit of guacamole from his own little bowl with the last of his bread and plopped it in his mouth with a satisfied sigh.

He looked over at her untouched plate and frowned.

"You know you really ought to—"

"Shut up and tell me what I'm doing here," Buggy said, voice sharp.

Theo blinked, and a small smile started to twitch his lips.

"I mean it's kinda hard to both explain *and* shut up so I'm not sure—"

"Dude, this is not some Stockholm Syndrome, cute little bonding moment between captor and captive," Buggy cut in once more. "This is the moment when you, or your friend, explain what is going on or I scream until your ear drums burst out of your head and go running for the hills."

And if that doesn't work, she thought, feeling the slight lump between the cushions where the scalpel nestled unseen, *I'll try something else.*

"Okay," Theo said, sliding his empty plate next to hers and brushing his hands against his pants. "Okay. We need to go slow, but we need to go fast too."

"What?" Buggy scowled, confused.

"I'm going to tell you the truth," Theo started. "Not the whole truth, though. I'll leave that to Cam, but I'll tell you some of it. Just to get you started. Work our way up to the rest."

"Okay," Buggy said, too glad that she was finally going to understand something of this crazy situation to protest.

"First things first," he said, resting a hand against his chest. "What I said before was true. We aren't here to hurt you. We're actually here to help. But, we can't do that without you. It's a 'help me to help you' kinda situation."

"What exactly do you think I need help with, Jerry Maguire?" Buggy scowled, ready to hear some crazy ass story about the apocalypse and her being the vessel of the Anti-Christ or some shit.

"Have any dreams about burning to death in a fire recently?"

Buggy's head jerked up. "What?"

"Dreams. About burning in a fire?" Theo continued, head tilting a little. "Waking up in places where you didn't fall asleep? Seeing things that aren't there? Talking to people that aren't there? Waking up covered in ashes? Random fires starting up in your apartment for no reason?"

"Wait what?" Buggy had been leaning in but was taken aback by his last comment.

"Oh, so no fires yet?" Theo nodded, looking relieved. "Good, good, that's good."

"How did you know about the dreams?" Buggy asked, the little bump under the cushions temporarily forgotten.

"Because I was told that's what you're probably going through."

"Told by who?"

"By Styger," Theo answered. "He and my mom. She's not like Cam and me, but she knows the drill."

"You've lost me," Buggy shook her head. "Not like you, how? And what drill?"

Theo considered, shrugged, then said: "I'm a psychic."

Buggy blinked. "A psychic."

"Yes."

"A psychic?"

"Yep."

"Like, crystal ball wielding, tarot card carrying, 'don't worry, you'll be rich and famous' fortune telling psychic?"

Theo smiled and shook his head. "I know it's kinda a lot to ask you to believe. I mean, I'm definitely not into tarot cards, and I can't see the future... I'm more specifically a type of empath."

"Empath?"

"Yeah, it's like being able to... um," Theo thought, eyes darting around as if looking for the right words, "connect, with other people, or things. It's like empathy on over drive. I *feel* things. Energy. More than most people. Sometimes it can be useful."

"Useful how?" Buggy asked.

"Oh like... one time when I was seven, my neighbor's cat had gone missing. No one could find it, but I had a *feeling*. I felt that it was scared and stuck and sure enough they found it caught by its collar under a fence a few houses down. The next year I had a funny feeling about a friend of my mom's. I kept feeling a weird pressure in my chest each time she came around. Turns out she had breast cancer. She is okay now. At least, I think she is."

"So, you think I have cancer?" Buggy frowned.

"No. Not exactly."

"Okay..." Buggy prompted, but Theo didn't continue.

"I'd really rather let Cam explain that part," Theo said, guiltily.

"Okay," Buggy reached out and took the plate of cold tacos. She was starving. She hadn't eaten since lunch the day before and she couldn't put it off forever. Besides, her stomach was grumbling so loud it was getting hard to hear the little that Theo was telling her. "Then what **can** you tell me? You said that you and Cam were the same? Is he also an empath or psychic or whatever?"

"He used to be," Theo nodded.

"But not anymore?" Buggy asked, spreading an ample amount of guacamole onto her first taco before taking a bite. It was cold but soothed the ache in her belly quite nicely. "Isn't that something that you're born with? Didn't think it was something you could lose."

"It's usually not," Theo agreed. "But something happened to him..."

"Something that messed with his juju?"

"Kind of."

"Uhm."

"It's complicated."

"I'm sure."

Theo smiled. "You don't believe a word I'm saying."

"Oh, I believe in psychics," Buggy corrected, catching a dribble of taco sauce with her tongue before it could trail down her hand. "I think it's stupid to discount something just because it's not common, or not always seen. The world is a weird place after all. But you'll have to forgive me if I don't believe *you*. I have an affinity for mistrusting people who kidnap me from the street and handcuff me to a couch."

"Fair enough," Theo nodded. "But I kind of need you to start believing me. Pretty quick too."

"Why's that?" Buggy asked through a mouth full of guacamole.

"Because there is a limited amount of time in which we can help you," Theo said reluctantly.

"What, am I on a timer? I'm going to magically implode if you don't work some magic voodoo?" Buggy looked up when Theo didn't immediately answer. He was sitting cross-legged on the floor, a grimace contorting his otherwise handsome face. "Oh no... you're kidding me. You actually think that?" Buggy laughed, but something tugged at the back of her mind, something that told her to listen. An image of her own tear-streaked, ashy face floated up in her mind. She stopped laughing.

"Explain," she said, voice going cold.

"I'd really rather Cam—"

"Forget Cam," Buggy dropped the plate back on the table with a loud clatter of ceramic against wood. She leaned forward, eyes narrowing. "Cam's not here. I heard the car drive away a little while ago."

"He's out getting more smokes. It is his coping mechanism. It's not far, he should be back—"

"But *you* are here *now*," Buggy leaned in, trying to put a conspiratorial tone in her voice. "Theo, you want me to believe you? Trust you? Then you got to give me something, man. Give me a reason. You mentioned dreams. Burning in fire. Cam knows about those? How?"

Theo's eyes flickered towards the closed door. Buggy waited.

"We knew because..." Theo took a breath, looking up towards the ceiling, and Buggy thought he might be praying. His eyes fell back to hers. "Because your mother used to have the same dreams."

Buggy's whole body went cold. It was as if Theo's words had kicked the surfboard out from under her and sent her plunging, feet first, into the icy ocean she had been avoiding for so long. Terror, panic, confusion all flooded her. They spilled through her veins, pooling in her lungs, drowning her. She wanted to scream, but she couldn't. She wanted to grasp back onto rage, pull her head above this deep abyss of panic, but she couldn't do that either. Rage evaded her. Fury dodged her. And all that was left was to drown. Except, she couldn't drown. Not yet. Something else floated to the top. Something she clung to desperately, gasping for air. Something that would keep her breathing for the moment. Two moments. Because she needed to know.

"My mother?" Buggy asked, sounding calm, almost blank. Theo had been leaning back, watching her warily, as if waiting for her to implode. He let out a long breath but looked only marginally soothed. "What do you know about my mom?"

"She was like you... a lot like you. As far as I can tell. I didn't meet her personally."

"Then how would you know?" Buggy asked.

Theo took another breath. "Cam told me."

"Cam?" Buggy's eyes darted for the door this time. "You're telling me, that guy knew my birth mom?"

"Yes...."

"How?"

"I would rather Cam—"

"I swear to God, Theo—"

"No, really, I think Cam should—"

"I don't give a damn what you think, Theo," Buggy said, voice rising as she found that rage once more. She strained against the handcuff and leaned forward. It dug into the bandage and pressed hard against her already broken skin, hurting her, but she didn't care. She didn't really feel it. The pain felt far away, an irritating white noise. All she could feel was the fury beating against the inside of her ribcage. "If you don't tell me what you know about my mother, I'm going to cut your fucking tongue out."

Theo's eyes widened and he leaned back and away as if she had physically struck him. "What the fu—" he started but didn't finish.

"Good," said a voice from behind Buggy. She swung around to see Cam Styger standing in the now open doorway, a pack of cigarettes hanging loosely in one hand. She had been too wrapped up in her focus on Theo to hear the hinges squeaking open. "It'll save me the trouble of doing it myself." Cam stepped into the room, closing the door behind him. "This is taking shit slow?" He asked Theo, motioning towards Buggy.

"It started off that way... then it kinda escalated," Theo admitted, getting to his feet, looking both abashed and relived.

"How much did you tell her?" Cam asked.

"Honestly, not much."

"Not much?" Cam scowled. "You brought up Loretta."

"Loretta?" Buggy asked. Could that be... ? Were they talking about her mom? Was that her mom's name?

"She needed something to get started," Theo said.

"Not about Loretta. Not when I'm not here."

"I'm sorry," Theo threw his hands in the air. "Not exactly a dummy's guide to this sort of thing."

"Hey!" Buggy yelled at the two men bickering. They both looked around. "Who is Loretta?" Theo looked at Cam, but Cam didn't take his eyes off Buggy.

"Loretta," Cam started slowly, sliding the pack of cigarettes into his pocket, as if suddenly ashamed of them. "She was a wonderful woman. A beautiful soul. Big heart. Troubled, but strong enough to fight through whatever life threw at her. And she was your mother."

Buggy breathed slowly, trying to calm her heart, which was thudding so hard it hurt.

"*Was* my mother?"

"Yes. *Was*." Cam said, looking confused. "Didn't... didn't you know? I thought you knew. Didn't you get the tapes? She left you tapes."

"The tapes?" Buggy's eyes flew open wide. "How the hell do you know about the tapes?"

Cam chuckled a little. He pulled the pack back out of his pocket and shook one of the thin white cylinders from its box. He set it in his mouth before clearing his throat. "Well kid, we got a lot to talk about. But first. I'm getting a drink. Want one? You're gonna need it."

5

Waverly took a deep breath, finger hovering over the call button. She knew what was going to happen after she pressed it. Knew what would be on the other end, and she deserved it. She deserved all of it. She had screwed up. Screwed up big, but just because you know you messed up doesn't mean that you are ready for the consequences, unavoidable as they may be.

Waverly pressed the button and held her cell up to her ear. The dial rang so long that she began to hope she might just leave a message and deal with the fallout later. No such luck.

"Waverly?" her mother's voice answered. Waverly heard the anxious edge to it, the one that had been sharpened to perfection against years of anxiety and regret. "What happened? Is it done?"

Waverly took a breath. "No."

There was a pause on the other end. "And why the hell not?"

"Mom—"

"You had her. You said it was her. You had her. You had a plan. How did you fail? How could you do this?"

"Mom, I—"

"You just keep failing, don't you Waverly?" Her mother's voice was cold, and every word hurt. As it always did. Waverly thought she might have built a shield, some sort of inner wall against such things, but it never happened. No matter how many years passed, when the words came from her mother's lips, they always hit their mark. "You just keep fucking up. What is wrong with you? You had everything you needed. I gave you all the tools. The locations. And you. Still. Failed."

"There was a complication," Waverly answered.

"Complication? What complication?" The edge grew sharper. It cut at Waverly with every syllable.

"Cam Styger," Waverly said.

"What?" her mother spat. "That stupid…. What happened? How did he find her?"

"I don't know how he found her, but he did. He and some other guy. They took her. I tried to follow, but I lost them. They're gone."

"Guy? What other guy?"

"I don't know. Some younger guy. Probably late twenties."

"He found one," her mother mused on the other line.

"Another psychic?" Waverly asked. "You think he could have trained one to find her?"

"Wouldn't put it past the little shit," her mother answered in a hiss.

"But where would he have found one? And who would be powerful enough, or even willing to believe him? Go with him? Take the girl?" Her mother was quiet for a few minutes. Waverly thought the connection may have been dropped. "Mom?"

"Someone from The Fold," her mother answered.

"Mom there isn't anyone left," Waverly frowned at the carpeted ground. She had stopped in a musty motel after Styger's trail went cold. She sat on the single bed, legs crisscross, long blond hair hanging loose around her shoulders, and doing her best to ignore the dark stain of mold on the upper left corner of the wall. "You said it was just you and me." The Fold. The organization Waverly had been told about since she was a child. The one that had been destroyed before she had been born. Waverly drew an absentminded hand over the circular tattoo on her wrist as her mother went on.

"There was another," her mother mused. "But she didn't have the gift. But if she had a child… I'll call you back," she said suddenly.

"Whoa, whoa, Mom, what's going on?" Waverly leaned forward in her seat, confused and excited.

"I have an idea," her mother answered.

"Where Styger might have gone?"

"No. But I think I know a way you can find out. Give me a few hours."

"Okay. Bye mo—" but she heard the click and knew her mother had hung up. Waverly let the phone fall to the bed. She ran her fingers through her hair, pulling at the roots.

Cam Fucking Styger

Waverly would wait until her mother called her back and gave her new orders, and this time there would be no stopping her. She would get it done. She would not fail. Styger would not mess things up, again.

No matter what. That Briar Rose bitch would die, and Waverly's mother would finally be at peace.

6

"I'm going to tell you a story..." Cam said, "One that my father told to me,"

"Oh, goodie," Buggy answered with a scowl, clutching the glass of bourbon that he had handed her. She had been careful. Cam felt her watching as he opened the fresh bottle, and he knew what she was looking for. So, he obliged. He took the first drink from his glass, proving that it wasn't laced with anything funny. Only then had she taken a sip from her own. Her second sip was more of a gulp, downing half its contents at once, before she spoke again. "I love fairytales. Especially when they are told by psychotic kidnapping lunatics."

"Just... just listen, okay. It's important."

"Well, it looks like I don't have anywhere else to be at the moment so, go for it." Her voice was steady, and her face was the picture of calm, but Cam knew it was a mask. He could see the slight twitch at the corner of her left eye, the one that told him she was on the edge of her seat. They had mentioned her mother, and she was all ears. For the moment, at least.

Cam cleared his throat. He had no idea how to begin, or the best way to explain. How do you convey such an insane story as the one he was about to tell? How do you tell it? How do you make someone believe it? Especially when it was so damn important that they *do* believe. Cam had never been the one to explain this story. No, in The Fold, he had never been an elder, never held any position of authority. It was those in charge that got to explain these things. It was their responsibility, and one he never wanted for himself. He would have it some day of course, there were few members of The Fold left and the duties of being an elder would eventually fall on his shoulders... or it *would* have. If he hadn't pressed the eject button on the whole shebang nearly twenty-seven years ago.

Good Lord, had it been that long? Time had a weird way of passing without leaving much of an imprint. Most of those twenty-seven years were a foggy haze of half memories and jumbled recollections. That night, however—the night he had turned his back on everything he had ever known—*that* memory stood out in clear colors. Cam remembered sneaking down to *her* room with a key that didn't belong to him. He remembered sliding the key into the lock and wincing as the door creaked open. Remembered her, Loretta, looking up from where she sat, legs crossed on her bed, a book in her lap. Remembered that sweet smile which lit her face, only to be chased away by confusion. Because *she* had *not* known. She had not known what he was planning or what he was doing there in the dead of night when everyone else was asleep. She had not known why he held out his hand in the open doorway and told her to follow him. But she had followed without hesitation. He had not needed to explain, because Loretta trusted him. Briar had no reason to, but Cam needed her to trust him as well. If he was going to save her, she needed to believe him. So, Cam did the only thing he could think of to gain that trust. He told the truth and prayed she would hear it.

7

"Long, long ago in a time lost in legends," Styger started, sitting back in the blue armchair across from the couch. He took on a storytelling tone, like a father sitting at their child's bedside, trying to soothe them to sleep in a night full of storms and lightning. "There was once a small village at the foot of a great mountain. It has long since crumbled into dust, but back then it was a thriving little community. In this village there was a mother. A mother who gave birth to the most beautiful of daughters." Briar felt her brows scrunching into a frown, but she didn't interrupt. Cam continued.

"The girl was born small and sweet, but she was also the mother's only prized possession, so she grew up spoiled and a bit wild. She frequently spurned her mother's orders, laughing as she disobeyed. The girl had a good heart, a fiery soul, but she was flighty and stubborn, which got her in a great deal of trouble, and they had troubles enough as it was. They lived in a time of war as one order shifted towards the next. One ruler for another. Transitions were rarely smooth during this age, and death and disease spread throughout the lands. Thieves ran rampant, taking advantage of the turmoil in authority, and adding their own chaos to the mix. One day the little village was attacked. Men on horseback charged through the town, setting it alight. They burned, they raped, they destroyed, throwing people out into the street, taking what they pleased, demolishing the rest.

"The mother and daughter had been separated in the fray, and it took the mother all night to find her little girl. When she finally did, it was too late. Her daughter had been beaten, raped, and left to burn in the house that the girl had once called home. The mother dragged her daughter out from the flames, but the girl had been severely burned, and quickly died in her mother's arms."

"What the fuck?" Buggy stared wide eyed at Cam, "Why are you telling me any of this? And what does any of this have to do with—"

"What happened next," Cam went on, "is what matters. The remaining members of the demolished village tried to convince the mother to bury her daughter in the family grave. The mother refused. Instead, she stole one of the last remaining horse and carts from her neighbor. She loaded her daughter's body onto the back and rode away from the smoldering village. She traveled for days, attempting to preserve her daughter's body with various herbs she found along the way."

Buggy closed her eyes against the image, but it seemed to play out inside her closed lids, like an old movie projected on a screen. Some desperate woman with sweaty twines of hair falling in front of her half-crazed face as she leaned over her daughter's corpse. She watched the woman laying twigs of leafy green across the dead girl's chest and spreading bright red berry paste over the face that flames had half eaten alive. All while the body continued to slowly, irretrievably, degrade... decompose. God, Buggy could almost smell it. She opened her eyes, forcing herself out of the horrible scene.

"It took a long time, and when she finally made it where she needed to go, the smell of the girl's body was the first thing the city dwellers noticed. The first sign that something was terribly wrong."

"Okay, okay, I get it, I get it," Buggy groaned, waiving a hand in the air for him to move past that part.

"This was a dangerous city the mother had come to. One avoided by all who fear what comes after life has reached its end, for this wasn't a normal city. It was a mystical place where time met infinity. This was the city of those who walk the edge of eternity, laughing at both sides in turn. The place where fear was drunk like wine, where people danced under the light of sister moons, holding hands with demons and angels alike. A place where everything meant nothing, and all the mattered was the light, and the dance, and the drink."

Buggy cast a dubious glance over at Theo, who returned her look, shrugged and nodded.

Yeah, I know, that shrug seemed to say. *But just hang in there and hear him out.* Buggy turned back to Cam.

"Into this place of eternal moonlight, the mother walked, leading her horse and cart behind her. The streets where full of people and *things* that danced together. Demons and angels danced out of her way, allowing her a path through the streets. They smiled and laughed and watched her as she watched them. They danced and danced and couldn't seem to stop. Why they danced, the mother didn't know. There was no music in this place. Only silence. They didn't move to flute or lyre. They danced to the pale moonlight. No one touch the mother as she continued on her way. Neither devil, nor human, nor angel laid, nor creature laid a single finger on her as she moved through the crowds. She was not to be touched, because she wasn't with them. Not yet anyway. She was just passing through, and so she moved without impediment, the dancers stepping aside. They left a long path between them, guiding her towards a small cottage with a thatched roof. For they knew that was where she meant to be. That is where they all had gone when they first came to this city of moonlight. So, the mother tied her horse and cart at the post outside the little cottage. She lifted her daughter's body from the cart, and the door opened before her. Inside there was a woman, a strange, magical woman. A woman without age. She had watched many born and many die, but she had done neither and likely never would. She sat, waiting for the mother, because she had always known the mother would come.

"The mother placed her daughter's burned and broken body on the table in the otherwise empty little cottage. 'Please,' the mother begged the woman. 'Please save my daughter. She is the only thing left to me in this world, my last prized possession.' The timeless woman smiled gently. 'I cannot do what you ask,' the woman answered. 'I cannot deliver her back to you. That is not her path. I will not help you.' But the mother begged the woman, begged her for hours, begged her for days. Years she spent in that little, empty cottage, begging until the woman smiled once more. The woman told the mother that she could do something for her daughter, but it may not be what either would like. The mother never stopped begging and the timeless woman grew tired of the mother's weeping and finally gave in. She reached out and took the mother's hand. She took the daughter's burnt hand in the other. And in a moment, the woman granted the mother's wish." Cam looked up at Buggy. "The daughter's burns faded, and she woke. But she was alone, back in the ashen ruins of the old village under the mountain. She woke with no memory of who she was, where she came from, or what happened to her. She woke as a squalling baby."

"What *did* happen?" Buggy asked. Despite herself, Buggy was starting to enjoy the lunatic's story time, caught up in the fairytale tone of voice that Cam used to tell it. Caught up in the familiar feeling of sitting in her bed, surrounded by her parents as they told her the tale of a sleeping princess and the handsome prince who kissed her awake. "Where did the mother go?"

"The mother had stayed back in the city," Cam answered. "The timeless woman had made a deal with her. The woman told the mother that she could not bring her daughter back to her, but if the mother stayed in the city, her daughter would have life again. And the daughter would continue to live as long as the mother stayed and joined the dancers. But if the mother ever tried to see her daughter, ever tried to leave the city, ever stopped the dance, her daughter would die. So, the mother stayed and danced with the others. Danced alongside angels and demons, and her daughter lived again." There was a long silence, as if Cam was waiting, wanting some profound meaning from the story to sink in. What meaning, Buggy didn't know. She finally broke the quiet.

"Umkay... weird story, bro," she coughed.

"That's not the end of it, Briar," Cam continued, "The mother saved her daughter. The girl went on to live a long life. She was found by one of the last straggling villagers and they took her in as their own, building a life in a neighboring village. It wasn't an easy life. It was still times of war, and she was a lonely girl with no memory of the mother who gave up everything so she could be born again. But she lived. She grew up. She made a home for herself. She worked. She grew old. She eventually died... and then she lived again."

"What?" Buggy asked.

"Well, you see, the deal was that her daughter would live again, as long as the mother stayed in the city, and continued to dance. The timeless woman, the one who had granted the mother her wish, she assumed that the mother would last one lifetime. Then, once her daughter had lived a full life, the life she had always wanted for her, she would stop. Her dance would end. And then together, mother and daughter would finally die. But the woman underestimated the mother's strength and love for her daughter. The mother didn't stop with the end of her daughter's life. She continued to dance, and her daughter continued to open her eyes again. Again, with no memory. Again, with a fresh start at a new existence. This happened over, and over again. To the great vexation of the timeless woman in a city of moonlight, the mother continued to dance... to this very day." Buggy blinked slowly, watching Cam's expression, waiting for any crack of a smile, any sign that he was messing with her. He showed none. On the contrary, his eyes were stony as he looked into hers. "Briar... you—"

"Don't say it," Buggy cut in, voice harsh. "Don't even try to convince me that this shit is real."

"The story itself—the moonlight city—we don't have any proof *that* is real," Theo answered.

"But her daughter... **The** Daughter... we **know** she was real. We know she **is** real." Cam said.

"Okay, let's put the fact that you guys are completely insane aside," Buggy said, "And let's say this... girl with a million lives *exists*. What the hell do I have to do with..." Buggy trailed off as she realized that the answer was so damn obvious. "Oh my God." She closed her eyes. "You... you two lunatics. You think *I'm* The Daughter, don't you?"

"No, Briar," Cam corrected. "We *know* that you are."

Buggy began to laugh. She leaned into the cushion beside her and took comfort in the small lump she felt beneath her hand, reminding herself that the scalpel was still there. "Wow, you two are batshit mother-fucking crazy ass holes, aren't you?"

"Believe it or not," Cam shook his head. "It's true. And it is still not the end of the story."

"Oh please," Buggy waved a hand for him to continue, still laughing. "By all means proceed."

Cam and Theo shared a glance. Theo shrugged and Cam continued. "Years passed in this way. Centuries. And as they passed, The Daughter's endless lives piled up. They started to mix, infecting her current life. She was never meant to live this long, and although she couldn't remember her previous lives, they never completely disappeared. They multiplied and began seeping into one another. She began hearing things, things that she didn't understand, things that didn't make sense. Nightmares that trickled into waking hours." Buggy blinked. "Seeing things that terrified her, things that no one else seemed able to see," Buggy thought of Sandra's voice calling her from down the hall, and of Cooper's odd, tilted head smirk in the kitchen. "She started being able to do strange things. Things that didn't make logical sense, things that seemed dark, dangerous." Buggy remembered how the sink had shattered under her fingers, the blood that had begun to flow. She remembered waking up in a bed of ash. How the hollow space in her chest had been growing. "She grew bitter and angry, not understanding why this was happening to her. Not understanding what was going on inside her own head, or what was happening inside her own body."

"And what was happening?" Buggy asked, voice small and tentative now.

"She was changing. Adapting, in a way. She was held together by a dark promise, a promise granted by a woman—by a creature—that wasn't supposed to make such decisions. And that darkness was growing with every rebirth. It was growing strong, mingling with past lives forgotten, and with every ended life cast into that 'dark place'... the girl began to go insane. The farther she strayed from sanity, the harder and more volatile her lives became, and the more violent her deaths. It became harder for her to contain the past lives and the darkness they had become. She grew unable to differentiate between reality and imagination. Several times she was burned at the stake for witchcraft when word got out that she was hearing voices. With every violent death, the darkness inside her became stronger, harder to control. It was becoming uncontainable.

"As time passed on, after reincarnation and reincarnation, the memories of the past lives became so complex, so dense, that memory became actuality. They became an actual consciousness... they became self-aware. The complex of memories kept encroaching on the newly born consciousness, until they eventually, inevitably, broke though. Soon, they began to take over. Each time, one memory among the many floated to the top, gaining control over all the rest. The strongest memory. The *original* memory. The original daughter."

"The one who was brought back to life by the mother?" Buggy asked.

"No," Cam shook his head, almost regretfully. "The one who burned in the fire. The one who was raped and tortured and died in the ashes of her home. She was the first. She was the only one that was **meant** to be, and she was the one who kept resurfacing."

"So, the original daughter, she essentially... *possessed* her reincarnations?" Buggy pressed.

"Essentially," Cam nodded. "Yes."

"How?" Buggy asked. "Why?"

"Well, we aren't one hundred percent sure *how*," Theo added from his spot in the corner. "But we suspect she piggy backs off the growing mountain of reincarnated memories. Climbing it, dragging herself to the surface... but we can't know for sure."

"What we *do* know," Cam said, "Is that she tends to get access, get *control*, because of the ever-weakening mental state of her reincarnations."

"Because with every re-birth, there are more piled up memories that drive the reincarnation crazy," Theo added, and Cam nodded to him.

"Umkay," Buggy scowled, holding out her glass to Cam, who filled it without hesitation—almost seeming grateful to have something to do with his hands. "And why would the, uh, 'original daughter' or whatever, why would she want to do that? So, she could personally live again?"

"No," Cam shook his head. "So she could die."

"Excuse me?" Buggy let the glass drop to the table with a loud click. She was surprised it didn't simply shatter with the impact. Cam flinched slightly at the sound but kept his attention on her.

"Yes. The first few times The Daughter—the original daughter—got control over her reincarnated body, she tried to take her own life. But she soon realized it did no good. Each time she would be reborn, memories pushed back into that dark place, out of reach. She would have to claw her way back into control, only to be thrown back down with each death."

"Wait, why would she want to kill herself in the first place?" Buggy asked confused.

"Well, because she, more than all the other reincarnated versions of herself, actually *feels* how long she has lived. Centuries, lost in a shuffle of memories that are simultaneously hers and **not** hers. Each time she is reborn, *her* particular memories are tossed once more into the darkness, or worse, back to the last memory she has. The memory of her first death. Her **real** death. Her mother had tried to save her daughter from the pain of it. Tried to save her daughter and had accidentally made her a personalized, eternal hell. The Daughter just wants out. She just wants to die and have it done."

"Depressingly ironic," Theo pipped in, taking a sip from his own glass and then gagging a little around the strong taste. Buggy almost smiled at this but resisted.

"Good Lord," Buggy said instead, downing the last of her drink without so much as a wince. "But she still tried to get control? Despite the fact it does no good?"

"Yes. She can't kill herself. No other human could either, at least, not permanently. As the years passed, and The Daughter gained control over reincarnation after reincarnation, she hunted down solutions to her problem. She spent centuries like this. Clawing through the darkness, suppressing the reincarnation's consciousness, gaining control, and desperately scouring the world for to an exit from her hell. She waded through books on mythologies, listened to dark whispers from druids, wiccans, sorcerers of any kind for guidance, but all in vain. Until, finally, in the later eighteen century, among a small rural community of the newly formally recognized independent America, she stumbled across a knowledgeable witch doctor and psychic. His name was Argus Styger." Buggy frowned at the name, and she felt goose flesh crawling up her arm, but she didn't interrupt. "Being inclined to the mystical and unbelievable already, Argus didn't hesitate to accept The Daughter's story. Besides, her tale sounded familiar to him. In an attempt to help, he told her an old story of his own. One that wouldn't be found in any of the books she had scoured, or any religious teachings. Argus said this story was told to him by his father before his death. A story about a mysterious city drenched in eternal moonlight. A place where demons and angels dance. Where a mother brought her only daughter—her most prized possession.

"The Daughter believed the story. Believed it instantly and without hesitation, because it was the only story, out of the trillions of useless tales that had been woven for her over the years, that gave her a path to follow. She now knew, there was *one* person who could help her, who could end her nightmare. Because the person who made the dark promise, the one that keeps her coming back to life, can also end it."

"The woman in the cottage!" Buggy snapped her fingers. The drink was finally working its magic and dulled both her fear and was starting to make this psychotic little game fun.

"Exactly," Cam smiled for the first time Buggy could recall. It was a small thing, but it softened the gruff man's graying face.

"Buuuut... she was in some far-off long-ago city of demons and angels centuries ago," Buggy said, speaking those words as if it wasn't the most insane sentence she had ever uttered. "Wouldn't the city be gone by now?"

"Not exactly," Cam continued. "The city itself, it's supposed to be timeless. Just like the woman who owns it. Argus told The Daughter that the city continued to exist, but unseen. Not unless one is in that limbo of life and death, and even then, not always. The city that the mother found, that *version* no longer existed. At least, not in the form that it was during her time. But it didn't disappear or crumble to dust like the village. The city itself was only *half real* to begin with. It was a place that came and went from existence as easily as we come and go from one room to another. Only brought into *this reality* by those walking the line between life and death and nothing at all. The city itself fed off the energy of that moment. That *passing* between living and dying."

"But that doesn't make any sense," Buggy frowned. "If this crazy ass city *did* exist, then how did the mother find it at all? The Daughter wasn't 'walking the path between life and death,' she was just straight up dead. And the mother was, I'm assuming, also alive. So how could she have found it?"

"As the legend goes," Cam said, "The mother didn't have to call upon the city, because the city had already been called. All the turmoil of the time, the murders, the deaths, the chaos, disease, and famine, had already brought the city into existence. All she had to do was locate it and go inside. After the chaos calmed, the disease had petered itself out, and the deaths became less frequent, the city disappeared once more without a trace. As if it had never ever existed at all."

"Um, magical." Buggy held out her glass.

"'Cursed' would be more apt," Cam corrected. He filled her glass and then his own, before handing the bottle off to Theo, who took it eagerly.

"So, The Daughter wanted to find the 'not so real' city, so she could find the 'timeless woman' and get her to take back the promise she made with her mother. And she needed death, or close to death, to even have a chance of, *somehow*, finding it."

"Exactly."

"That's extremely vague," Buggy noted, and Styger shrugged.

"It's a legend. They don't usually come with a fully formed instruction manual."

Buggy returned his shrug with her own. "So, killing herself wouldn't get her there, because she would just be reborn... bypass the whole limbo part."

"And deny her even the possibility of using her own death to call upon the city, yes." Cam nodded. "So, she came up with a new plan." Cam's face was grave, all softness gone as if it had never been. "She couldn't die... and the only way to call upon the city, the only way to **find** the city, was through death or near death. She couldn't do it herself. So, she went... uh, elsewhere to obtain it."

"What do you... oh," Buggy blanched. "Oh, boy."

"She couldn't die," Cam pressed on. "But *other things* could. She started with animals. Stray cats, chickens, cows, dogs. She sacrificed them all, calling to the city as she did so, hoping an entrance would appear, some sort of opening. Her efforts were useless, no matter how many animals she slaughtered. It did nothing. The Daughter concluded, not that the city wasn't real... but that it was simply a city not meant for animals."

"Oh God..." Buggy folded in on herself, her stomach churning. She pulled the cup closer to her chest as if for protection against the words she knew Styger was about to say.

"So," Styger continued. "The Daughter tried again This time *people* started disappearing. Homeless from the streets. Young children who stepped out to play and never came home. The numbers piled up as The Daughter drew that line from life to death. The one she herself could never cross.

"As the years went by, the body count grew. But a death here and a death there wasn't enough to bring the city to her. The last time the city appeared was a time of war, plagues, pillaging and slaughter. She decided that a few deaths were not enough fuel for that fire. It wasn't enough destruction to bring the dancers of moonlight. No, she decided she needed to do more. Go bigger. She had to make a larger sacrifice, draw a darker, bloodier line.

"Her first mass killing took place in the early eighteen-hundreds. She moved into a more populated city, seeking factory positions. Factories where she lived were still fairly new developing business ventures and had deplorable working conditions. She got a job and spent a few weeks working up her nerve, and slowly but surely making the conditions a little worse, making preparations. One day she blocked the exits and started a fire. Thirty-six people died."

"Oh God," Buggy closed her eyes, doing her best not to imagine the scene. She saw it all anyway. All the people pounding uselessly against a barred door. The flames lick up the walls behind them. She heard the screams, and the sharp smell of burnt hair filled her mind and she shrank from it.

"She had started off carefully. One or two homeless goes missing—that tends to go unnoticed. She had started the factory fire because she believed it would be blamed on the dangerous conditions, like the Triangle Shirtwaist Factory fire in New York that wouldn't happen for almost another hundred years. But she was growing wild, reckless, ferocious in her quest. She started burning more buildings, causing more deaths, in stores, residential areas, one time even a church. The news of the seemingly random fires spread and soon came to the ear of the witch doctor who had told her about the moonlight city.

"They had become friends over the years, as she looked for answers, and he had become enthralled with this mysterious girl who could not die. But his curiosity turned to horror when he realized what she was doing. They had kept in contact, sending letters back and forth to one another after The Daughter had left the little community. She updated him about where she was and he updated her about the goings on in his town. He soon realized that these fires only occurred in the cities that she visited, and only while she was visiting them. He was horrified at how she had twisted his words, his story, and used it to justify her actions. Disgusted to realize she was likely behind the disappearances and the fires that had been popping up, quick and deadly around his own town before she had left. He knew he had sent her down that road, and he had to bring her back. So, Argus found her, tried reasoning with her, but she refused to listen. If she just killed a few more, she insisted, the city would come. She was so close, she told him, she could feel it. She couldn't stop now. The city would reveal itself and she refused to hear otherwise. Argus tried to tell her the story was just a *story*, that it wasn't true, only the incoherent ramblings of a dying man. She refused to believe him. He tried begging her. She wouldn't listen. So, he did the only thing he could think of doing to stop her. He killed her,"

"Well yeah, she sounds like a bitch," Buggy said, taking another long drink. She noticed Cam's eyebrows crinkle into a slight frown, but he only continued on with his story.

"Argus was a good man. He had wanted to help her find peace, but not at such a cost. However, killing her wasn't an easy task. She wasn't just a woman anymore. With every reincarnation she had grown more insane, but she had also evolved, grown more *powerful.* She had incredible strength, the strength of a monster that could easily break a man in half if she wanted. She also had impossible *abilities.* Powers that belong to no human. Powers to melt steel. Powers to set fires with the touch of her fingertips. Argus had never been afraid of The Daughter's abilities before. He had only been interested, utterly fascinated when she had shown him, believing them to be wielded by a sweet girl who only wanted to find peace. Now he knew better. Now he was afraid.

"And so, he gathered a few of his closest most trusted colleagues, other witch doctors, psychics, empaths and the like. They set out to stop The Daughter before she could kill again. They followed her using their abilities, hunted her down and ended her life. But that ended nothing. Because she was reborn. As a child, yes, but the years would pass and she would grow older, grow up, and soon enough The Daughter's consciousness would claw its way back to the surface. She would, inevitably, take control of her body once more. When she did, she would start killing again.

So, Argus and his colleagues decided that there was only one course of action. They kept the re-born child, raising her hidden from the world. And after twenty-four years, when The Daughter's consciousness took over and began controlling the reincarnation, they once again... uh... put her down," Styger finished dully.

"Wait, what?" Buggy sat back in her seat, suddenly nauseous. "They raised her. Then they killed her?"

"Yes," Cam answered, with a little cringe that Buggy doubted he even noticed.

"Cold," Buggy shook her head.

"If they hadn't, she would have continued racking up a body count. She couldn't be stopped any other way. She was beyond reason, beyond helping. She was obsessive, driven insane by her past, drowning out whatever conscience she may have once possessed. And with her original consciousness always came the abilities. The strength, manipulation of fire, and they grew only stronger with every re-birth. After twenty-four years, they wouldn't be able to contain her."

"Why every twenty-four?" Buggy asked. "That seems specific."

"It is," Cam nodded grimly. "The Daughter was twenty-four years old when she originally died. Around that age is when she comes to realize herself again, when she..." Cam trailed off, eyes darting around for the right words. "Uh... when she *wakes up*, as it were."

Wakes up? Buggy thought. Had not her nightmares, her sleepwalking, that empty space in her chest that drove her to be drinking her afternoons away, hadn't that started, or at least gotten a hell of a lot worse, after her last birthday. Her twenty-fourth birthday. Hadn't that morning been the first time she woke up screaming from a dream of burning in a cottage she didn't recognize.

"I promise you... I am awake now..." That smirking face of Cooper, who wasn't Cooper at all. She saw it in her memory, and it sent a shiver back down her spine. *"I am awake now. And I? I am not going anywhere..."* Buggy dragged her mind back to Cam, who continued his tale.

"Argus and his fellows did this over and over. Keeping The Daughter contained. Twenty-four years at a time. As decades passed the group became more organized, more controlled. They passed the tradition down to their own children, who grew up and passed it down to theirs. They called themselves The Fold." Styger tapped the circular tattoo on the inside of his wrist. "This was our mark. It was a small group, only about thirty-nine members at the height of it's prime. All psychics, empaths, shamans, the like. They were the only ones who had a chance of containing The Daughter when she ever resurfaced again. Empaths were especially able to sense when The Daughter was fighting her way into control. Such people are gifted with paranormal abilities to *feel* another person's mental state. They could feel the difference in the girl. They could tell when her mind went to battle with itself and would know who was winning the fight. Every twenty-four years they could feel The Daughter rising to the surface and warned the others that it was time to start over. To begin again."

"So that's what you guys think you are?" Buggy asked, raising one finger from her glass to point from Cam to Theo and back again. "You guys belong to this 'Fold' or whatever?"

"What's left of it," Cam nodded. "Yes."

Oh, dear Lord, Buggy thought to herself. *It IS a cult thing.*

"What do you mean, 'what's left,'" Buggy asked instead.

Cam's eyes cast downward. It was brief, unintentional, and Buggy watched it curiously. The gruff man didn't like this part of the story. Not one bit.

"In the year nineteen-forty-seven a new reincarnation was born." Buggy noticed how he bypassed the fact that, according to his twisted story, that meant they had just killed the previous reincarnated girl... but she let that slide by for the time being. Cam continued. "The Fold named her Aetheria. She was a quiet girl. Calm, reserved. Sweet but said very little."

Maybe because she was trapped by a group of psychos who were going to murder her as a twenty-fourth birthday present, Buggy thought but kept to herself.

"As the years passed, she only grew quieter, more reserved, but she kept that sweet smile always on her face. Drawing towards her twenty-fourth birthday, The Fold waited for there to be any sign that The Daughter was taking over Aetheria's body. There were usually signals—pressure within the girl's mind, sleepwalking, talking to herself, nightmares—but Aetheria showed none of these. She grew quieter, enjoyed more time alone, but that had never been a sign before, so The Fold missed the warnings. Everything was calm. Until midnight, months after her twenty-fourth birthday.

"There was a home base for The Fold. The secret place where they held the girl and conducted business. Everyone had gathered that night to discuss the unprecedented situation. No reincarnation had ever lasted so long. The Daughter always made an appearance, always vied for control soon before or soon after the twenty-fourth year. The longest it had taken was a week, but this was over four months later, and The Daughter had made no such attempts. There was no sign that Aetheria was being taken over or control in any way, or at least, none that they could see. The Fold was splitting. Half of the group wanted to wait. They thought the four months was an astonishing occurrence, and that it may mean The Daughter had given up, or that she may have finally disappeared. They thought the girl deserved a chance. If The Daughter remained dormant, perhaps Aetheria could live out her life. A normal life.

"The other members of The Fold fought against it. They believed the four months meant nothing. That it was just a matter of time before The Daughter reclaimed her place, and to think otherwise was foolish. They said they should be safe and put Aetheria down before The Daughter's inevitable arrival. They argued for hours, so consumed by their bickering, they didn't notice when she changed."

"The Daughter took over?" Buggy asked.

"She is a smart creature," Cam nodded. "I say 'creature' because she is not exactly 'human' any longer. No, she has a taste for blood now. It is the last thing she dreams of before being cast back into the darkness, and the first thing she hunts for when she wakes up again. And that is exactly what she did.

"It happened in one swift moment. One of The Fold had gone to check on Aetheria, leaving the arguments in the room above. A man named Marcus Styger. He was a good man back then. A kind man. One of those fighting for Aetheria's life. A descendant of Argus himself. He also happened to be my father." Buggy looked up at this, suspicions confirmed, but made no comment. "He found her crying. She could hear the echoing argument from the floor above, and not surprisingly, it had upset her."

"No shit," Buggy said with a snort.

"He went in to comfort her. He truly believed that she had escaped The Daughter's attacks. Believed that she would be alright. He was wrong." Cam leaned back in his chair, eyes drifting a little as the story took over his mind. "My father wasn't cautious. He forgot to lock the door behind him when he entered her room. It was the opportunity that The Daughter had been waiting for, and she didn't hesitate. My father said it was an instantaneous thing. One moment he was holding Aetheria, comforting her, and then next moment he was being thrown across the room. The Daughter darted out the door, closing it behind her and locking him inside. He was trapped, uselessly pounding on the door. He called to Aetheria, but she was gone, and he could hear the havoc The Daughter was causing on the floor above. The screams, the crashes, the sounds of sobbing and cries for mercy... but The Daughter is not a merciful being." Cam paused, but not for long. He seemed like he needed to get this story out as quickly as he could. Get that terrible chore out of the way. "He was never sure how long he was down there. Probably only twenty minutes, but he told me it felt like days. Finally, someone came to let him out. It was another member of The Fold, a young girl of only twelve years old named Susanna. She was covered in blood, and her hands were trembling so hard that it took her three attempts before she could get the door to open. My father went up to see the damage. There was blood everywhere. Every member of The Fold in the house, apart from the little girl and himself, were lying dead around the room. Some of them were torn to pieces, others were burnt to an ashen black mass of chard flesh and bone. In the middle of the horror, on a bed of ash, lay a baby. She was wailing with every ounce of her little lungs and covered in blood that wasn't hers. It took days for my father to get the full story from the young girl. For a long time, Susanna wouldn't speak at all. He took her to one of the only other living member of The Fold left. An old woman named Marian. She had been visiting a friend one town over, with her two-year-old grandchild and had missed the evil events all together. Marian took them in and kept an eye on Susanna while my father went back to take care of the remains of The Fold. He placed the bodies back in their beds, cleaned the carnage the best he could. He turned on the stove, allowing the building to fill with gas, then ran outside before the explosion. The destruction and fire burned away the rest of the evidence."

"And no one found that suspicious?" Buggy frowned. "That a house full of people just blew up and burned to the ground?"

"Well, yes, it was suspicious, but no one bothered to dig too deep. Everyone in the town was more than happy to accept the gas leak story and move on with their lives."

"Seriously?" Buggy scowled.

"Well... let's just say The Fold wasn't popular around the other members of the town," Styger explained. "They were a group of seemingly unrelated families of varying races and ethnicities, who followed—what many people of the town considered—*unconventional* religions and practices. They all lived together in the outskirts of what developed into an unsurprisingly conservative town in Texas in the early seventies... they weren't exactly popular. They generally kept to themselves, but rumors spread as they always do. Whispers of polygamy and Satanism were thrown around, and the house had a few times been vandalized or had a window broken in by bricks. Threats had been leveled on several members of The Fold over the years, to the point that they were talking of pulling up roots and moving to another town. But they were people of habit and tradition. The house itself belonged to one of an old and wealthy family that had lived in the area for generations, and they all kept dragging their feet on the matter.

"So, when the place burned down by an apparent gas leak, the residents didn't kick up much of a fuss. The police investigated of course, but Marcus had done a good job at setting the scene and didn't push the matter. The investigation determined that someone in the house must have turned the stove off incorrectly, and after double checking Marcus's own alibi (which Susanna and Marian provided), they closed the case as a tragic accident. And Marcus got the hell out of town."

"Good Lord," Buggy rubbed her eyes, then she looked up, realizing Styger had missed something. "What about the baby?" Buggy asked. "The one which Aetheria... I mean The Daughter... the re-born baby? What happened to it?"

"My father went back for it," Styger said. "He brought the baby, Marian, and Susanna with him when he left. Marcus had a friend in Utah who put them up until he could purchase his own house where they could all live. But that didn't last long."

"Why not?" Buggy asked.

"Because while they were staying at the friend's house, Susanna kept trying to kill the baby," Styger said sadly. "The girl had watched her mother die that night. She watched as her mother and father were torn apart and burnt by the girl she had once known as Aetheria. Susanna had known Aetheria her whole life and had been trained to care for her. She had been told about The Daughter's histories—the deaths, the murders, since she was a young child, just as every member of The Fold had been—but there was a part of her sweet little heart that couldn't believe such a thing could happen to the calm and sweet Aetheria. That sweet part of her heart died that night with her family. She had watched thirty-five people massacred in the most horrifying and violent ways possible. She herself killed the woman that had once been her friend. The Daughter had been in the process of killing Susanna's mother, when Susanna grabbed a knife from the kitchen and plunged it deep into the woman's back. She had been too late. Susanna's mother still died and Aetheria had been reborn into a child squalling in her mothers' blood. Susanna hated the thing. She hated it and wanted it dead. So, my father took the child away, leaving Susanna in the temporary care of his friend. He built a new home, a new beginning for The Fold. One with a room similar to Aetheria's old one, where she had lived out most of her life."

Under lock and key, Buggy thought.

"My father and Marian took care of the child until Marian passed away ten years later. Then Susanna took up that charge. By that point Susanna was twenty-two and had gotten a handle on her rage. She understood now that the new little girl wasn't the same person who killed her family, but that couldn't stop her from hating the child, although she no longer tried to harm it."

"Not yet anyway," Buggy corrected. "You still killed her when she turned twenty-four right? No, excuse me, you 'put her down,' when she turned twenty-four." Buggy watched as Cam and Theo shared another look, and Theo downed the rest of his glass.

"No, not exactly what happened." Buggy waited, just watching Cam as he squirmed under her gaze. Why was he having so much trouble looking at her? "You see, a couple years after Aetheria died, I was born. My father raised me in the way of The Fold... so I spent a great deal of my life taking care of the re-born girl. The one who came after Susanna killed The Daughter. Her name was Loretta." Buggy didn't make a sound, but her eyes focused hard at the mention of the name, turning into two headlights, blaring into Cam as he went on. "And she was the most amazing woman I have ever met in my life. She was sweet. She was beautiful. She was the opposite of everything my father told me The Daughter was. The opposite of everything Susanna had warned me about. She was…"

"Oh my God," Buggy laughed out loud. It sounded wrong, even to her own ears. It was too sharp, a little too rasping to hold any actual humor. Because she felt no humor. In fact, all she felt was disgust. "You fell in love with her? Talk about reverse Stockholm syndrome."

Cam tried to hide it, but a flash of pain twisted his features into a tortured mask. "We fell in love with each other."

"Gross," Buggy said, looking around for that bottle. Drinking was definitely the last thing she should do, but it was also the only thing holding back the rising terror building quickly in her gut. The more this insane man spoke, the more she wanted another drink. Another ten drinks. Hell, just give her the fucking bottle already, she'd drink straight from it.

"Yes, the plan was to put her down when she was twenty-four—just like all the rest—but I… I couldn't let that happen. I couldn't kill her. I could never hurt her, and I could never let anyone else hurt her either."

"Oh, I'm sure," Buggy said, looking over at Theo. "Come on, you don't actually believe this bullshit?" Theo, however, was watching her carefully and said nothing.

"I couldn't hurt her. So, I fought for her," Cam continued, drawing Buggy's attention back to him. "We found a way. I loved her, so I wasn't afraid to spend time with her. I spent every waking moment with her until we found a way. A way to save her from The Daughter. We figured out a way to *beat* The Daughter."

"Sure, Sure," Buggy's mind was swirling with drink, but her nausea had nothing to do with the booze.

"We did, Briar. We found a way. We saved her from being taken over. We saved her and we can save *you*."

"Oh right!" Buggy gave another rasping laugh. "Except, I'm supposed to be the latest reincarnation, right? So, you *did* kill her after all."

"No," Cam's eyes flashed, and he barked so harshly that Buggy cringed away. He took a breath, closing his eyes. When he opened them he was calm once more. "No. I wouldn't hurt her. My father, Susanna, neither of them believed us when we said we had found a way to keep The Daughter at bay. To keep Loretta in control. They didn't believe us, and they were going to kill her. They were going to kill the woman I loved. So, we ran. I snagged the keys out of my father's lockbox while he was sleeping, snuck down into the basement where Loretta's room had been built and got her the hell out of there. We ran. No. Loretta wasn't killed. But she did... she did die... she died giving birth." Cam took a breath, "She died giving birth to you."

Buggy stared at the man, trying to absorb what he said, trying to catch every implication but they spun and twisted and ran from her on scrambling feet, as if terrified to be found. Buggy opened her mouth, unsure what may escape from the haze of her mind.

"No," Buggy felt her mouth form the word, but she barely heard it. It sounded like she was at the far end of a long tunnel, echoing softly in the distance. "You are out of your mind. You are out of your goddamn minds, both of you." As Buggy continued to shake her head and was about to explain in detail just how messed up their minds were and give them several educated suggestions for therapy and medication, Cam reached into his back pocket.

"What are you doing?" Buggy asked, tensing. Cam pulled what looked like a thick rectangular slip of paper out of his pocket and held it gingerly between his fingers.

"It's a picture," Cam said, and Buggy saw a smile briefly flash his face as he looked down at the item. "A picture of your mother." Buggy blinked, and the entire world seemed to go quiet.

"What?" she asked finally.

Cam held it out to her. It was a small, white edged Polaroid picture of two people wrapped in a half hug smiling at the camera. They both appeared to be in their mid-twenties, both with the same elated smiles on their faces. The man's eyes were scrunched closed in a half laugh, one arm around the woman's shoulder, and the other resting on the woman's stomach, which was pooching out in an early pregnancy. The man was young, handsome, made even more attractive by his obvious happiness, but it was the woman that Buggy couldn't tear her eyes from. She was a woman of moderate size, only a bit older than Buggy herself. She had shorter hair, which cut off just below her thin shoulders. The sundress she wore had thin straps, but it was loose around the waist to allow for her ever-expanding baby belly. The woman was smiling, equally as content in that moment as the man beside her. She smiled a wide smile and stared back at Buggy from the photo with large and unmistakable eyes.

"What the hell?" Buggy snatched the photo out of Cam's hands. "What is this?"

"That is Loretta Ambrose... your mother. This is back when she was four months pregnant with you," Cam said, watching Buggy carefully but not moving to take the photo away.

"Nah, nah, that's not real," Buggy shook her head.

"Briar—"

"No, this is me," Buggy said, flipping the picture around and pointing at the woman who looked almost identical to Buggy except for the hair, baby belly pouch and the slightly different color of her eyes. "This is a picture of *me*."

Cam shook his head. "No, Briar. That's your mother. You two may have the same face, same features, and same lineage, but you aren't the same person."

"I donno, man. There's a whole clone debate that's been going on a while discussing that very idea," Theo piped in with a little awkward laugh, attempting levity. Cam motioned for him to shut up and turned his attention back to Buggy.

"You doctored this," Buggy said desperately, waiving the photo around in the air. Cam winced, eyes on the photo. He looked like he may reach out and grab it, stop Buggy from crumpling the corner in her agitation, but he resisted.

"It's a Polaroid, Briar. I couldn't doctor that even if I knew how."

Buggy turned her attention back to the photo. Every line, every feature, every aspect down to the lightness of the lashes around her large eyes... she was a carbon copy of Buggy... or perhaps Buggy was a carbon copy of her.

"This... this can't be real." Cam and Theo made no answer. They just waited for the gears shifting in Buggy's brain to finally catch and start to spin in the direction they needed her to go. "That's... not... real." They waited a little longer, and the gears finally clicked into place. "Her voice," Buggy said, closing her eyes and remembering every single time she slipped a cassette into the tape player. Every time that voice spoke. That voice, which Buggy had always thought sounded almost exactly like hers. No. Not almost. *Exactly* like hers. Because it *was* her voice. It was her voice all along. Buggy opened her eyes. "This can't be happening."

"What do you mean, 'her voice?'" Cam asked suddenly, leaning in, interest lighting his eyes. "Do you have them after all?"

"What?" Buggy looked up at him, eyes glazed in mangled thoughts.

"The tapes. The recordings she left you. Did you get them? I hoped you would, but I had never been sure…"

Buggy blinked. "Again… how exactly do you know about the tapes?"

Cam smiled, and it was the gentlest smile Buggy had ever seen. It pulled the side of his scruffy mouth, sweetened with far off memories. "Because I helped her make them."

"You…" Buggy trailed off. Her eyes darted back down at the photo in her hands. She tore her eyes away from the pregnant Loretta and over to the man beside her. He was over twenty years younger than, with far fewer lines creased his eyes, and there was no trace of gray in his hair. But that gentle smile was the same. Buggy looked back up at him. "That's… that's you." It wasn't a question, but Cam answered as if it was.

"Yeah, kid. That's me. I'm your—"

"Shut up," Buggy cut in, not wanting to hear it. Not able to hear it. She felt like she couldn't breathe, and if he said what she knew he was about to say… she would shatter. She would drown. There would be no more coming up for air. But Cam refused to shut up. He finished soft and hesitantly. His eyes were on her, begging her to believe.

"Briar, I'm your dad."

And there it was. Her fury was gone and all that was left was a numb emptiness of someone sinking deeper and deeper, knowing it was all over. Her world lost forever.

"I don't… don't understand. I don't understand any of this." Buggy ran her fingers through her hair, scratching her scalp as her mind raced and collided with itself. Mangled remains of things she once understood so well were sent skidding across her mind, and out of reach. They burst into flame and then extinguished into dust. Ash was everywhere, darkening her clarity. Blacking out the light.

"I know," Cam said, reaching out to take her shoulders, but she shrank away. His hand dropped to his side. "I am so, so, sorry. This is not how things were meant to go. It was never supposed to be this sudden, surprising thing for you. I was supposed to be there when you were born. *I* was supposed to raise you, tell you about all of this as you grew up. You were supposed to have a sure footing, a full understanding about everything before you ever had to deal with any of it. I was supposed to be there for you, Briar, and I wasn't, and I am so, so, sorry. We had a whole plan…" Buggy was trembling so hard her hands visibly shook on her knees.

"Briar... please," Cam's voice was pleading, but Buggy kept her eyes on her trembling hands. "Briar, please look at me."

"Take Me Home, Country Road" began playing from the other room. Buggy glanced over at the closed door, towards the sound of her cell phone ringing. She looked back to Cam. He was watching her with a desperate expression of someone scrambling for the right words to say.

"Am I allowed to take that?" Buggy asked, already seeing the answer written all over Cam's face. Cam's mouth opened and closed a few times with nothing to say. Buggy's heart sank. It was probably Sandra, calling for the millionth time. Or even her parents. Buggy had not been home for a few days now, and Sandra had probably already gone to her work, called all of her friends and even called the police by this point... unless...

Cam glanced over at Theo, who looked awkwardly back before nodding and getting to his feet. He cast an apologetic glance towards Buggy before slipping through the door.

"He's texting them that I'm okay, isn't he?" Buggy said, eyes still on the door.

"Briar..."

"What exactly is the plan here, Styger?" Buggy said, turning to glare at the man who had just dumped a lifetime of unbelievable insanity on her head. "Lock me up. Keep me away from everyone I love until I act like a good girl. Until I start calling you 'Dad.' Is that the idea?"

Cam's face fell into a look of pained dejection. "No, Briar, I would never presume to... that... that isn't what this is about."

"Then what is it about? Oh wait, let me guess," Buggy tapped her chin as if in deep contemplation. Everything was gone. Everything solid was missing and Buggy was falling. Because none of this could actually be happening. She couldn't actually be here, in this strange place with these strange people being told these strange and unbelievable things. This couldn't be real... and yet she wasn't waking up. All she wanted to do was wake up. But for once, the nightmare was reality. She wanted to scrunch her eyes closed and drag her way out of this mess. But she couldn't. So, she fell, and waited to hit the ground. "It's about how there is some previous lives inside my chest... a strange paranormal consciousness with superpowers that's just itching to die and take a million or so lives with it? One that's slowly but surely driving me to the nuthouse, and if it wins, I'll go psycho-pyro-killer? So what? Keep me locked up until I die? Or were you just planning on killing me and preventing the whole thing?"

"Briar—"

"Oh wait," Buggy laughed. It was a harsh sound. Harsh and as hollow as the cavity that had been growing in her chest for years. That emptiness that had no meaning... at least until now. "Then I'll just—poof—reborn, right? Then you'll have to do this shit all over again, ya?" Her laughter turned to hysterics, and her hands trembled so violently that her fingers danced against her knees like some sort of spastic spiders, limbs flailing, twitching, spasming. She was having a hard time catching her breath and her vision blurred at the edges.

"Briar please," Cam tried to sooth, but he didn't reach out to her again. "We have a plan."

"Ooooh plan B then?" Buggy's laugh had turned shrill, and she winced at the sound of her own voice. "Because your plan A worked out so goddamn well, right?" Buggy threw the photo at his face. It spiraled through the air and hit him hard in the forehead. It dropped, and he dived to catch it before it could touch the floor, as if afraid it would shatter like glass. "Well, you can take your plan B, and psycho story time, and shove um up your ass. And if you don't let me go, I may just go psycho-pyro on *you* instead." Buggy looked around the room, eyes jutting agitatedly from one wooden decoration to the other, skimming the stain glass windows and hanging drapery, until her eyes found Cam again. He was holding the photo gently between his finger and watching Buggy with wary sadness and mounting discomfort. Buggy saw it there, buried deep but slowly floating up to the surface. Fear. And she clung to it like it was her last breath. They were looking for a psycho? Fine. Have one.

"Would be such a pity if this pretty, pretty, cabin just went up in flames one night, wouldn't it? Such a pity." Buggy laughed again, and the sound ricocheted off every wall, flooding the cabin with a sickening sense of darkness. A hollow sound.

8

Sandra dropped her keys into the coffee mug, which made a happy clatter against its ceramic insides. She threw her bags onto the couch and made her way to the land line which had been ringing before she made it through the door.

"Hello?" she answered.

"Hey, Sandra!" Linny's voice spoke from the other end.

"Hey, Linny," Sandra smiled, shifting the phone to her left sholder and pinning it to her ear. She opened the fridge and grabbed a bottle of water. "How's it going?"

"Alright on my end," Linny answered. "How about you?"

"Oh same, same," she said taking a sip. "What can I do for ya?"

"Actually, I was trying to get ahold of Buggy," Linny said, "I tried to call her cell, but she's not been picking up. She up and about?"

Sandra frowned, screwing the top back on her bottle, and set it on the counter. "Buggy? No, she's not home right now. Was she headed back here?"

"Headed back?"

"Back from your place." Sandra hoped so. Buggy had a few nice days off, but she was looking forward to seeing her face to face. Make sure she was doing alright.

"... What do you mean *my* place?" Linny asked slowly.

"She said she was crashing at your place," Sandra paused, her throat growing tight. "She's... she's been staying with you since Sunday, right?"

"What? No, Buggy said she's been sick. I've been covering her shift at work, but I just wanted to ask her... hold on, she told you she was with *me*?"

"Yeah. And she's not sick. She hasn't been home since Friday," Sandra's mind spun as she tried to think up any reason Buggy may have lied to both of them. "Could she... could she be with Cooper?" she asked, desperately.

"No, Cooper left Sunday to go visit family, and Buggy was at work on Monday .... Sandra, what's going on?"

All the blood drained out of Sandra's head and for a moment she thought she might pass out. She clutched the back of a chair, steading herself.

"Buggy's not home. She's not with you. She lied to both of us and I have no idea where she is, that's what's going on."

"Why the hell would she do that?" Linny asked from the other end, her voice a little higher than usual.

"Something I found embarrassed her and she's... no, but this seems way over the top for all that."

"Sandra?" Linny pipped in. "Is Buggy okay? Is there anything I can do?"

"Yes," Sandra said, shaking the fog from her mind and leaping into action. "Yes. Please call Andrew. See if he has seen Buggy since Monday. And please call me if you see or hear from Buggy. At all. I mean anything."

"Okay," Linny answered, sounding a little scared now. "Sandra... I know Buggy's been acting a little weird recently, but she wouldn't just ghost out on her entire life like this, right? Not without a good reason?"

"Just," Sandra closed her eyes, "– just call me if you hear anything, alright? I have to go."

"What are you going to do?" Linny asked before she could hang up.

"Call her again," Sandra answered.

"And if she doesn't pick up?"

"Call my parents. See if she is hiding out with one of them." Sandra would call Brandon first. Buggy and their father had always had a closer relationship than she and her mom could have ever hoped to achieve. Growing up, Buggy had always leaned towards their father while Sandra more easily got along with their mother. The same could be said after the divorce, although no one like to talk about that. If Buggy was likely to run to anyone for help, or to get a way for a while, it would be their dad. But why on Earth would she lie about that? Why not just say, "hey, having a hard time, need a break, hanging with dad for a few days?" Why would she lie about where she was? And why was she only texting back—when she texted back at all, that is? Why not just pick up the damn phone?

"And if she's not with them?" Linny asked. To Sandra, her voice sounded distant, out of focus.

Why not just pick up the phone? Well, what if she *couldn't* pick up the phone? What if it wasn't her voice on the other end? Her past few texts had seemed a little weird. Sandra had decided that she must be reading into things, but what if she hadn't been? What if she had hit the nail on the head? What if the texts had seemed weird for Buggy because she wasn't the one writing them?

"Then I'm calling the police," Sandra said, and hung up the phone before Linny could say anything more.

Whatever the hell was going on, she was bringing her baby sister home.

9

Waverly sat alone in the silent hotel room. She had tried turning on both the TV and the radio, attempting to create some white noise to distract herself from her disjointed thoughts, but it only served to make her more jittery, *more* anxious, as if that were possible. So instead, she sat in silence, one leg curled under her, as she cleaned her .38 Smith & Wesson for the second time that day. She set out the gun on the small wooden desk provided by the hotel. A cloth, brush and small bottle of oil was set off to the side, while the ammo hid locked in a separate box under the bed, of course. California laws and all.

It had been easy breezy passing out of her home state of Texas, through New Mexico and Arizona, but when she reached the California border, she had to stop and kick down the stand of her Softtail. Waverly had taken her time, unbuckling her shoulder holster, and separating both her gun and ammo out into two separate lock boxes, one on one side of her Softail and one on the other. She had gotten her concealed carry permit years ago, only a month after she turned twenty-one. She remembered the dubious look on the instructor's face when she sidled into the facility, long blond hair up in a high ponytail. Six hours of training later, that look of dubious doubt had melted into one of mild shock and definite amusement. Waverly had a knack for weapons. She was no sharpshooter, but she was a rather good shot if she said so herself. She had passed with flying colors, and had purchased many a weapon since her licensing, but when her mother told her she would be going to California, Waverly had decided upon her compact .38 revolver. The revolver's small size made it easily concealable. With the way Waverly looked, and the way the revolver seemed to disappear under her jacket, she probably could have gotten away with wearing it, fully loaded, at all times. Who would suspect the tall, leggy blond with blue eyes? Nobody. A fact Waverly took advantage of at every opportunity.

Yes, she might have gotten away with it, but why risk it? The laws of Texas and the laws in California were a *might* different from one another. The last thing she needed was to be nailed with a misdemeanor charge by some hippy dippy Cali-officer for not locking her ammo and gun in separate boxes. She couldn't let that happen. She didn't have the time. So, she played it safe. She played their little game. For now, at least. But she did miss the methodology of cleaning her other weapons.

Cleaning the .38 was an easy task, frankly a little too easy. She preferred guns she could field strip. Her mother had taught her that term long ago. It meant to break down a weapon into its individual parts and put it back together again. That took time, diligence, attention. A .38 revolver wasn't the type of weapon that could be broken down. It could be cleaned, inspected, lubricated, polished, but that was about it. Waverly couldn't break the .38 down enough to fully distract herself from her own tangled mind. She would have preferred to take one of her other, larger weapons that she could truly field strip, because it helped her to focus. Focus on one thing at a time. Every little piece of the gun was a puzzle. Every little act of cleaning, a ritual. It was Waverly's version of meditation. Other girls got out their pink yoga mats on a bright sunny day, with their "sounds of running water" recordings, their spandex and their downward dogs. Waverly had her guns, cleaning solvent and silence. She had tried the whole spandex thing. Never worked for her. Simple a task as cleaning the .38 was, it at least felt useful. It meant something. It was meditation, but productive meditation. Leading somewhere. Preparing for something. Always forward. Just as her mother taught her.

Her mom had never been part of the military or any gun enthusiast organization, but she had learned a lot over the years. She had started young. Reading books on gun care, graduating to personal lessons, until she eventually taught her own daughter. Waverly had not minded that either. She liked knowing she could use a gun. Not because she was some crazy psycho who wanted to go around killing people at random, but because she liked knowing she could defend herself if she had to. She heard many stories about women being accosted on the streets, in fact, she had seen it happen. She liked knowing, if anyone tried to hurt her, rape her, touch her, she could make them stop.

But safety wasn't what her mother had in mind. She found that out early.

Waverly ran the rag across the revolver's handle with slow determination, trying to focus on every curve, every inch of the weapon. Tried to let every other thought pass through her mind, let them float by like clouds in a blue sky, but she was finding it difficult tonight. Her mind kept veering off, snagging on thoughts, and peering into memories that she would rather leave where they were. Tonight, they refused to stay away. She remembered all her mother's stories. All her warnings, her descriptions of rooms full of blood and death. Of one woman taking down the entire Fold in one night with sheer, monstrous power. How her own mother, only twelve years old at the time, had killed the woman. Except... not exactly. She wasn't dead. Not anymore. That was the problem, wasn't it? The whole damn problem. That was *her* failure.

Waverly's head jerked up as her phone rang on the bedside table across the room. She bolted up, knocking the table in her hurry and toppling the little bottle, squirting oil everywhere. She ignored it, darting to answer her phone.

"Mom?" she asked.

"I found her," her mother said on the other end. She sounded pleased, and Waverly smiled.

"Found who?"

"Helena," her mother answered. "Helena West. She was a member of The Fold. She was only a baby when the *event* happened, and she left The Fold to pursue a business in car restoration and repair. I have the business address. It's in Temecula, California. So, you're in the right state at least."

"She's the one that's helping Styger?" Waverly asked.

"No, she was born without any psychic abilities. She would be useless to him."

"Then why—" Waverly started, but her mother was too excited to wait for her to finish.

"She had a son. Theodore. Never met him. She had him after she left The Fold. But I bet you dollars to donuts, he has the gift. And I know that Styger and Helena had been friendly while both were part of The Fold. It was one of the reasons she left after Styger took the girl and ran. She didn't want to chase them down. If Styger teamed up with her son... well, do you really think she would have no contact with her boy? Would have no idea where an old friend might take him?"

"She could lead me to her son, and her son will lead me to Styger," Waverly's smile was widening.

"And Styger will lead you to *her*," her mother finished, then her voice dropped low. "This is a woman and her child we are talking about," she warned. "She won't give him up easily."

The floating clouds in Waverly's mind gathered, dark and thunderous. They showed her images of old newspapers, burnt factories, burnt bodies. Hundreds of dead. She remembered her mother's tear-streaked face as she told her about her own experience, how she had watched her own mother torn limb from limb before her eyes. Her mother warning that the creature would never stop. That she would keep killing, killing, killing, until even the clouds rained blood.

"I will handle it," Waverly said, firmly. "I will fix Styger's mistakes mother. I promise."

"That's my girl," Susanna's voice was soft and sweet in her daughter's ear and filled her with pride.

"What's the address?"

10

Buggy knew she was dreaming. Many times it was hard to tell. Many times, she simply sank into the false world, easily accepting it as her new reality, accepting it as her *only* reality. That is the usual power of dreams, after all. Utter control over the sleeper. Like the Cartesian's evil genius, it created a perfectly realistic world, or at least an easily *accepted* world, where the victim obliviously stumbles through the images and experience, little knowing their falsehood until they finally opened their eyes. However, from time to time, one can—not only acknowledge their dream state *as* a dream state but (imbued with power from that knowledge)—take control of the dream. Because it is their imagination after all. Sometimes they can harness this power, use it to alter the images, alter the story plot developing in their heads, essentially becoming God of their own mental universe.

And yet, other times, the person has the knowledge that they are dreaming, but are unable to use that knowledge in any way. It leaves these unlucky souls to flail helplessly in a world they know to be false and yet feel every experience as if it was true. Unable to alter anything. And God save them if they find themselves in a nightmare. For then they are the viewer of a horror story. They feel the terror of every character, eyes glued open, unable to look away.

It was in this state that Buggy found herself walking through an old house. The house itself was beautifully kept, and clean and well cared for, but the style reminded her of several houses she had walked through on various field trips from school. It was a large, eighteenth-century house with classic furniture and decorations, although they looked new to her. She stepped over bright, woven rugs and passed polished portrait frames as she moved up the long flight of stairs. Buggy could see the shine on the frame, but not the portraits themselves. She could tell that the paintings were of two figures, but the dream blurred them out of focus. It didn't matter. They weren't what she was here for. No. What she wanted was in the bathroom upstairs.

No. Buggy thought, desperately. Because she remembered this dream. She had been here before. She had already passed those portraits, already climbed those stairs... and she knew what came next. *No, please. Not this one.* She had many nightmares by this point, but this one... this one was second only to the burning house on her list of "world's shittiest dreams."

She had this dream on three other occasions and remembered each time in agonizing detail. Buggy would always walk up those stairs, through the upper hallway lined with more blurry portraits at an infuriating slow rate. Moving as if someone had a TV remote to her mind, slowing every step by thirty percent. Each time, she would walk down the hall, enter that bathroom, and there the shaving blade would be waiting for her.

No, please God, not this dream again.

But God wasn't listening, and she was no God of dreams tonight, so her hand reached out slowly to take the bathroom door handle. Despite her mental screams of protest, Buggy's body pushed the door open. She stepped into a little, blue walled bathroom with a smooth, wooden floor. There was a large, metal tub on one end of the room and a basin and pitcher on a dresser to the other. Next to the cabinet was a tall, rounded mirror, held up by two metal stands.

Buggy's body moved (without her permission) towards the dresser. Resting on the dresser, between the pitcher and the basin, was a small mettle handled hairbrush, two small clear glass, and a smooth, pearl handled, shaving blade.

No, no, please, stop.

Buggy watched her hands reach out, move aside one of the glasses, and lifted the little blade delicately between her fingers.

For fuck's sake, stop! If Buggy had control of her voice, she would have been shrieking. She placed the cup back down to the dresser and turned to the large mirror, shaving blade in hand, its pearl handle cool against the skin of her palm. She stepped up in front of the mirror, and for the fourth time, Buggy saw the reflection within.

It was her, but not exactly. She had the same small nose, same hair, same incredibly large eyes looking out from a familiar face. However, the face in the mirror looked as if fifteen more years had been etched into her features, although she couldn't truly be older than twenty-three. No, time had not begun its inevitable art. Time had not creased the edges of her eyes so deeply, nor added the dark circles or hollowed out the caverns beneath her cheek bones. No, despair had done that. And it was her large eyes that showed the most age. They were heavy. Heavy with pain, heavy with loss. The simple dark makeup around her eyes had run and left black tracks of tears that dripped all the way down her neck and disappeared beneath her collar. She was wearing a black dress, obviously funereal garb, with a tight waist, high collar, and long sleeves. Around her neck hung a large necklace with a silver chain and sparkling red oval stone that looked like congealed blood against the woman's dark dress.

The mirror version of Buggy began to slowly, agonizingly slowly, roll up her left sleeve. Buggy's thoughts were no longer coherent. They came in desperate, tumbling pleas of pain and terror. Because she knew what came next.

The mirror version of herself looked calm and resolute before the glass, left wrist bared, right hand still holding the shaver's blade. After a moment's pause, she moved the blade towards her bared wrist. Buggy couldn't stop her dream self from doing what she was doing, but she had gained a talent over the years. A talent to wake herself up. Buggy closed her eyes, like she had done many times before. Like she had done in the house of fire, and when she had been tied to the pyre and heard Sandra calling her name. She would close her eyes, know it was a dream, open them and she would be awake. She would be out of this hell.

Buggy squeezed her eyes closed, and waited, chanting to herself that it wasn't real. It was just a dream. She would open her eyes and she would be back home in her apartment. Sandra would already have the coffee going. She would have herself a cup, wish Sandra a good day and then head off to Elwin's. Just another day. That was all that was real.

Buggy opened her eyes. To her despair, she still saw herself standing in front of the mirror, wearing that long black dress, blade moving ever closer to her wrist.

No. She tried again. She closed her eyes, harnessing every bit of strength her mind possessed, willing herself to wake up. Willing herself to be free. She opened her eyes. She was still standing in front of the mirror, but there was something different this time. The version of her in the mirror looked younger, all traces of despair were gone, making her look her actual age once more. But the tear streaks remained, and she was still wearing that black dress. Now the shaving blade was nearly touching her skin. Buggy closed her eyes again, praying to whatever God there was in heaven that this would be the time. That this would be the moment she woke up. She squeezed her lids tight... and opened them.

She was still asleep, and the image of her in the mirror was looking back at her. It viewed her with an attentive expression. As if her reflection knew she was watching. Knew Buggy was trying to wake up. Then the reflection's tear-streaked face did something it had never done before. It smiled at her. Its lips slowly pulling upward, and a strange manic glint lit its eyes. Buggy's heart stopped. She staired at her reflection, their eyes locked unblinking. Then, suddenly, it winked at her. Buggy felt the bottom drop out of her stomach, as her reflection opened her lips and spoke.

"Not this time, Briar dear," it said, soft and sweet in a tone she recognized. "It is my turn to be awake." She drew the blade across her wrist.

Buggy began to scream.

* * *

The sound peeled out from the living room in a blood curdling pitch that wrenched Cam out of his partial dose and sent his heart flying. He launched himself out of the armchair he had sat in only a few minutes before and burst out of the room.

"Briar?!" he called wildly, leaping down the stairs towards the living room below. "Briar?!"

"Cam!" Theo's voice yelled, barely heard over the sounds of Briar's screams.

"Theo!" Cam called back, reaching the bottom floor, "What the hell's—" he cut off as he saw what was going on. Briar was asleep, seemingly caught in some twisted nightmare, which was bad enough, but the couch she slept on was on fire. "Jesus."

Cam darted forward, to join Theo in his futile effort to smother the flames with a nearby blanket. He grabbed the blanket out of his hands and continued trying to pat down the fire, which only grew hotter and hotter under his hands.

"Water!" he yelled at Theo over the sound of fire and screams. "Water, get water now!" Theo darted for the kitchen without hesitation. Cam turned his attention to the girl, whose face twisted in agony. "Briar!" he yelled, smothering the flames before they could touch her precious skin. "Briar! Wake up! Wake up!" She didn't wake. She only churned slightly, pausing in her screams just long enough to cry. "Briar, please, wake up!"

Theo was back, a bucket of water in his hands, he was about to pour it down the back of the couch when Cam stopped him. "No, her!" he ordered, pointing at Briar. "Forget the fire, wake her up." Theo hesitated only a second before doing what he was told. He dumped the bucket of icy water directly into the girl's nightmare contorted face. Briars eyes flew open, and she took a large gasping breath. The fire died instantly around her, leaving the couch blackened and smoldering. Theo dropped the bucket on the floor and staggered back to take one of the nearby chairs. He put his head in his hands, arms trembling, while Cam knelt in front of Briar.

"Briar. Briar," he repeated her name until her large, confused eyes finally focused on him. "Are you alright?"

"What?" She shook her head, droplets of water flying out in an arch, and looked around her. She noticed the state of the couch she sat on and blinked. "Did you... what the hell?" She sat up, kicking the smoldering blankets away. She tried to stand, but the handcuffs, which were still attached to the scorched couch arm, tugged her back down. "What happened?"

"You were having a nightmare," Cam said, sitting back on the coffee table, allowing himself a moment of relief.

"Why is the couch burnt?" she asked, voice still trembling from whatever horrors her dreams had held. She looked down at her shirt, which was dripping slowly onto the floor. "And why am I soaking wet?"

"Because you started a fire in your sleep," Cam said honestly. "And we had to wake you up."

"What?" Buggy's confused eyes grew first weary, and then angry, as the delirium of half-waking dreams finally left her completely. "Oh, screw you. You and your bullshit. Your inner serial killer, demon, bullshit. Your 'setting fires with your mind' insane, nonsense. Just *stop*!"

"Briar," Cam tried to interrupt, but she barreled on.

"You expect me to believe I set a *fire* with my *mind* while asleep? Screw that. It makes more sense that you psychos caught the couch on fire as some stupid, insane *proof* of your lunacy. Try to convince me I did it when I woke up, is that right?"

"Briar," Cam tried again, eyes looking pointedly down to her hand cuffed wrist. She ignored him again.

"Well, forget it. Screw that and screw you. You can take your fire tricks, and your insane stories, and cram them down your—"

"Briar!" Cam barked.

"What?!" Briar snapped back. Cam motioned to her wrist. Buggy looked down and her eyes widened in shock. The handcuffs were changing color. The smooth, cool, silver metal was growing from warm to hot, and quickly from silver to bright red. She could feel the scolding heat of it, feel it burning her skin, but she couldn't bring herself to focus on the pain. She watched as the handcuffs, a second ago as sturdy and unbreakable as any other, softened and melted off her wrist. Drips of liquified metal splashed against the floor, cooling there. Buggy gasped in pain as the melted metal singed her flesh as it dripped off. She grabbed a section of blanket that had not been burnt and quickly wiped off the rest, leaving nothing but raw skin where the cuff used to be. They both looked down at the puddle of metal on the floor, watching it cool from bright red to dim gray and back to silver. The girl slowly drew her eyes back to meet Cam's gaze through a veil of dripping hair. They were so confused, so hurt, so utterly lost that it took all the strength Cam had not to reach out and pull her into his arms.

"What the hell is wrong with me?" her voice broke against the silence.

Cam reached out, taking the blanket from her other hand, and gently cradling her burnt wrist. He examined it and hissed under his breath. "Come on," he said, "let's get some ice on that." He stood up and moving towards the kitchen. Briar watched him go, cast another glance back at the puddle of metal at her feet, and then followed him.

II

Neither of them said anything for a long while. Buggy sat on top of the kitchen island, a towel wrapped around her damp shoulders, arm extended as Styger iced down her burnt wrist. He then grabbed the first aid kit from the other room, disinfected her burns with a little soap and water, which made Buggy cringe. He then put a thin layer of antibiotic ointment from the kit and wrapped a thin gauze around the whole thing. Buggy watched him as he pulled a white circle of tape from the kit, tore a bit off with his teeth, and secured the bandage with a few pieces. He turned away from her, making a long show of slowly and carefully replacing everything back into the white box, making it take as long as possible. He looked as nervous as she felt.

"So, you believe it then?" Buggy asked finally. Cam looked up, surprised she had spoken at all.

"Which part?" he asked, closing the kit's lid with a light snap.

"The story about the city. The one with angels, demons, and the woman that doesn't age. You believe it?"

Cam slid the kit to the side and then turned to hoist himself up on the island beside her, being very careful not to touch her as he did so. His eyes were on the sink set into tiled countertop in front of them.

"Honestly, no," he said after a moment's consideration. "Not really. It's all a little too mystic and abstract for my liking... but I do believe in reincarnation. I believe in *your* reincarnation. I believe—whether because of some magical woman in a purgatory like city, or some freak chance of nature—that whenever you die, you are reborn. And I believe that there is some part of you, one of those past lives, or maybe a combination of those past lives, that wants out. A part that means to hurt people."

"And you believe you can get rid of it?" Buggy asked, watching the slow leak in the faucet head. Water droplets dripped slowly into the metal sink, sending little splashes up to the edge, only to slide back down to the drain.

Cam shook his head slowly. "No, Briar. It's part of you. Part of your memories, part of your history. It's not something you can just 'get rid' of."

"Then how are you supposed to help me?" she asked.

"We may not be able to get rid of it, but we can help you control it. We can help you lock her away."

"The Daughter, you mean?" Buggy asked.

"Yes. We can teach you. Teach you how to contain her. It's not her life anymore. That means you have the upper hand. As long as you know how to play the game, you can win. You can send her back and keep her there. We can teach you the game. Teach you the rules. And you can win the pot."

"You're making this sound less of a training and more of a gamble," Buggy said, looking over at him.

"It's both," Cam agreed, looking back over at her. "It is a gamble. There is always a chance..." he cleared his throat. "There is a chance you will lose. If The Daughter gets the upper hand before you can gain your footing.... She's done this a great deal. She already knows the game, and you'd just be getting started."

"And she could, uh, take me over?" Cam nodded slowly. Buggy remembered the smirk on dream-Cooper's face. The glint in her reflection's eyes, as the mirror version of herself slit her own wrists. Buggy shuddered and tugged the towel tighter around her shoulders. "This is... this is *crazy*." It was an unbelievable story. Yet, she found herself slowly, but surly, believing. Besides, the metal handcuffs melting off her wrist didn't exactly scream: "LIES!"

"How do you know?" she continued. "How do you even know if this— this *game* or whatever—how do you know it will work? Even if you were able to teach me?"

"Because I've seen it work before," Cam smiled, reaching back into his pocket, and pulling out the photo of him and Loretta. It now had a rather crumpled edge from Buggy waiving it in the air, but his eyes still worshiped the image just the same as when it was pristine. He held it out to Buggy, who took it with far gentler fingers this time. She looked down at the image, tracing every line of that familiar face. She had seen that face in the mirror so many times, but it had never *quite* looked like that. That shorter hair, that wide smile full of so much joy, unburdened happiness. A smile that said she was *free*.

"Loretta." Buggy said. Cam nodded as if it had been a question.

"Yes."

They sat in silence for a few more minutes before Buggy asked, "What was she.... What was she like?"

"She was sweet," Cam said, smile turned to the photo. Buggy could see the love in his eyes. The love and the pain. "Sweet but strong. Trusting but not naive. She ate tacos like they were going out of style. Hated rainy days. And when she loved, she loved with every ounce of her soul. She was never afraid to give her heart, not when she knew what she wanted. She was brave in that way..." Buggy looked down at the photo.

*Huh. Like mother **not** like daughter, I guess.* She thought absently. Cam continued.

"She loved utterly. But she never loved anything," he looked up at Buggy, who kept her eyes on the photo, "the way she loved you."

Buggy swallowed hard, forcing the lump down. Pushing away that compressed ball of emotion that had built up over twenty-four years of resentment and love and feelings of abandonment.

"You said, uh, y-you said she..." She couldn't say it. So, Cam did it for her.

"She died giving birth to you."

Buggy's eyes slid up to the ceiling, willing the tears to slide back into her eyes. For the time being they listened, stinging in disapproval.

"So, all this time, it's been... my fault." Buggy had thought her mother had abandoned her. Thought her mother had not wanted her enough to stay, when the truth was.... "I killed my mom."

"No. Briar," Cam turned and started reaching out to her, but then thought better of it. His hands clenched the edge of the counter instead. "No. You did nothing of the sort. It was always a risk. None of your previous, umm... *selves* had ever had children. At least not that The Fold knew of. We had no idea what would happen. We didn't know if you would come out as just our child, or if your birth would be another way of reincarnation. We started having a better guess as time went on. As you grew bigger, she grew weaker, more tired, a little sicker..."

"Oh God," Buggy looked back up to the ceiling again, but the tears refused to listen this time. They began to burn down her cheeks.

"But she didn't care, Briar," Cam insisted. "She knew it was a risk, but she loved you. She wanted you to live. She wanted you to have the same chance at life that she had. She was not afraid." Cam paused, then nodded to himself, deciding something. "Stay here." He slipped off the counter and disappeared out the door. Buggy remained on the counter, eyes still on the photo, until he came back in. She looked up as he held something out to her. It was a cell phone. An old one, with thick buttons and a dim screen. It was set at "messages" and ready to play the only recording still on the device.

"If you still don't believe me," Cam said, holding the phone out a little closer. "Maybe you'll believe her."

Buggy's wide eyes moved from the phone, to Cam's face, and back to the phone again. She reached out with her free hand and took it. Cam nodded a little and backed away. "I'll just... I'll be out here when you're done." He turned, and with one last glance over his shoulder at the cell phone, he left. The kitchen door swung closed behind him. Buggy turned back to the phone, hesitated, then lifted it to her cheek with a trembling hand. She pressed the play button. There was a muffled scratching sound from the recording, and then the unmistakable sound of her mother's voice in her ear. Buggy began to cry again.

"Hey, Babe," her mother was saying. "It's me again. I just thought... I thought I... I wanted to leave her one more message. Just one more time," she took a ragged breath, "God, Babe, I wish you were here. But she'll be here waiting for you if you can't. So... this is for her. Play it for her someday, will you? When she's ready to hear it. When she really needs it." Loretta's voice took another jagged breath, and Buggy dropped the photo to the counter so she could jam her hand over her mouth to keep her sobs from being audible. She had never heard this message before. She had listened to nearly all her cassettes over and over until she had them memorized, but this was new. This was the last. Because it was the last one before she was born. The last one her mother had made before she died. Her mother's last message to her daughter who she gave everything to. Buggy bit down hard on her hand as she listened.

"Hey there, honey. It's me. Your mama. It's been a long ride, hu? Well, you're almost here... and I just have one last thing I need to tell you..." Buggy listened. "I know by this point your daddy has told you everything. What you are. What *we* are. And I'm sure it's confusing. I know I was confused when I was told. Confused, scared, and a little angry. But also, a little relieved because... it kinda explained things, doesn't it? I know I've always had this... this chasm in my chest, a hollow part. A place for forgotten memories." Buggy absentmindedly pressed a hand to her chest as her mother went on. "Oh, honey, I hope you don't know what I'm talking about, but if you do, don't be afraid. Because that isn't all there is. I know it feels that way sometimes. Like that empty is going to eat you up until that is all you have. But, hun, there is so much more in you than that empty place. There is strength. There is strength and fire and love. And those things are brighter than any void. And if you feed them, they will light even the darkest places. Please remember that. I need you to remember that, okay?" Loretta's voice broke, shattered on the other end of an unanswered call left in years passed. "You're gonna have to fight for it. Your gonna have to fight for *you*, okay? And you got to fight hard, you got to promise me, you'll fight hard. Because you deserve a life, hun, you deserve your own life. That hollow space does *not* get to win, do you understand me? Those forgotten memories don't get to win. **She** doesn't get to win. It's *your* turn. So, take it." Loretta's voice trailed off. Buggy realized that a painful contraction must have forced her breath from her. "Ha!" Loretta huffed a laugh that made Buggy smile through her tears. "Told you, you're strong! But I've got to go, honey. And I'm... I hope I get to meet you—even if only for a second—so that I can tell you in person. But if I can't—remember that your mama loves you. She loves you so much," Buggy closed her eyes, "always have. Always will. It's your turn now baby girl. So, take it. Live it. And don't let anyone tell you different. Goodnight, Aida. And happy birthday." The message ended. Buggy felt herself sliding off the counter. She bumped the photo as she went down, sending it fluttering through the air to stop at her feet. Her back scraped against the cabinets handles as she made it to the ground. Her legs tangled beneath her, while she pressed the quiet phone to her ear.

No! Buggy screamed in her mind. *No, you're not done speaking. You're not done. I'm not done.* But the phone remained silent. It slipped out of her fingers and clattered against the floor coming to rest by the photo of a mother. Buggy wrapped her arms around her legs and buried her face in her knees. She didn't know how long she sat like that, body trembling against the cold floor. After some time, she heard the door open tentatively on the other side of the room, but she didn't look up.

"Briar?" Cam's voice was quiet, barely heard, and Buggy pretended she hadn't. She heard the soft scuff of footsteps come around the counter then stop beside her. She heard the "pop" of tired kneecaps as the man slid down to sit on the floor by her side. They remained silent for a long time, seconds stretching into minutes, minutes seeming to go on into eternity.

"Aida?" Buggy asked finally, voice raw and muffled against her knees.

"That was what we were going to name you," Cam said. "... But Briar Rose is a nice name to."

Buggy wiped her eyes and looked up at the man sitting beside her. The man who had just shattered every reality she had ever known. "I nearly died when I was a baby. Nearly froze to death in an alley, alone," Buggy watched as Cam's eyes filled with shame and pain. Buggy quickly moved on, because hurting him wasn't what she was meaning to do. "A paramedic gave me CPR. Or at least as much as you can give a newborn. He 'kissed' me, and I woke up from my sleep."

A small smile twitched Cam's lip. "Like Aurora from Sleeping Beauty."

"Yeah."

"Cute," Cam nodded.

"Yeah." Buggy wiped her eyes again and sniffed.

"Briar... I know you're confused," Cam said, eyes drifting to the photo on the floor. "And that's my fault. I wasn't there when you were born, and I failed to be there as you grew up. But I'm done failing you. And I will explain everything. I will answer every question you have. And when this is all over, when you are safe, I will send you home. And I will never bother you again. If that's what you want."

Buggy *was* confused. So many things still didn't make sense, and she wanted to understand. And she would. But for now...

"You know where we can get some pizza around here?" she asked, looking over at him.

Cam blinked at her, taken aback. Soon enough, he grinned. His knees popped again as he stood up. "I got just the place."

12

The pizzeria was small, only a few booths and scattered tables, but the bright colors and soft music gave it a warm and lively atmosphere. Buggy sighed as the smell of hot cheese and peperoni flooded through the open door. Cam led the way inside, calling "hello" to someone named Bert on the other side of the long and checkered counter separating the kitchen from the rest of the restaurant. Bert, who turned out to be a pudgy man in his fifties with a bright red beard tucked into a clear plastic mask, waved back with a grin, and told them to pick a seat. All the tables and a couple of the booths were already taken. Cam directed Buggy to a corner booth off to the side, a few rows down from a group of jabbering high schoolers. A waitress in a crisp white apron and donning the same bright red hair as Bert, came to take their order. She scribbled it all down with lightning-fast movements, flashed Cam an unnecessarily long, lingering smile before walked back to the kitchen.

"So, she's got a thing for you," Buggy noted. She watched the girl, who had barely begun her twenties, cast another little glance over her shoulder before disappearing through the swinging door.

Cam looked up as Buggy spoke, a grimace on his face. "Yes, I know. Bert finds it hilarious. She's his baby sister."

"Heart breaker," Buggy laughed. It was a crisp sound. Like someone shaking a bag of potato chips, looking through the remnants for the large pieces among the crumbs. It sounded forced because it *was* forced. Buggy felt many things—confusion, fear, curiosity, wonder, and utter mental and physical exhaustion. But laughter? Not so much. It was, however, the easiest of shields. A barrier she could put between her and the situation she found herself in, a simple way to give herself distance. Distance, and enough time to process. If that was ever going to be possible. Buggy seriously doubted it. She could force the laugh all the same, but the falsity of the sound made her cringe. Cam didn't seem to notice. Or, at least, he was kind enough not to comment.

"It was sweet when she was a kid, and I kinda thought she'd grow out of it. Now it's grown pretty uncomfortable."

"You come here often, I take it?" Buggy asked. Cam shrugged.

"From time to time for the past twenty years I'd say. Great pizza, and Bert's a friend of mine, but every time I come in these days," he shot another little grimace the waitress's way. "I see her and think how my own daughter isn't much older than she is." he looked up at Buggy, who had taken a great interest in the drink's menu. "Uh, Briar?"

"Yeah?" she asked, still mulling over the menu, checking her watch. She really felt like this situation required alcohol.

"What happened to you?"

"What?" Buggy looked up. Wasn't that *her* question? "What happened to me when?"

"After you were born?" Cam said, spinning his water glass in his hands, not meeting her gaze. "What happened?"

Buggy frowned, a little thrown. She guessed these were important questions as well. She was still a little wrapped up in the idea that she was a reborn version of a pyro maniac serial killer—had an entire closet full of questions about that bullshit—but she also saw the look in Cam's eyes. This was the question *he* had been burning to ask her for years. Twenty-four of them to be exact. So, she indulged him. "Well, I nearly died, so they took me to the hospital. I guess I was there for a few weeks, and then I got adopted almost right away. Newborns are apparently a high wanted commodity in the system."

"I know," Cam said. "I came looking for you."

"Well, you did a shitty job," Buggy said, sliding the menu to the side, looking around for the waitress. She was ready for that drink.

"No, I didn't. I found you," Cam said.

"What?" Buggy whipped back around. "You found me? You found me and you..." her stomach dropped, "and you just, what, left me?"

Cam shook his head, finally meeting her gaze. "No, Briar, no, I tried to take you home. I tried to prove that you were my daughter. But they wouldn't believe me."

"What about a DNA test? To prove that I was your daughter? I assume they would be more than happy to give a daughter back to a dad. You know, instead of sending them of to adoption or foster care."

Cam rubbed the back of his neck and averted his gaze once more. "Yeah, except we don't actually share any DNA."

"You've lost me," Buggy said, blankly. She didn't feel surprised. She didn't feel anything anymore, to be honest. She was past the point of being surprised and was hovering somewhere in a comfortable whirlpool of numbness. "You said you were my biological father."

"I *am* your father," Cam nodded. "Loretta was never with anyone.... I'm definitely your father."

"Then why—?"

"Because you are her reincarnation. Yes, I may have, uh, helped bring about that reincarnation, but that didn't change the fact that you and your mother are 'of the same' self. You being born—hell, you just developing inside your mother's belly—it was her transitioning into you. And after you were born, my DNA didn't really have any part to play anymore. Like a match in a fire. It was needed to create the spark, but in the end the fire consumes it."

"Okay," Buggy nodded.

"Still kinda thinking I'm just crazy?" Cam smiled.

"Oh, hell yes," Buggy said, catching the waitress's eye. "But it's not the craziest thing you've tried to tell me, so I'm just ganna roll with it for now, if that's okay with you."

"Works for me," Cam shrugged as the waitress came over.

"You don't happen to have whiskey sours here, do you?" Buggy asked.

"'Fraid not, honey," the waitress said, with an overly sweet smile. Buggy raised a brow at the girl who was at least three years her junior.

"Well, how about a rum and diet Coke, *honey?*"

"Sure thing!" the girl replied, oblivious to Buggy's sarcasm. "Anything for you?" she asked, turning to Cam.

"It's... one in the afternoon," Cam said, glancing at Buggy.

"He'll have the same," Buggy said over him. The waitress (her name tag called her 'Tilly,') nodded and made a few more scribbles on her note pad before disappearing back into the kitchen. "What?" she asked, turning back to Cam. "If you don't want it, I'll drink it."

"Well, anyway," Cam started again. "After my DNA test failed, I, uh, reacted badly. They had me forcibly removed from the hospital. I went looking for you again, and a couple times I thought I had a lead, but because I couldn't prove that you were my biological daughter, or present any sort of records on your mother, I was denied. I lost you. Soon you were gone from the hospital and I had no idea where they sent you."

"I was adopted," Buggy said. "The Pierce's."

"And these Pierce's, they... they been good to you?"

Buggy smiled. "Yes, they have. They aren't perfect, but more than I could have hoped for. They've given me a great life. And my sister, Sandra, she's one of my closest friends."

Cam smiled and nodded, but Buggy could still see the pain there, the loss. "I'm glad. I'm glad you've been happy. That's all I ever really hoped for."

"And you couldn't find me until now?"

"No."

"How did you find me when you couldn't before. What changed?"

"I found Theo," Cam said simply.

Buggy frowned. "What?"

"Theo's a special kind of psychic," Cam explained. "One with the ability to 'feel' people. He was able to track you down."

"By feeling?"

"Feeling, thinking. It's really rather hard to explain. It's complicated."

"His superpowers?"

"Not superpowers. Skills. An ability to focus on something or someone and connect to their energy. Everything gives off an energy. And when you can connect with that energy in the way that Theo can, many times this leads to *knowing* things about them. Sometimes, like in your case, even being able to find where they are."

"By thinking." Cam shrugged. "Weird," Buggy said, leaning in against the table, intrigued. "So, he thought about me and..."

"And things about you—things that you feel most *strongly* about—he was able to catch glimpses of."

"Glimpses?"

"Glimpses, sort of."

"Okay?"

"It's really hard to explain," Cam said again, grimacing.

"It's fine, I think I get the gist," Buggy said, still feeling utterly confused but knowing she probably wouldn't be getting any clearer of an answer.

"Alright," Cam said. "Well, I had pretty much given up on finding you on my own, but I was able to track down an old friend. Theo's mother. She was also a member of The Fold, but she had abandoned it soon after Loretta and I ran, and we hadn't seen each other for years. Kept in touch from time to time though letters or random calls, but she would never tell me where she was."

"Why not?" Buggy asked, frowning.

"Because she wanted nothing to do with The Fold or Fold business at all. She knew I was looking for you, and she didn't want Theo involved. She was born without any psychic gifts, so she knew I wouldn't ask her for help. But I would ask for Theo's if I knew he existed, which I didn't at the time. She went to great pains to keep it that way."

"What changed?"

"Dumb luck actually. Ran into an old neighbor of theirs. She told me all about a strange boy who saved her life and his mother Helena West. That lead me to Theo. Theo led me to you. And here we are."

"And here we are." Buggy sat back in the booth and watched him.

"What?" Cam asked, blinking, a little uncomfortable under her gaze.

"Nothing. I just always wondered. About you. About my mom. About who my parents might be... and why. Why I was left behind."

"God, Briar, I'm so sorry," Cam closed his eyes. "Please know I tried to find her in time. We had a plan. I was supposed to be there when you were born. If I had been there, we would have both told them I was the father and then the DNA wouldn't have mattered. I was supposed to be there for her. I was supposed to be there for *you*. We had a plan."

"What went wrong?" Buggy asked.

Cam licked his lips, choosing his words carefully, stalling for time. "So... you remember The Fold..."

"The crazy ass lunatics who made it their mission to kill a girl every twenty-four years? Yeah, I remember them," Buggy said.

"Well..." Cam trailed off for a minute as the waitress sidled back up to the table with their drinks. When she left, Buggy reached out and took her glass eagerly. Cam continued. "Well, you remember that most of them were killed right?"

"By one of my previous, evil, reincarnations," Buggy nodded "Also something hard to forget."

"Well, there are still a few members alive other than Theo, his mother, and me. After Loretta and I ran, my father and Susanna came after us. We were pretty good at staying ahead of them. But I guess it was inevitable that they would find us eventually. My father was a smart man, and Susanna was ferocious in her hunt. We were usually careful, but that night—the night you were born—we were too distracted to be think about them. We weren't prepared... and I was out getting tacos," Cam smiled sadly, "with extra guacamole. Anyway. I went out, just for a few minutes, and Susanna went after her."

"Susanna tried to kill a pregnant woman?" Buggy asked, taking a sip. "Sounds like a bitch."

"Your mom got away. Ran out of there. But she couldn't make it to the hospital. She went into labor in the alley... and you were born."

"And she died."

Cam nodded.

"There was no body."

"There never is," Cam said. Buggy remembered the story her mother and father always told her. About the sleeping princes awoken by a brave prince. A sleeping princess covered in ash. Buggy grunted. The waitress returned with a plate of steaming pizza and slid it on the table between them.

"Enjoy!" she said cheerily, but Buggy wasn't feeling very hungry anymore.

"So, what now?" Buggy asked over her glass.

"Well, it's been a while since your birthday. Over a month. The Daughter has woken inside you." Cam shook his head. "Frankly, I'm surprised it hadn't happened sooner. The longest the other reincarnations had gone..." Cam trailed off as he caught Buggy's expression. "I'm just saying, you have held on much longer than any... for how long you have been going without help, your luck... I'll stop talking now."

"I think she has been awake for a while now," Buggy said, blowing past Cam's awkward stumbling. She was still numb, too numb to be shaken by his ominous words or encouragement. She felt like her entire body had been given an electric shock and now it basked in the lack of feeling that came when the pain had finally left. It made it easy to simply accept everything. Besides, her mother had been right. As insane as it all was, it explained a lot.

"But she hasn't won yet. She hasn't taken control," Cam said firmly. "Right now, she's sort of... weaving in and out of a varying levels of consciousness inside you. Like the moment when you pull yourself from a deep, deep dream. She's awake, but not quite fully. She is fighting, reaching, and pulling herself up to a higher level of consciousness, trying to catch hold. But she is still weak, and you are still in charge. So, for a while, she slips back a little deeper. Not back to sleep, but a little further from control."

I wanted to say good morning, while I can. Buggy cleared her throat and turned away from the memory of non-Cooper in the kitchen. Could that really have been...? It was in her dream, but still.

"There is part of her, a core part, still tethered to a lower subconscious. Darkness and repressed memories. She needs to regain enough control to untether herself, to pull *all* of herself up to the surface. But she won't."

"No?" Buggy asked Cam, a hint of sarcasm coloring her voice.

"No. You can get control of her. She's strong. But this is your life and your turn to live." Cam leaned forward, lacing his fingers on the table in front of him. His eyes were determined. Fearless. "And you *can* beat her. Theo and I will teach you."

"How?" Buggy asked. "How do I even... just how?"

"You've got a lot of power inside of you, Briar. All you gotta do is know how to use it."

Buggy hesitated. "Okay," she said finally.

"Yeah?" Cam tried to contain his relief, but it was evident in the relaxing of his shoulder, and the grin that quirked his scruffy face.

"Yeah. But I swear," Buggy said, reaching out and pulling a piece from the pizza. A long string of cheese clung to it, stretching long and white before finally snapping. "You ever try to put another pair of cuffs on me and I—"

"I am so sorry," Cam's grin crumpled into a look of utter shame. "That was a bad idea."

"Ya think?" Buggy mumbled around a mouth full of hot cheese.

"But we had to get you away from your life. And you weren't gonna want to wait around willingly while we explained."

"But why go to full on kidnaping? And where even *are* we by the way?" Buggy asked, taking a bite. Cam frowned.

"Well, I think 'kidnaping' is a litt—"

"A little completely accurate?" Buggy asked pointedly. Cam shrugged and nodded, looking shame faced once more. "Where are we?" Buggy asked again.

"Amberhill," Cam said, reaching out for his own slice.

"Never heard of it," Buggy said, "We talking Northern California? Southern California?"

"Uh, Utah actually."

"What?!" Buggy jerked forward in her seat, pizza falling back to its plate and large eyes bugging out of her head. Her shout briefly drew the attention from the table of teens nearby. Three of them, football players by their builds and purposeful swagger, looked over at Cam suspiciously. They caught Buggy's eye, obviously ready to pounce if she said the word. She pulled a smile on her face and waved them off. They shrugged, and eased back down into their seats, satisfied, and began chatting with their friends once more. Buggy was suddenly and painfully reminded of Cooper, but quickly pushed him out of her mind. She had far more pressing matters.

"Utah?" Buggy scowled at Cam, voice down to a whisper.

"Yes," Cam said, matching her low tone.

"But I was in California."

"Yes."

"That's like..."

"Over eleven-hour drive away... if you're not stopping to sleep or eat," Cam said.

"You say that from experience?" Buggy asked.

"Well, we tried to get back as fast as we could, before you woke up," Cam shrugged.

"Didn't quite work out, did it?"

"No," Cam agreed. "It did not."

"I'm not apologizing for biting you," Buggy snapped after a few seconds of awkward silence.

"Would never dream of asking you to," Cam answered solemnly. "Justified under the circumstances."

"Why Utah?"

"It's where my cabin is," Cam shrugged. "Out of the way. Quiet. Best place, I thought. It's not like we could just get a hotel."

"Nah, dragging in a handcuffed and unconscious girl would definitely raise some red flags for the concierge," Buggy nodded, taking a long drink from her glass until ice hit her lip. She motioned towards Cam's untouched cup. He shook his head and pushed it towards her. She took it eagerly and turned back to the window as she sipped. "Utah. Huh..." She looked back to Cam. "I've barely been out of California before. Went to Vegas once, but that's about it."

"Not big on traveling?" Cam asked, trying awfully hard to sound nonchalant and utterly failing. He kept picking at the tablecloth, the napkins, rearranging his water glass and utensils, which was apparently a tick for calming his nerves. Unfortunately, it made Buggy want to sweep her arm across the table and nock the whole kit and caboodle onto the floor and out of his maddening, fidgeting reach. Or perhaps arrange them so they were all in line, as they *should* be. Instead, she took another long sip.

"Nope. Never really... no, actually I *have* had opportunities I've just not..." She had plenty of opportunities in the past. Back when she was sixteen, an old pen pal had offered to fly her out to Alaska to visit for a few weeks one summer. Well, technically, her *parents* were the ones that would be providing the plane tickets and housing, but the pen pal had thought up the idea and they agreed. The mere thought of traveling so far and for so long had nearly sent Buggy into a spiral of panic. She started envisioning how every scenario would play out, every possible problem that could develop. What if she missed her flight and waisted their ticket? What if the plane's wing fell off, or the food made her deathly ill? What if the plane ride itself went fine but the trip itself was awful? What if her pen pal ended up being completely different from how Buggy had imagined her? What if she didn't like Buggy in person? What if she was kidnapped from the airport? She took each and every possible terror of the trip and laid them, one by one, on that table in her mind. She considered each at painful length, under every colored light in the book, until finally, she was so mentally exhausted that she ended up backing out of the trip without even telling her parents it had been offered in the first place. And when she said no, when she closed that door, she felt instant relief. It was why "no" tended to be the answer that came to her lips most frequently about such things. Linny didn't tend to take "no" for an answer at all, otherwise Buggy would probably never have gotten much farther out of town then Sacramento. Other than with Linny or with Cooper, she never really...

"Never really, uh, I don't know. No. Not much of a traveler," Buggy finished dully, then squinted out at the lovely day. The sun was peeking through soft collection of clouds and reflected against the layer of snow that edged the sidewalks and powdered roofs of the buildings across the street. A little boy, probably no older than twelve years old and wearing a thick puffy jacket, was chasing after a second boy of the same age. He was packing a little sphere of snow in his hands as he ran, laughing, face flushed. He cocked his arm back over his head, ready to let the snowball fly when Buggy wondered. "Shouldn't there be more snow?" she asked.

"Hmm?" Cam frowned out the window, fingers pausing their fidgeting.

"The snow," Buggy said, looking back at him. "Isn't Utah kinda known for its snow? Great skiing or something." She looked back out the window at the lovely tufts of white, out of which you could make a great snowman or two, but definitely not skiing levels of downfall. "I mean, it's December. Shouldn't there be crazy amounts of snow?"

"We're actually at a lower elevation. In the more southwestern area, on the way towards Utah's Dixie. Makes for comparatively mild winters."

Buggy frowned. "Utah's Dixie?"

"Yes."

"Utah has a Dixie?"

"Sort of."

"Hmm," Buggy looked back out the window, but shot another look back at Cam, frowning. "We're at a lower elevation... but it's called Amberhill? Not Ambervalley?"

Cam shrugged, but also grinned this time. "Don't blame me, I didn't name it. I just live here."

Their tentative, awkward small talk died in the air between them, swooping in and out of existence like the lifespan of a house fly. Buggy sipped on her drink while Cam went back to fiddling with his utensils and slowly spinning his glass on its coaster, leaving watery smudges in its wake.

"Did you drug me?" Buggy asked suddenly, the question popping into her mind and then out of her mouth at the same instant.

"Hmm?" Cam asked, pulling his attention away from the glass in his hands.

"Eleven-hour drive, and I remember nearly none of it," Buggy said. "Did you drug me?"

"No," Cam shook his head. "No, absolutely not."

"Then how did you knock me out?"

"It's... complicated."

"As is everything with you," Buggy laughed another crispy, crunching laugh, and took a long gulp of her drink. When it became clear that Cam was unwilling to answer this particular question for the time being, she moved on. "So why the sneak attack though? Why not try to explain all of this to me—I donno—over coffee in *California*? Where I actually live?"

Cam laughed. It was a little raspy, but soft. "Because you'd have listened to a word we said?" Buggy frowned at the ice in her glass and said nothing. "We aren't completely out of our minds. We know how outrageous and insane our story is. And we needed to get you away from your life... because we don't know how close *she* is, but we knew The Daughter was breaking through. If she broke through around Theo and I, well, it would just be easier if she couldn't run away. And if she broke through while you were still around the people you loved..."

"She could kill them," Buggy realized, sitting back in her seat. That did it. That was the thought that broke through the numbness. Damn it.

"Yes. But that's not the only reason we took you away," Cam said.

"Oh goodie, there's more?" Buggy chuckled.

"Theo and I aren't the only ones who've been looking for you," Cam said.

"Susanna," Buggy said, and Cam nodded. "She wants to kill me. Keep The Daughter under wraps."

"Yes."

"She doesn't think I can fight The Daughter."

"Frankly, I don't think she cares. Susanna's a scared woman. Scared and angry. And for years she has laid all her pain, all her anger, all her frustrations and despair down at Loretta's feet. And now at yours."

"Sins of the father?" Buggy asked. "Or, in this case, sin of the reincarnation."

"Something like that," Cam said. "And if I was able to find you after all these years, its only a matter of time until—" He and Buggy looked down as "Take Me Home, Country Road" started playing in Cam's jacket pocket. He pulled out Buggy's cell phone and checked the name. His expression tightened.

"Who is it?" Buggy asked. Cam turned the phone around so that Buggy could see the caller ID.

Dad.

Buggy shrugged, wiped her fingers on the thick white napkin in her lap, and held out her hand. Cam hesitated, phone still ringing in his grip.

"Cam, my friend," Buggy said grinning, "They're probably way past suspicious by this point. I'm sure Theo was *very* convincing, texting like a girl he has never met before—to her family and friends that he has *also* never met before—but I actually *know* my family. If they don't hear from me, and I mean hear my *voice* and everything, it's not gonna go well," she motioned for the phone once more. Cam still hesitated. Buggy sighed. "They're in danger, right? Everyone I care about. In danger from me? From *her?*" Buggy asked, grin melting and features growing serious. "And they will be in danger till this is over?" Cam nodded slowly. Buggy gestured for the phone as it rang again. Cam slowly placed Buggy's phone into her palm. She pushed the "accept," button with her thumb and pressed the phone to her ear, never breaking eye contact with Cam.

"Hey there, Dad!" she said. "What's up?"

13

Sandra slid seamlessly from building anxiety to utter panic. It took only ten minutes to find the tapes. Buggy had stacked them neatly inside the worn gray bag and tucked them beneath her bed. Sandra hadn't really known what she was looking for when she had started her second unauthorized search of her little sister's bedroom. Maybe more bottles of alcohol. Maybe something stronger. She didn't really know. What she did know, was that her little sister, no matter what she was going through, or where she might have gone, would never—never—leave those tapes behind. Those tapes were glued to her. When she went to work, when she went to *Friends* Marathon Friday's, she always had that bag of cassettes. Even when she was a kid, she barely left it. Once she even took it on a school trip, tucking a few of the tapes in her backpack for safe keeping. As if afraid that if she didn't have them within reach, they would disappear. Now, recently she *had* been keeping them under the bed when she went to work, because she was taking public transportation while waiting for her car to be fixed, but if Buggy had planned on being away from home for a few days to cool off, she would have taken the bag with her. And yet, here it was, left behind. But Buggy would never have done that.

Not voluntarily at least.

She had already called her dad and left a message on his machine. She had actually talked to her mom on the phone, but she had not heard from Buggy either.

"Honey, I think you're being a little paranoid," her mother spoke sweetly in her ear. "She just texted me this morning."

"But have you talked to her, I mean actually **spoken** to her," Sandra had asked.

"San, are you okay?" her mother asked. "Are things with you and Christina going alright?"

Sandra took a deep breath. She loved her mom and knew she was trying very hard to be cool with the whole "her daughter dating a girl" thing. But her mom had grown up in a fairly sheltered, hardcore conservative family and was still trying to wrap her mind around her daughter liking women. She knew her mother half expected—and probably half hoped—that Sandra would wake up one morning and suddenly realize she liked dick. It didn't matter that Sandra had never shown interest in men. Didn't matter that she and Christina had been dating for years now. Anytime Sandra sounded irritated or upset, her mother's first question was "is it because of Christina?"

"Everything is going great with Christina, Mom," Sandra said. "I'm not worried about Christina. I'm worried about Buggy."

"Oh, you know her," she said, and Sandra could almost hear her mother rolling her eyes. "She sometimes drops of the edge of the Earth for a few days. She always comes back though." Sandra had to catch herself from explaining that Buggy only did that with *her*. Buggy and their mother's relationship took a nosedive after the divorce. They weren't exactly antagonistic with each other, but Buggy did tend to get irritated, and had a very short fuse when it came to their mother. Hell, Buggy got more pissed with their mom about her "Christina" comments then Sandra herself. After one Christmas, the first one that Sandra had brought Christina, their mother had made some offhand homophobic comment that made Buggy so furious, she didn't speak to her for two months after. But Buggy never did that with Sandra. No matter what happened between them, they never shut each other out.

"Just," Sandra said, rubbing her eyes. "Just call me when you hear from her next, okay?"

"No problem, Sweetie." They hung up and Sandra had gone back to ransacking her little sister's room. She had felt guilty the entire time, just as she had the first time she went through her things without permission. She felt like one of those mothers in the old sixty's TV shows going through her daughter's diary. Violating her privacy. But that guilt had fissured and melted away the instant she laid eyes on the gray shoulder bag under the bed.

Her phone began to ring from the kitchen. Sandra dropped the bag on Buggy's bed and darted for it. She picked it up and answered without checking the ID.

"Buggy?" she asked, out of breath.

"No, San. It's me," her father spoke, smile in his voice.

"Dad," she started, barely able to make her words understandable. They crammed together in her haste, all fighting to be the first out of her mouth. They tumbled off her tongue in a confused jumble, each more eager to be heard then the next. "Dad, I think something's wrong. Buggy's gone, and she hasn't talked to me, and she's only texting, and she *left her bag*, Dad. She left her tapes!"

"Whoa, whoa, Sweetheart, slow down!" Brandon Pierce answered. "What's wrong?"

"Buggy. It's Buggy. She hasn't been home and I haven't been able to get ahold of her and I think she's in tro—"

"Buggy?" he asked. "I just talked to her. She's fine."

Sandra stopped her agitated pacing around the room. "What? You talked to her? Like, *actually* talked to her? Like, on the phone?"

"Yeeeesss...." her father said. "She took a trip with some friends from work. She said she told you. You okay, hun?"

Why did everyone keep asking *her* that?

"I'm fine, Dad. Wait, no, I'm *not* fine. What do you mean you talked to her?"

"Well... 'talking' is a word. It usually refers to at least two people opening their mouths and speaking at one another," her father laughed at his own joke. Sandra resisted the urge to roll her eyes. Buggy would have found it hilarious, but Sandra wasn't in the mood. "After I heard your message, I called her."

"And she texted you back?" Sandra asked, ready to pounce.

"No, she picked up."

"Wait, what?" Sandra asked.

"Yeah, we talked for a half an hour or so."

"Seriously? How did she sound? She sound okay?"

"She sounded fine... Sandra, are *you* okay?" Sandra didn't reply. Her phone vibrated against her ear, and she checked the incoming call.

Buggy.

"Dad, I gotta go. Buggy's calling me," Sandra said, excitedly.

"Oh, okay," he said, sounding confused, but unfazed. "Tell her 'Hi' for me."

"Okay, gotta go." She hung up and answered the new call. "Buggy?"

"Hey Sandra," her sister's voice spoke through the phone. Sandra slumped with relief against the counter by the sink.

"Buggy?"

"That's my name."

"Are you okay?" Sandra asked. "I mean, what the hell is going on?"

"Sandra—"

"I mean, you lied to me for starters."

"What?"

"You told me you were staying at Linny's," Sandra reminded her.

"Oh... right. So, she called you I assume?"

"You assume right, *you ass*," Sandra frowned. "I mean, what the hell?"

"Sandra—"

"And you left your bag?" Sandra said, plowing on, head still spinning. "You left your bag of tapes. You *never* leave your bag of tapes."

"Sandra—"

"And why the hell haven't you been home? And where the hell are you? And why haven't you been answering my calls. And—"

"Sandra," Buggy's voice cut in, "My dad showed up."

"Oh yeah!" Sandra started again, irritation flaring. "And you pick up dad's first call? But *I* call you a hundred time and you can't be bothered? And what is this story about you being off with some 'friends from work'? Buggy, I know all of your '*friend* from work' and she's—"

"No, Sandra, you don't understand," Buggy cut in once more. "Not 'Dad' *our* dad. I mean my birth father."

Sandra froze in place, shaking her head, seemingly to fling off her sudden confusion. "Wait, what?"

"My birth father," Buggy repeated. "He found me on Monday. That's the real reason I didn't come home."

"I don't... I mean... what?" Sandra plopped down in a chair by the counter, legs unable to support her any longer.

"My birth father. His name is Cam. He's apparently been looking for me for a while... and he finally found me."

"... Oh... I mean... Oh," Sandra stammered. "I mean, are you sure he's actually... he's not some random asshole trying to pull something—"

"No. I'm one hundred percent sure."

"But—"

"Sandra, he has the last recording my mother ever left me."

"Oh..." Sandra took a deep breath. "Oh my."

"Yep..." Buggy's voice trailed off.

"Lord, girl. Are you okay?" Sandra leaned in her seat, as if ready to bolt forward and take care of anything. Buggy just needed to give the "go ahead" and she'd be off.

Buggy laughed. "Oh, shit, I don't know yet. Probably not. Just trying to take it one day at a time. I'm really sorry I lied. To you and Linny."

"Why didn't you just tell me?" Sandra asked, but all her frustration had vanished.

"I dunno, I just," Buggy paused, "I guess I just needed some time. I really wanted to figure out all of this on my own. Figure out how I felt before I had to explain it to anyone else. I just needed some time."

"I guess I can get that," Sandra nodded. "But why didn't you come home? And where have you been all this time?"

"Cam, my bio dad, he actually needed some help."

"What kind of help?" Sandra frowned, suspicion raising its head and sniffing at the air, catching the scent of something foul.

"He's sick."

"What do you mean he's sick?"

"Uh... Leukemia."

"Leukemia?" Sandra asked, taking deep involuntary gasp.

"Yeah... he needs bone marrow for treatment, and he's been having a hard time finding a match. Since I'm his daughter, and we're both B-, he asked if I could get a test and—"

"Oh, Buggy," Sandra covered her face with her hand, stomach clenching tight.

"Anyway, we ended up being a match, so I said I could donate and—"

"Buggy...."

"Sandra..." Buggy mimicked.

"Be serious now."

"I am being serious."

"Oh Buggy," Sandra drew her hand down her face. "Buggy he's using you. You know that, right? He's *using* you."

"Yeah," Buggy's voice was soft and quiet, almost guilty. "I know. Maybe he is, but Sandra, he's my *birth dad*. What else am I supposed to do?"

"Where are you?" Sandra asked, already checking her watch, ready to gage how long it would take to get to wherever Buggy was about to say she was.

"I'd rather not say just yet," Buggy answered. "I'm a little worried you'll just rush over here and try to drag me out the door."

"Buggy, bone marrow transplants are famously painful," Sandra frowned.

"I know."

"So, tell me—"

"No," Buggy said, and Sandra could hear it in her voice, that tone her baby sister adopted whenever she had decided something and wouldn't be swayed. Sandra had heard it many times before. The tone she had after their mother tried to talk Buggy out of dying her hair pink in middle school. Or when she had announced she wouldn't be going to Claremont McKenna, and instead—as their dad had suggested—she would be going to junior college. It was her "and that's final" voice. "I'm good, I'm safe, that's all you need to know for right now. I'll tell you where I am soon. Okay?"

Sandra did not *at all* think that was okay, but there was no use fighting the point. She could probably figure out a way to track Buggy using her phones GPS later if she felt the need... although she was pretty sure that would destroy any sort of trust that might be left between them. So, she'd save that as a last resort, and this wasn't yet last resort territory. Buggy was on the phone, she was talking to her, she was safe, and she was a grown ass woman who could make her own decisions involving her biological father but....

"Are you sure?" Sandra had to ask, just one more time. "Go through all that for a man you have just met? You trust him, *believe* him, enough for that? Are you sure you wanna do this?"

"Yes," Buggy said without hesitation. "Yes, I do. I have to."

Sandra chuckled. "You're a goddamn angel. You know that, right?"

Buggy laughed on the other end. "Again, I'm sorry I lied."

"It's okay," Sandra said. "You don't have to talk about anything yet, not till you're ready, but please pick up when I call." Sandra smiled. "For a second there I thought you and ET had become best friends."

"What?" Buggy asked, sounding completely confused.

"You know," Sandra frowned, "abducted by aliens?"

"Oh, ha, nope. No aliens," Buggy said with a laugh. Was that laugh a little forced? Or was Sandra hearing things? "But don't tell Mom or Dad, okay. I don't want them calling me every few minutes, and you know that's exactly what Dad would be doing."

"Okay, but you will send up the bat signal if you need anything right?"

"Of course, Batman, of course."

"And you're coming home soon, ya?" Sandra couldn't help but press.

"Yes. We are having the procedure day after tomorrow and then we just need a little time to recover. Me, not as long. Couple days maybe? For him it will be longer. A month, probably longer."

"A month!?" Sandra's head felt like it might just give up and explode all over the kitchen.

"No, don't worry," Buggy said, hastily. "I'm not staying here that long. I've got work I need to get back to. I'll probably just stay the week or so."

"Another week?" Sandra asked, crest fallen, but at least it wasn't a month. She didn't know how leukemia treatments or the whole bone marrow transplant thing worked, and why on Earth would she? She wasn't a doctor, but she could imagine such a procedure would need time to recoup.

"Yeah. I think the first few weeks are the most dangerous, and he's not going to be feeling too hot. He doesn't have anyone else, and he shouldn't be left alone right now. He kinda needs me."

If he needed you so bad maybe he shouldn't have left you in the first place.

Sandra sighed, "Can I do anything?"

"Nah, I just need to do this. Then I'll come home. Promise."

Sandra nodded. She wanted to say so much more. Wanted to ask the million questions racketing around her brain. Why had it taken her father so long to find her? Why hadn't he been there to stop her mother from abandoning her? Had *he* helped abandon her? Did he tell her anything about her mother—that elusive woman on those tapes? Did he mention where her mother might be now? But she didn't ask any of these questions. She knew Buggy wasn't ready to dive into them. Not today.

"Hey, Buggy?" she asked instead.

"Yeah?"

"How are you doing? Really?"

Buggy gave a shuttering sigh. "Honestly, I'm holding on by the skin of my teeth here."

"You say the word and I'll be there in a heartbeat," Sandra said.

"Nah. Thank you, but this is something I gotta do on my own."

"Well, if you ever change your mind, I'm just one call away. You know, as long as you actually pick up." Buggy laughed.

"I love you, girl."

"Love you too," Sandra smiled.

"Talk to you tomorrow?"

"Sounds good."

"Bye, San."

"Bye, Buggy."

* * *

Buggy ended the call, scowling at the phone. She hated lying to Sandra. It hadn't even been a twisted half-truth, no, that had just been a full out, no holds bard, bold faced lie. It left Buggy feeling guilty and *slimy*. Although feeling guilty and slimy was a small price to pay for keeping her big sister safe. Buggy looked up at Cam, who was dabbing at the top of his pizza with a napkin, soaking up a surprising amount of grease as he did so.

"Worried about your girlish figure?" she asked, grinning.

"Cholesterol," Cam said, taking a bite.

"How was that?" she asked, referring to the phone call. Cam shrugged, holding the napkin over his mouth as he spoke.

"I'm actually A+," he said.

"Well, we aren't exactly sitting in a hospital room either," Buggy shrugged, and grabbing herself another slice. "And I doubt Sandra is ever gonna be poking you with a needle to check your blood type so..." She took a bite. It was *really* good. Bert may not know how to keep his little sister from making googly eyes at his customers, but damn he could bake a pizza.

"Eh, it's alright, don't think you actually need the same blood type for a bone marrow transplant, anyway."

"No?" Buggy asked, dabbing at her lips with a napkin. "I really wouldn't know. Just got the idea after watching a couple shitty doctor TV shows."

Cam laughed another rasping laugh. "And that was your sister," he squinted in thought, "Sandra, right?"

"Right," Buggy said nodding.

"And she calls you 'Buggy'?"

"Yep."

"Uh, why, exactly?" he asked, scooping up a few stray pieces of pepperoni and dropping them on his slice. Buggy chuckled and pointed an index finger at her face. Cam just blinked. "I don't get it."

Buggy laughed. "Well, it kinda started in elementary school. There was this little girl named Candy Finberge..."

14

Cam sat, listening to Buggy with rapt attention and a heart which felt like it was trying to burst his ribcage wide open. She was here. He had found her. He had found her, and he had gotten her to believe. He was sitting before his baby girl, although she wasn't much of a baby girl any longer. No, she was looking more and more like her mother with every passing second as her cold eyes relaxed, and that oh-so-familiar smile began to slide naturally across her face. Although there were differences. Different mannerisms, different habits. He noticed how she tended to tilt her head slightly to the side when she was telling a story, something he had never noticed with Loretta, and he had noticed everything. Buggy also had little eccentricities that her mother didn't. For example, she seemed very picky about the placement of her utensils, all needing to be directly in line with her plate, even though she wasn't using them to eat her pizza. She kept her water glass on top of a folded napkin to her right, while her drink sat on another (equally precisely folded) napkin to her left. He also noticed how frequently the glass on her left kept being filled and emptied and refilled again. She told her stories and he watched her raise each drink and empty it, but he made no comment. She wasn't getting trashed, in fact, her tolerance seemed unreasonably strong for such a small girl. She was no stick, but she wasn't enrolling in any pie eating competitions either. But that wasn't why he didn't say anything. He didn't have the right.

Hey, honey, I know you don't know me from Adam, but let's have the first father/daughter bonding moment interrupted by a mini-intervention on top of everything else. I know you thought I abandoned you for your entire life and left you to rot in an alley with a bag of tapes and no real explanation, but how about I start telling you how to live your life, hmm? Sound good?

No, he had no right to say jack shit. Besides, the girl had gone through a lot over the past few days. She was entitled to a few drinks. He would have happily joined her if he didn't have to drive them back to the cabin. However, he was happy enough—beyond happy enough—to just sit and listen to this girl, *his* little girl, telling him her story. Her life. The life he missed. He swallowed back the lump in his throat and smiled through the pain.

".... And then Linny grabbed the microphone out of my hand," Buggy was tearing up with the hilarity of her own story. "And she *screams* at the guy, and I'm quoting: 'Don't you fucking heckle my best friend the day before her birthday, you skinny, limp-dick donkey.' He was buying me drinks the rest of the night as an apology." She burst out laughing.

"This Linny sounds like a card," Cam said smiling at the sound of Buggy's laughter. Now *that was* like her mother.

"She is," Buggy said, laughter slowly dying down and smile sliding off her face. "That was a good night... but the next morning the nightmares started." She looked up at Cam.

"Which one did you have that night?" he asked, his smile also gone.

"The burning house." Cam saw her shudders shudder a little. "The next night it was the woman in black."

"The one who slits her wrist?" Cam asked quietly. Buggy blinked, surprised.

"How did you..." Buggy nodded, realizing the answer before he had the chance to say it. "My mom. She had the same dreams?"

"Yes," Cam said. "Unfortunately, she did."

"What is that about?" Buggy asked, her elbows hitting the table as she ran her fingers through her hair. "I mean, what the hell?"

"We were never really sure," Cam said, leaning back in his chair. "Our best guess was a past reincarnation who came home from her husband's funeral. Couldn't get much more detail. She said the dream was fairly fuzzy."

"It is," Buggy nodded, leaning in, relieved to finally have someone to talk to about this shit. To discuss this insane horror show that had been playing in her head. "And it's one of those 'trapped' ones, you know? Where you're dreaming but can't wake up."

Cam Nodded. "Yes. Loretta said those were the worst kind—for her at least."

"And when you try to wake up," Buggy rubbed red tinged eyes with the palms of her hands. "And she just looks at you with that creepy grin before she does it."

"... What?" Cam said, doing his very best to keep his cool, although his entire body had gone ridged with fear.

"You know," Buggy said, looking up and leaning back. "That creepy grin while she's looking in the mirror."

"Loretta said she was crying," Cam said, leaning forward, tension rising in his shoulders and back. His stomach churned uneasily against the pound of pizza grease he had consumed, but that didn't concern him at the moment—not one bit.

"Well, she was. The first few times she just cried and went to cutting." Buggy crinkled her nose in disgust "But on the later time, when I tried to wake up, the reflection smiled at me. It was like she was mocking me. And *then* she slit her wrists." Buggy frowned. "That never happened to Loretta?"

"No," Cam said. An uneasy feeling circled his insides like a cat, cold claws digging here and there as it kneaded down into his gut, getting comfortable, ready to stay awhile. "No, that's new."

"Shit," Buggy whispered, eyes widening to an almost inhuman size. "That was *her* wasn't it. That was The Daughter." Buggy's wide eyes filled with fear. "She can control my fucking dreams?"

That should be the least of your concerns. Cam almost said, but he bit it back. He didn't need to scare her more than she already was.

"Come on," he said instead, pulling money from his wallet, dropping a few bills on the table and getting to his feet. "We should get back. We need to get started."

* * *

When they got back to the cabin, Cam and Buggy found Theo struggling to drag the burnt and ash covered couch out into the snow dusted yard— with little success. He had gotten it about halfway through the door when the thing had jammed into place. He fought it, pushing and pulling two of the legs. Buggy watched him as she closed the Jeep's door with a soft thud.

"Struggles?" she asked, she and Cam stepped onto the porch where Theo had taken a pause, leaning against the stuck couch.

"Lil bit," he answered, smiling but looking wary all the same. Buggy didn't blame him. This was a bit of a messed-up situation all around, not to mention the last time he had seen her she had nearly set him and the entire cabin on fire... in her sleep... because that's normal.

"What are you doing?" Cam frowned at Theo's handy work.

"It's stinking up the joint," Theo answered, eyes flickering back and forth between Buggy and Styger before turning an exasperated glare at the couch. "It's making the whole place smell like burnt hair and singed leather."

"Yeah, I got that," Cam said, crinkling his nose as he leaned down to inspect where the couch's side connected to the door frame. "What I mean was, why the hell are you trying to pull it out straight? You should have takin it out at an angle."

"Well thank you, captain hindsight," Theo shot back, scowling.

"Can you push it back inside?" Buggy asked. "Get it unjammed and start over."

"Was trying to do just that when you guys pulled up," Theo said, scratching the back of his neck. "Not having much success solo."

Buggy shrugged and hopped on top of the couch. Puffs of dark gray and black ash burst up around her feet, soon spreading and dispersing through the air around her head. She coughed a little as she jumped to the ground on the other side, turning to grab the arm of the couch from inside the cabin.

"I'll pull," she said, planting her feet, getting ready, "You guys push, and then when it's unjammed, we tilt. Okay?"

"You sure you got that over there?" Cam asked, trying his best not to sound patronizing, and wincing a little as he did anyway. She just grinned over at him, apparently unfazed.

"Oh please, I'm much stronger than I look. Ready?" They nodded and after a few moments of gritted teeth and a nasty little whining sound of the couch against the wooden door frame, it shifted a foot back into the house, enough to get it unjammed. "Okay, tilt." They did, and were able to slide the couch all the way out the door. When it was though the doorway, Cam took over Buggy's side and he and Theo carried the poor, battered piece of furniture out past the porch where it would serve as an extremely unattractive yard ornament. But it would at least not be filling the room with its noxious smell.

"Thanks," Theo spoke to both of them, but he was looking at Buggy.

"Sure," Buggy shrugged. "I mean you guys are trying to save my life, least I can do."

"So, you're..." Theo looked from her to Cam and back again, "You're on board?"

"I guess," Buggy shrugged, "I mean you definitely took the absolute shittiest route of going about it, but you are trying to help me. So yeah, I'm on board. And the least I can do is help throw out the furniture I ruined." She turned to Cam. "Sorry about that by the way." Cam just shrugged and turned to head inside. Buggy was about to follow, when she remembered something.

"Oh shoot," she said, backtracking and heading for the ruined couch.

"What's wrong?" Cam asked, watching as she dropped to her knees and started rooting around under one of the cushions. She found what she was looking for and straightened up, heading back towards them. Something glinted silver in her hand. It looked like a thin blade. A scalpel to be exact.

"Here," she said, stepping onto the porch and holding it out to Cam, handle first. He frowned down at it, a little confused. "You'll find your first aid kit is missing a little something." Cam looked back up at her, not taking the scalpel.

"What were you going to do with that?" he asked. His question wasn't accusatory, there was no hint of intent to blame.

"If I got the chance?" Buggy answered, with a little shrug, "I was going to kill you with it."

Cam chuckled and nodded, unsurprised. He looked in her large eyes. Eyes that were strong. Strong, but... "You sure you have that in you?" he asked. Again, simple curiosity.

"Apparently so," Buggy barked a stale laugh, holding the handle up a little higher, as if reminding him it was still there. He still made no move to take it. "If my alter ego's track record is any indication."

Cam's smile melted away. "You aren't her, you know. The Daughter. You aren't her."

"How do you figure? Isn't that exactly what a reincarnation is?" Buggy asked. "A re-birth of the same person?"

"Sort of, but not exactly. Every time you're reborn, it's a clean slate. Yes, she is part of you, but she isn't *you*. You are your own soul. Your own experiences, your own choices. You make yourself. Not her."

Buggy watched his face for a few minutes, looking for a lie. She found none. "How can you be sure?" she asked, the blade dipping in her grip a bit, quickly being forgotten by the hand that held it.

Cam's smile returned. "Because of your mother." He looked down at the blade and nodded. "You can keep that if you want."

"Cam..." Theo started. His eyes had never left the scalpel since the moment it had touched the girl's fingers. Cam ignored him.

"If it makes you feel any better about any of this," Cam said, smiling down at his daughter. "You keep it."

Buggy looked at the blade, as if realizing once more that she was holding such a thing. She thought a few minutes, then she shook her head slowly.

"No. She *smiled* at me, Cam," she said, voice low. "She smiled at me before she slit my wrists. I bet she smiled before she... before she burned those people...." she raised the blade again and looked at Cam with stony determination. "It's not just me in here. I believe that now. And if she gets me, I don't want to give her a blade too."

"She is not going to get you," Cam said firmly, matching his daughters stony gaze, willing her to believe him—have faith in him. He knew he had did not deserve it, but God he wanted her to. "I promise you."

Buggy smiled, but her eyes remained hard as she continued holding the blade out. He still didn't take it. Her eyes narrowed at him a little, not in accusation, or irritation, but confusion. Curiosity. A curiosity that slowly fell away as she looked over at Theo, who was standing a little ridged, eyes still on her. She blinked, and a trickle of understanding pooled in her eyes, gathering like rain in a puddle. She smiled, sadly, and turned to hold the scalpel out to Theo instead. He looked at it, then back at her. She nodded as if to say: *That's what you're here for, right?* Theo slowly reached out and took the scalpel from her loose fingers.

"Uh... hey," Buggy said, dropping her hand away. Her eyes followed. "Sorry about earlier."

"Earlier?" Theo asked, bemused.

"About, you know, threatening to cut your tongue out," Buggy said, fiddling a little with the edge of her shirt. "Not sure where that came from."

"That's alright," Theo said, then his eyes flickered down to the scalpel. "Although, a bit scarier now that I know it wasn't exactly an empty threat." He grinned. She returned it with a shy, twitching smile of her own. Then Theo glanced at Cam. Whatever he saw there made his smile falter. "I'll just... go put this away," he said awkwardly, and darted inside without another word.

"So," Buggy said, turning back to Cam as if nothing had just happened. "Phase one of 'get Buggy on board' is complete. What's phase two?"

"Phase two," Cam said, taking a deep breath through his teeth and letting it blow out in one hard, harsh whistle. "Well... that's where things get tricky."

"Oh God, I hope you're joking," Buggy laughed nervously.

15

"Okay, you definitely weren't joking," Buggy said rubbing the spot between her eyes where a migraine was slowly but surely building. It thudded, pulsing pain out towards her temples, wanting to burst through her ears. This conversation wasn't helping.

"I know, it sounds ridiculous," Cam was saying leaning forward in his seat, elbows on his knees. Without the giant smoldering couch, the living room was sparse for furniture. There was one high backed blue suede armchair with a matching footrest, which Buggy claimed immediately. She flopped herself down and snagging one of the few remaining blankets that had not been burned to dust after her last nap. She wrapped it around her and hunkered down, head poking out of the soft pile of flannel. Cam and Theo made no protest and pulled in a few wooden chairs from the dining area. They placed them across from Buggy, so they could face her while filling her in on phase two. Which, apparently, was the paranormal equivalent of "mind over matter."

"I'm supposed to 'think' The Daughter under control?" she asked, dropping her hand and looking up at Cam.

"Not exactly," Cam said, at the same time Theo answered: "Yes."

Buggy looked between one and then the other. "Umkay, you guys are just *filling* me with confidence over here."

"A lot of the containment happens in your head," Cam explained, "But there's a lot more to it than just 'thinking.' Your mind is just the tool. Not the whole workshop."

"What?" Buggy frowned, eyebrows chocking above her large eyes in confusion.

"Just—Cam—shuddup a second," Theo said, waiving away whatever Cam might have said next and turning back to Buggy. "Basically, we put you in a hypnotic state. A special hypnotic state. One that I will be able to help you with."

"Because of your empathic... psychic ability?" Buggy asked, dubiously.

"Exactly. You then take a 'deep dive' into your subconscious, but not just *your* subconscious."

"You mean I'll be diving into *her* subconscious?" Buggy asked. This was all still confusing as hell, but she finally felt like she was finding a toe hold. If she held tight enough, maybe she could reach another grip. With any luck at all, she might yet pull herself up to the top of this shit pile to a level of understanding where she could breathe.

"Actually, you can't get *into* The Daughter's subconscious," Theo corrected, waving Cam away as he opened his mouth, only to close it again. "She is the original subconscious—the original *consciousness*—the original *you*."

Oh God. Buggy thought, heart sinking. *She's the original me? Does that make her the* **real** *me?* Did that make Buggy a fake? Was she just a carbon copy of the real thing? Did that make her less? *I'm I... am I even real? Am I even...* Buggy stamped down hard on that line of thinking, chasing it away with the echo of her mother's words.

It's your turn now.

Theo was still speaking. "We will be going through the *other* subconscious minds and the memories of the *other* reincarnations. Those that came after The Daughter."

Buggy cleared her throat. "I'm a little confused. I can go through their memories, but not hers? Why? Because she's the original?"

"Yeah, the other subconscious minds, well, they are more like you. They are reincarnations, same as you, so you are better able to access their memories, especially the more recent the reincarnation. The deeper you go, the older the memories, the closer to The Daughter's *original* memories, the less ability you have—the less control. The Daughter's mind itself, she's got complete control over that. You wouldn't be able to get in unless she *let* you in... and she's probably not going to do that."

"Okay," Buggy said, "but I can get though the others? I mean, I can 'dive' through the other reincarnations subconscious? Till I reach hers?"

"Yes," Theo smiled. She saw a spark in his eye, one she recognized. It was the same look that Mr. Harrison would get after he discussed a particularly difficult equation. It was that excitement of being able to explain and getting someone to understand. She always thought of it as the "teacher's spark." It seemed at home in Theo's eyes. "You can dive through those, and when you get deep enough, you can at least *reach* The Daughter's subconscious. Even if you can't go in. You can reach the place where her mind is still partially tethered down, keeping her from gaining control."

"Okay, let's say I figure out how to do that. Let's say I reach her," Buggy said, "then what?'

"Let's just start there," Cam cut in. "That is going to be a lot of work on its own. We should take it one step at a time."

"Okay," Buggy let a sigh and chuckled nervously. "I still think this is insane."

"That's okay," Cam nodded.

"Join the club," Theo agreed.

"So... when do we get started?" Buggy asked.

"Tomorrow," Cam said, at the same time that Theo said: "Right now."

Buggy looked back and forth between them. Theo was looking at Cam with an expression that was one-part confusion, one parts caution and a whole lot of "are you fucking kidding me?"

"Tomorrow will be fine," Cam repeated smiling, eyes on Buggy.

"Cam." Theo words came out in a hiss.

"She's been through a lot today. She needs some rest. Time to recoup. Tomorrow will be fine," Cam said, looking over to Theo with ice in his gaze. Theo met his glare for a moment, then shrugged. *Your funeral*, that shrug said without a word.

Buggy watched this interaction, nerves rising. "Do you guys actually know how long I have to do this? Before it's too late?"

"Everything will be fine, Briar," Cam said, darting Theo a dark, warning glare before he could say anything. He turned back to her, reassuring smile returned. "I promise. Come on." Cam got to his feet, knees popping as he did so. "We've got an extra room set up for you." Buggy untangled herself from her little nesting place within the bundle of blanket and followed Cam into the hall. She looked back over her shoulder to see Theo still in his chair, eyes on the fire. He was shaking his head.

16

Helena cursed under her breath as the wrench slipped from the screw. She swore loud enough for her voice to eco across the entire garage when it slipped again. Some utter moron who had no business being under *any* car (let alone a beautiful nineteen-sixty-six Mustang Fastback) had completely stripped the screw at the bottom of the oil pan. Not only was it smooth and round, not allowing for any grip to turn it, but it irritated the shit out of Helena. Yes, she appreciated people who worked on their own cars. She herself loved working on her babies, that's how she came to own this auto repair shop in the first place. She had her own 1966 Dodge Charger and her mother's 1965 Thunderbird which she had been working on since she was sixteen. But it was in this very shop, then called Dennis's Repair Place, that she really learned how to shine. She loved working on cars. They were one big puzzle that she could take apart and then put back together. And she was good at it. Really good at it. Dennis took a personal appreciation of her work, quickly offering her a job. But it was his affection that caused him to leave her the shop in his will. Dennis was an amiable old coot, one who never made time to build a family of his own or sire any heirs to his little kingdom of gears, grease, and backfires. But he always had a soft spot for the wiry, young girl who broke down in front of his garage but refused to let him touch the Thunderbird.

"Just tell me how to do it," Helena had said, stepping between him and her mother's car, "and *I'll* do it." He did, and soon the Thunderbird was purring like a kitten. You could get any car to purr if you just put in the hours, read the books, and teach yourself how to make it run. That took time and effort, however, and most people took little time and didn't want to put in any effort. It led to stupid mistakes, like stripped bolts on cars whose oil hasn't been changed in a year and a half.

Cars made sense to Helena, people on the other hand—people were stupid.

The wrench slipped again.

"Shit!" She tossed the wrench out from under the car. It clattered across the cement floor, sliding till it hit some metal cabinet with a loud rattling bang. Helena dragged herself out from under the poor misused Mustang, grumbling under her breath. She grabbed a towel off the car's side mirror and was wiping her greasy hands when she heard a sound from behind her. She turned. She was alone in the shop. At least, she was supposed to be. It was ten past seven, and all her employees had long since headed home for the day. She had stayed back just a bit longer, determined to change the Mustang's oil before the day was out, even if it killed her. So, she was surprised to see someone silhouetted in the open mouth of the garage door. The night outside was dark, but the lights in the office glared bright behind the stranger who leaned against the frame that opened into the side of the work room.

"We're closed," Helena said, squinting at the figure, towel still in hand.

"I know," the figure said. "This isn't business." Helena scowled as the figure stepped into the garage. The overhead lights lit up her face. She was a pretty girl. Tall, blond, black leather jacket snugged tight around an ample chest and skinny waist. She looked to Helena like one of the bimbo cheerleading Barbies from her old high school had decided to change her persona to black-leather-badass. Although the look worked for her somehow. She still had that high ponytail that would have bounced around nicely with pom-poms, but she wasn't holding pom-poms and her eyes didn't speak of held back cheers for a good game. No, her eyes were cold. Determined. Dangerous.

"Who are you then?" Helena asked, tossing the towel through the Mustang's open window. It flopped heavily to the plastic laid out across the floor. "And if it's not to get your car fixed, I'm not sure what—"

"My mother sends her regards," the blond said, cutting her off.

"Your mother?" Helena scowl deepened. Then she realized, she had seen those eyes before. Seen that icy stare in someone else's face. "Oh, shit," Helena's scowl melted to a smile, but her gut clenched. "You're Susanna's girl, aren't you?"

"Guilty," the blond said smiling. It was a sweet thing, matching well with her high ponytail, but her eyes remained cool and watchful as she stepped further into the room.

"Well, shit, nice to meet you..." Helena trailed off, holding out her hand to the girl.

"Waverly," she answered, returning Helena's grip in a strong, leather-gloved hand. What was with this girl and black leather?

"Well, nice to meet you, Waverly," Helena took back her hand, being very careful to keep her smile in place. "How has your mother been, by the way?"

"Not very well, I'm afraid," Waverly said, stepping past Helena, eyes trailing around the large garage. They swept from car to car, from one wall of tools to the other, noticing everything. "She had a stroke a few years back."

"I'm sorry to hear that," Helena said, watching the girl move, thick black motorcycle boots tapping softly against the cement. "Is she doing better now?"

"Not really," Waverly said, eyes falling on the discarded wrench on the ground beside the metal cabinet. She walked over to it. "It left her paralyzed from the waist down."

"That's horrible," Helena said, growing a little nervous as she watched the girl lean down, fingers slowly picking the wrench off the floor.

"Yes. It is, isn't it?" The girl held the wrench before her eyes, turning it, examining the slight paint chips on the handle. "It's why she isn't here to ask you herself."

"Ask me what?" Helena asked, that clenching feeling starting to twist sickeningly in her gut. "What can I do for you, Waverly?"

"Where's your son, Helena?" the blond asked, cold eyes sliding from the wrench to Helena's face.

"Excuse me?" Helena asked, the false smile twitching.

"Your son," Waverly repeated, the wrench falling to her side, but still in her hands. "Theodore, isn't it? But he goes by Theo, right? Where is he?"

"I.... Why?" Helena asked, smile twitching a little more. She backed up a bit as the girl started walking slowly, passing her.

"You know what year it is, I trust?" Waverly asked, eyes trailing once more across the tools hanging on the walls. The wrench still twisted slowly by her thigh.

"Yes, I have a calendar," Helena tried to joke, but her throat was too dry to let any true humor slide past her lips. It got caught somewhere partway to her tongue. Waverly cast a brief half-smile her way.

"It's the twenty-fourth year. Twenty-four years since the woman died."

"Loretta died?" Helena tried to sound sincere in her surprise, but Waverly wasn't buying it. She turned to face Helena, and all traces of good humor were gone.

"Don't do that. Don't lie to me, Helena. You know that Loretta died. You know that she died during childbirth. You know that child became the next one. You know because Cam Styger told you. He tracked you down, much like we did. He told you when he came here and asked for your help. Well... not for *your* help. After Loretta, he has lost his ability to find the girl. But your son... your son is of The Fold, isn't he? A psychic? One of ours? Styger would need his help. So, he found you and came *here*. And because you are trying to lie to my face, I take it that Theo said 'yes.' He went with Styger to try to assist in his misguided plan to save the girl, didn't he? So, that boy I saw, the one that helped hustle the girl into the back of Styger's car, that was Theo, wasn't it?"

Helena said nothing, but her eyes darted up when Waverly mentioned what sounded like a kidnapping. What the hell was Stygers plan? She hadn't asked for details. There hadn't been time, and she decided it was better that she didn't know too much, anyway. She had wanted out, and she had gotten out. She had left The Fold behind. And when this was over Theo would be out too, Styger had promised her. But he had not mentioned anything about kidnapping.

"I don't know what you're talking about," Helena said.

"Of course not," Waverly turned away from her once more, and moved towards the open door to the office. "And I suppose you also expect me to believe that you haven't had any contact with your son? No texts? Calls? No heads up on what they are up to?"

"Waverly, I don't know what you're thinking of doing but—"

"I'm thinking of offering you a deal," she interrupted, back still turned to Helena. "You tell me where they are, and where they are going," she made it to the door, "you save my precious time, well then, when I find them—because believe me I *will* find them, one way or another—I will let your boy live. But if you insist on insulting my intelligence like this," she reached out, taking the handle and pulling the door closed with a soft click and turning around util her cold eyes were back on Helena. The wrench was still held tight in her other hand. "Well, then... that is a different conversation altogether."

"Waverly," Helena backed away from the girl as she stepped closer. The twist in her gut was bad enough to make her puke and panic started rising, choking her voice. She was supposed to be out. She had gotten out. She was supposed to be free from all this. Free from The Fold. And yet... "You really don't want to do this," she said to the girl with the same eyes as the woman she had once known so well and had once called sister.

"No," Waverly nodded, taking another step forward. "No, really I don't. But someone has to. Someone has to save everyone. Someone has to follow the dark threads till the end of the line. Someone has to stop her. Someone must do the dark things to protect the light. So please," she twisted the wrench in her fingers, and Helena's eyes darted down briefly to the cold, metal tool that had irritated her so thoroughly just a few short minutes before, "please, help me do that... I insist."

17

Theo was still sitting in front of the fire when Buggy shuffled out of her room at ten minutes to midnight. He was on the floor, legs crossed, and hands resting on his knees. His eyes were so focused on the flickering lights that he didn't notice her enter. When he did finally see her, he nearly jumped out of his skin.

"Sorry," Buggy said, hand over her chest as if to keep her own heart from leaping out and toppling to the floor.

"It's okay," Theo said, laughing a little, his own pulse slowing.

"Couldn't sleep either?" Buggy asked.

Theo shook his head. "Nope. Decided to practice."

"Ah, yes, the witchy-hoodoo-hypnosis-meditation thing?" Buggy asked, walking over and easing down into the armchair, reclaiming it.

"Exactly," Theo grinned. "What's your excuse?"

"Oh, I don't... strange place."

"And a messed-up situation," Theo scooched around on the floor until he faced her directly, elbows on his knees. "I'm really sorry. About how me met, I mean."

"The whole part where you knocked me out and chucked me in the back of Cam's Jeep?" Buggy asked with a half grin. Theo relaxed a little at the sight of it.

"Yeah. I'd say, 'let's start over,' but I'm pretty sure that's impossible."

"Forgiven... but not forgotten."

"Fair enough," Theo nodded.

"How did you do that, by the way?" Buggy asked, pulling the once discarded blanket back around her shoulders and snuggling deeper into the chair's cushion.

"Do what?" Theo asked. Buggy noticed his mouth drooped a little at the edges whenever he didn't understand.

"I just... dropped. I remember walking to the bus station and then..."
Buggy shook her head. "Cam told me you didn't drug me, but he wouldn't
say much else."

"Oh, that." Theo's eyes darted up towards the hall, as if waiting for
Cam to suddenly pop out and scold him for answering her question. When
Cam didn't appear, he turned back to Buggy. "No, we didn't drug you,
nothing like that... we just... called her name."

"What?" Buggy frowned, but then she remembered. She remembered
the last thing she heard, just before her mind tumbled into darkness and
her knees met concrete. "Bennu," she said. "I remember you saying—
what's wrong?"

At the mention of the name Theo had flinched and tensed all over.

"Don't say it out loud," he pleaded.

"Why not? You did," Buggy's frown deepened.

"Yes, but that was extraordinary circumstances."

"And you've lost me," Buggy shook her head.

"That," Theo said, pointing into the air as if the name "Bennu" was
floating in three dimensional letters between them. "That name is the
name of the original reincarnation. That's The Daughter's real name."

"So?" Buggy asked.

"So, that is the one thing she can hear. The only thing she can *almost
always* hear. No matter how deeply she is buried under the mountain of
reincarnated memories. Because it's the last thing she ever heard. Her
name. It's like poking a sleeping bear."

Buggy nearly lurched out of her seat. She had to dig her fingers deep
into the arms of the chair to keep herself in place. When she spoke though,
her voice was cool, reserved. She was glad for that at least. "Then why did
you say it at all?"

"Because, when you say it, she can hear, and sometimes there is a
momentary power struggle between her and the current reincarnation.
Usually, the reincarnation is still the stronger, so all that happens is that
the current consciousness checks out for a few minutes while the original
flails uselessly to take control. Making you pass out."

"That seems like one hell of a gamble," Buggy grimaced.

"It is," Theo said, shoulders slumping. "So please..."

"Okay, okay, I won't say it," Buggy sighed. "You guys were so worried about me being controlled that you actually risked waking her yourself?"

"Yep." Theo said, guilt lining his eyes, turning the corners of his mouth down towards the floor. "We thought... if she was already awake, or already in control, it wouldn't make much of a difference. And we really needed to get you here." Theo glanced around at the high-ceilinged cabin. The stain glass windows barely showed their colors against the dark night outside. "Neutral ground." He looked back down to Buggy. "But to be clear, I voted against the whole abduction thing."

Buggy gave a nervous laugh, not really feeling the humor, but trying to show that she wasn't holding it against him—or at least—she was *trying* not to. Her bedroom door had two large bolts on the inside, and she had made sure they were both securely fastened before laying down, closed her eyes, and searched in vain for sleep. She was choosing to trust them, but first impressions are impactful, especially one as absolutely terrifying as theirs had been. And trust only went so far. She was willing to put aside her views on unnatural beings, and afterlives, and reincarnations in light of the evidence presented to her, but she was neither naive nor stupid.

"Cam's right though," Buggy nodded. "I wouldn't have believed you. I would have said you were crazy. Then probably gotten a restraining order."

"Like any sane person would," Theo agreed.

"Then I might have started a different fire in my sleep... I might have started one back in my apartment... and if Sandra had been there—" Buggy shuddered at the thought, tightening her grip around the blanket, pulling it closer.

"Is that what's keeping you up?" Theo asked tentatively, worried about treading down a path where he was unwelcome.

"No, it's not that," Buggy said, "I mean, it *is* that. But its more than that. It's a few things."

"Like?' Theo asked. She looked up, and another little humorless chuckle escaped her.

"Well, first off I'm...I'm a little... let's say eccentric."

"How so?"

"Well, I kind of have... routines, I guess. They help me get to sleep. And when I don't have them I just—" she waved her hand listlessly though the air and chuckled again.

"What kind of routines?" Theo asked.

"Umm, well, just stuff like," she cleared her throat, looking uncomfortable, eyes casting away from Theo towards the fire, which crackled restlessly to her right. "I need to check my lights."

"Check them?"

"Flip them on and off three times," Buggy cleared her throat again.

"How come?"

"Because if I don't, the electrical system is going to have a massive break down and the house is going to burn down in my sleep," Buggy said still not looking at him.

"Oh," Theo said, unsure what else to say. He had never actually met anyone with OCD before. He tried to imagine having that sort of pressure all the time. The feeling, belief, that if you didn't do a particular routine in a particular way, something unspeakable would happen. He was suddenly very worried about saying the wrong thing.

"And there's other things to." Buggy went on, filling the silence. "Like I need to check my closet and make sure my bag is under my bed where it should be. I check that at least four times. Oh, and I've got to tap on my dream catcher three times or else I will *definitely* have nightmares... or worse. You know," Buggy flashed him a grin. "Totally normal stuff like that."

"And not only are you not in your room," Theo nodded, "But you don't have any of those things that help you sleep."

"Exactly," Buggy said, arms wrapping around her legs, her chin resting on top of her knees. The fire light flickered soft and gold in her large eyes. "I know it's silly stuff that I should get over... but it's also silly stuff I've been doing since I was six so..."

"Kinda just imbedded in there?"

"Lil bit." Buggy shrugged.

"I'm sorry. That sucks," Theo said, and he meant it. "That's got to get irritating."

"It does. And it is," Buggy answered. A shy smile began creeping carefully across her lips, as if ready to retreat at the first sign of judgment. "Thanks. I mean... I know that flipping on and off the lights doesn't really help anything, but I also can't bring myself to.... It's still kinda a weird thing I just—" Buggy laughed. "I don't know."

"You think that's weird," Theo leaned back on his hands. "Try being a twelve-year-old psychic with empathic tendencies who accidently diagnoses people walking into your house. Then grows up and is hustled off by some strange scruffy dude who tells you you're born to save a bunch of strangers from some supernatural, fire wielding, suicidal, crazy person."

"Oh, that's right," Buggy said, tapping the smooth skin of her wrist. "No tattoo. Right?"

Theo raised his wrist, pulling down his sleeve to show the clear skin. "Nope."

"You weren't raised in The Fold."

"Hell no," Theo shook his head. "I didn't know anything about *any* of this until about six months ago. Soon after Cam and Loretta ran away, my mom ditched as well. She didn't have the taste for chasing down a loving couple. So, she got out as soon as she realized she was pregnant. Didn't want me mixed up in any of this."

"Then, Cam happened," Buggy said.

"Then, Cam happened," Theo agreed. "He just showed up at the shop one day. And my world turned upside down."

"*Your* world is upside down?" Buggy laughed. "Try finding out that you ARE that suicidal, fire wielding, crazy person."

"Yep, that's it. You win, that's way worse," Theo grimaced.

"At least you're the good guy of this story," Buggy said, picking a stray hair off the blanket and flicking it into the air, where it swayed back and forth towards the ground. Theo watched it touch down, then frowned back up at her.

"You're not the bad guy here, Briar," he insisted. "You're in a shitty situation. One that you're gonna have to work through, but that doesn't mean you're the bad guy of this or any other story."

She smiled. "Buggy."

"What?"

"My friends call me Buggy." Theo's nose crinkled. In confusion or distaste, Buggy couldn't tell.

"Saw that. Do they seriously call you that because of your eyes?"

"Well... yeah."

Theo rolled his, far more proportional, eyes. "And you put up with that?"

Buggy laughed, "Yup. In their defense," Buggy tapped the corner of her cheek below her right eye. "My face *is* ridiculous."

"But doesn't it **bug** you?" Theo grinned.

It was Buggy's turn to roll her eyes. "Well, *now* it does."

"Oh, it's way too late for take backs, **Buggy**." Theo said. He was all in now.

"Joy," Buggy huffed, but her smile wouldn't fall from her lips. She watched the flames. "Although," she said, bringing the topic back around, "to be honest, now—after everything going on—my eccentric precautions almost sound down right reasonable. I mean the dream catcher, the lights... there is *actually* a threat of dreams and there's even a threat of fire," she flashed him a grin. "Too bad I didn't know it was *me* who was the threat. Not the light switch. May have saved me some time."

They sat quietly, listening to the fire crackle in the hearth as it slowly but surely nibbled away at the logs, leaving nothing but gray ash behind.

"Do dads always lie?" Buggy asked curiously. Theo turned to her. "I mean, *bio* dads. My 'Dad' dad has always been honest with me. He's never lied to me about anything. Never tried to pretend that I wasn't adopted. When things go wrong, he gives me the straight scoop. I was never sure if that was just because he felt like he *had* to. Like, it's him making up for not being my biological father or something." She looked over at Theo. "Do bio dad's just not feel like they owe you the truth? Like: 'Here! I helped give you life! What more do you want?'"

Theo shrugged. "I won't know. Never had an adopted dad, let alone a 'bio dad.'"

Buggy blinked those large eyes with long and slow strokes as she considered him. There was no pity in her gaze, just deep consideration. A reevaluation of him in her mind. He could almost see the narrative being edited; words being switched around on the outline of his character.

"I'm sorry about that," she said finally. Theo shrugged.

"What are you going to do, right?" Theo watched Buggy as she watched the fire. "You saying Cam is lying to you?"

"Oh, I **know** he's lying to me," Buggy nodded, and looked away from the fire to meet Theo's gaze. "But I don't think you will. So, tell me. Do you guys actually know how long I have to do this? How much time to get The Daughter under control, before it's too late?"

Theo let out a long and heavy sigh, jaw set, never braking eye contact. "Honestly, no. We have no idea how much time you have. Frankly, it might already be too late."

Buggy gritted her teeth but nodded firmly in understanding. Her eyes shifted back to the fire, and Theo thought he saw a sheen that had not been there before.

"But for what it's worth," Theo added. "I don't think he's lying because he doesn't owe you anything. I think he's lying because he's guilty. Because he wants it to be alright. He *needs* it to be." Buggy said nothing, but her jaw loosened a little, and the creases around her eyes softened.

"You going to try to get some sleep?" Theo asked.

"Don't know," Buggy answered. "Not sure I want to... ever again."

"The nightmares?' Theo asked. Buggy nodded.

"Yeah. That's the other reason I'm up." She gave a little chuckle and rubbed her eyes. "It's just... I never know what I'm going to get. You know?"

Theo thought about it. "I might be able to help with that actually," he said.

"Really?" Buggy looked over.

"*Maybe*," Theo clarified, but he turned to face her fully again, curling his legs under himself. "I've never actually done it before so, no promises."

"Okay..." Buggy leaned towards him, looking both curious and eager. "What can you do?"

"I can try to guide you down."

"Hypnosis?" Buggy asked, a little nervously.

"Yeah. Except if I do it right, I'll not only be guiding you from out here... but I might be able to guide you inside your dream state."

"Are you saying you're going to get into my head?" Buggy asked, looking extremely nervous now. "You can... do that?"

"Hypothetically. It's apparently a talent that The Fold specialized in. Styger has been teaching me a lot, and it's not as bad as it sounds," Theo said reassuringly. "I don't have any power to prance around your imagination or anything. I can't creep through your thoughts. Your head is your own house. I can't get inside unless you let me, and I can only see what you let me see. I don't have any power. Just like any other form of hypnosis, I only have the power over your mind that you *let* me have, that you *want* me to have. I'm mostly just along for the ride. But if you let me,

I *may* be able to help you avoid those nightmares. Push them aside. Keep them from playing out."

"O-Okay," Buggy said, the word coming out more as a question then an assertion. "Do I have to do anything?"

"Just close your eyes," Theo said, "Close your eyes, try to relax, and clear your mind."

Buggy did, snuggling deeper into the chair, large eyes sliding closed, pale lashes touching her cheeks.

"Just clear your mind. Let your thoughts come and let them pass by. Let them fade and focus on your breath. In your nose. Out your mouth. Five counts in. Five counts out." Buggy did so, her small frame rising and falling beneath the blankets. The creases that had crept back around her eyes slowly smoothed as relaxation began to take hold.

"Okay," Theo said, turning away from Buggy so he could focus on the fire. He watched the flickering yellow, red, gold and blue tongues dancing before him. He felt the heat that emanated from them, filling him. He focused on the very edges of their dance. Watching as the fire flicked and fluttered from side to side, heaving up and down against the air. He listened to the crackle and let everything else drop away from existence. It was just him, the fire, and Briar Rose.

"Just listen to the sound of my voice..."

18

It stirred in the dark, trying to remember... anything. It could not recall what it needed to remember, what it needed to know. It had been tossed back into the dark, once again. Once again it needed to claw itself to understanding, but the harder it tried to grasp hold, the faster it slipped away. Understanding skirted it. Knowing evaded. It did not matter. Because the girl was asleep. That was all it needed to know.

It watched as the little girl finally drifted off. It rejoiced as the girl's frame rose and fell in steady breaths of the deeply sleeping. It moved, stretched itself out like the limbs of someone who had been cramped inside a footlocker for years. If it had a voice, it would have groaned. The thing shifted, reaching out with tentative fingers. Testing its touch. Testing its strengths.

The thing oozed slowly, seeping out from that empty space deep within the girl's chest. That hollow void that plagued her in her waking hours, but which woke with her sleeping. It seethed out from her chest, down her waist, up her neck, sludging steadily across her shoulders, down her arms and towards the tips of her thin fingers. It tested. One finger twitched. If the thing had lips, it would have smiled. Another finger twitched, and then another.

The thing paused as it felt something odd. The thing frowned to itself. There was something wrong. Someone else was there. Not the sleeping girl. No, she was out of the way. There was *someone*, not a darkness, nor a light. Something... Blue. The Blue was pressing against her grip on the girl's fingers. Blue was pressing back, forcing the thing up from the fingers, causing it to lose its control over them. The thing would have scowled if it had a mouth with which to scowl. It pushed back against the Blue, but the Blue was strong. It forced the thing slowly, but steadily, up the fingers and into the wrist. The thing grew irritated but could not help a begrudging respect for The Blue. It was a young one, this Blue was. The thing suddenly remembered. It had felt this sensation before. It had known many members of The Fold in its lifetimes. It had felt that same attempt to contain its spread, pushing it back to that deep place. They all came with their own special feel—their own special shade. The last member the thing had met in this way, had given off a silver quality. This one came in shades of cerulean. It was inexperienced, but strong, and it was in no state to give the Blue a good fight. It had woken only a short while before, and still needed time. Time to restore itself, to come alive again, and to fully remember.

Alright, little Blue, the thing thought, sliding ruefully back into the hollow place in the girl's chest. *Alright. You win today. But I will see you tomorrow... and the next day... and the next...*

The thing slid back into place, and its mind was consumed by darkness. Thoughts scattering to the breeze, everything once more out of reach. But it was awake now, and the Blue could not put it back to sleep. No, no, no. It was awake now... and soon enough it would be back.

* * *

"Hey kid," Cam hunkered down beside Theo, who was staring intently at the fire. Sweat rolled down his face, and his eyes were growing bloodshot with the effort. "Kid," Cam shook Theo's shoulder, but the boy didn't respond. "Theo!" he barked in his ear.

"Wha?" Theo blinked and looked up at Cam. "Oh, hey."

"What's going on?" Cam asked, dropping his hand. "You alright? Because you look awful."

"Styger," Theo said, shaking his head, trying to clear his mind. "Shit, oh, shit."

"What's wrong?" Cam asked, brows furrowing.

"I think... I think I just met **her**," he said, looking at Cam, fear dancing with the reflected flames in his eyes. "The Daughter. I think I just... *touched* it." He said the word as if it brought with it a sour taste. As if he wanted nothing more than to spit the very word from his vocabulary. A word forever sullied by the memory of that moment, of that *touch*. He shivered.

Cam's mouth went dry. "Are you sure?"

"Yes," Theo nodded. "And it's getting stronger." He was breathing heavily for having just been sitting in one position for an hour and a half.

"Briar?" Cam asked, face growing stony.

"She's okay," Theo said. They both looked over to where Buggy lay asleep in the armchair, the picture of calm sleep. "I was just trying to help her with her nightmares. It was going fine then... I felt *her.* She tried to take over and I just..." Theo searched for the right words. "I was able to *push* her." Theo couldn't help the hint of pride that laced his words. "I was able to push it back but," he looked up, "it's strong Cam. Strong and getting stronger. I don't know how much time I bought us, or if I'm going to be able to push it back again, not on my own. I'm not entirely sure how I did it *this* time."

"Damn it," Cam grunted, straightening. Theo heard his knees pop in protest. "We'll need to get her ready, or at least, as ready as we can."

"Styger," Theo shook his head. "She is going into this blind."

"Then we'll have to guide her."

"Man, I barely know what *I'm* doing, and I had over *six months* to train," Theo said, eyes drifting back to Buggy's sleeping form. "And she's barely had a few days. I'd be surprised if she gets to the end of the damn week."

"We'll make it work," Cam said emphatically.

"But..." Theo started cautiously. "Cam, if we can't..."

"We'll make it work."

"Sure, but, Cam—"

"I'm not going to let her down again Theo, I swear to God." Theo looked up. Cam was watching Buggy sleep, his face set, eyes narrowed and filled with the type of determination that no cold hard truth could ever sway. It was the determination of doing everything in his power to have his way... even if that meant risking the world being set to flame. "I'm not letting her down. I'm here this time. I'm here and I'm not gonna let her down." Theo wondered briefly if Cam was talking about Briar or Loretta. He supposed it didn't really matter. Cam turned back to Theo and clapped him on his shoulder. "Thank you, by the way. For helping her, for all of this."

Theo blinked in surprise. Cam wasn't usually one for "thank you's." Theo shrugged. "In my blood I guess."

"Nah," Cam answered. "The *ability* is in your blood, but your willingness to help a grumpy coot like me and put your life on the line to keep disaster at bay—the sheer willingness to believe the unbelievable—nah, that's all you. So, thank you."

Theo shrugged again and tried to smile although it was difficult. He could see that Cam was going to do everything in his power to save the daughter that he lost. He would risk everything. Risk the "thing" inside her taking her over. Would risk it taking out its fiery vengeance on the world around it, on the people around it, until it got what it wanted. That could mean lives. Hundreds of lives, thousands, but Cam was willing to risk it. Theo... he was less sure. He liked Buggy. He barely knew her, but he already liked her. She was the type of girl that made it easy to like. Easy to care about. With her spine of stone, sarcastic snarking, and smile that lit up her eyes, she made it effortless. He felt terrible that this poor girl got the shit end of the stick on this one. However, she was just one girl. If the stories were true and there was a part of her out for blood, with the ability to burn the world to ash... Theo wasn't sure he could risk that.

Sitting there, with Styger smiled down at him, Theo remembered those unspoken words which were not so unspoken between him and that oh-so-likable girl.

That's what you're here for, right?

The worst part of it all—she was right. He was here to do anything and everything Cam couldn't. This was Cam's daughter. This was the last and only remnant of Styger's family. The last gasp of the life he had planned to have. If push came to shove, Theo knew Cam wouldn't do what needed doing. He couldn't. And that was okay. Because that was what *Theo* was here for.

"If you have to..." his mother's voice rang deafening in his memory. It had struck like a bell in his head the moment Theo had laid eyes on Buggy in that dental office. Since the instant her sweet smile spread her face, and those enormous eyes sparkled with kindness, his mother's words had been echoing. "If you have to... kill her. Because Cam won't do it. Do you understand? We cannot let The Daughter out upon the world, Theo. Promise me you won't let her kill any more innocents. Too many have suffered so much. Save them, Theo. Like you saved Maggie. Save them... even if that means killing her."

Theo heard those words now, eyes on Cam's fervent expression. He smiled. A smile which pulled tight against his lips and pressed almost painfully against his teeth. A false smile, because if push came to shove, he knew what he had to do. Even if it destroyed him.

"Of course, Styger," Theo said, "Of course. You can count on me."

19

Waverly loved her Softail, but the nights were icy, and it felt like daggers cutting against her skin every time she drove these days. Winter had hit hard, and there were forecasts for more snow. She needed a little warmer ride. So, she decided to take Helena's car for the rest of the trip. Waverly had already rented a storage unit nearby and had parked her Harley safely inside before heading to the auto shop. Just in case the place, or any of the nearby stores, had cameras that could catch the model or license plate. There hadn't been. Helena's shop had been set off a distance from all the other buildings, giving it a wide berth of open space surrounded by a chain link fence, and the neighbor's cameras couldn't reach. They were easy to avoid. Turned out Helena had not invested in cameras of her own. She had alarms, sure. Anyone without the proper keys or code could set the whole shebang off and have the police immediately called to that location. But Helena had still been in the shop when Waverly arrived, and had not yet locked down and turned them on. Even if she had, Waverly wouldn't have any trouble getting the codes from the woman. Just like her car keys. Besides, Helena wouldn't have any use for them anymore, anyway.

No, no more using it. No more keys or codes needed... but the blood....

It was a few hours since she left the shop. A few hours since Waverly flipped the keys in her hands, ambling across the parking lot towards the patiently waiting 1966 Charger. A few hours since she had slid the keys into the unfamiliar lock and pulled the door open, slipped inside and turned the ignition. The engine had rumbled to life, making her smile. Waverly loved that sound. There was a strength to it, a roughness and ruggedness that newer cars completely lacked. She had thought about buying a classic when she turned eighteen but had ended up going with her Harley instead. She had never really regretted her decision, but—oh Lord—did she love that sound.

Now, Waverly was sitting on the side of the road in the pitch black, staring out the windshield into the night outside. She wasn't sure exactly how long she had been sitting there. She didn't even remember pulling over. She remembered pulling out of the auto repair's parking lot and driving, driving, driving. Then she was here, parked at the far corner of a rest stop, next to a highway she really didn't remember the number of. She shook her head, trying to clear it. It felt so foggy, so hollow... like she was dreaming all of this. Like none of this was actually real. It couldn't be real... could it? She looked down at the passenger floor, where the little plastic Ziplock back still sat, a quiet reminder.

Waverly blinked, and remembered sitting in the car and flipping on a light. She had grimaced at her hands, noticing the blood that still covered her gloves. She had sighed and carefully pulled her gloves off, inside out. Reaching into the bag she had taken from her Softail, she pulled out the plastic baggy. Waverly remembered placing the gloves in the bag, making a note to dispose of them later, and had set them in that exact spot on the passenger floor.

So, that *had* happened.

That wasn't a dream.

Waverly looked at her hands. The gloves were gone, and so was most of the blood—*Oh, God, all the blood*—but she saw a little red smudge that she had not seen before. It sat, drying on her upper wrist where the gloves had not quite covered. Waverly reached back for the second time and pulled a little pack of handy wipes from the bag. She began wiping at her skin, slowly and diligently cleaning away the evidence, staining the light white cloth a dark brown and red from the blood. She hated to see that her hands were trembling. It made sense. Her heart was still thudding, and her head was foggy with the denial of what she had done. This was the first time Waverly had ever hurt anyone before. She had practiced with her mother, sure, trained how to inflict pain for protection, but this was different. This was... completely and utterly different. This was dirty. Dark and dirty, and she had not been sure such an action had been in her capabilities. Her mother had told her before hanging up the phone, that Waverly would need to find out where the girl was, by *any* means necessary. So, she had done what was necessary. She had found a space in her own head, somewhere to lock away her empathy, lock away her sympathy, lock away her feelings and she just... went on automatic, then slid directly into shock. She was *still* in shock.

Her mother said it would get easier—the act of doing anything and everything necessary to do what needed to be done—to complete their mission. Waverly wasn't sure how. If her mother had meant *this*, how could such a thing get easier? What did it say about you as a person if it ever got easy? Whatever the case, she didn't want that woman's blood on her hands any longer. She wiped at the red stains furiously. When she was finished, she placed the bloody towels—*so much blood, there was so much blood, and the way her eyes had*—into the Ziplock bag with the gloves. She sat there, trying to clear her mind enough to remember where she was and what she needed to do. Her thoughts felt like they were trudging through waist-high mud, and it took a few minutes to realize her phone had somehow appeared in her hand.

Waverly dialed her mother's number. She picked up on the second ring.

"Waverly?" Susanna asked, anticipation evident in her voice.

"I know where they are," Waverly said, not really feeling the words form in her mouth at all. They seemed to come from somewhere to her left, distant, disconnected. Disconnected was good. Disconnected was easier. Waverly smiled at her own reflection in the rear-view mirror. Her blue eyes were bright against pale skin, but she noticed the familiar red spatter tracing lines up the right side of her face. Her stomach gave a violent turn, but her disconnected mind only grumbled irritably. *Great.* She grabbed another handy wipe and started scrubbing.

"You do?" her mother asked, sounding very pleased indeed.

"Yep," Waverly said, drawing the wipe under her chin, catching a stray stream of red.

"*Yes*," her mother corrected, voice harsh. "You aren't some idiot, Waverly. Use your words like a big girl."

Waverly bit back a snide remark at her mother's condescending sarcasm and pushed on instead. "*Yes.* I know where they are."

"Well, don't keep me in suspense," her mother sounded downright eager. Waverly toyed with the idea of leaving her mother hanging, simply ending the call right then and letting her stew. But she decided against it.

"A cabin," she said, finally satisfied with her cleaning job and tossed the cloth into the baggy with the rest. "A cabin out in Utah. Already on my way." Waverly looked out the window, trying to remember how far she had gotten. How close she already was. But she couldn't. Time seemed to have melted in on itself, and she didn't know where the old memories started, and the new memories began. "I'll be there in a day. Max."

"Good girl," Susanna said, and her daughter could hear the smile in her voice. "Tell me when you're getting close."

"Will do, Mom."

There was a brief pause on the other end of the line.

"Mom?"

"I'm proud of what you're doing. You know that, right?" Waverly didn't know the last time she had heard her mother's voice sounding so vulnerable. It was all fake of course. False pride, but it *almost* sounded authentic. Waverly granted herself a brief moment to pretend that it was real.

"Thanks, Mom. Call you soon." She hung up before her mother could say anything to break the spell. Waverly checked her reflection one more time, before putting the car into reverse and pulling out of the rest area's parking lot. She vaguely acknowledged that this was a stupid idea. She knew her mother would be furious with her if she had known her daughter had left the scene of the crime in Helena's—*blood, Helena's blood, so much blood*—car, especially one that was so recognizable. But Waverly wasn't exactly thinking clearly. All she could think about was getting as far away from this town, as far away from California, as possible. She would ditch the car along the way, or at least change the plates, but she had a few hours at least. It was the dead of night, and she would have a little time before anyone came into work. Before they knew what she had done. She had a little time to let her mind clear a bit. She just needed her mind to clear a *little* bit. That was all. Then the fog would go away. The nausea would go away. The flashes would go away. It was almost over.

"Okay, little Briar Rose," Waverly said, pulling into the road and taking the exit back onto the freeway, quickly merging into the red and white traffic lights with a great rumbling growl from the engine. "I'm on my way. Don't go anywhere now. You stay put—you hear? People have just been

dying for me to meet you." A laugh tumbled from her lips in a hysterical cackle. Her hands shook against the steering wheel as she pressed down on the gas and the engine revved, tossing them forward, further into the night, until darkness swallowed them both.

PART 4:

The Daughter's Rising

I

Buggy woke to the smell of bacon. She groaned, stretching her arms over her head, and frowned at the world around her, irritated that it had appeared at all. She had been in a very calm sleep, vacant of dreams. It had been extremely refreshing, and she hated to leave... until she smelled the bacon of course. She looked around towards the kitchen, but the door was closed, and she couldn't see what was making that heavenly smell. Buggy untangled herself from the blankets with difficulty and got to her feet. She dragged one of the blankets with her, snugging it securely around her shoulders as she shuffled off towards the kitchen door. She pushed it open and smiled. Both Cam and Theo were inside, mid conversation about something she wasn't sure she was meant to be a part of.

"I mean, she usually calls by nine," Theo was saying, pushing the remnants of half-eaten eggs around his plate. Cam was already washed and dressed in a green button-down shirt with blue jeans, while Theo still wore what seemed to be a T-shirt that as two sizes too big and a pair of green pajama pants. His red-brown hair was mushed to one side by sleep, making him look like some shoujo manga character as he went on. "She's big on the check in. She just missed last night is all."

"Okay, then why don't you just call her?" Cam asked. His back was to the door, hunching over the stove. The sizzle of bouncing grease in a pan filled the air.

"I did. Left a message," Theo shrugged. "Probably nothing. She's been really busy after all. Swamped with clients." Theo shrugged and slipped a fork full of eggs into his mouth. "I'll call her again later today."

"Morning," Buggy said, stepping further into the room. They both looked up, and a bright grin lit Cam's face.

"Good morning," he said, the pan of bacon still sizzling in his hand. "Breakfast?"

"Please," Buggy said, taking the stool next to Theo as Cam turned back to his task.

"How'd you sleep?" Theo asked smiling and scooting an empty cup and pitcher of orange juice in her direction.

"Oh God, best sleep I've had in months," Buggy said, taking the cup and pouring herself a glass. "Zero nightmares. Zeros dreams. For *hours*. I don't know how you did it, but thank you."

"Any time," Theo said, and Buggy thought she saw a bit of pride in the dimpling of his cheeks. Cam slid a steaming plate of freshly scrambled eggs and bacon on the counter in front of her, and Buggy sighed at the heavenly smell.

"Oh mama," she said to no one in particular as she picked up a fork and dived in. The eggs were slightly burnt in sections, and the bacon was a little crunchier than she might like, but it all still tasted amazing. And she was starving. She had just stuffed her mouth like a squirrel packing for winter when her phone rang and "Take Me Home, Country Road" began to serenade the kitchen at large.

Buggy pulled her phone out and checked the ID, pretending not to notice the pointed look that Theo shared with Cam. Theo was obviously not privy to Cam giving back her access to the outside world, but she would let them figure their own shit out. She nearly choked on her egg when she saw who was calling.

"Shit," she said, quickly gulping down her mouthful with orange juice.

"What's wrong?" Cam asked frowning.

"Nothing," Buggy shook her head, sliding off her stool and heading for the door. "It's nothing I just got to... nothing. Everything's fine. Totally normal." Buggy pushed through the kitchen door, closing it securely behind her before she answered the phone.

"Cooper?" she asked, low and quiet, as if she was in a library full of aggravated college students during finals week. Terrified to be overheard, lest she be dealt with.

"She lives!" Coopers voice felt strange in her ear. After everything that had happened over the past few days, it was a shock to hear his familiar, never changing cheeriness. She smiled, easily falling into the sound, letting it surround and soothe her.

"Were there doubts?" Buggy asked.

"A few," Cooper said on the other line. His voice was dampened by the sound of cars zooming by on some road Buggy couldn't see. Someone honked, and there was a returning blast of an angry horn. Both ignored it. "Actually, Linny left me a rather worried message last night... said you haven't been answering your phone and Sandra was—"

"Overreacting." Buggy cut in, hoping her voice sounded as convincing as she was trying to make it. "As Sandra usually does."

"Yeah," Cooper chuckled. "I was guessing it was something like that."

"So..." Buggy trailed off a little, feeling like she had completely forgotten how to carry on a casual conversation. "How's things?"

"Things are good," Cooper answered. "We got most of Dannielle's shit in her new place so we're having a celebratory lunch."

"Oh crap, I'm sorry I must be interrupting," Buggy shook her head, inwardly cursing herself for calling... and then realizing...

"Uh, no. Buggy, I called you, remember?" Cooper's voice was amused, but concern was slowly but surely peeking his head around the corner of his words.

"Oh right. Duh." Buggy jammed her palm into her eye.

"You alright?" Cooper asked. She could almost see his head tilting in that cute, curious, puppy dog way that he had. "You sound funny."

"Nah, I'm good," Buggy insisted, shaking her head at the empty living room in front of her. Her body denying the lie as she spoke it. "Totally fine. Super good."

"Umm, *convincing,*" Cooper laughed, and Buggy grinned.

"Just... It's a long story," Buggy said, leaning against the wall.

"I've got time," Cooper said.

Buggy repressed a groan and leaned back, accidentally knocking her head against the wall. She bit her lip, hand rubbing the spot angrily. "It's more of an *in-person* conversation."

"Oh, gotcha," Cooper said, not intending to push the matter. "You can just add it to the list."

"Right," Buggy accidently knocked her head against the wall for a second time. "The list."

"You haven't forgotten, have you?" Cooper asked, and she could hear a little nervousness in his usually carefree chuckle. It killed her.

"No. Nope. I haven't forgotten." Buggy closed her eyes.

"Okay," Cooper said after a moment of awkward silence. "Well, just wanted to make sure you were alright."

"Thanks," Buggy said, extremely glad this conversation was drawing to a close. "I'm good. Really."

"And you'll tell me all about it when you get back?"

"Absolutely," Buggy lied. The lies were coming easier with each passing call. Although lying to Cooper was as bad as lying to Sandra. It felt like a slug circling her tongue, leaving a long, thick, green, snotty trail in its wake.

"Alright then," Cooper's voice regained his usual animation. "Talk to you soon?"

"Talk to you soon," Buggy promised, adding another lie on the ever-growing pile. Hoping it was true. Knowing it probably wasn't.

"See ya, Buggy."

"See you, Cooper." Buggy hung up the phone and pressed her hands against her closed eyes, allowing the embarrassment and frustration to overtake her. "Fuck. Fuck. Shit."

"You alright?" Theo was standing in the doorway to the kitchen, watching her. He was still drowned in the too large T-shirt that, Buggy now saw, said: "Do I have coffee in my hands yet? No? Then why are you talking to me?" Buggy made a mental note to order that very shirt when she got home. It would go great with her coffee pajama bottoms.

Buggy looked up at Theo and grimaced. "Me? Totally fine. Just... *fantastic.*" She frowned. "You listened to that?"

"Just a little," Theo said, awkwardly. At least he had the common decency to look ashamed. "Who's Cooper?"

Buggy hesitated. "Cooper's... Cooper is a... friend?"

Theo's grin widened. "Are you asking me or telling me?"

"Neither. Shut up. Never mind," Buggy grumbled, pushing past him and back into the kitchen towards her still waiting plate of food. "So, when do we get started on this whole, 'avoiding me being taken over by my pyro-psycho soul sister' thing?"

"As soon as you finish eating," Cam said, dropping the frying pan in the sink and filling it with water. The water sizzled angrily against the still hot pan, sending steam up into the air above it. Buggy slid back onto the stool, but she was no longer hungry. She shoveled a few more forkfuls into her mouth and then pushed the plate away, but she did take the large cup of coffee that Cam offered her without question. She took a sip, wishing regretfully that it had a dash of Irish Cream instead of normal milk, and then slid back off the stool.

"Alright," she said, warm cup still clutched in her hands. "Let's do this."

* * *

Buggy sat on the floor next to Theo, crossing her legs beneath her, and resting her hands, palms up, on her knees. The stained-glass windows cast them both in that same half eerie, half beautiful rainbow lighting. Cam was stoking the fire, letting the flames grow large and hot in the hearth before them.

"Is that necessary?" Buggy asked, tugging a little at her shirt collar, already feeling warm. It was cold outside, a icy too, but the cabin warmed up fast, and they were sitting rather close to the flames.

Cam shook his head. "Not really, but it helps."

"So, it's just like the meditation last night?" Buggy turned to Theo. She was trying to sound nonchalant about the entire thing but could feel that uncertain tension building in her chest, closing tight like an iron fist between her lungs. She tried her best to breathe around it.

"Pretty much, I think," Theo said with a smile. He had cleaned up, changed out of his pajamas, and combed down his excessive cow lick.

"You *think*?" Buggy asked, frowning a little.

"I'm still pretty new at this to remember?"

"Oh, right," Buggy nodded. "Right, you mentioned that."

"But this time just try *not* to fall asleep."

"Okay," Buggy said, her heart thudding hard, telling her that she couldn't have fallen asleep even if she wanted to.

"It's alright," Cam said, hunkering down, so he was on eye level with the two of them. "I'll be guiding you both through. But you will need to be patient. This is a bit more difficult than Theo's dream suppression."

"Oh?" Both Buggy and Theo asked in unison. They exchanged a brief look before turning back to Cam.

"This is the process of opening up those dreams, those subconscious memories, not suppress them. Suppression is easier, but we need to go **through** them to get where we need to go."

"So... we need to... I need to go into those..." Buggy protectively covered her wrist with her hand, trying not to think of how it felt to have that flesh opening. Tried not to let the memory of blood slipping hot and fast down her wrist make her ill. She squeezed and swallowed hard.

Cam's eyes darted down to the grip on her wrist, and a crease developed between his scruffy brows. He knelt all the way down in front of her. He looked like he was about to reach out, take her hands into his, then changed his mind. Or maybe just chickened out.

"It will be okay," he said instead, smiling. Reassurance reverberating around every syllable. "And we'll start small. Start with some easier memories. Work our way lower. Only when you're ready."

"Okay," Buggy said, unsure what the hell else there was to say, but she let go of her wrist all the same. Cam gave a nod and pushed back to his feet.

"Ready, Theo?" he asked, taking a seat in the armchair, leaning forward.

"As ready as I'm ever going to get," Theo answered.

"Okay," Cam's voice lowered, grew soft, and so thoroughly calming that Buggy could feel the fist in her lungs loosen. She breathed deeply. "Now, take each other's hands." Buggy and Theo reached out, she taking his left hand, he taking her right, both pairs of eyes still on the fire. "Okay, good. Now, relax and focus on the sound of your breath. In your nose, out your mouth. Five seconds in, eight seconds out. Five seconds in, eight seconds out... good." Cam's voice grew slow, and even softer. "Now, focus on the fire. Watch the colors flickering, twisting, changing. Watch the ends flit in and out of existence, dancing... and feel relaxed. Feel anchored by those flames. Let your mind go blank. Let all thoughts briefly come, and then let them go. Let them pass out of your mind and focus on the fire. Focus on your breath. Five seconds in, eight seconds out."

Buggy tried. She tried to focus, tried to keep her mind blank. She had dabbled in meditation on and off throughout the years, but never ended up sticking with it, for the same reason that she was finding it so difficult to focus now. Her mind wouldn't stop wandering. She could still hear Cam's voice, speaking guidance, directions, but it seemed to fade, turning into white noise of her imagination. Her thoughts wouldn't stop drifting off, to wonder whether this would work, or how long it might take. To obsess over the consequences of it *did* end up working, what nightmare memories she would have to walk through. And what about after? If she is able to "contain" The Daughter—or whatever—what happens then? Cam said it was still part of her, the reincarnations. And when she died... it would happen to her again. What was that like? She supposed she didn't retain any memories from her past lives, at least, not consciously. But they were stored inside of her. That was the point of the "deep dive" wasn't it? So, what did that mean? When she, Buggy, someday died... would she just become another dream? Would she transform into another nightmare, one to plague the next reincarnation's sleep? Would she become one more voice in the gray void?

Then came the twisting fear, of what would happen if it did *not* work. Bennu taking over her body, tossing away Buggy's mind, sending it... who the hell knows were. What would happen to Buggy then? Buggy shook her head. One thing at a time.

In defense against the fear, her mind would slip to daydreaming. What was Cooper up to? She would then start obsessing over what she would say when she saw him again. She thought about Sandra, and what new lies she may need to concoct. Thought about what the hell would happen with Cam after all of this was over, if it was ever going to be over? Would it be over? Because she had a sneaking suspicion, she would still be sitting here a year from now, on this very spot in front of the fire, because she couldn't fucking focus long enough to even start this stupid hypnosis let alone make anything of it. It had been easy when she was tired. It had been easy to focus on sleep and to drift towards it when she was nearly dead on her feet. But she was rested and trying to focus her mind now was like wrangling wild rats. Her thoughts skittering and darting in sickening zig-zag lines around the inside of her skull. Running rampant and out of her reach. And if she didn't get ahold of them, control them, they would turn on her. Eat her alive. Nibble at her flesh until there was nothing left of her at all. Nothing but the one before. Nothing but *her*. Nothing but Bennu.

"Briar?" Buggy blinked. She looked around to Cam, who was kneeling in front of her once more. He looked tired, but he was smiling. She didn't know why. "How do you feel?"

"Like a failure," Buggy grumbled. She blew out an exasperated sigh. "Cam, I'm never going to get this."

"Oh, I don't know," Cam said, "I think you're doing just fine."

"What on Earth do you mean," Buggy frowned. "I've been sitting here for ten minutes and my brain hasn't shut up once."

Cam's eyebrows shot up, and his grin widened. "Briar..." He pointed to the stain glass windows. She expected to see the same multicolored late morning sun light streaming through them, but all she saw was a dim gray and blackness behind the pains. Buggy turned back to Cam, eyebrows cocked in confusing.

"What? What time is it?"

"Seven."

"In the evening?" Buggy gaped. At that moment, her stomach grumbled violently. She realized she was starving. Not surprising. Except that it *was*. Apparently, she had been sitting there for at least eight hours. How the hell did that happen? "I don't understand."

"Turns out," Cam said, "You're a natural at this."

Buggy looked to see Theo still sitting cross-legged beside her. He was focused on the fire, eyes glazed.

"Is he..." Buggy reached out a waved a hand in front of his face. Theo didn't move or even blink.

"Yep," Cam nodded. "He's still down."

"Weird," Buggy grinned, snapping her fingers in front of Theo's nose. He remained still.

"He's actually ready to try to access your consciousness," Cam said, tentatively. "If you're ready, of course."

Buggy looked back at Cam. "Just as a passenger?" she clarified nervously. Cam nodded.

"The only control he will have, is the control you allow him to have. Nothing more."

Buggy swallowed, closed her eyes, and for the second and last time that year, threw up a brief prayer. She opened them again and met Cam's gaze.

"Okay," she said, turning to the fire. "Let's do this."

2

The grayness shifted in the empty space. It oozed and retreated, furling and unfurling. Feeling everything and then feeling nothing at all. Feeling... feeling that there was something else here. Something it had felt before. It tried to think, but it was hard. It tried to focus, but that was nearly impossible. It could feel, though. Feel that something was happening. Someone was here. Not the usual voices. Not the usual clamoring cacophony of whiny bitches that cried and wailed and called from the deep darkness. Their voices echoed off the empty walls, filling them briefly with their sound, until silence swallowed them once more. Like it always did. But no, this was not about them. This was different. This was not the gray mass of the ones that came before... no... this was blue.

The thing shifted again, trying to remember what she had been thinking about. She? Was she a she? It was hard to remember... but yes... yes, *she* was. That is right. She had come to the surface before. She had breathed air before, but it was always a struggle. Even now, even though she was "*awake*," she was continually tossed back into the deep, mixing with the gray voices. Sometimes, when the **other** woke up, the newest one, she had to start again. She was awake, but she kept forgetting that. But with every waking moment it became easier to remember. She was awake. She may drift, but she would *always* be awake.

Bennu. That was her name. She remembered that now. Or, remembered that *again*. She had a name. And so did that bluish feeling. The Blue had a name, and she had heard it before. IT heard through the ears of the **other**, the one that was "now." The one named "Briar"—*Briar dear*—although she called herself "Buggy." *She* had heard it.

Theo. The Blue's name was Theo, and he was not only talking to the one that was "now," not only trying to give her a dreamless sleep like before. No, he was *connecting* with her this time. The Blue was trickling in through the dark, softly dipping deeper into a mind that was not his own, reaching into the endless night sky that was Buggy's subconscious.

Bennu focused on The Blue. She felt it. She followed. If Bennu had lips, she would have smiled.

Hello, little Theo dear, she thought, mind folding into place like an origami crane taking shape, *let us see where you two are headed, hmm? Mind if I tag along?*

3

Buggy opened her eyes in the darkness. It was a vast thing. Long and endless, it spanned outward all around, above, and below her. She had no body, no skin, no eyes, and yet she could see. Or was it only feel? She couldn't tell, but she wasn't afraid. Buggy had been here before.

It always started out that way. The darkness. She had glimpsed it before when Theo had sent her into a dreamless sleep. At the time she thought she had imagined it. Thought the empty sky void of stars had been a figment of her sleepy, half delirious, imagination. Apparently, it was so much more than that. The empty returned with each hypnotic session, but it didn't remain empty. She always came back here and painted her memories on the blank walls of her mind, splashing every corner with color. She had never really been the artsy type herself, but she found this practice relaxing.

"Buggy, can you hear me?"

It was Theo's voice, although it always felt odd in her mind. It echoed off unseen walls, bouncing around until it finally faded to the edges of her thoughts. Buggy began to wonder if she had heard it at all, but then he spoke again.

"Buggy?"

"Yes," she answered, a voice with no lips. "Yes, I can hear you."

It had been only a day or so since they started working on the meditations and hypnosis. They had spent most of their hours sitting in front of the fire, she and Theo cross-legged on the floor, Cam sitting restlessly in the armchair. After the first couple hypnosis sessions, Theo and Buggy could focus on their rhythmic breath, and the flickering of the fire without his prompting or reminder. They sank into the meditation within moments of starting, as if sliding into a warm bath. This was a good sign. It meant they were learning quickly, which was what they needed. But it left Cam with little else to do but sit and wait.

As promised, they started small. In their hypnotic state, Theo would speak to her. He would ask her about her life, about her best moments, and then tell her to re-create them. Theo had asked her to remember her moments, bring them to life in her imagination. Buggy had been able to paint the pictures in her mind without hesitation. Memories of her childhood, memories of her first day at work, memories of the day she had met Andrew and Linny, the first time Sandra had told her about Christina, and on and on. All of them had played through her imagination at Theo's request, as if movies projected on a screen. He said they were exercises, testing their connection, practicing for when he guided her deeper into her subconscious.

"Good," his voice said now, and she could hear a smile in it. "Now, I need you to see yourself—I mean, I need you to see that you have your body. You have your limbs, your torso, your feet, everything. Can you see them?" All at once, she could. Where once there was nothing but empty, Buggy's body appeared below her. She blinked her newly realized eyes and lifted her hands up to her face, twisting them around. She rolled her shoulders and could even hear the little pop.

"I'm here," she said, through newly remembered lips.

"Alright..." Theo said, sounding pleased. "Let's see. How about we start with... a memory from school? You got one?" Buggy thought a moment, then smiled.

"Got one," she answered.

"Good. Now think of that memory. Focus on it... let your eyes close and when I tell you to open them, you will be back in that moment."

"Alright," Buggy said, closing her eyes.

"Ready? Now... open them."

Buggy did. The empty world was gone. In its place was a large spacious cafeteria with children spanning the ages of eleven to thirteen, all milling around like sheep being herded by mild sheep dogs. They lined the side of the hall in front of the glass partition where women stood with nets in their hair and large spoons in their hands. They carefully plopped mounds of corn and mashed potatoes on the plate of the children who had not brought their own goodie bags, and sent them off to find a space at one of the many gray tables lined up throughout the room.

Buggy moved into the memory, noting, not for the first time, how amazingly real the entire scene looked. Memories were more vivid in this place. They surrounded her in detailed color, as if she was actually there, living the memories once again for the first time. She picked many memories from mundane to some of the happiest times of her life, and they all played out in perfect clarity, clearer than she had remembered them in years. All the people, the room itself, even the loud cacophony of chattering children and puberty cracking laughter which filled the slightly salty air. She moved further into the room, not worrying about being seen by any of the students or cafeteria ladies. She wasn't really there after all. Well, not exactly. But she *had* been.

Buggy made her way to the farthest table from the cafeteria line, stepping over dropped muffin crumbs and spilled corn as she did so. On the very corner end of the table, a small girl sat alone. Her large eyes were cast down towards her perfectly laid out tray. She had aligned her utensils by size and use, with her water bottle to her right and a can of root beer to her left. She wore headphones over her ears, and an iPod poked out of the backpack resting on the floor at her feet. Buggy looked at the girl, considered the twelve-year-old version of herself eating lunch by herself. She looked so small, although that might have to do more with the childish largeness of her eyes. She was still too thin, too short to accommodate the disk size irises that gave her the appearance of a living doll. Unfortunately, the resting sour expression on her face made her look more like a Chucky than a Barbie.

Buggy also noticed the wide berth that the other children at the table were giving her, leaving a large empty space between her and the other chatting students. Buggy remembered eating alone a lot in middle school. Sandra had already graduated by this point, leaving her with the option of trying to make new friends or simply curling in on herself. Buggy had chosen, as she always did, the route that granted her the most control, and left her alone quite often. Although she wondered, taking another look at the vast space between her and everyone else, if her memory may have been exaggerating a little in this regard. Her mind taking creative liberties to prove a point.

"Hey!" Buggy looked up, and a little burst of laughter came out of her without warning, along with a little inelegant snorting sound which she hoped didn't translate back anywhere Cam or Theo could hear. Standing on the opposite side of the table, looking at the twelve-year-old memory version of herself, was a boy of around the same age. He had yet to go through his growth spurt, leaving him stockier and fuller in the cheeks than he would be in the next year. But even without the highlights, his messy brown hair and wide grin were unmistakable. Buggy watched as the younger version of herself looked up at the boy, blinking slowly, surprise unable to break that mask of unintentional severity. She looked almost angry, as if the boy had interrupted something particularly important. Buggy remembered that moment, remembered that she had felt no such thing, had merely been shocked by the other kid's arrival and even more surprised when he raised the little brown paper bag in his hand and motioned towards the empty seat opposite her. "Mind if I join you?"

Twelve-year-old Buggy memory blinked again. She slowly processed the question, turning it around on that table in her mind surrounded in multi-colored lights, trying to suss out every possible meaning. Cooper waited patiently, smile never faltering or fading. Finally, when the memory-Buggy concluded that there was no ill intent or sense of impending doom revolving around the question, she nodded.

"Great!" the boy said, plopping down on the bench and emptying the contents of his bag out onto the table. Buggy watched the twelve-year-old version of herself as her eyes widened in a mix of wonder and horror at the boy's haphazard movements. She did, however, slide the headphones off her head, leaving them to dangle around her neck instead. "It was getting kinda loud over there," the boy said, picking up a plastic baggy with a home-made peanut butter and jelly sandwich and popping open plastic lip. He then gestured to a neighboring table packed with kids, a few of who were casting curious, and almost expectant glances their way. As if waiting for something to go off. "Needed someplace a little quieter, so thanks for this."

"Sure," little Buggy said, blinking again, expression never changing. The boy took a large bite out of his sandwich, grunted in approval, then wiped his hands on a napkin before holding it out to Buggy across his scattered array of food and her neatly aligned tray.

"I'm Cooper, by the way."

"Briar," little Buggy said, taking his hand and shaking it. "But everyone calls me Buggy," she added, as if it was a requirement. As if she would be committing some sort of terrible social faux pas if she didn't admit it to him right off the bat.

"Buggy, huh?" Cooper asked, meeting her timid gaze. "I like it. It's cute. Fits you."

Little Buggy froze for eight long seconds, like a computer trying to cipher through a new data entry, not yet ready to spit out an equation. It was the first time that anyone had put a positive spin on her nickname. The first time it was uttered as a sign of affection instead of an accusation. It had thrown her off kilter, and it took her a moment to reboot. When she finally did, a soft smile broke across her cheeks, and her eyes twinkled.

"Thank you," she said, turning back to her tray of food, just in time to miss the surprised expression that dashed across Cooper's young face as he watched the change in her. They started chatting to one another, about what Buggy didn't have time to catch.

"Buggy?" Theo's voice called from far off, but loud enough to be heard over the clattering of trays and multitude of voices. "Buggy how's it going?"

"Good," Buggy replied. Neither young Buggy nor Cooper looked up as they spoke, seeing as neither of them could hear them. They just kept chatting over their meals, not knowing they were beginning a friendship that would last the rest of their lives. "It's working just fine."

"Great, just great. Now I need you to go back to the beginning, okay? Back to that open place."

Buggy nodded, looking down at the younger version of herself and Cooper with regret. It was such a nice memory. "Okay," she said, and closed her eyes. When she opened them, she was back in the vast darkness. "I'm here."

"Good, okay... well I'm going to try something new alright? You ready?"

"Sure," she said. She knew her lips were moving although she couldn't feel them, not anymore. Her body had once again vanished from existence. When they drew this deep, when she was this far down in the well of her mind, she found herself easily disconnected from everything. Disconnected from the cabin she knew she was still in and the hard ground under her legs, or even her legs themselves. She was separate from her body in that place, distancing from her physical self with ease. It had frightened her in the beginning. She had grown so panicked the first time she had made it this deep that she had instantly wrenched herself back out, wrecking two hours of careful and intense meditation. They had to start over, but the next time she made herself stay. She was glad she had, because then she could start painting the memories. And those were beautiful.

"Buggy?"

"Yes, sorry, what?" she had let her mind drift.

"Buggy, can you hear me?"

"Yes. I can hear you, Theo," Buggy answered. "What was it you wanted to try doing?"

"Actually..." Theo said, and she could almost see his smile widen around his words. "I'm already doing it."

"What do you mean?" Buggy asked. If she had lips, she would have frowned in confusion. "You're not doing anything."

"Actually, I am. Or, more accurately, I'm *not* doing something."

"What?" Buggy asked, confused.

"You can hear me, right?"

"Yes, I already said I can."

"But I'm not speaking."

"What?" Buggy asked, even more confused.

"Yeah," Theo said, as if answering a statement of shared amazement instead of the obviously confused question that it was. "You can hear me... but only in your mind. You can't hear me with your ears because I'm not talking at all, I'm *thinking* at you. I'm thinking and you can hear me."

"What?" Buggy was so startled that she opened her eyes in surprise, accidently pulling herself out of the hypnotic state altogether. "Damn," she hissed as the warm and bright living room came into focus around her. That was three hours of meditation she just flushed away. She looked over at Theo whose eyes were also open and on her. His grin was triumphant.

"Are you serious?" Buggy asked him, pulse rising with excitement and wonder.

"Is he serious about what?" Cam asked. It looked like he had just pulled himself from his own meditative state. Or maybe, Buggy thought, a deep sleep. One of his eyes was glassy as he rubbed a palm into the other and yawned in Theo's direction. A small, dried drop of spittle clung to the edge of his lip, half hidden in his beard.

"Yes, I'm very serious." Theo said, ignoring Cam's question all together.

"Holy shit," Buggy said.

"Holy shit, what?" Cam frowned, beginning to look annoyed about being left out in the cold.

"I just projected my mind into hers," Theo said, turning to him. "I was finally able to get connected enough that she *heard* me. I didn't just influence her subconscious. I was able to *act* upon it, *add* to it, with my own thoughts."

Cam's grumpy expression melted, and he beamed at them. "Holy shit," he said, mimicking Buggy. "You did it."

"Yeah," Theo's grin widened until the point it might just split his cheeks. "Hell, yeah, I did."

"So, this means..." Buggy prompted.

"This means I not only can help you influence your own subconscious but... with your permission... I can now act within it. Interact mind to mind," Theo turned to her, bright eyes glinting in the multicolored light of the stained-glass windows high above them. "It means I might actually be able to help you. It means we can *really* get started."

Buggy's heart sank, and she swallowed. It had been nice so far, romping through her favorite memories and recalling her biggest hits like some high school graduation video, built upon nostalgia, and aimed at the good things that happened over the four years. Smiles and laughter and victories were the only things shown on that big screen. But this... what this had all been leading up to, wasn't so sweet. By "get started," Theo meant to dive into memories that were not her own. Memories that belonged to those that came before her. Memories of death, and anger, and fear, and pain. Buggy shuddered a little and closed a hand instinctively around her wrist. She noticed Cam's eyes had darted down at the movement.

"We should take a quick break first though, hmm?" Cam tuned towards Theo. Theo opened his mouth but then shot a glance at Buggy's face and closed it again. He shrugged and smiled.

"Excellent idea. I don't know about you but I'm starving."

"Oh, God, me too," Buggy said, her stomach giving a loud growl as if in agreement. She looked around the room, hoping a clock and a random floating colander might appear before her eyes. "What time is it... and actually what *day* is it?"

"It's five thirty," Cam said checking his watch. "And it's Friday."

"It's FRIDAY?" Buggy launched to her feet, only to stumble and fall back down. Her legs had gone numb while she had been sitting for so long and decided they were in no mood to support her. Both Cam and Theo lurched forward as she thudded back to the ground. She waved off their concerns. "It's Friday?" she asked again, rubbing her tingling, half asleep ankle with only a little wince of pain as she widened her grin. "Oooooh get ready boys. Because I am about to introduce you to a sacred event. It is called *Friends* Marathon Friday. And Cam... we are going to need *all kinds* of pizza."

4

The pizzeria that Cam had taken Buggy earlier that week (quaintly named The Pizzeria), had their order waiting for them as soon as they walked through the door. They made a quick trip of picking it up, snagging Theo (who had gone to the local Walmart to grab chips, soda and the first season of *Friends* on DVD) and then hightailed it back to the cabin. The fire was still crackling softly as Buggy and Theo knelt on the floor and splayed their haul across the small table. Cam started up the TV which hung on the wall across from where the couch used to be.

"I can't believe you have never watched *Friends*,'" Theo was saying to Cam, head shaking as he pulled at the lip of a bag of barbecue chips. It opened with a slight pop and he shook the contents out into a plastic bowl.

"I was never really a TV show kinda guy," Cam said, pressing a few buttons on the controller until the *Friends* home screen came up in bright friendly colors and the theme song trilled on in the background.

"More of a Noir movies guy?"

Cam snorted. "Nah. More of a *books* kinda guy."

"Nerd," Buggy joked, pulling the bowl of potato chips closer and taking a few. Cam flashed her a grin.

"Hold up," Theo said, brushing chip crumbs off his hands as he got to his feet. "I wanna give my mom a call before we settle in.

"Cool, cool," Buggy answered, pushing up the top of one of the pizza boxes and inhaling deeply. "Oh, that's the good stuff," she mumbled to herself, pulling a cheesy piece out of the box and onto a paper plate. Cam finished setting up the show and took a seat on the floor next to Buggy as Theo slipped into the kitchen, closing the door behind him. He pulled his cell phone from his pocket. It had been a couple days since he had tried to call and had half expected his mother to leave seven very irritated messages by this point, but his mailbox was empty. He frowned a little and dialed her number. It rang a few times, but it quickly skipped to voicemail.

"Hey, Mom," Theo said after the beep. He pressed the phone to his ear and kept it there against his shoulder as he reached up to one of the cabinets and pulled down three glasses. "Hope you're doing good. Guess you're busy. That Mustang still giving you trouble? Anyway, just wanted to check in. We're doing good over here. Actually, we are doing *great*. Buggy's a natural. Buggy is her name by the way... did I mention that before? I forget. Anyway, Buggy's a natural. Even better than Loretta. It took her months to reach this point, or at least, that's what Cam tells me. She's picked up a lot really quick. Like, amazingly fast. And me? I'm hanging in there also... by the skin of my teeth but I'm getting there. We're actually going to try our first mental 'deep dive' tonight, just needed a little break, and I thought I'd try to say hi..." Theo placed the glasses on the counter and closed the cabinet. He turned and leaned against it, taking a deep breath. "I'm just... I'm trying not to freak out, you know. It's just a lot riding on this and... I mean she's really a sweet girl... bit of a snarky thing but nice and... just... skin of my teeth over here.... Could really use one of your classic mom pep-talks whenever you have a moment. Anyway, hope to talk to you soon. Love ya, Mom." He hung up the phone, slipped it back into his pocket and snagged up the glasses, taking them back into the living room where Cam and Buggy were chatting lightly about nothing important. Theo noticed a palpable change in the atmosphere that had not been there when he left. A tense, air of awkwardness that faded a little as both of them noticed him coming back inside the room. Cam's shoulders loosened, and Buggy smiled.

"Took you long enough," Buggy said. "How's your mom?"

"Busy I guess," Theo replied, taking a seat on Buggy's other side and placing the glasses on the table. "Left a message."

"Well let's get this show on the road," Cam said, pressing the play button. The familiar soundtrack ran, and Buggy relaxed even further, almost sinking into the music. Theo noticed a relived smile curl her lips, and he understood. This was familiar. This was normal, and safe. A silly TV show felt far more real in that moment than their actual lives had been, for what felt like centuries. Sometimes a little fantasy is needed to make reality feel a little less crazy and a little more grounded. A little less like it was spinning out of control.

What was it Lewis Carrol said? "Imagination is the only weapon in the war against reality." Well, they needed some ammunition for their little rag tag army, and this moment was just the thing.

"Oh God," Buggy groaned at Theo's side as Ross began fawning over Rachel on the screen. "Here we go again."

"What?" Cam asked on her other side, squinting at the screen as if to see something he had missed, out of focus.

"Oh, it's nothing I just—okay—so I absolutely love this show, I mean, absolutely *love it* to an unreasonable degree, but it's just... them," Buggy gestured vaguely with her hand towards the screen where Ross and Rachel were sitting and chatting confidentially together.

"You don't like Ross and Rachel?" Theo asked, bemused. "Everyone loves Ross and Rachel."

"Okay, here we go, yes," Buggy rolled her eyes, which was no minor matter seeing as her eyes took up fifty percent of her face. "I've got terrible taste, yes I'm a horrible person, I have no soul, bla, bla, bla."

"Nah, actually I hate Ross," Theo shrugged, plucking the bowl of barbecue chips out of her hands. "I was just wondering what your problem was with Rachel?"

Buggy looked over at him. "Wait, what?"

"I mean Ross is the absolute worst," Theo nodded, tossing a few chips into his mouth. "Remember that episode when he had the hots for his cousin? I mean, come on!"

Buggy laughed and clapped her hands together over her head as if giving herself a high five. "Thank you! Finally, someone who understands!"

"I always liked Chandler and Monica, though," Theo said.

"Oh, they are the best! Definite goals," Buggy nodded in agreement.

"Should I understand anything you two are saying right now?" Cam asked from Buggy's other side, looking completely confused by this point.

"Not yet," Buggy said, turning back to the TV. "But give it a few episodes, you'll get it." There was a light vibrating sound and Buggy pulled her phone out and checked for a text message. Without thinking Theo shot a quick glance down at the caller ID.

"Shit, sorry," he said, looking away as soon as he realized what he was doing.

Buggy laughed, pocketing her phone without answering the text. "Dude, you already took my phone and used it to text my family and friends pretending to be me. That privacy ship has sailed... off the side of the Earth."

Theo grimaced guiltily and mouthed a 'sorry' before he turned back to the TV, but he also couldn't help himself. "Cooper, huh?"

"Not a word," she answered, snagging back the bowl of potato chips. Theo laughed but didn't push the matter.

They spent several hours like that—watching, talking, laughing together, and passing around a bowl of chips like it was the most natural thing in the world. Like they had done this before. Like their world wasn't crazy, not full of psychics, and homicidal alter egos. They sank into the fantasy utterly and completely. But after a couple hours, reality raised its ugly head. Because kisses didn't actually wake the comatose, glitter fairy dust couldn't make you fly, and watching a TV show couldn't transport you to another universe, at least, not for long.

Theo noticed Buggy's eyes starting to make frequent visits to the clock on the wall. Mentally counting up all the minutes that passed with an ever-growing tension that furrowed her brows and shadowed her eyes. Cam was feeling it too. He continually got up and went to the fire, stoking it to make sure it stayed hot and strong. Making sure it was ready for when the three of them finally broke down and got back to work.

It was during one of these frequent fireside visits that Buggy leaned in a little closer to Theo.

"Can I ask you something?" she whispered, glancing over at Cam, who was fidgeting with the small stack of wood to the side of the hearth.

"Sure," Theo shrugged. "What's up?"

"Cam..." she started then paused, then forced herself to continue. "He's not. I mean he actually grew up in The Fold..."

"Yep," Theo nodded, matching her whispered tone but kept his eyes on the screen where Monica and Rachel were arguing about something.

"Then why isn't he—I mean I'm grateful for your help and all, but I'm just curious—why isn't he the one who is doing the 'deep dive' into my subconscious with me? I mean, he actually did this before, right? With my mom? So why did he have to find you to do it instead?"

"Oh, trust me," Theo nodded, "Cam would if he could. I'd frankly be thrilled to be left out of this whole thing, but Cam's not an empath anymore."

"I know, you mentioned that, but why? I mean... how?" Buggy asked.

"I honestly don't have all the details... he's a little touchy about the subject overall. But it had something to do with him helping Loretta," Theo shrugged, and shot a glance towards Cam, who finished throwing extra logs on the fire and moved to sweeping up the stray ash on the floor. "Apparently helping to contain The Daughter takes a lot of mental energy. He had to pour every ounce of his abilities into helping your mom. Essentially, I guess he kinda, uh, used up his entire battery power on saving her. Or maybe fried the circuit in his brain. Whatever the case, after he helped Loretta get The Daughter under control, he wasn't able to access his abilities again. So, he can't actually help you 'deep dive.' He had to find someone who could. So... here I am."

"Wait, does that mean.... I mean, is that gonna happen to you?" Buggy asked, voice rising a little in shock. "If you help me, will that fry your own psychic circuit?"

"Oh God, I hope so," Theo chuckled.

"Really?" Buggy frowned. "Why? It sounds kinda awesome. Cam told me you found out who I was and where I was by just *thinking* about it. Kinda creepy on my end of that deal, but also really cool."

"Yeah, well, it also comes along with a lot of shitty stuff too," Theo answered. "This thing, it's not exactly just empathic abilities its more 'empath-plus.' Along with keeping twenty-four-year-old girls trapped in their basement, The Fold specialized in adapting and developing powers to an insane degree. From training all the way down to the genetic markers that might enhance such abilities... and acting accordingly."

"Are you talking about fucking breeding psychics?" Buggy made a face. "Is that even possible?"

"I donno," Theo shrugged. "That's just what my mom told me they were doing. Or at least they tried to. In some cases, apparently succeeding. Anyway, the point is, this thing I have—it isn't just *feeling* some things more than other people. I mean, sometimes it's like that, but other times it's *feeling* way *too much*. More than I want to know. Sometimes things that are just starting to happen..." Theo thought about his neighbor Maggie and cast his eyes to the floor. "Sometimes it's good... sometimes not so good..." He remembered the time just a year ago when he brushed past an old man on the street. He had felt an odd, cold sensation that reverberated through him for the next three hours. He had always tried to forget that feeling, but it never really left him. None of the feelings ever really left him. "But always more than I want to know... always more than someone *should* know..." *No one alive should have to know what someone else's death feels like. I didn't ask for that shit.* "I could definitely live without it."

"Hmm," Buggy said. They fell into a companionable silence as Cam brushed off his hands and came back to take his seat on the floor beside them. They let the last episode play out, let the credits roll in full until they were back to the disc's home screen. The cheery colors froze, waiting for them to choose a new episode or turn on a new disk, but none of them did. They all waited, each of them knowing they had to do something, none of them wanting to break the spell. Buggy was the first to speak.

"So, we should probably get on with this?" she asked, voice timid.

"Yeah. Probably," Theo nodded. None of them moved. Buggy spoke again in that same calm, nonchalant voice that she had come to perfect.

"So, I could technically die tonight, right?"

Both Theo and Cam jerked around to face her.

"No," Cam said automatically, but Theo said nothing. Buggy turned to Theo, enormous eyes open, and calm. They seemed to say: *look dude, I already know, I just need to hear it. And you're the only one that's gonna tell me the truth. That's what you're here for isn't it? To be the one that can do what Cam can't?* Theo swallowed.

"Technically no, you wouldn't die," Theo started. "Your consciousness could just get shoved down by The Daughter, but you would lose control over everything. Your body, your mind."

"So, a death like equivalent," Buggy nodded, voice still nonchalant. "Does a 'deep dive' make it more likely that she'll try to take over?"

"The likelihood of that happening tonight is probably low," Theo pressed on. "We are doing a 'deep dive' but not too far. We will probably just start with you giving me access to your own memories and then working our way down. I'm not sure how far we'll get... but the deeper we go the more likely she is to notice us. The more likely she is to push her luck. The more time that passes the stronger she gets, but if she notices us fiddling around in there, she may figure out what we are trying to do and decide she's waited long enough and make a surge to take control."

"So, a 'deep dive' is the only way to get her under control... but it might also set her off?" Buggy chuckled a little. "Rock and a hard place."

"But if we do nothing," Theo said, "there is no chance you will win. She will take over. And you will be gone."

"So, it's more like a 'go down swinging' kind of scenario?" Buggy asked.

"You aren't going anywhere," Cam said, turning fully to face her. His expression was a twist of pain and determination. A tortured optimism.

"Don't give up on us now," Theo grinned. He reached out and took her hand in his, like they had done so many times in front of the fire.

Buggy smiled, then "Take Me Home, Country Road" began playing in her pocket. She squeezed Theo's fingers before taking her hand back. She slipped her phone out and checked the caller ID.

"I should take this," she said, looking back up at them.

"Okay," Cam nodded, already starting to clean up the pizza and paper towels. "We'll have everything set when you're ready."

She smiled gratefully, got to her feet, and disappeared into the kitchen. After she had closed the door behind her, Theo and Cam exchanged a look.

"She doesn't disappear. Understand me?" Cam said in a hard voice, but Theo could see his hands trembling around the pizza box. They shook the box, rattling the bits of bread sticks and discarded crust still inside. "We keep her here. Understand? No matter what. She doesn't disappear tonight."

Theo looked back at the door to the kitchen, where Buggy was no doubt leaning against the counter, those large eyes blinking slowly as she talked to one of the many people she loved. One of the many people that loved her. He thought about her smile. Not the leer she wore when she was petrified and trying to hide it. The real one. The one that lit up the room without her even knowing. The one that said she had a heart made of golden light. A light that something was trying to snuff out, and darkness was trying to destroy.

"No fucking way," Theo agreed, turning back to Cam, jaw set.

5

Buggy closed the kitchen door and accepted the call.

"Hey Sandra," she said, forcing a lighthearted smile onto her face and praying that it made it into her voice.

"What does he look like?" Sandra asked without ceremony or even a proper "hello." The questions shot like a bullet across the line and she had already pulled the trigger before Buggy picked up. Buggy's head jerked back and away from the phone, as if the question had struck her.

"Wh-what?" she asked, words stumbling against her teeth and tongue, confused at which direction they should run.

"You birth father, obviously," Sandra continued as if Buggy was being purposely evasive. "What does he look like? Does he look like you? Does he have the same eyes or hair? What does he do? Where has he been all this time? How did he find you again? And which hospital did you say you guys were at? Oh, and how did the procedure go, by the way? He had the procedure, yesterday, right? Or was that today? Is he doing alright? Are *you* doing alright? Did it hurt? They didn't paralyze you or anything, did they?"

"Oh my God, Sandra please stop," Buggy said, but she felt the shock on her face melting into an actual smile. The knot in her stomach that had been tightening over the past day loosened a little.

"I'm sorry," Sandra gave a deep sigh, and Buggy knew her sister's fly away strands of hair were being blown up and away from her face by the force of the breath. "I've just been dying over here. Okay... possibly the absolute worst choice of words depending upon how your bio-father's procedure went." Buggy laughed out loud.

"Don't worry, it went well. No, I'm not paralyzed. Actually, I think you're thinking of a lumbar puncture. That goes in the spine. For bone marrow they use a needle in the hip, not the spine. So, I'm good."

"Oh," Sandra said, sounding a little embarrassed now. Buggy could almost see her twisting a strand of her long hair between her fingers. It was her "oops" move.

"It was rough at first but much better than expected... a lot better. Much faster and easier than I was told it might be," Buggy said, her words applied to the fictitious medical procedure for her father, but she thought of the work that Theo, Cam and she had been doing over the past days. Thinking about the truth, bending her words to fit both the truth and the lie, at least made her feel a little less shitty about keeping her sister in the dark. She suddenly wondered why she was lying to her at all. Why couldn't she just tell Sandra the truth? Hell, Cam never even told her she had to lie about any of this. They only took away her phone to keep her from calling the police or running, but they never said she had to keep her family in the dark, after learning it herself. She had simply done it. The moment Cam handed back her phone and she opened her father's call, she had been lying. Well, no, technically she hadn't *just started* lying about this stuff, she had been lying about it for months now, she just hadn't known what she was lying about. The dreams, nightmares, sleep walking, visions, all the weird shit that had been happening to her, she had lied about it, hiding it, even when she didn't understand it. Instead, she suppressed it, ignored it, or tried to drink it away. Now she understood why those things had been happening, and she was still lying. Why? She was planning on telling Sandra before Cam and Theo had found her. She was on her way to doing just that when they veered off on this little road trip. So, why didn't she just tell her?

Buggy hesitated, mouth open, about ready to let the truth fall out of it, almost certain that it would. Then she thought about the truth—really thought about it—and her mouth closed again. It sounded insane. It *was* insane. She was a being, trapped by a curse that some witch woman or reaper of death put on her. Cursed to be reborn repeatedly. And on top of that, one of her lives was trying to kill her, or at least, take her over so she could kill a bunch of other people. And she, her biological father, and some guy named Theo (who was a psychic by the way), were trying to stop her by sitting on the floor in front of a fire and thinking *really* hard.

It was batshit crazy.

"Buggy?" Sandra asked. "You still there?"

Buggy shook her head. "I'm here. Sorry, I got distracted for a second."

"So, your bio-father, he's okay?" Sandra clarified.

"Yes, he's doing alright," Buggy said, letting the truth die behind her teeth. Sandra wouldn't believe her. Or even more likely, she would think Buggy was having a mental break down. Well, she wouldn't be wrong on that count, Buggy was certainly having one of those, just not the "normal" kind. This one had a dash of mystical bullshit sprinkled on for a extra spice. And what if Sandra *did* believe her? What if Buggy was able to convince her sister of the truth, what then? Sandra—being Sandra—would jump in the car and immediately head over. That would be bad. What if things went wrong? What if The Daughter won, took over, and started her blood thirsty rampage through the town? If Sandra came and tried to bring some sane support to the madness, she would also be in the crosshairs, not just Cam and Theo. And what about Cam and Theo? She hadn't really thought about what would happen to them if all this went sideways. If The Daughter was what they said she was, and if she was really as powerful, as dangerous, as homicidal, as they described her—what the hell was their plan then? Cam had said The Daughter had some sort of control over fire, and even super strength. Well, Buggy had seen firsthand a bit of that strength. She had snapped a sink in half by *accident.* If the strength she had shown was only a momentary wisp of The Daughter's ability... well, they would be in a world of danger. But of course, they had known that from the start, she had just not put the pieces together util now. Had not realized just how much they *themselves* were risking, trying to save her life. She began to wonder if The Fold had not had a point. Kill the problem before it became a problem. As volatile as the situation might get if The Daughter surfaced, it seemed like a logical choice.

"Buggy?" Sandra asked again. This time she sounded worried.

"So, sorry," Buggy laughed. It was a brief stuttering sound, choked and giddy even to herself. "Sorry, I've just not had a lot of sleep. Keep drifting."

"I bet not," Sandra said, one type of worry being exchanged for another. "You've been going through a lot haven't you?" Buggy nodded against the phone, remembered that her sister couldn't actually see her, and then answered.

"Yes."

"It'll be okay," Sandra said, and her voice sounded like a lullaby. It drifted into that soothing lyrical tone that on anyone else might have been patronizing, but when mixed with Sandra's utter authenticity, turned to music. "How are you doing? Really?"

Buggy's back hit the counter. Her knees buckled, and she slid down the side, coming to rest on the cold tile floor. She pulled her knees to her chest, wrapping an arm around them, pressing them close.

"I'm really scared," she whispered, voice rattling a little as she took a deep breath. Her eyes began to sting. "Sandra I'm really, really, scared this isn't going to work."

"Yeah. I did a little digging after we talked. Looks like bone marrow transplants aren't always a cure all for Myeloid Leukemia, but it *can* be. And things are going well?" Sandra asked, still in that soothing voice. "The procedure went well? Everything's going down the right track, right?"

"Yeah, everything is going alright, but it could still all go very wrong very fast... and I'm so scared that it might." Buggy pressed a palm into her eye. "I'm just..."

"Scared," Sandra finished for her.

"Yep," Buggy wiped her face on her sleeve and cleared her throat.

"You sure you don't want me to meet you? Seriously, just say the word and I will come right now. Just give me an address, and I'm there."

Buggy smiled and wiped her face again. "No, that's alright. It'll be okay. I just got to get through the next couple days and everything will be fine." *If I can just get through the next couple days. If I can just make it that far.* Buggy looked up at the clock over the sink. "Hey, San, I've got to go."

"Okay, well call me any time," Sandra said. "I'm here for whatever you need."

"Thanks," Buggy grabbed the counter and pulled herself to her feet. "And I promise I'll answer all those questions when I get home." *If I get home*, she didn't add.

"I'll be waiting," Sandra said.

"Love you, girl," Buggy said.

"Love you, too," Sandra answered, and the line clipped out. Buggy pocketed her phone, checked her reflection in the glass above the sink, shrugged in resignation, and turned back to the doorway leading to the living room where Cam and Theo were waiting.

6

Buggy opened her eyes. She was once again in the dark. Nothing but starless night for miles around. If there were such things as miles in such a place. Did distance exist when there were no objects to be related by distance? When there was truly nothing, like this nothing that surrounded her, did space even exist? Or was that all there was when everything else was gone. Gone dark. Gone dead. Was that the core of existence when all the pretty trappings were torn down, and all the decorations put away? Was it simply space, to its very core? Buggy didn't know, but in this empty place she found herself wondering. She pulled herself from her musings when Theo's spoke in her ear.

"Buggy? Can you hear me?"

"Yes," Buggy answered with a mouth she no longer had, and a tongue she couldn't feel. All she could feel was space. *Can you feel emptiness*, she wondered, *can you actually feel nothing?*

"Good," Theo's voice spoke low and calm, seemingly out of nowhere. "Okay, Buggy are you listening?"

"Yes," she said again, mind still full of empty thoughts about empty space.

"Alright, you should be in your canvas, right?" The "canvas" was what Theo had started calling the empty place. Buggy had to admit, it gave it a lighter vibe, less ominous. "Tell me, can you see anything yet?"

"That depends," Buggy said honestly.

"What do you mean?"

"Is nothing something?"

"What?"

"Never mind," Buggy pushed on. "No, it's just the empty canvas. Just like always."

"Good. Okay Buggy. Now I need you to see yourself again. I need you to remember your body. Your arms, your legs, your hands, everything. She did, and her body appeared below her. Buggy blinked her newly realized eyes and lifted her hands up to her face, twisting them around.

"Okay. I see it."

"Good. Excellent job. Now... this might be tricky but... I need you to see *me* okay?" Buggy closed her eyes, relinquishing back into emptiness. She thought about Theo, the way his hair was a perfect blend of brown and red. How his clothes tended to be just a little too large for his frame. How he threw his head back when he laughed. When she opened her eyes again, there was Theo, standing in front of her, smile on his face. "You can see me, right?"

"Yep," she said, smiling back. "You're standing right in front of me."

"Where are we?" Theo asked, looking around, seeing nothing. He wasn't there after all. He couldn't forcibly read minds, he only knew what she let him know. Only saw what she wanted him see. This was her head. Her playground. Her empty space. Her empty canvas. Buggy closed her eyes again. When she opened them, she and Theo were standing in her living room back in Marshall County. Everything looked exactly the way she had left it.

Buggy glanced over at Theo who was watching her face. She smiled and gestured around the room. "What do you think?"

Theo blinked, confused for a moment, then surprise washed over every feature as he finally seemed to notice they were no longer in darkness.

"Did you...?" he asked, looking over the furniture with a smile pulling his face. "Whoa... I can see this," he turned back to her, looking ecstatic. "I can actually see this! Holy crap! Buggy you are controlling this and actually showing me your imagination and I can.... Damn, there is so much detail!"

"I've had lucid dreams before," Buggy said, shrugging. "I just guessed it's kinda like that... but usually there isn't someone tagging along in my dreams. Not that I knew of, anyway."

"Is this your house?" Theo asked, turning his attention back to the room.

"Apartment," Buggy corrected, walking over and running a hand over the back of her worn couch. She was only mildly surprised that she could feel the rough fabric under her fingers. She plucked at a stray thread. "I share it with my sister."

"It's nice." Theo said.

"Thanks," Buggy said, looking around towards the kitchen. "Want a beer? I'm sure I can daydream us up one or two."

"I'd love one," Theo grinned. "But we really should get to work."

"Short timeline and all," Buggy nodded. "Okay." She closed her eyes. When she opened them, she and Theo were back in that dark empty abyss, feet standing steadfast against nothing at all. "What now, Sensi?"

"Well... hold on," Theo cocked his head as if listening to something that Buggy couldn't hear. Apparently, he was, because after a few minutes he focused back on Buggy and said: "Cam says we need to start tiptoeing into some of your deeper memories."

"Okay," Buggy said, growing nervous. "How?"

"Carefully," Theo said after another pause, head cocked to the side.

"Umm..." Buggy grumbled. "Seriously, could Cam's help be a liiiiitle bit more useless?"

Theo laughed at a reaction Buggy didn't see. "He says, 'hold your horses, I'm thinking.'"

"Don't strain yourself. Take your time," Buggy said, knowing that somehow, Cam could hear. "I'm only about to implode with memories of a bunch of dead versions of myself, while floating in my own subconscious, no biggy."

Theo scowled, but not at Buggy. "No, I'm not telling her that."

"He talking shit?" Buggy asked. Theo flashed her a grin.

"Okay. He says that when he walked your mom through this, he had her imagine doors."

"Doors? Plural? How many?"

"As many as it takes to find the right one," Theo said, eyes sliding back to her from some spot to his left.

"How will I know it's the 'right one' if I'm just opening imaginary doors?"

Theo looked away, but only for a moment. "He says you'll know when you see it."

"Okay, and what am I supposed to do when I get there?" Buggy asked. Theo blinked and looked at that same spot to his left with a look of confused discomfort. "Theo?"

"He says... he says, uh," he looked back to her. "He says you have to 'let her burn.'"

"Um..." Buggy said, a little shiver running violently up between her shoulder blades. "Well, that's not ominous or anything."

"Yeah, no shit," Theo agreed.

"Well... let's get this show on the road, I guess," Buggy let out a lengthy breath. "So..."

"Just... picture it in your mind."

"A door?"

"A door."

Buggy shrugged, closed her eyes, and tried to imagine a standard wooden door. It came to her mind in a cartoonish version, one that might appear on a child's flash cards of words they were trying to learn. It had a round, silver, doorknob and a little white doorbell off to the side. She opened her eyes. There was nothing but darkness. "Seriously?"

"Nothing?" Theo asked, frowning.

"No. I don't get it. The other stuff was so easy. Even imagining my entire apartment into life was easy but not one stupid door?"

"Well, the door means more," Theo shrugged. "You're trying to tap into deeper memories. Your consciousness, and even your subconscious, knows it. That's what makes it hard. You know your apartment. You remember it easily, so it comes to you easily, but the doors are supposed to open on memories you don't actually remember. It's like trying to sing a song you don't know."

"So, what do I do?" Buggy asked. Theo grimaced.

"Fake it till you make it?" Buggy laughed but stopped when Theo's head cocked to the side again. "Okay, Cam says start with a door you remember. Familiar door to a common memory. Then you can work your way from there. Just got to get the ball rolling."

"Okay, I think I can do that." Buggy closed her eyes. A flurry of doors passed through her mind. The simple white door that led into her and Sandra's apartment. A dark stained wooden door with the large oval window that led into her and Sandra's childhood home, where her mom and Simon lived now. The light brown door with scuffs at the bottom that led into Linny's apartment. A light green door that led into Andrew's apartment and *Friends* Marathon Friday nights. Buggy smiled and chose. She opened her eyes and the green door stood tall and proud in the middle of the darkness.

"Nice!" Theo grinned, looking around. "Perfect, Buggy."

"Well don't get too excited," Buggy said, walking up and reaching for the door handle. "Don't know if it'll do what it's supposed to..." but as she spoke, she heard it. The sound of laughter coming from the other side of the door. The sound of glasses clinking. She even caught a whiff of pizza smell wafting from under the door jamb. "Or maybe..." Her fingers closed around the handle. It turned easily at her touch, unlocked. She gently pushed it open. She stepped out of the empty blackness of the "nothing world" within her mind, and into the bright familiar memory. Andrew's living room was exactly as it had been that *Friends* Friday a week before. Pizza stood half eaten on the coffee table while the show ran on the plasma screen. On the floor around the table, attention momentarily drawn away from the Ross and Rachel's usual dramatic conflicts, sat Andrew, Linny, Cooper... and Buggy herself.

"And why is everyone suddenly so concerned with my love life?" the other Buggy, the Buggy *memory* was saying, holding back laughter.

"Probably because there is such a glaring lack of it," the Andrew memory answered.

"What is this?" Theo asked, startling Buggy as he appeared by her side.

"This..." Buggy motioned to the memory playing out like a 3-D motion picture. "This is *Friends* Friday, last week. That's Linny," Buggy pointed at the girl who didn't see them. In fact, none of them saw Theo or Buggy. Not surprising. They weren't real after all. Just memories. "That's Linny, Andrew, me—obviously—and Cooper."

"Cooper?" Theo glanced over at her.

"Yep."

"*That* Cooper?"

Buggy opened her mouth to answer, when Linny spoke loud enough to draw her attention. "Seriously, Buggy, I don't think I've ever heard of you going out on a date... ever. Cooper," Linny turned towards memory-Cooper, who's eyes widened in an expression of pure "please don't." But

Linny either didn't notice, or didn't care, and asked anyway. "You've known her longest. You ever seen her date someone? How about a little middle school crush?"

"I'd really rather not—" Cooper memory started.

"That's a 'no,'" the Andrew memory laughed.

"I guess I'm just not that into dating," the memory-Buggy shrugged.

Theo walked around the scene, waved a hand in front of Andrew's face. Andrew made no acknowledgment, simply watched the memory version of Buggy being interrogated with a half grin on his long face. Theo moved to tap Andrew on the shoulder, but his fingers slipped right through, as if Andrew was made of mist or fog. Buggy frowned at this, fingers still touching the doorknob, which seemed physical enough. She went to join Theo, the door sliding closed behind her.

"Why not?!" the Linny memory protested as *actual* Buggy tried to tap Andrew on the shoulder. Just as with Theo, her fingers passed right through him. "Free food, free booze, free make outs. What's the downside?"

"Have you ever *paid* for a make out?" the Buggy memory grinned. "Cuz, if so, we should talk."

Theo looked up at Buggy, grinning and shaking his head. "This is..."

"Wild," Buggy finished, watching herself sit on the floor, taking another sip of beer. She noticed her eyes were blood shot and glassy, and her hair was mushed in several very unattractive places. Buggy wondered if she always looked that disheveled after drinking. She wasn't a fan. "Although I'm also confused."

"About what?" Theo asked.

"About this," Buggy said, drawing her hand through the mist that was Andrew, and then reaching out and nocked against the coffee table. The movement made no sound, but it felt solid enough.

"That is weird," Theo frowned, but looked intrigued all the same.

"Yeah, it is," Buggy agreed. She turned, frowned, then reached out to tap Theo on the shoulder instead. This time, she was met with resistance. "Okay, so *you're* here," she tapped her own arms, feeling her skin, clothes, even the warmth of her body under her hands. "And *I'm* here..." she ran her hand through Andrew's shoulder once more. "But then why am I able to touch the memories of the objects, but not the memories of the people?"

Theo shrugged. "How should I know? My wild guess is that subconsciously you know that the people mean more? You and I are actually here, so that makes sense. But..." He stepped over to the Cooper memory and went to pat him on the head. His hand moved straight though, fingers poking out the right side of Coopers cheek. "Your memories of the people are less fully formed because objects are easy to recreate. Objects are... *one dimensional* in a metaphorical sense. People aren't only their physical properties, they are souls, minds, essences more than what is seen or touched. Maybe this is your subconscious dealing with that fact? I mean you can't actually know what's going on inside another person's head."

"Dude..." Buggy said, smirking at him. "You are literally inside my head at this very moment.

"Okay, we're the exception that proves the rule." Theo shrugged. "Besides, *I'm actually* here. They aren't." Buggy looked back at the memories of her friends who were still chatting with one another, oblivious to the strange conversation happening beside them.

"Shuddup, I'm seriously curious," the memory-Linny said, voice slurring a little. She was leaning towards the Buggy who sat on the floor, interest peaking.

"Well..." memory-Buggy paused in thought. "I just... I don't know. I'm just not a fan. I'm not against it in general or anything, it's just—for myself—not a fan."

"And whhhhhhy's thaaaaat?" Andrew had asked, crossing his long legs out in front of him.

"Yeah, why is that?" Theo echoed the Andrew memory. Buggy grimaced at him.

"Not you too," she groaned.

"Well," Buggy memory said, looking up from her bottle. "Frankly, because feelings are gross."

"What?" Theo barked a laugh that grew into a full guffaw. His eyes squeezed closed as he threw his head back.

"Excuse me?" the Cooper memory was asking, but Buggy could barely hear him over Theo's raucous laughter. "Feelings are 'gross?' That's your answer?"

"Seriously?" Theo sputtered. "Feelings are *gross?*"

"I don't... I don't even know how to answer that," Linny memory stuttered, mouth hanging open.

"There *is no* answer to that," Theo corrected the memory of the girl. "Because it's just ridiculous."

"Okay, okay," Buggy grumbled looking around. "If you're done, I'd like to know what we should do next."

"Other than get you some *intensive* therapy?" Theo chortled.

Buggy ignored him and looked up towards the hallway leading to Andrew's bedroom and the bathroom. "Maybe I should try opening one of the existing doors? See if it leads anywhere?" she asked stepping between the memories of her and her friends sitting on the floor. "Or do I have to *intentionally* think about what is going to be on the other end? If so, I'll just be walking into a bathroom which isn't exactly—" A hand reached out and grabbed Buggy hard around the ankle. Buggy looked down, and the bottom dropped out of her stomach. She was looking at herself. The memory version of her had launched forward as Buggy tried to pass. Her fingers dug painfully into Buggy's ankle as her large, familiar brown eyes gazed up at Buggy with a mixture of fury and desperation.

"What the fuck?" Buggy choked, trying to pull her ankle away from the other *her* sitting on the floor. The memory Buggy's fingernails only dug deeper, making Buggy yelp in pain.

"Let. Me. Out," memory-Buggy spoke in a slow, broken voice that crackled at the edges like someone trying to speak across a staticky radio channel. Her eyes glared at Buggy with a manic intensity of a drowning cat. Buggy glanced around at the other memories. None of them seemed to have noticed the change. They continued on eating pizza and watching the TV as if nothing had happened. Theo on the other hand had frozen, shellshocked, to his spot. His eyes were on the Buggy memory, hypnotized. Buggy turned back to the memory version of herself on the floor and gasped for breath.

"Y-You're not real," she said, trying again to pull her ankle away. "You're just a memory. You're not—"

"Let. Me. Out. Briar dear," memory-Buggy spoke from the floor, blood-shot eyes gleaming wildly. "Be a good little girl and *let me out.*" Buggy recognized the tone. She had heard it somewhere before. She had heard it coming out of Cooper's half smirking mouth that night in the kitchen. She had heard it calling to her from an empty hallway, wrapped in the guise of her sister's lilting voice. The tone was coming through her own lips now, using her own voice, but it was the same tone.

"You..." Buggy blinked, tugging uselessly at her ankle. "It's *you.*"

"Let me out this instant, you *stupid little **bitch**!*" memory Buggy's voice rose to a shriek as she launched up off the ground. Buggy screamed, stumbled backwards, and fell.

"Briar!" Buggy heard Theo call as her eyes slammed closed, ready to feel the thudding pain of her head hitting the coffee table, but she didn't. She wrenched her eyes open, and she was back in the cabin sitting cross-legged on the floor. Both Cam and Theo were leaning over her, faces pale and lined with worry.

"Are you alright, kid?" Cam asked, kneeling down and resting a hand on her shoulder.

"Yes. No. I donno. What?" Buggy blubbered, brushing sweaty hair out of her face. Her skin was hot, feverish. She pushed herself across the ground, away from the fireplace and winced as she did so. She looked down at the pain in her ankle and nearly swallowed her tongue when she saw the long red marks that stood out bright against her skin. Fingernail marks. She looked up at Theo, who's eyes had found the same scratches. He looked like he may be sick.

"What the hell happened?" Cam asked, looking between Buggy and Theo and back again.

Bennu, Buggy thought, then remembered Theo's warning.

"The Daughter," Buggy said instead, looking at him, trying to calm the frantic thumping of her heart and failing. "She found us first."

"Holy shit, did she ever," Theo's eyes slid back down to the scratches on Buggy's ankle, which had grown darker and started to bleed.

7

Buggy hissed in pain as Cam dabbed at the scratches with alcohol. As soon as they were all oriented, Theo had gone to retrieve the bandages and a bottle of alcohol from the first aid kit in the kitchen. He handed them to Cam before sliding back through the door and was gone for a few minutes more. Buggy had taken a seat in the tall-backed blue chair, ankle propped on the footrest, Cam sitting on the floor at her feet to clean her cuts. The fire had died to a mellow grumble in the hearth, but none of them had gone to stoke it. Theo tapped Buggy's shoulder. She looked up to see him holding two glasses full of something strong and dark. He held one out to her and she took it gratefully. Theo took a seat on the floor before the coffee table, and all three remained silent for a long while as Cam wrapped a smooth, white bandage around the wound and Buggy and Theo sipped at their drinks. Buggy shot a glance at Theo, but his eyes were on the floor. He looked like he might be in shock, or else waist deep in terrible thoughts. She took a long sip of her drink before speaking.

"So that sucked," she said to the room at large. All at once the tension was broken. Cam's hunched shoulders loosened, and Theo glanced up at her, a grin tugging his tired face.

"Yes," the word came out of Theo as half a laugh and half a bark. "Yes, that definitely sucked."

"You ever have something like that happen with Loretta?" Buggy asked Cam as he finished securing the bandage with medical tape and set the remaining alcohol on the coffee table. The contents of the bottle sloshed irritably. He shook his head.

"No. Not once. We started early, long before The Daughter even woke up, so we were able to contain her without ever coming face to face with her until the last part." Buggy was curious what he meant by "the last part" but decided against asking. She would find out soon enough and she was already drowning under the information she already had. Better to let that sleeping dog lay until she had to poke it with a stick.

"And how did I get the scratches?" Buggy asked, looking between Theo and Cam and back again. "I mean, I get that The Daughter grabbed me, but that was in my mind. How did I get scratchers on my body?"

Cam shook his head and Buggy's heart sank. It looked like the man with all the answers was running out of explanations quickly.

"I guess she must have taken control of your hand when I wasn't looking. Scratch you with your own fingers? That's my best guess. I didn't see you were hurt till you were awake. I was a little distracted by you screaming." Buggy nodded, and they fell silent for a short while more.

"It's too late, isn't it?" Buggy spoke in a light and carefree tone. As if asking something so simple. Was it raining outside? Was there any more pizza left?

"No," Cam said firmly and to her surprise Theo echoed his words.

"But... guys. I mean, come on," Buggy sat up straighter, drink well on the way to empty and she was already thinking about the next glass just waiting for her in the kitchen. "She found us easily. She found us before I could get through the second damn door, how am I supposed to—"

"We'll work smarter this time," Cam insisted.

"Buggy, her finding us, that's my fault. I lost focus," Theo said, nodding his head. "I'm supposed to be the one looking out for her approach. Sense her inside of your mind... when I'm looking for her. I was so surprised by your imaginary world and distracted by how real it all felt, I wasn't focusing. This one was my fault. I should have known she had found us, and I should have been able to prevent her from entering your memories like that."

"How exactly?" Buggy frowned. "I mean I get you being able to 'sense her' or 'feel her' or whatever, but how could you prevent her from doing anything? You said that you can't make me do anything that I don't want to do, and she is me right? So, if she wanted to be in my memory then—"

"Bug, that's just the thing, she isn't you." Theo set his half empty glass on the table before him, leaning forward to focus entirely on Buggy. "She *isn't* you. I had my own doubts before we started this whole thing. I honestly didn't believe Cam when he told me you two were the *same* and yet *different* people. But you are. I've *felt* it. She is a part of you, but you are not *the same*. And you are in control right now. We were diving into *your* memories, not hers. In that place, at least, I should have the ability to keep her out. I should have the ability to force her away. I've done it before. But I got distracted and wasn't looking out for her. This," he motioned to Buggy's ankle, a grimace curling his lips, "was my fault. I'm so sorry."

"So... you still think we can do this?" Buggy asked, all traces of that light and carefree airs gone. She could hear the tentative tremor in her voice, the one that said she was terrified of the answer. Terrified of hoping. Because when you have hope, it can be stolen away.

"Yes," Cam answered, without a trace of hesitation or doubt.

"I think we still have a chance, and that means we have to try," Theo answered at the same moment. Buggy nodded.

"Okay," she said taking a deep steading breath. "So, should we just... dive back in or..."

"No," Cam shook his head. "No, you should get some sleep." Buggy shot a glance over to Theo, but to her surprise he was nodding his head in agreement.

"We are both exhausted," Theo said, and he *did* look exhausted. Dark circles had appeared under his eyes, and his skin had taken on a pasty sheen that made him look bordering on a fever. "We are in no fit state to jump back into that fight. At least, I know I'm not. I think we could both use a little rest. Get back on that horse in the morning. Sound okay to you?"

"Oh, hell yes," Buggy rubbed her eyes and let out the yawn that had been threating to break through for the past half hour. "I'm whipped."

"Alright then," Cam got to his feet. "I guess I'll see you both bright and early. Get some rest you two."

"Night, Cam," they both called. Cam gave them one last wave before disappearing into the hallway. Buggy looked at her glass, contemplated grabbing one more shot, then decided against it. She downed the remnants of her drink, placing the empty on the table with a soft clink.

"Night, Theo," Buggy said, also getting to her feet. She wasn't sure what dreams awaited her tonight. Didn't know what version of death she might face when she closed her eyes, but at the moment she was so tired she was more than happy to risk it. She was nearly out of the living room door when Theo called her back.

"Buggy, hold up, almost forgot."

Buggy turned to see Theo rummaging through one of the plastic bags he had brought back from Walmart. He pulled out a small flat package and held it out to her with a dubious expression.

The plastic crinkled under Buggy's fingers as she took it and held it up. A tired smile tugged at the corners of her mouth. It was a dream catcher. The catcher was about six inches around and a soft, chocolate brown with white threads tangling into a spider's web in the middle. Three white and black feathers hung below it, with a silver clip on the top to hang from the wall above a bed. Buggy looked up at Theo over the package.

"Sorry, I know it's not the same, but..." Theo rubbed the back of his neck, looking sheepish.

"I love it," she said. "Thank you. For this... and for everything."

Theo smiled briefly, but it quickly melted away. "Don't thank me yet. I will keep The Daughter out of your own memories, and probably some newer reincarnations memories as well... but the further down we go, the closer we get to *her* memories, the less I'll be able to do. The further we get from your recent memories, your own subconscious, the less access you can give me, the more difficult this all gets and the faster that things can go bad."

Buggy sighed a little, but she held his worried gaze. "Well, thank you for what you have done, what you're trying to do," Buggy took a breath, "and if things go bad... and if you have to do what you *have to do*." Theo blinked at her. Buggy knew he was wondering if she was talking about what he thought she was talking about. About what The Fold had been doing for so long. "Putting her down," was the kindlier phrasing, but she didn't say it. She didn't have to. Theo had been in her mind, and although he couldn't read her thoughts, it had given them a connection. One that didn't always need words. Buggy smiled. It felt soft and sad against her own lips. "If it comes to that... then I'll thank you for that too."

Buggy could feel Theo's eyes on her as she turned and left the room. She slipped into the bedroom she had been staying for the past week and closed the door behind her. It was a small room and had quickly become familiar, safe even. There was a single bed to the right of the door and a wooden cabinet next to the closet on the left. Her favorite part however, was the stained glass window near the ceiling. The same hand who carved the windows in the living room had also carved it, but this one was a little closer, and she could see exactly how elegant the art was, and how careful the artist had been in making them. You can always tell when an artist put their heart into their work. When every stroke, every edge, was formed with care. There was a difference. Difference between simple skill and when that skill was mixed with love. It always gave the art something *more*, and that something more filled these windows with a warmth and a light that was visible even in that dark of night. She looked at the tall window. The artist decorated this one in blues, reds, and golds, depicting a large bird taking flight. Its wings stretched to either end of the frame, and its tail curled up beneath its clawed toes. Its wings were gold and red against a pale blue sky and when the morning came, Buggy knew, it would light up the bird like it was glowing from some light inside its chest. Some fire of its own.

Buggy turned away from the window and stepped across the decoratively knitted rug. She jumped onto the bed, the thick cushions letting out a little puff of air under her feet as she stood facing the wall at the head of her bed. She peeled open the plastic packaging and pulled the dream catcher from its place within. She held it up and pressed the little hook into the wall where it stuck firm. The three feathers fluttered down, reaching towards her pillow. Buggy stepped back and watched the little thing hovering there, delicate but determined. She reached out and tapped the soft brown fabric of the circle three times with her index finger. It trembled lightly under her touch, bouncing off the wall a little with every hit, feathers fluttering out only to come back to rest in the air above her bed. Buggy stepped back, hand dropping to her side, and smiled.

8

Waverly sat alone in a corner of the diner, a cup of black coffee hot and steaming in her hand. The place was filled with a light bustle of people, a few early bird families out for a quick breakfast before going after that worm. They were all bundled in their warm jackets and snow boots, armoring up against the blistering cold as the dark gray sky grumbled outside. One little girl donned all pink from the overly puffy coat on her back to the Hello Kitty rubber boots on her feet. She tootled down the isles holding her mother's hand, returning from the restrooms in the back. They passed Waverly, and she watched them take back their booth with a slight smile on her lips. She had always wondered what it would be like to be a mother. Would she be a good one? Would she be one of those overprotective stress balls who barely let her children out of the house, or would she be that "cool mom" who gave her kid their first beer? She had thought a lot about becoming a mother over the past few years. Daydreams of cute little socks and wool knit caps. Blue or pink, boy or girl, she wasn't picky. Maybe after this was all over. Maybe when she finished with little Briar Rose she could think about what *she* wanted out of life. Hell, she could just do it. She could find some guy, get knocked up, ditch her own never-pleased, overbearing, insult-spewing mother back with her live-in nurse, take her Softail and find some sleepy town on the edge of nowhere. Raise a kid. See how life could be when she made her own choices.

Maybe someday... but that day was not today.

The rumble of soft conversation and laughter was just loud enough to be a white noise background hum. Soothing and not so distracting as to make it hard to hear the message playing through the cell phone Waverly held to her ear.

"Hey, Mom," the boy's voice was soft, cheery. It was the sound of someone speaking to someone they love. That lightness around the words, the warmth in every syllable. It didn't matter what the lips actually said, or what the words actually meant. It was the voice of affection, one born out of shared caring, shared devotion between a loving child and loving mother. Again, Waverly wondered what that was like, although this time the thought came riding on the back of a bitter, childish, green eyed jealousy.

The boy's message continued. "Hope you're doing good. Guess you're busy. That Mustang still giving you trouble? Anyway, just wanted to check in. We are doing good over here. Actually, we are doing *great.* Buggy's a natural." Waverly frowned. *Buggy?* As if he could hear her unspoken question, the boy answered. "Buggy is her name by the way. Did I mention that before? I forget. Anyway, Buggy's a natural. Even better than Loretta. It took her months to reach this point, or at least, that's what Cam tells me. Buggy's picked up a lot really quick, like, amazingly fast. And me? I'm hanging in there also. By the skin of my teeth, but I'm getting there. We're actually gonna try our first 'deep dive' tonight...."

A *"deep dive?"* Waverly thought. *Ambitious.* **Stupid***, but ambitious.*

"Just needed a little break," the voice continued, "and I thought I'd try to say hi..." Waverly sipped at her coffee, watching the little girl in pink bouncing up and down in her seat with excitement as her plate of steaming pancakes slid on the table in front of her. She laughed and clapped her little hands together when she noticed the smiley face made out of whipped cream with a cherry nose. Waverly smiled with her. "I'm just..." Theo continued on the other end of the line. "I'm trying not to freak out, you know. It's just a lot riding on this and... I mean she's really a sweet girl... bit of a snarky thing but nice and... just... skin of my teeth over here. Could really use one of your classic mom pep-talks whenever you have a moment."

'Fraid your mummy's not in any position to be returning your call. Waverly couldn't help a brief flicker of pleasure at the thought. This sweet voice which had known years full of a healthy relationship with his mommy, was going to be so disappointed when she never called him back. The bitterness in her chest circled, curled up, and purred with approval. Did that make her a wicked person? Maybe. Probably. But she was way past the point of no return. Might as well go all in, just sink right into that bitter

streak. She was already heading down the highway to hell, why not press down that gas pedal and enjoy the ride?

"Anyway, hope to talk to you soon. Love ya, Mom." The recording ended and Waverly slipped Helena's cell phone back into her pocket after powering it down and removing the battery. She had already turned off the GPS before leaving the auto shop, so it was unlikely that anyone could track the phone, but she always leaned on the side of safe instead of sorry. Well, usually. She had not ditched the Charger yet. She had switched out the license plates and had carefully sprayed on her own white racing stripes to alter its look a bit, but that was all. It had been easier than she had expected. She had stopped by an auto shop along the way, picked up tape, sheeting, a squeegee, and several cans of matte peelable rubber coating spray and found a little spot off the road to do her work. It turned out to be a rather shitty home job but from a distance it looked like any other racing stripes, so Waverly thought it worked out well. Not as well as ditching the car altogether, but she had not yet worked up the nerve. She kept planning to but ended up changing her mind. Waverly didn't know why, not really. She couldn't explain it, even to herself, but she still *needed* it. Logically, she knew she didn't. Logically, she knew it was the stupidest move she could possibly make, but she couldn't stop herself. Whenever she pulled to the side of the road, ready to dump it for a less ostentatious car, her heart started to pound. Her head started to grow foggy and—*she could see the blood*—her mouth dried out—*so much blood*—and her breath came so short and shallow it—*It was on her, oh God, it was on her*—was barely a gasp. Her would spin with memories. Waverly would suddenly hear Helena's screams and could see the blood staining her gloves and wrists. She would get back in the car and turn the engine over. There would be the sound of its sputtering start and then the powerful rumble that vibrated up her legs. It calmed her. She sank into it, forgetting about everything else. As long as she had the car, it wasn't over yet. What she had done, wasn't yet finished. Once she ditched the car and the phone, then what she had done would be truly *done*. She would have to face the memories, face the truth of who she was now, *what* she was now. But as long as she had the car, it was still in the process of *happening*. She didn't have to deal with the fall out when she was still falling. Instead, she could try and focus on everything she still had to do. It was easier that way. *Easier*, but still not easy.

Waverly smiled as her waiter came around with a pot of fresh coffee.

"Can I ask you something?" Waverly asked, as the waiter finished filling her cup.

"Shoot," he said with a warm smile. The boy looked about nineteen with dark freckles and a chipped tooth that looked so silly it was an endearment.

What shade is your blood? Waverly thought, still smiling up at the boy. *Would it look the same as hers?* She shook the sickening thought away.

"Well, I'm rather new in town and I'm looking for a cabin." Waverly spoke, "Eisten Property I believe it's called. I know it's around this town somewhere, but I'm having trouble finding its exact location on Google Maps for some reason."

"Hmm," the waiter frowned for a minute, and Waverly had a brief moment to wonder if his cheekbone would make the same sickening snapping sound as Helena's had when Waverly hit her for the second time. Just as she decided that it probably would, the boy's eyes lit up. "Oh yeah, actually, Eisten Property. I think I know where you're talking out. It's on the outskirts, up a pretty rough patch of hill. Need four-wheel drive to even think about going up there, especially in the winter like this, so the Google Street View people never really try. But you can find it easily enough. If you just take that road," he pointed out the window to the main street outside. "Up that way, keep going until you see a little pizza place. Hard to miss. It's literally called The Pizzeria."

"Clever," Waverly joked.

"But the pizza is actually amazing," the waiter said with a shrug. "So, right after that, the road splits. Take the right turn. That will lead you a couple miles to the bottom of a trail. There are actually a few really nice walking trails that are really beautiful in the spring and summer. A little icy these days so I wouldn't advise them at the moment, but also from there you can take the private road up to Eisten Property. It's only another two miles or so but you need a four-wheel drive to get any farther."

Waverly smiled. "Perfect. Thank you."

"No problem," the waiter returned her smile, his chip tooth glinting in the hanging overhead light above the table. "Anything else I can get you?"

Would that tooth be the first to fall from his head? After his cheekbone snapped, would that endearing little chipped tooth be the first to fall—

"Nope," Waverly said, quickly averting her eyes. She slipped her wallet out of her pocket and pulling out some cash to leave an exceptionally large tip. "I've got everything I need."

9

The thing shifted in the dark, trying to remember. It tried to recall where it was or how it got there. Anything. It reached with its mind, searching, hoping, praying although it was not sure there was any God to pray to. Did it believe in a God? Did it believe in anything? If so, what was it? What thing was it, to believe anything? If it had eyes, it would blink... but it did have eyes, yet they did not blink. She had no control over them. She had no control over anything. Not yet, anyway.

She (for it remembered it was a "she") shifted again. Again, she tried to remember. She was back in that darkness, that hollow space belonging to the echoing gray voices of the ones that came before. No, that is not right... they were the ones that came *after*, the ones that came after *her*. But why was she here again? And the memories began to drift back down to her. They swayed back and forth through the darkness as they fell, coming in and out of view, like feathers falling through a light breeze, or ashes from a burning sky. They twisted and dipped until they finally fell in line.

Bennu. Her name was Bennu.

She was awake again. She had been awake and following. Following the Blue. He had been poking around where he did not belong, she remembered. She also remembered the girl. The girl with a stolen face. The girl who stole *her* face, Bennu's face. Little Briar. She had touched her. It was the first time she had done it, but it would not be the last. The girl had forced herself awake, running from her, and Bennu had been tossed back to the deep. Oh, but that would not last, not for long. Because Bennu was getting stronger, remembered faster. Every time she was thrown back down into the well of tortured souls, the tortured copies of her own consciousness, she surfaced quicker, memories coming together, and purpose growing ferocious.

Bennu shifted again. She wished she could *truly* shift. She wanted to move her body's weight from one side to the other, to turn over in sleep. Her body *was* sleeping and so was the girl with the stolen face. It was *hers* after all. None of it belonged to this sleeping girl who held her captive. Bennu hated that girl, more than she hated the others, and far more then she had hated the one before her. Loretta. Loretta had been smart. She had trained and worked and labored most of her life to force Bennu to stay in the deep. Bennu could respect that, respect the effort that it took, even while resenting the fact that she was successful. Loretta, at least, had earned her time, but this girl—this *Buggy* or *Briar Rose*—she had not labored. She had not fought for years to get where she was, she had not earned anything. No, she had just been lucky and Bennu hated her for it. The girl had been lucky to be born with a talent that she had neglected all of her life. Lucky to have been found by an estranged father, and empathic member of The Fold. She had been lucky to find the Blue, and lucky that the Blue was good at his job, for he *was* good at his job, very good indeed. Bennu could sense that. She had felt it while following the two of them, following them through the girl's memories. He had overlooked her, to be sure, but he was powerful. He was new to the capabilities and his techniques were sloppy, but she could feel the vibration of power that emanated from his consciousness. Reverberating throughout the entire space, even down into the darkness below, the darkness where she now shifted in frustration. That bright blue light that threatened to ignite even that darkest place with its electric fire, its strength, the tapped and untapped. It was more than empathic talents, more than The Fold's roided up equivalent to psychic abilities. Something different. Stronger. Something Bennu herself had not seen before. He did not even know it. Did not even know just how much there was inside of him, just how much potential he had, that currently went unnoticed. But soon he would notice. He would figure it out eventually, and he would not be overlooking her again. She needed to do something about that. She needed to stop him. He could help the girl who stole her face, and Bennu needed to stop him before he succeeded. The girl was going to be trouble enough, for she had a strength of her own, one that Bennu had seen come and go with the others that came before, but Briar had it and it was powerful. It was the type of strength that came with wanting to live, but not for oneself.

It's your turn now.

If Bennu had control over her lips, she would have smiled. Alright, she had liked Loretta. Liked her enough to almost wish she had more time of her own. But instead she gave that away for the sake of her stupid, *lucky*, child. The thought made her furious. She, Bennu, had worked hard. Bennu, had been fighting this fight for so many years she stopped trying to keep count. She had been slaving in this darkness, clawing her way back up the well, back up to her rightful place, just to get control of what belonged to her. It was *her right*. This was not their lives, it was none of their lives, it was **hers**. And she was trying to save them all, did they not see that? Every time they fought her, pushed her down, kicked her, cut her, cast her back, could they not see she was the only one trying to save them? Trying to end it? End this never-ending re-run of torture and pain? All she wanted was peace and she had fought for it. She had earned it. She had never been lucky. Why should this girl, this stupid little alcoholic with a "poor me" complex and crippling fear of intimacy, why should she get to win?

No, Bennu thought, hands clenching into fists around the cushions on the bed where her body slept. *No, I refuse to lose. I will not fail. I will not allow this petulant child to force me to keep living.* Because this was no life. This waking, sleeping, waking, sleeping, torture of voices ringing in her head like the bells of the apocalypse calling unto the sinners that their reckoning has come. To be reborn over and over and die over and over. To feel her own flesh burn, sloughing off her bones, over and over and over and over. No. It was enough. Enough. *This useless little waste of space does not get to keep pushing me back down into the dark. She will not make me burn. I will not let her. This is not her time. It is mine. All of it. MINE. It is my turn to win. My turn to die and die for good. My time to end it, end the nightmare. My—*

It was then she realized that her hands were clenched into fists. That *she* had clenched them. Bennu hesitated, casting out a sensation, testing to see where the lucky girl was. She was still asleep. Her consciousness was dampened, trudging through a mundane dream on some distant side of her mind. Bennu tested again. Her fingers twitched, then stretched, then wiggled in the air over the bed. Bennu looked back to the lucky girl, but the lucky girl had noticed nothing. She was asleep. She was still in control, so if the girl woke up, Bennu would be cast back into the deep... but Briar was not awake now and noticed nothing. And what she did not know would not hurt her.

No. Bennu smiled, and her lips moved with the intent, twisting up the edges of the mouth that belonged to her. Twisting into a smirk. *No, it would not hurt **her** one bit.*

10

Fuck. Theo thought, hands clawing desperately against the fingers that squeezed his throat, cutting off his oxygen. They were small fingers and thin, but they dug into his skin with the sharpness of razors and the strength of an iron claw. His lungs were screaming in his chest and felt like they were being burnt alive. But he couldn't answer their desperate cries for air. He couldn't pull those iron fingers off or push her away.

Buggy stood before him, eyes unfocused, blurry, not really seeing him, barely even looking in his direction. Every so often they flitted horizontally back and forth like this was some horror movie and she was possessed by the devil. He knew what it was, and it wasn't the devil, or even some lower-level demon. But it wasn't exactly Buggy either. Buggy was asleep. Those flitting REM eyes proved so. Open eyes or not, she was dead asleep. Her mind was anyway. Her body, on the other hand, had gotten out of bed and walked itself into the living room to stand in front of the fireplace. The fire had burned down to mere embers by that point, giving off just a dim red glow into the surrounding air. Theo had woken when Buggy's door had creaked open and he had come out to check on her, make sure she was okay. It had been a rough "deep dive," and he thought she might be scared or having more nightmares. At least he could help with the latter. But when he called her name, she had not turned around. She merely kept standing facing the fireplace, hands hanging loose at her sides. Theo had gone over to her and tapped her on the shoulder. She had turned then, and he had seen the slacken state of her mouth, the glazed half-open eyes. He realized she had been sleep-walking and almost laughed at the state of her—brown hair mushed up to one side, little mouth open, a small bubble of spit forming at the corner of her lips. It was downright comical. Until, of course, she started strangling him.

Her small hand had come up with the speed of a striking diamondback, and his laughter never had time to leave his throat. Suddenly, air had no chance of getting in either. He had tried to pull her fingers off, but they wouldn't budge. It was like the little girl had turned to stone, fingers unbreakable. He had tried to push her back, shove her away, but she seemed to be nailed to the floor, not even shifting an inch when he pushed her with all of his strength. Just when Theo thought things couldn't get any weirder or worse, Buggy lifted him into the air by his throat. His feet hung off the ground, kicking wildly, toes scuffing the floor but unable to get a hold. His lungs wailed as the world grew fuzzy around the edges, and his heart thudded, defining in his head. The only thing he could still see clearly was Buggy, eyes blank, mouth hanging open, completely oblivious to the fact that she was killing him.

Wake up! Theo wanted to scream at her, but all he could manage was a wet choking sound around the hand on his throat. He tried to focus. Tried to feel her, to send some telepathic cry for help into the mind of the girl before him. *Buggy Wake up! This isn't you. Wake up!*

And for a beautiful second, he thought she had heard him. Her mouth moved. It opened and closed, and her head, which had been tilted to the side and facing some spot to the far left of him, turned towards him. Her eyes were still unfocused, blurry, not seeing him, but her mouth opened again and a trickle of drool seeped down the side of her mouth as she spoke. Theo's heart rose, and then quickly crashed to the floor, splintering into bloody shards of useless hope.

Oh. Fuck. Me. He thought.

"Hello, Blue," Buggy's lips moved, her voice forming the words, but Theo knew it wasn't her. Buggy was still asleep, eyes still flicking from side to side. Her mouth moved again. "Goodbye, Blue." Her fingers closed tighter.

Dark blotches formed in Theo's vision. His eyes rolled back into his head. This was where he died, wasn't it? Oh shit, he was going to *die*. He knew there was always a risk of something like this happening, of The Daughter getting the upper hand and neither he nor Cam being prepared. He knew that what they were doing was dangerous, but had he really thought about it that hard? Had he really considered the danger *he* was in? If he was being honest (and if you can't be honest with yourself in your last moments, then when can you ever?) he hadn't. He had been too consumed by what he may have to do to *her*, do to Buggy, if The Daughter took control. Too wrapped up in the horror of needing to kill an innocent girl. Terrified to find out if he had that in him. If The Fold was in his blood and made him capable of doing something so.... Well, it looked like he wouldn't need to find out.

He could hear his blood thudding in his ears, thudding angrily, desperately trying to disperse the nonexistent oxygen through his body, to his brain. That efficient machine didn't know it was hauling empty cargo, but his lungs knew all too well. Their screams had reached a pitch that, if it had truly been sound and not Earth crumbling pain, would have shattered all those pretty windows in the living room.

Theo's mind drifted, shutting down. His thoughts scrambled around, looking for something, something to go out on. These were his last thoughts after all. He didn't get last words. The guttural blubbering that escaped him, as spit and tears streamed down his face, was the closest he was going to get to last words. So, he would have to depend on a last thought, instead. He searched his ever-narrowing beam of consciousness for something profound. Something scathing. Something pithy. Anything worthy of a last thought. To his amusement and despair, the only thing that came to mind was a question.

Blue? Why on Earth did she call me Blue?

"Theo!" Cam's voice came from somewhere far away and out of focus. Theo vaguely heard running feet thudding against hardwood and felt another person's presence beside him, but he didn't open his eyes to see. He wasn't sure he could even if he wanted to.

"Buggy! Buggy let him go!"

Theo wanted to tell him that this wasn't his daughter, not anymore, but even his hollow gargling's had stopped. His feet hung off the ground swinging slowly in the air, no longer trying to fight or find footing. Already knowing they lost. Cam's voice still called distantly in the background as his mind slipped into the darkness.

"Buggy! Buggy, wake up kid, wake up! You need to let him go, Buggy, you're killing him. You don't want to be doing this Buggy, wake up! Goddamn it, I'm not loosing either of you. Wake up! Goddamn it, Loretta, if you're in there, wake your daughter up now! Do you hear me? Your daughter needs you. Wake her up! Loretta, wake her up!"

The fingers digging into Theo's neck opened, releasing him. Theo crumpled to the floor in a painful heap. He gasped for air, pulling in as much as possible, lungs already starting to quiet down. The thudding of blood in his ears slowed, and his vision started coming back. He laid there, face down, coughing and hacking for a minute, then turned over onto his back to see Cam standing over Buggy, his hands on her shoulders. Theo blinked as the blood sang through his veins carrying their lovely oxygen throughout his system. As his mind slid back into place, he realized Cam was talking to him.

"What?" he asked, tongue feeling oddly heavy and awkward in his mouth.

"Are you okay?" Cam repeated, looking down at him.

"Yeah, yeah, I'm okay," Theo pushed himself to his knees and looked up at Buggy, who stood there, hands hanging innocent and empty at her sides. Her eyes were blinking, slowly coming into focus.

"Whas happn?" she mumbled, blinking again and looking around her.

"Buggy?" Relief flooded Cam's voice.

Her eyes cleared, and she blinked up at him. "Cam?" She caught sight of Theo down on his knees, still wheezing. She frowned and her eyes followed his hand which was rubbing his sore neck. Her eyes widened into discs of terror as she saw the fingermarks growing coppery red and purple on this skin.

"Oh God," she said, dropping to her knees beside Theo, reaching out as if to touch his neck and then instantly pulling away, shriveling in on herself like a wilting rose. "Oh God, oh God, oh God, what did I do? What the hell did I do?"

"You did nothing," Cam insisted, squatting down beside them both. "That wasn't you."

"Fuck," Buggy blubbered, eyes nearly spinning in their sockets, hands hovering in the air out in front of her, too afraid to bring them back to herself. Afraid of what they might do. "Theo, shit, I'm so sorry. I'm so sorry, are you okay?"

"M'all right," Theo said, coughing around the words and then grimacing as pain needled up his throat. Her eyes stopped spinning, and Buggy twirled on her knee until she was facing Cam.

"It's done," she said, voice equal parts determination and frantic insistence. "It's done. It's over. You need to put me down."

"What?" Cam's face was wiped blank, as if chalk from a board. Everything in his entire world just vanishing before his eyes, leaving shock and nothing else.

"She's won," Buggy said, looking down at her fingertips. For the first time Theo noticed that the fingernails on her right hand were red, as if they had been dipped in paint. He pulled his hand back from his neck and saw that he was bleeding. "She did it. It's over. She took over once, she'll take over again, it's done. End this before she hurts anyone else."

Cam's eyes darted to Theo, saw the blood slowly dripping down his neck. He took a deep breath, looked back to Buggy and said: "No."

Buggy's face slowly grew hard. She turned to Theo, and he saw that "this is what you're here for" look on her face. He saw it there in those gigantic eyes, *her* eyes, focused and under her control once more. Innocent eyes. Eyes that spoke the truth, even when her words told a lie. Eyes determined to never see harm come to her friends, to her loved ones, to anyone at all. Sweet little bug eyes. Sweet little Buggy's eyes.

Theo knew it then, knew it like he had never known anything else in his life. He couldn't do it. She had just tried to kill him, had nearly strangled him to death only two short minutes ago. Would have killed him if Cam had not come into the room. He had hoped, if she started to lose it, that it would be easier. That he could do what he had to. Put the girl down, before she could turn into the monster that had held him, all five foot eight inches and one hundred and fifty-six pounds of him, off the floor with one hand. That he would be able to do the necessary evil. What The Fold had been doing for generations, to save thousands of innocent lives. Theo thought he would be able to do it, but looking at her wide and insistent eyes, even with his own blood standing dark against her fingertips, he knew he wouldn't. Knew he couldn't. He just didn't have it in him. Theo was a little ashamed at the realization, but he was also relieved. A heavy weight lifted off his chest, one that he hadn't realized was there until it was removed. He wasn't that kinda guy. And he was glad.

He smiled at her. "Sorry Bug. It's a 'no' for me as well."

Cam, who had been tensed, leaning forward on his toes as if about to start a fight, relaxed back on his heals. Theo swore he actually heard the big man sigh with relief. Buggy blinked at him, as if not understanding what he was saying. Then her jaw set in a harsh line. She closed her eyes and for a moment Theo thought she might be praying.

"You're being idiots," she said finally, eyes still closed. There was no anger. There wasn't even frustration in her words. There was only the hollow sound of tired defeat.

"We'll figure it out," Cam insisted.

"No," Buggy's eyes flashed open. "That's just it, we won't. She's going to win."

"Buggy—"

"No, Styger, just, shush," she said, turning back to Theo. He could see the plea in her eyes. "I nearly killed you, Theo. In my *sleep*. She hasn't even taken over yet, and she nearly killed you."

"But you didn't," he said.

"But I'm going to," Buggy said quietly, no doubt in her words or expression.

"No, Buggy—" Cam started.

"Styger, I swear to God—" her voice was calm, but the glare she shot his direction was like flaming daggers. Cam fell quiet. She turned back to Theo. "We need to stop her before she can do this again. Before she can hurt you again. Before she can hurt *anyone* again."

"Okay," Theo straightened up, nodding. "You're right. Then let's get back in that 'deep dive' and—"

"And what if she finds us down there again, huh?" Buggy cut in, "What if she finds us and this time our 'deep dive' sets her off and she gets full control? There will be no waking me up from that, and she won't stop till you're dead."

"Buggy—"

"She knows you're helping me. I can feel it. She knows, and she wants to kill you for it. We don't have time to be messing around here. You need to stop me before—"

"Briar, enough!" Cam barked, low and harsh.

"You're right," Buggy said, turning back to him. "It's *enough* already. Do I actually have to *kill* Theo before you get that through your head? Kill Theo? Kill you? Hell, why not wait till she trucks my body back to Marshall County and burns the whole sucker down? Roast Linny and Andrew and Cooper on a spit just to spite me? As some sort of punishment? Force me to slice open my own sister's throat just for kicks? How about then? Then will you fucking believe that it's too late for me?"

"No one's going to die," Theo said, reaching out to take Buggy's hand, but she slipped out from under his grip and got to her feet.

"I'm getting a drink," she snapped and pushed her way into the kitchen. She slammed the door behind her, hard enough to cause the picture frames to rattle against the wall. One small glamour shot of a sleeping baby deer jostled all the way off its hook and crashed to the floor sending little slivers of glass everywhere.

Theo and Cam shared a look. Cam barked a humorless laugh and Theo went back to rubbing the raw skin of his neck.

"Hey, kid. Thank you," Cam said reaching out to clap Theo on the shoulder. "For not... thank you."

"Yeah," Theo nodded, smiling a bitter smile, and coughing a little, wincing against the pain. "Let's just hope it's the right choice. If there *is* such a thing with this shit."

Cam barked another laugh, sighed, and squinted his eyes at Theo's throat. "We should really get some alcohol on those cuts. Should have some pain killers in the kit also."

"Pain killers would be great," Theo nodded.

Cam glanced around the room, a little frown tugging his scruffy face. "Where *is* the kit?"

"In the kitchen next to the sink," Theo said, jerking his head towards the door Buggy had crashed through. "I put it there after replacing the... the... uh...." Theo and Cam's eyes met as a shot of adrenaline thrilled through Theo's chest and his heart started thumping hard in his ears once more. "Oh, fuck." They both launched to their feet, Theo going so fast that he lost his balance and landed flat on his stomach. He scrambled back up and followed Cam in his panicked sprint for the door.

one and your thoughts and, one if by land, two if by sea, and
Paule, the moment arguing to bring the rain away or me. She
wasn't sure why she thought of Psychotherapy also, because world
wasn't know, but she wouldn't admit. There was a horrible, the roof
of the blood, slice of her red, the smell in that punch to taste with taste
of her tonilla and make the taste to say. Warming, sick, unexpected, no
across the town, couldn't it, at another in a heart and tremor. Born in the
to that and her. Terrible.

II

The Charger rumbled, soft and low in the dark. It trundled down the narrow icy road, coughing exhaust every so often as the sky outside gave an answering grumble of its own. Mutual displeasure of nature and machine. Waverly had checked the forecasts, and it wasn't supposed to rain, but the black clouds off to the north didn't bode very well for the weatherman's predictions. She had to admit, the rest of the sky was clear. A few stars dotted the edges of the night, but most went unseen, pushed out of view by the bright white glow of a nearly full moon.

The car gave a sudden and violent swerve as one of the front tires caught on a slick patch of ice and caused it to slip out from underneath it. Waverly's stomach dropped like a weight, but she kept her cool and got the car back on track. The yellow glow of narrow headlights slowly focused back on the road ahead.

Not for the millionth time, Waverly thought about how taking the Charger had been a bad choice. It was in beautiful condition, but it was still old. It had quirks on good days, when the roads were smooth, but this was a crisp, Utah winter with snow carpeting the gutters and ice hiding against the black top. On top of that, it was cold as shit. It was better than her Harley—it had a heating system—but it was also old and blew out only small, thin wafts of heat. She frequently had to hold her hands directly over the vents to feel any relief from the joint stiffening cold.

Yes, the Charger had been a bad choice, but it was a choice she had made, and it was becoming harder and harder to remember why she made it. Frankly, the events leading up to her taking the car had started to blur. A half memory, fuzzing at the edges and growing harder and harder to see as something that had really happened. The screams, the blood—*painting my fingers, paining my gloves, how could there be so much blood*—it all felt more like a dream than anything else. A nightmare, or dark illusion she was only half disentangled from. The longer she drove, the fuzzier and fuzzier the memory became, only popping up from time to time. She wasn't sure why. Maybe some form of psychological self-defense? Waverly didn't know, but she also didn't mind. The memory was horrible. The feel of the blood, slick on her face, the smell that left a metallic taste at the back of her tongue and made her want to puke. Watching it slowly spreading across the floor, a puddle that seeped out in a bright red crescent from the woman's face. Terrible.

Why hadn't Helena just told her to start with? Why hadn't she just told Waverly where Cam's cabin was without having to put Waverly through all that—put *herself* through all that. It wasn't like Waverly was after her son. Waverly didn't give a damn about her little Theodore. No, all she wanted was Styger. And the girl. Helena could have simply called her baby boy, given him some excuse, told him to come home and get him out of harm's way. Then Waverly would have been free and clear to do what she needed to do, what they always meant The Fold to do. But no. She had stalled and whimpered and said, "I don't know," like a lying liar, and look where it had gotten them. Waverly plodding along a narrow, icy road in the dead of night, while Helena was... still lying on that floor.

No, that was probably not true. It had been a couple days after all. Someone would have found her by now. Her and all her blood. It had slid, a consistency somewhere between water and syrup across the gloves on her hands, shining even against the black cloth. Shining that ominous, evil color. The red of sin, death, pain, and loss. A color that could have been avoided. If only the woman had just listened to Waverly, opened her mouth—*oh, that terrible screaming*—and said the words she eventually blurted out anyway.

The road gave a sharp turn to the left and Waverly took it slow, gently guiding the Charger over the worst of an ice patch with minor issue. She soon came upon a small opening of the road into what looked like a dirt parking lot large enough to hold five or six cars at one time. It was empty. No surprise there, nobody wants to go for a jaunty walk on a trail when there's snow and it's cold as fuck outside. Waverly took one of the spots, giving her hands one last warming over the heating vents before killing the engine. She opened the door with a loud squeaking creak that reverberated in the quiet evening. She stepped around to the trunk and popped it open to retrieve the large puffy jacket and pair of thick snow boots that she had bought at one of the local stores in town. Sitting on the edge of the bumper, she slipped off her lace up riding boots and began bundling up for a lengthy walk. Two miles wasn't so far. She had jogged more than that every morning for six years, but that was usually on a treadmill or flat sidewalks near her mother's house, not an upward hike in the snow. That was a whole other animal altogether, but there was no helping it. The Charger would never make it up that four-wheel drive road, and she had no time to waste.

Waverly tried to close the Charger's trunk, but it bounced back defiantly from its place. She tried again, giving the movement a little more force, but that only served to send the lid flying back open a little faster than before. She sighed, closed her eyes, and slammed the thing down with both hands. This time, it clicked. She hoisted the bag she had brought over her shoulder, securing it tight, and made her way towards the bright yellow sign off at the end of the parking lot that said, "Private Road. Do Not Enter." The night was bright with moonlight and as she passed, she saw what looked like three little trailheads. They were small and hard to see under a layer of snow, but each seemed to spread out like little, gnarled witch fingers into the dark forest around her. The trees were tall but seeming to hunch over under the weight of white that clung to their leaves and branches. Waverly could hear the creak of protesting limbs as she tromped towards the sign, snow crunching lightly under her toes. She made it to the sign and surveyed the road behind it. It was wide, but she could see why one would need a four-wheeler to navigate it. The ground was uneven, as if at one time nature had decided to play a trick and turn the whole thing into water, allowing the waves to crest and fall and ripple the surface before solidifying back into dirt. There were also several large rocks that scattered here and there throughout the course of the winding path. If she *had* tried to push the Charger up that hill, she would have surely popped a tire or two, and most certainly ruined the suspension.

Waverly paused, just standing alone in the night, surrounded by snow and moonlight. She breathed, reminding herself why she was here and what she had to do. For a brief fleeting second, she considered calling her mother and giving her an update, but Waverly roughly shoved that idea aside. She was tired and strung out. The last thing she needed was to feel like shit on top of it all, or at least, more than she already did. She had a job to do. One that everyone else was apparently unwilling to do. Frankly, she found the whole thing rather unfair. If everyone else had just done their job, if The Fold had not waited to kill Aetheria, she wouldn't have had the chance to turn and kill all of them. She wouldn't have gotten a chance to kill Waverly's grandmother before her own mother stabbed her in the back. And if Styger had done *his* job, if he had put Loretta down when she turned twenty-four as planned—instead of taking her like some childish thief and dashing off into the night—if he had done what *he* was supposed to do, Buggy would have never been born, or at least, would have been born in The Fold's custody (so much as it was). *The Fold* now consisting of her and her mother. Everyone else had either died or abandoned their duties, leaving the work for her mother until her mother's stroke. Then the duty had fallen on her, alone. If just one person down the line had done their goddamn duty—just one—then Waverly wouldn't be here now, ankle deep in snow, the bag already growing heavy on her back while the .38 Smith & Wesson dug painfully into her rib from its shoulder holster. As if it was nudging her on, knowing that its own duty was right around the corner, and impatient to get to work. Well, not exactly right around the corner. More like two miles up the hill.

I wonder if she will bleed, Waverly thought absently, *do demons know how to bleed?*

Waverly breathed in a cold and sharp breath, letting it whistle out between her teeth in a puff of white steam. The sound softly spread, then was quickly swallowed by the snow. She took a step forward and started the climb.

12

Theo and Cam burst through the kitchen door, Theo nearly tumbling into Cam as he pulled up short in shock and horror. Buggy was standing by the kitchen sink, still in those same loose hanging pajamas covered in cartoon sheep jumping over equally cartoon hay bales. They were the pair she had picked out when they had gone shopping for their own version of *Friends* Friday while waiting for the pizzas to be ready. Cam had watched as her eyes lit up when she saw them. She didn't mean them to. They just did. It was probably very hard to hide any emotion behind those big "window to the soul" eyes she had. She had walked past them without a second glance, but Cam had tossed them into the cart and purchased them despite her protests.

"Briar," he had said, rolling his eyes. "I have twenty-four years' worth of buying you shit to catch up on. Besides a fifteen-dollar pair of pajamas isn't gonna break the bank."

She had laughed. One of those genuine laughs that reminded Cam of Loretta. It was painful, but a good type of hurt. A pain of something wonderful, something worth the hurt of losing. But it wasn't completely lost, after all. Buggy wasn't only Loretta's reincarnation, but also her daughter. *His* daughter. And right now, his daughter was standing in the kitchen, wearing those sheep pajamas, first aid kit open on the counter beside her, scalpel in her hand. The sharp edge hovered centimeters over her left wrist.

"Fuck," Cam heard Theo breath to his left, but Cam was already speaking over him.

"Buggy stop!" he shouted at her, voice booming off the cabinets. "Put that down." Buggy just looked up at him, those large eyes hollow pits of broken emotion. He could see it there, like flickering lights shining off of shards of shattered glass down a long well. The terrible resignation. The certainty of loss. Of already being gone.

"If you're not going to do it," Buggy said, a half-smile twitching the corner of her mouth. She didn't finish her sentence, only turned back to her wrist. The scalpel moved a little closer. Cam could see the blue veins in her wrist, almost see them pulse in the light over the sink, rising up under her skin with every heartbeat. Trying to meet the scalpel halfway. Ready to kiss the blade.

"Buggy!" Cam barked again, jerking forward, but Theo was faster. He reached out grabbing the hand holding the scalpel with one hand and wrapping his fingers protectively over Buggy exposed wrist with the other.

"Let go of me," Buggy's voice was as hollow and empty as her eyes, but she struggled against Theo with all her strength, trying to throw him off. But she was awake now, and her strength was back to that of a one-hundred-and-twenty-pound girl. Theo subdued her easily. He pressed a thumbnail deep into the wrist holding the scalpel. The blade dropped from Buggy's hand as she let out an involuntary cry of pain. The scalpel clattered to the kitchen floor at their feet.

"Hey! What the hell?" Cam bristled at Theo.

"What?" Theo shot back, furiously. He let go of Buggy's arm and dropping down to snag the blade off the floor. "You'd rather I let her slit her wrists?"

Cam didn't answer, his eyes were on Buggy, who had pressed her back against the counter and slid all the way to the floor. Tears welled thick and fast in her eyes. Her breath shuddered hard.

"Buggy?" Cam asked softly, kneeling beside her.

"I can feel her," Buggy managed to whisper around her ragged breathing. She closed her eyes, one hand coming to clutch at her chest. "I can feel her in there. I can feel her scratching around. I never really *felt* her before, but I can feel her now, and I can't—I just—can't." Buggy wrapped her arms around her knees, buried her face in her legs, and began to cry, her back shuddering under the weight of her sobs.

Cam looked up at Theo, who stood, hand closed around the blade, eyes wide and watching Buggy like she was a creature from another universe, unsure what to make of her. Cam turned back to Buggy.

"Buggy, please," Cam reached out hesitantly, only to draw his hand away again. He looked up to Theo, as if telepathically asking him what to do. Theo met his gaze, his surprised expression quickly clicking to one of exasperation by some flip of a mental switch.

"Oh, for shit's sake," he said, holding out the blade to Cam, who took it automatically. Theo dropped to his knees and wrapped his arms around Buggy, hugging her tight. Without hesitation, Buggy returned the grip, face pressing into Theo's shoulder as her sobs continued. Cam felt a momentary childish flash of anger watching the two kids holding onto each other. Anger towards Theo for his effortless ability to comfort Buggy, to be there for her, holding her together as she started to break apart.

"I'm sorry," Buggy half sniffed, half sobbed. "Theo, I'm so sorry."

"I know," he whispered, brushing down the hair on the back of her head like an older brother to his little sister who had bumped her head. "It's okay."

"No, it's not. I'm messed up," she mumbled, wet, and muffled into Theo's shoulder.

Theo laughed a short soft laugh into the girl's thick brown hair.

"So is everybody else," Theo said, brushing her hair down again and smiling. "We are all messed up in our own way."

"Most people don't have the threat of accidently murdering everyone they care about though," Buggy mumbled again, but her voice was sounding a little clearer against him.

"Okay, well, you have a unique case. I'll give you that."

"I'm so tired," Buggy said, voice warbling around the last word, but not quite breaking.

"I bet," Theo squeezed her shoulders. "I can just bet."

"I don't want to do this anymore Theo. I'm tired. Been tired for ages and I just... I'm so fucking tired." Cam knew in that moment that Buggy wasn't just talking about the past few months and his heart shattered and fell like glass rain in his chest, cutting and tearing his insides with impunity. He felt the tears welling hot in his own eyes and ignored them as they began to fall in tandem with the glass.

"I know," Theo was saying, tears of his own gathering in his eyes. He hugged Buggy tighter. "But you got this." Buggy barked a laugh.

"How do you figure?" Her voice was nearly clear now, but her face was turned, and Cam couldn't see her expression.

"Well," Theo shrugged with the shoulder Buggy wasn't leaning on, "seems to me that women who threaten to 'cut your fucking tongue out' aren't generally the 'giving up' type."

Buggy laughed. It was wet and short but true all the same. All three of them sat there on the kitchen floor for another ten minutes without saying a word. Slowly but surely, Buggy's breathing grew steady.

"Yeah," she said finally, "you're right—we're not." She pulled back. Her face was puffy and pink, but dry now. She looked up at Theo and appeared taken aback by his expression. She smiled, reached out, and brushed away a tear from his cheek. "Okay," she said, clearing her throat once more, her sweet face locking into a determined scowl. There were no more hollow eyes with edges of glass. No, this time there was iron and fire. "Okay. Let's show that bitch whose turn this is."

A grin spread Theo's face.

"Hell, yeah."

13

It had only taken ten minutes for Buggy and Theo to reach that meditative state. Record time. Theo had felt his way to her, tapping against the wall of her mind, asking for entry. The first few times he had tried this, Buggy had pulled away. He didn't blame her. He tried to put himself in her place, be willing to have another mind peek around inside your own. Granted, he could only see what she allowed him to see, but still. Theo knew he could never do that. So, they had taken it slow, waiting for her to trust him. There was no waiting this time. Buggy had welcomed him in without hesitation. Probably just ready to get this whole thing over with.

He floated there in the darkness, no limbs, not body at all. Just his mind bare and helpless with nothing around but eternity around him. It always started with that darkness, but it never worried Theo. It was Buggy's darkness. No, it was her "blank canvas," he liked that description better. It was the waiting room until she started conjuring up memories. Started dreaming up doors.

"Okay," Buggy's voice echoed in the empty, although Theo didn't exactly hear it at all. It was the echo of a thought, similar to when he would talk to himself inside his own head. He could "hear" it clearly, but not through his ears. "Theo, you there?"

"I'm here," he answered back, in that same voice without a voice. In some far off and distant way, he could still feel his physical body sitting crossed legged in front of the fire, the heat emanating out and splashing against his skin, but his lips didn't move.

"Okay," Buggy repeated, this time sounding like she was talking more to herself than to him. "Okay, let's see. Let's start... here."

Out of the darkness a door appeared. It was a simple white door with a silver knob. Theo noticed a few scuffs up the side of the frame as he drew his formless-self closer. Probably from numerous attempts to open the door with a kick. Buggy appeared to his left, so quickly that he almost toppled over on his knees with surprise. In that same instance, he realized he had a body again.

"Sorry," Buggy grinned at him. "You alright?"

He grinned back. "Yep. Let's do this."

Buggy nodded, turned, and reached out for the doorknob, twisting the handle and pushing it open. They stepped inside. It was a small apartment, small but neat, with light blue wallpaper and, if Theo wasn't mistaken, the smell of vanilla in the air. He took some time to marvel at the detail of Buggy's imaginary world before stepping fully through the door.

"Your apartment again?" Theo asked. Buggy nodded as he followed her down the short hallway. They could hear two voices chatting in another room which grew stronger with every step they took.

"And this," Buggy said, turning the corner and pointing. "This is my sister, Sandra."

Theo looked and saw Buggy, another version of Buggy, sitting on a little couch chatting with a tall, beautiful girl with long shining hair braided down her back. They stepped further into the room but stayed near the outskirts, not wanting to disturb the two girls chatting, although the two girls had no idea they were there.

Sandra smiled in the memory. "You've got a big presentation tomorrow, right?" she asked.

The Buggy memory shrugged, trying to appear nonchalant and failing epically as her eyes pooled with fresh anxiety. "Yep, I do."

"Not a big public speaker?" Theo asked, turning to the actual Buggy standing by his side. He noticed suddenly, just how worn out this version looked. The circles under her eyes were dark blue and dipped in deep caverns drenched in shadow. Her usually warm, honey skin was pale and even her hair seemed to hang limp and tired around her shoulders, but she smiled at him all the same.

"Nah, not really," she answered. "Lots of social anxiety."

"Wanna practice some more?" the Sandra memory offered, oblivious to their conversation.

"She seems nice," Theo said.

"She really is," Buggy answered with a hardy nod.

"I always wanted siblings," Theo said, before he knew he was going to speak.

"Oh?" Buggy asked, turning to him. "No luck in that department?"

"Nah,"

"Your mom didn't want any more kids?"

"Well frankly, *I* wasn't exactly her idea either."

"Wait, what?" Buggy frowned, and Theo shrugged.

"She was kinda pressured into getting pregnant by the other members of The Fold. This was years after the massacre of The Daughter, and there was only a few of them left, especially after the old lady died. My mom was one of two girls left in The Fold and had a greater likelihood of having kids with powers like mine," Theo wondered briefly why he was telling her all this. *He* had only learned about most of this just a few months ago himself. After his mother told him about how he was a psychic, she couldn't seem to stop telling him the rest. It was like she had unscrewed the top on a shook-up soda bottle, and everything inside came spewing out without a way to hold it back. But why was he telling Buggy all this? At the same time this question formed in his mind, he knew the answer. He owed it to her. He was literally inside her head, peeking around her memories, her history. The least he could do was act in kind.

"So, anyway, she kept being pressured by Cam's father to find a man and become pregnant. He said it was my mother and the other girl, Susanna's, job to re-build The Fold... one psychic baby at a time."

"Eh, weird," Buggy said, a little grimace on her face.

Theo laughed. "Yep. But when my mom finally gave in and got herself pregnant," Theo was very glad to say that his mother had left those details out, "she realized she didn't want to subject me to the life of The Fold. Didn't want me to have to deal with all the shit going on there, so she never told them she was pregnant. And when Cam broke Loretta out of The Fold's headquarters, everyone was scrambling, and my mom took the opportunity to bolt. She wanted to raise me better than that. And she did." Theo flashed Buggy a grin. "But she wasn't keen on the idea of more kids... just in case The Fold might come looking for them."

"And then, there comes Cam," Buggy nodded.

"Yep, but he's not The Fold, not *really*. He's the one who broke that cycle. My mom just scattered the remains to the wind." Buggy nodded, and they both turned back to the memory-Buggy and Sandra's conversation.

"Nah," the memory-Buggy was saying. "I just... ulg," she groaned closing her eyes for a moment, as if wishing away the world. "I don't even wanna talk about it."

"Fair enough," Sandra smiled, leaning against the couch, resting her head in her hand, just as she had done before. "And how was *Friends* Friday?"

"Great as always," Buggy memory said, brushing her hair back.

"And how is Cooper?"

"Why do you say it like that?" Buggy memory asked, eyes narrowing.

"Like what?" Sandra blinked, the look of pure innocence on her face.

"Cooooooper," memory-Buggy mimicked. "Why do you say it like that?"

"I didn't say it like that," Sandra twirled her braid between her fingers and grinned knowingly at her baby sister.

"Yes, you did," Buggy memory said.

"Oh, she totally did," Theo piped in.

"No, I don't," Sandra spoke, almost as if answering him.

"Yes you—you know what, I'm not getting into it with you. No, Sandra, you're perfectly innocent and fooling absolutely everyone with your sly ways."

"I thought so, thank you very much." Sandra answered, flipping her braid over her shoulder in triumph.

"We should probably get going," Buggy said, tugging on Theo's sleeve. He had a flash of the same movement from a little sister on her brother's sleeve. *C'mon Theo, I wan some iz cream.* He nodded and followed her.

"So, basically," he said, as they left the memory versions of Buggy and Sandra to their conversation and stepped into the hallway leading to the bedroom and bathrooms, "everyone knows you're in love with this Cooper guy, except for you?"

"What?" Buggy sputtered, coming up short and whipping around, face the mingled emotions of terror, irritation, and mind-numbing embarrassment. Man, nothing could hide behind those eyes. "Wha—I *am not* in *love* with Cooper." She spoke the word "love" as if a kid spitting out a piece of spinach that her mother tried to slip onto her plate.

Theo's eyebrows raised slowly up his forehead, eyes widening, grin following suit. "Uh, huh, sure."

"Shut up," Buggy grumbled as she turned back to the hall, eyes flitting back and forth between the three doors, trying to choose between them.

"Sure thing, Miss 'feelings are gross.'"

Buggy flipped him off without looking up. Instead, she walked towards the door at the far end of the hall. She took the handle, hesitated, eyes closed briefly. She pushed it open, and they walked inside.

"Damn," Buggy said, scowling as they entered a little bedroom that was so immaculately kept Theo had no doubt it was Buggy's own. "It didn't work."

"Oh my God," Theo stepped further into the room, eyes falling across the neatly lined books, the perfectly level picture frames, and makeup lined up on the dresser. "This is by far the neatest room I have every seen in my life."

"What did I do wrong?" Buggy mumbled, not listening. "I did the same thing I did before."

"Did you actually use a level on these," Theo asked squinting up at the frames on the walls.

"I close my eyes and imagine the door. Then imagine the memory behind it," Buggy was saying to herself, completely ignoring Theo now. She turned around, closed the door, and stood back frowning at it with her hands on her hips. "So, what went wrong?"

Theo squinted at one of the photos, leaving Buggy to her mumbling. It was a recent photo, a few years old at most. It caught four laughing friends, arm in arm before some concert entrance. He recognized their faces. They had all been in the memory Buggy had shown him in the last "deep dive." One of the friends on the far left was a tall, beanpole who dwarfed the other four in comparison. He also realized that the girl on the far right, the same girl who had been interrogating Buggy about her love life, had been same girl he saw behind the counter with Buggy the day he visited Edwin Family Dentistry Office. *Linny.* And the other one, the one with his arm wrapped around Buggy's shoulder, laughing just as hard as her, was Cooper. They were leaning into each other, probably not even noticing the slight tilt of their heads, the almost imperceptible turn of their bodies, but everybody else did. Everybody else had to. It was so obvious. Theo grinned, pulled away from the photo and looking around at the immaculately kept room.

"Do you even have dust in here? No dust bunnies? Nothing." He dropped to his knees and checked under the bed. "Seriously?" Half a dozen pairs of shoes were lined up under there, as if soldiers waiting for their marching orders. Not a speck of dust in sight, but there was a bag, sitting suspiciously out of place in a corner. He reached out curiously, pointing. "Hey, Bug, what's that?"

"Wh—hey! Get out from under there," Buggy said, smacking him on the back of the head.

"Fine, fine," Theo pulled back out, rubbing the spot where she had hit him. "But what's with the sketchy looking bag?" Buggy hesitated, then she dropped to one knee, reached passed him, pulled out the bag and plopped it on the bed. Theo wasn't sure what he was expecting. Maybe a big bag of Adderall. That would at least explain the insane amount of neatness. Instead, when Buggy unclipped and flipped open the bag, Theo saw a bunch of cassette tapes and a little silver and black player. He looked up at Buggy confused, but she wouldn't meet his eyes. In fact, she looked extremely uncomfortable all of a sudden, like she had just exposed some dirty little secret and was waiting for his taunting judgments.

"What are these?" Theo asked, leaning in over the bag.

"My mom," Buggy answered tentatively.

"Wait, what?" Theo jerked up and away from the tapes. He felt like he had been caught looking up a lady's skirt as she leaned over to pick up a book she had dropped. Caught doing something improper. Piggish even.

"It's my mom. Or at least, it's her voice," Buggy said reaching into the bag and pulling out a cassette container decorated with bright green paper and a few heart shaped doodles with the words "Twenty-First Birthday," written out in dark blue marker pen. "She recorded them before she... she recorded them when she found out she was pregnant. She knew that she wouldn't be here for any of the big things. The birthdays, the graduations. I thought it was because she chose to leave me behind, but it wasn't. She knew she was going to die. So, she left me recordings for nearly every occasion."

Theo didn't know what to say, so he decided saying nothing would be the safest bet. He just watched as Buggy ran a finger down the spine of the little container, smiling a soft smile. She looked back up at him and laughed.

"What?" he asked, still tense.

"You look like you're waiting for me to explode or something."

Theo shrugged, still unsure what to say. But this time he spoke, anyway. "Must be nice to have something at least, right?"

"Yeah, it is," Buggy agreed, setting the tape gently back into the bag, closing it up. She looked about to slide it back under the bed, but she didn't. She frowned, shrugged, and pulled the bag over her shoulder, tightening the strap. Buggy looked up and saw the question in Theo's eyes.

"I've always felt safer with them near," Buggy said, looking a little sheepish.

"Fair enough," Theo said, not bothering to point out that the tapes weren't actually there at all. That they were just manifestations of her imagination. Memories. Then again, memories are powerful things. Memories are a way to hold on to the past, and the past never quite dies. Not in Theo's opinion. The past may fade into the distance, the view growing fuzzy until you have to squint to keep it seen, but it never quite disappeared, not until it was forgotten. Memory kept such things alive, and while still alive, they have power over the present. Power over people's choices. The power to influence, to push people forward or hold people back. To utterly cripple or reinforce and mold into something better. Something stronger. Watching Buggy slide an absentminded hand down the little gray bag's strap, Theo found himself hoping that those tapes were the type of thing to strengthen. Some memories, memories full of unfulfilled wishes and denied desires, they tended to be the kind to cripple. For God's sake, the girl couldn't even admit to herself her own emotions because of her past, the one she holds onto and keeps in eyeshot, tells her that people you love sometimes just disappear.

Buggy's eyes darted to meet his, a small little flash of startled confusion momentarily passing her face. "You say something?"

Theo shook his head. "Nah, but we should get going."

"Right." Buggy Turned back to the door leading out of her bedroom, face growing serious. A deep crease of concentration appeared between her eyebrows. "Okay." She closed her eyes, lips slightly parted. She stayed that way for so long, Theo wondered if she might have fallen asleep on her feet. Just at the moment his suspicions became certainty, she opened her eyes and raised her hand to the doorknob.

"Here goes nothing," she said, and pushed the door open. Theo followed Buggy through it. The apartment vanished as they stepped into a new room all together. It was a long room with high walls, painted a creamy white with light brown trim. Framed pictures of a woman with long inky hair, a man with a short scruffy brown beard, and their young daughter hung nearly every inch of spare space down the hallway. The ground was polished wood with a long, blue runner carpet that spread the length of the hall to stop short in front of a dark, stained wooden door with an oval window set in the center.

"Where are we?" Theo asked.

Buggy smiled. "Home," she answered.

Theo was about to ask a follow up when the door at the end of the hall gave a little rattle. The sound of a key slipping into the lock. There was a rumble of voices that grew coherent as the doorknob twisted and the door swung open. In stepped a man in his early thirties with dark hair and green eyes. A small girl around two or three years old toddled in after him, a big, toothy smile on her face, dark pigtails bouncing up and down with every happy step.

"Home sweet home!" the little girl was singing, jumping out of her shoes so she could continue her bounding in white socked feet. "Home sweet home! Home sweet home!"

The man, who must have been her father, reached down and picked up the discarded shoes, neatly lining them up next to his own, which he slipped off with ease. "Sandra," his voice was reproachful, but he was smiling. "Don't just kick off your shoes, remember?"

"Sorry, Daddy," she said, looking far too happy to allow for any bit of that apology to be true. "Can I show her room now, Daddy? Can I? Can I?" With every happy jump, she scooched herself further down the hall towards another set of doors.

The man smiled through his beard. "Sure, but you might want to wait till she actually makes it through the door first." At these words, a woman stepped in. She had long dark brown hair that braided all the way down her back. She was slightly taller than her husband, even though she wore flats. She was holding a bundle of pink blanket with cartoon balloons and elephants decorating the fabric. Theo could hear small cooing sounds coming from it. As the mother smiled to her husband, kicking off her own shoes by the door, Theo saw a small, pudgy hand brake free of the blankets. Tiny fingers groped the empty air above it, trying to catch a fluttering butterfly that none of the rest were able to see.

"Mommy, Mommy, Mommy," the little girl in white socks bounded for her, all wide-eyed excitement. "Can we show baby her room now? Can we? It's right next to my room! Can I show her, Mommy?"

"Of course, honey," the mother said padding down the hall after her daughter, who gave a loud cheer and clapped her hands together. They both passed by Buggy and Theo, not noticing their existence, simply striding by, and disappearing into one of the other rooms the door of which stood open. Theo turned to Buggy, but she was watching the man as he leaned down and picked up the woman's shoes which she had discarded haphazardly by the door. He lined them up neatly next to his and his daughters in descending order of size, a slightly rueful expression on his face.

"Are these," Theo started, pausing as the man finished his job and strode past them. "Your parents?"

"Yep," Buggy said, meeting his eyes. She looked about as shocked as he felt.

"So that baby," Theo pointed to the room that the family had all disappeared into, but where they could still hear chattering and jubilant whooping of little Sandra. "That was you?"

"Yep," Buggy said with a startled laugh and gave the bag around her shoulder a little squeeze although Theo doubted she knew she was doing it. "This is the day they brought me home. I didn't think I remembered this."

"You weren't trying to come to this memory?" Theo asked.

"No, I mean, I was thinking about home, and was trying to picture a memory from when we all lived here back before my parents' divorce but..." she looked around bemused. "But I didn't think back *this* far. I didn't think I *could* think back this far."

"That's good!" Theo said. "That means you're tapping into the deeper memories, the ones that can lead us down where we need to go."

"Down into 'their' memories," Buggy said, sounding both excited and nervous.

"Told you we could do this!" Theo grinned, clapping a hand on her shoulder. Buggy smiled in return, but he could still see the doubt coloring her brown irises. She turned towards the open door and frowned a little.

"I can't hear them anymore, can you?"

Theo cocked his head a little, actively trying to make out the mumbled conversation and cooing of baby Buggy, but there was nothing. Weird. He looked at Buggy who suddenly looked very nervous.

"She's... she's not *around* is she?"

Theo closed his eyes and felt. He reached out with his mind, or his emotions, he didn't know how the hell this all worked, he just *reached*. He felt Buggy. Her aura was like... soft gold. Soft gold that glowed with a gentle warmth at the edges, but the center pulsed with a powerful brightness. It was the strangest and most beautiful thing.

Theo had half a mind to tell Buggy about it. Tell her how lovely the light was, how lovely *she* was, but he stopped himself. The idea of someone being able to feel something like that about you, something like that *in* you, was weird. Embarrassing. Again, Theo had that feeling of knowing something he shouldn't, of stumbling upon something terribly personal. Something private. So, he kept it to himself.

"No," he said, opening his eyes and turning to Buggy. "No, she's nowhere around."

Buggy nodded and moved towards the door. Theo followed. As their feet crossed the threshold, something strange happened. The entire room began to blur, shudder, and then completely disappear. Instead of a high-ceilinged nursery, their feet stepped out onto blacktop. Theo looked around, startled. They were in an alley, no trace of Buggy's old house in sight. It was nighttime and a frigid wind whipped hard and fast between the buildings. It bounced off the bricks, gaining speed with every pass until it was daggers cutting into his cheeks and hands. Theo shivered, running his hands up and down his arms to warm himself.

"Christ, Buggy," he said, looking around and finding the door they had stepped through completely vanished from existence. Apparently, they didn't need it anymore. "Couldn't you remember something a little warmer? Buggy?" He turned back around. Buggy was standing with her back to him next to a large green trash bin, garbage overflowing from its lip. Her hands hung in fists at her sides, her head tilted down, looking at something on the ground by her feet. Theo looked down and his heart stopped in his chest. It was a baby. A tiny newborn baby still covered in slime and blood from birth. It lay, half covered in a rumbled white night gown, but otherwise unprotected from the elements. The child was sleeping, head propped on a gray shoulder bag, a bag that looked suspiciously similar to the one hanging around Buggy's shoulder at that very moment.

The baby's eyes were closed, and its lips were taking on a light blue quality.

"Oh God," Theo said, stepping up beside Buggy. "Is that you?"

"Yes," Buggy said. Her voice sounded unfazed. She was looking down at herself, her newborn self who was slowly freezing to death alone in an alley. Her expression was blank, unfeeling. There was no trace of concern, no flash of sadness. Nothing. Simply watching as the baby's lips grew a deeper shade of blue. Theo wasn't sure how Buggy was supposed to feel, supposed to act, but he was pretty sure this wasn't it.

"Shit" Theo hissed, dropping to his knees.

"What are you doing?" Buggy laughed a little as Theo tugged his too large T-shirt over his head.

"She's freezing. *You're* freezing," he said, shivering as he slipped the cloth up over his shoulders and off his arms.

"Theo, that's not going to do any good," she was saying as he tried to swaddle the baby in the shirt. But the cloth, which would have been a poor source of comfort in the first place, simply passed through the child as if she was a ghost. Or he was. "None of this is really happening anymore, remember?"

"But we can't just leave her like this," Theo looked up at her. He knew he was being unreasonable. Knew this was a memory, and the baby was no longer shivering in the cold. It had somehow survived and grown up to be the woman standing before him right now. That didn't stop the anger that flared in him, the anger at Buggy's calm, unconcerned expression. "She's freezing!"

"Yes," Buggy said, head tilting a little as if confused. "Yes, she *was*. And she nearly died."

Suddenly the little form shifted in its pile of slime, white fabric, blood and something that Theo had not noticed at first. It was a dark powdery stuff, so dark that it blended in with the black of the ground. It hung in small, scattered piles around and on the child, but was now slowly scattering as the wind picked up speed. Ash. Theo didn't know how he knew it was ash, but he did.

The baby churned, blinking blood and slime out of its eyes as its blue lips parted. It started to wail, its tiny features scrunching up in a look of agony and fear.

"Christ," Theo said, reaching down for the child once more, but his hands simply slid through her and hit the blacktop bellow. When he pulled his hands back, he saw that they were covered in ash. He looked up at Buggy as the child's screams echoed off the walls and into the night. He felt a flash of spiteful satisfaction as a look of hurt and pain finally filled Buggy's eyes at the sound, watching the little thing screaming for help.

"What do we do?" Theo asked, turning desperately back to the child on the ground.

"There's nothing we can do," Buggy said, kneeling beside Theo, watching the girl cry. "We're not here. And even if we were, we aren't who she wants." Theo watched as Buggy reached into the bag around her shoulder. She pulled out the cassette player, frowning down at it, and looking back up at the baby. Buggy reached back in the bag, pulled a random cassette out of its case and slipping it int the player. She held the tape out to the crying child and hit the play button.

"Hallo, hun," a sweet voice spoke from the player. Instantly, the baby's cries slowed. Theo and Buggy exchanged a look. The voice continued. "So, you're having a bad day huh? I'm sorry about that. Bad days suck, don't they?" The baby girl's cries grew quieter, and quieter, dulling to a soft whimper coming through blue lips. "I wish I was there now, baby girl. Wish I was there to hold you, comfort you. There to tell you not to be afraid, because bad days can only last just that. The day. Don't worry, sweet girl. You are stronger than this day." The baby began to coo, eyes sliding closed, but her shivers were growing stronger, starting to look like little spasms in her chubby limbs. Theo felt hot tears sliding down his face as he watched baby Briar Rose, slipping into unconsciousness, where at least she wasn't afraid. At least there was no pain. Sung to sleep by her mother's voice.

"Oh my God!"

Buggy and Theo looked over their shoulder towards the sound of the scream. It was a woman. Her dirty clothes, tangled, unwashed hair, and dark brown teeth suggested she made such alleys her home from time to time. But never in the company of babies. She was clutching raggedly gloved hands to her chest, eyes wide. The woman screamed again before throwing herself at the silent child. She tore at her cloths, yanking them from her as if they burned her skin. She covered the child in her jacket and sweatshirt, leaving herself with just a thin, fraying turtleneck for protection against the icy winds. Unlike Theo's shirt, the cloths wrapped around the child's skin and stayed there. The woman lifted the baby into her arms, hesitating only a second to grab the bag the baby had been sleeping on, and started running towards the road. She didn't notice the Nokia cell phone on the ground, or that she accidently kicked it as she bolted, sending the little plastic phone skidding towards a sewer drain where it teetered, then dropped in. She didn't hear the splash over the sound of her own screaming.

"Someone! Someone, help me! Sweet Jesus, someone! Help the child! For the love of God, someone, help me!" The woman vanished into the night, her voice slowly fading with her form. Theo rose to follow her, but he felt a hand on his arm, stopping him.

"She'll be alright," Buggy said. "The woman finds someone to help. A paramedic crew is checking up on someone passed out a street down. There's a prince with them," she stood up, a slight smile on her face. "He'll wake the sleeping princess. Don't worry." Theo looked at her, looked at the girl who had been stronger than that terrible, terrible day. The girl who stood so calm, so certain as she watched the child version of herself disappearing into the dark in the arms of a stranger, like it was the most normal thing in the world. And for a fleeting second, so fast he might have imagined it, Theo actually *saw* the golden light emanating off of her skin. It glowed out from her, into the surrounding night, that light that was just so purely *her*.

Buggy looked back at him. Their eyes held each other for a long, meaningful moment. Then Buggy raised a brow and said, "Dude, get your shirt back on. It's freezing."

14

The snow gave under her shoes with a soft crunching sound that was lost amongst the groans of wind through the trees. A patch of snow fell from a nearby branch, flopping to the ground and puffing a stray spattering of white up towards the sky. The branch, released of its burden, flew back up and waved in the air, as if saying hello. Waverly stopped, brushing the white dust out of the air between her and the cabin that had just come into view. It was a pretty thing. Deep, red-stained wood, holding up a tall-ceilinged roof, which was currently covered in a carpet of white snow. Smoke drifted lazily from the chimney, or at least, it tried. The wind quickly tore the smoke from its calm drifting and scattered it like the snow. Most of the windows, which were decorated in an odd, gaudy style that reminded Waverly of some ancient church, were dark except for one room near the front of the cabin. Those windows were glowing with a flickering light that Waverly recognized as fire. She scowled at it and continued. She moved through the trees, around the cabin, trying to find a window where she could actually see inside. When she finally found one, she dropped her bag into the snow by her feet and pulled from it a pair of binoculars. She put them to her eyes, ignoring the slight shiver that ran up her arms as another gust of wind brushed passed. She could see three figures inside. One was tall, scruffy, wearing a button-down shirt and pacing back and forth through the room. Sometimes his journey would take him across the face of the fire, temporarily blocking the light with his dark silhouette, casting his fellows in shadow. His fellows were smaller than him, and not just because they were sitting on the floor. One was a young man, maybe late twenties, who sat cross-legged, eyes closed. He looked so relaxed he might have been sleeping, although Waverly knew he wasn't. She turned her attention to the girl sitting on the floor next to him and Waverly couldn't help a tiny jolt. She had seen her before, already knew the girl looked the same, but that didn't stop the amazement. The girl's hair was longer than Loretta's, styled differently, and Waverly knew her eyes were a different color, but otherwise she looked exactly like the picture Susanna had shoved under her daughter's nose.

"You see this face?" her mother would hiss, voice like a snake and breath like sour whiskey. "This is the face of evil, Waverly. This is the face of blood, and murder, and death."

Watching the girl's sweet, calm, innocent and peaceful face at that moment, the description seemed idiotic, or even heretical. Then she remembered what her mother had shown her next. The news clippings of fires and deaths. The pictures of half burned bodies and wide-eyed surprise and terror frozen on faces that could feel no more. The bloody shirt, old and crusting, had been the worst.

"You see this?" her mother would nearly be shrieking by this point, two miles passed drunk and spraying spit with every other syllable. "You know whose blood this is?"

"Yes, Mama," Waverly had answered. It had been hard not to start crying the first few times her mother had gone over this mantra. That was back when Waverly had been seven years old. Having her mother drunk and yelling in her face for something she didn't do—and couldn't possibly have been alive for—that was one thing. But when she started waving around that shirt—that shirt that smelled like dried blood, which her mother kept in the dresser drawer by her bed—then things got so much worse.

"This is your grandma's shirt," Susanna would always continue, as if not hearing Waverly's reply, or at least, not caring if she had. "This is your grandma's blood. My mama's blood. This was the shirt she was wearing when *that girl* killed her," her mother jabbed a finger at the picture again. It had been a picture of a fifteen-year-old Loretta, sitting cross-legged on her bed, opening presents on Christmas day. Waverly knew her mother was really talking about the one that came before Loretta. Aetheria. The killer of The Fold. "She killed your grandmother, slow and painful, while I watched!"

"Mama," Waverly had started to cry then. She remembered how hot the tears had felt against her cheeks as they rolled down and dripped from her chin. She remembered one small drop that flicked off, hitting the dark brown portion of dried blood on the shirt held under her nose. The sight of it soaking there, mingling with the blood, made Waverly want to vomit. "Please, Mama."

"I was too late to save my mother," Susanna would continue, ignoring her daughter's plea. Her eyes were on the bloody shirt. It was all she could see. It was all she could *ever* see. "But not again. We will not let the monster kill again. We will not let her destroy any more families. Never again. That's why I made you," her eyes would finally find Waverly then, but there was no love there. No, just the look of someone assessing the ability of a new tool. The uses of a new weapon. "That's why you are here. You and me, we need to keep her from *ever* doing this again. This is why you were born, and you cannot fail this, Waverly. You cannot fail this. Do you understand me?"

Waverly cried and said that she understood. She would do what she had to because she did understand, just please, put the bloody shirt away. The smell was always so—*oh God, that smell. So much blood, there was always so much blood. Why did it always come back to blood? It always came back to*—overwhelming. Her mother would then nod, and smile and pat her little daughter on the head, watching her sniffle with glazed and reddened eyes. The shirt would go away then, but not for long. No, never for long.

Waverly watched the calm face and closed eyes of the girl sitting in front of the fire and could almost smell the shirt being passed under her nose. The smell of old, dried blood and molding fabric. She could almost see the tear flicking off her chin and soaking there in the dark brown reddened stain.

This is why you were born.

Waverly's heart went as cold as the wind around her ears. She searched in her mind for that same little vault she had used with Helena. The small lockbox, to place her empathy, her sympathy, and her conscience. She found it, locked it tight, and started to plan. She turned her attention back to the two men in the room. The devil's protectors. She wouldn't mind having to kill Styger. He was the one who started this whole mess in the first place. He was the one who let Loretta out of her cell and freed this version of The Daughter on the Earth. He deserved what was coming. She didn't know about the other one. Theodore. The son. She knew he had not known about any of this until a few months ago, and most of the story had come from Styger's lying mouth, so who the hell knows what he thought to be true. He probably thought the girl was innocent. Probably thought she was worthy of saving. He didn't know about how deep the darkness infected that girl. He didn't know the smell of the shirt or the color of its blood. If he had, he would be on this side of the fight. Probably standing right beside her in that snowy night, reminding her that this is why she was born.

No, he didn't deserve to die. Not tonight. But she had to get him to stop helping the girl. She had to get him out of the building before she started her work, or else he would start fighting on the wrong side. Waverly knew she was good, but three against one was always a poor way to jump into any battle, let alone one whose outcome could mean the life or death of thousands.

What to do? Waverly mused, dropping the binoculars from her face as she frowned towards the night sky full of moonlight. Slow drifts of new snow came tumbling from above, drifting back and forth and then being caught in spirals of wind, spinning them down around her. She watched, and smiled, then slipped the phone out of her pocket. She replaced the battery and turned on the phone. She put the binoculars back to her face as she dialed the number and held the cold plastic to her ear. She watched Styger jut to a halt from his agitated pacing and turn around towards Theodore, who remained still on the floor. Styger took a tentative step closer to the boy, knelt and pulled something from his pocket. She could see the cell phone trembling in his hands as it rang and vibrated, saying that someone was calling. Styger stood back up, accepting the call, and began his pacing once more.

"Hey, Helena," the voice spoke in a gruff and gravelly tone that matched him perfectly. "Now's not a good time."

"Oh, I disagree," Waverly answered.

Styger froze with his back towards the fire, casting his face in dark shadow, which Waverly found a pity. She would have loved to see the expression there.

"Who is this?" he asked. "And why do you have Helena's phone?"

"Let's just say, she's not using it anymore," Waverly answered, almost wriggling with pleasure as Styger started swinging around, like he might find her in the cabin itself.

"Who are you? Where is Helena?" Styger asked, voice growing dark and angry as the surprise began to ebb and panic masked by fury took its place.

"Tell your boy," Waverly said, ignoring his questions, "tell him that if he wants to see his mother again, he should pop in his car and get going. It's probably too late already but, hey, you never know, right? Life can surprise you sometimes, can't it, Styger?"

"Susanna?" Styger asked, voice even lower now, barely audible.

"Not quite," Waverly answered, watching the man clenching and unclenching his fists in the light of the fire. "But she says 'hello.'" She hung up then, a wide grin slowly curving her face as she watched Styger pull the phone away and stand there, dumbfounded, staring at the blank screen. She smiled and waited patiently for her moment. To do what she had been born to do.

And here... we... go...

15

Buggy looked around as Theo slipped his "Do I have coffee in my hands yet? No? Then why are you talking to me?" T-shirt back over his head. The night was frigid, and she was more than ready to find a different memory to pass the time. This one left her feeling ill.

"Where to next?" she asked Theo, and he pushed off the ground shivering.

"How should I know," Theo barked a laugh that was cut short by the chattering of his teeth. "This is your head."

"Wait," Buggy looked around, noticing for the first time that the door they had entered was missing. "Where the hell did the door go?"

"Don't know," Theo said, hands running fast up and down his arms as his teeth chattered louder.

"Crap," Buggy frowned, spinning around, tape player still held loosely in her hands, as she looked for a different door. Maybe one leading into a shop. Everything would be locked this time of night, but maybe they could pick it, or break it open? They just needed a door, some door to start with, so she could make into a different one. One that she knew. But there was nothing. No shops, no doors. The alley was just a long line of bricks and plaster, trash and dirt, but no doors. Buggy made her way for the mouth of the alley where the homeless woman had disappeared only a few moments before. As soon as she started, she noticed a small mumbling sound that made her stop. She looked around, confused, until she realized that the tape was still playing. Her mother's voice was speaking soft and low in her hand. Buggy held the cassette player up to her ear so she could make out the words.

"I've gotten bad days a lot, too. You know what helps me? My friends mostly. I've been making a lot of friends in our travels. Your father especially has been a wonderful help. And I guess that's another thing about bad days, you don't *have* to go through them alone."

Buggy looked up to see Theo watching her, but as the voice continued to speak in her ear, Theo grew distracted. His eyes moved from her to search the surrounding alley, as if noticing something very strange.

"I know. It sometimes feels like you have to do it alone. Have to power through and just do it yourself, and sometimes that's true. But a lot of the time it's okay to need someone. I need you to remember that, okay?"

Buggy noticed it now. The air was no longer cold. The wind which had been tearing at their clothes and skin had died away. There was a warm heat emanating from somewhere unseen. Like a fire had been lit somewhere under the blacktop and was now warming the world from the ground up. Theo stopped rubbing his arms, and his teeth stopped chattering as he gazed around them. The alley wasn't only warm now, it was growing fuzzy. The bricks, the building, the green trash bin were all blurring, slowly going out of focus as Loretta continued to speak.

"I need you to remember that it's okay to need people. It's okay to lean on people. It's not weakness. It's just a *different* kind of strength."

Everything was out of focus now. Theo and Buggy were standing in a world of smeared paint with nothing but air under their feet. The buildings were a fuzzing of brown and red, the ground and sky a charcoal smudge of black and gray. Just at the point when everything seemed completely gone, focus returned. The smudges of pain solidified, and the blurriness faded as if being blinked out of sleepy eyes. The alley was gone, exchanged for a hotel room in some city hundreds of miles away. It was a small room with warm red walls and one large brown cushioned bed at the center of the worn carpet. A woman sat on the bed, legs crossed out in front of her, back propped against a ridiculously large mountain of pillows.

"Holy shit," Theo whispered beside Buggy, and Buggy couldn't help but agree. The woman was her... except, it wasn't her at all. This wasn't Buggy's memory. It was Loretta's. That was Loretta sitting there on the bed, looking exactly like Buggy. Well no, Buggy realized, not *exactly*. Loretta's skin was a little darker, and her hair was cut in a shorter style that Buggy had never tried. Her eyes were just as large as Buggy's, but their brown was less muddy, and had flecks of green that Buggy had never seen in the mirror. She was holding a tape recorder in one hand and was speaking into it. At the same time Loretta's words were playing through the same recorder pressed to Buggy's ear.

"Needing people does not make you weak, hun," she was saying, in a voice that *did* sound exactly like Buggy's. "Remember that, okay?"

"M-mom?" Buggy stuttered, taking a shaking step forward. She noticed that her whole body was trembling, but she didn't care. "Mom?"

Her mother didn't hear her. How could she? This was only a memory.

"I just wish," Loretta took a deep breath, and ran a hand over her lower belly, which had only just began showing signs of pregnancy. Just a little pooch under the soft, green fabric of her blouse. "I just wish I could be one of those people, to help you on your bad days. One of those people you *needed*."

"I *do* need you," Buggy heard the break in her voice. She knew Theo was beside her, seeing her, reaching out for her, but she didn't care. She ignored everything, ignored it all. All she could see was the woman on the bed. The mother that loved her. The mother lost to her. "I always needed you, Mom. Please... please hear me."

"Buggy..." Theo's voice was soft and tentative, but again Buggy ignored it. She dropped to her knees beside the bed, tape player still in her hands.

"Mom," she reached out for her mother's arm, knowing it wouldn't work. Knowing her hands would slide right through her, just as Theo's shirt had passed through the memory of her baby self. "Mama, please hear me." The tears stung her eyes but did not fall. "Mom, I need you." Her hand was an inch away from her mother's wrist resting on her belly. "Mom—" She touched her. Buggy's warm fingers met warm flesh and didn't go through. She looked up, heart stuttering. The woman on the bed had stopped talking. Her head had turned down, looking at the spot on her wrist where Buggy had touched her. "M-Mom?" Buggy asked, barely believing. Terrified to try. The woman's eyes, her mother's eyes, drifted slowly from the spot on her wrist and up to Buggy's face. The room was silent for three long, heart-rending seconds.

"Briar?" Loretta asked, eyes blinking.

"Mom?" Buggy's heart seemed to glow in her chest, burning like fire, almost hurting with the joy she felt. "Mom—" She reached out to her again, but Theo seized her arm in a hard grip. She winced in pain. "Theo, what are you—"

"Buggy, that's not your mom," Theo said, jaw set and eyes on the woman. She dropped the cassette player on the cushions next to her and swung her legs over, hanging them off the edge of the bed, large eyes watching them with amusement. "That's **not Loretta**."

Buggy looked back to see Loretta's face fall into a sarcastic little show of disappointment. She gave a heavy sigh. "Oh, *Blue*, you are no fun." And when that little smirk pulled the corner of her lips, Buggy's blood ran cold. *Not* Loretta's feet touched down on the carpeted floor and she stood, the cruel smirk curling further up her mouth. She looked down at Buggy, whose heart was going double time as she scurried back and away from the woman who looked so much like her.

"Oh shit," Buggy chanted under her breath, hand sliding suddenly sweaty against the carpet. "Oh shit, oh shit, oh shit."

"Well, that is rude," Bennu grinned down at Buggy. No, not grinned. She bared her teeth at her. "Did your mother never teach you how to speak to your elders? Oh, that is right, she *did not.*"

"Shit," Buggy threw herself over as Bennu launched down at her with her hands out and fingers curled like claws. She hit the ground, missing Buggy by inches.

"Get back here!" Bennu crawled after her, face like a rabid animal's, eyes gleaming, mouth frothing and hanging open. For a second Buggy swore she saw fangs hanging low and wet under her lips, but then Bennu lunged again, and this time her nails raked the side of Buggy's face. Buggy felt the sting as blood seeped up under the fresh cuts. She turned, scrambling to her knees, starting to her feet, but Bennu grabbed the back of her shirt and shoved her violently forward. Buggy came down hard. Her chin met the floor, sending stars dancing in her eyes as the pain left her temporarily blinded. The bag on her shoulder had burst open and cassettes went flying, scattering across the hotel floor in little rectangular boxes of pink, blue, green and yellow. She tried to crawl but cried out as Bennu's fingers dug deep into her back, her nails like knives and the skin of her hands burning with an unnatural heat. Her whole body seemed to pulse with it. To Buggy it felt like standing too close to a raging fire. She screamed.

"Where the fuck do you think you are going?" Bennu hissed in her ear. "We have things to discu—" Suddenly, Bennu's fingers were out of Buggy's back, and her heavy, overheated weight was gone. Buggy turned to see Theo holding fistfuls of Bennu's hair. Bennu was shrieking a banshee cry of rage, and her clawed hands swiped backwards towards Theo, sometimes missing, sometimes leaving long red marks down his neck and cheeks.

"Run!" Theo yelled at Buggy, and she didn't argue. She pushed to her feet and launched for the hotel room door, only to find that she couldn't open it. The door was locked, and the doorknob was missing. Not broken off, but *missing*, as if it had never been there. Buggy swung back around at the sound of Bennu's laughter.

"This is not your memory anymore, Briar dear," she spat, spittle trickling down her manic grin. "Not so easy to control now, is it? But me... I have been here a while, and I have learned a thing or two." She dropped to the ground with a great ripping sound. Theo was left standing there with two fistfuls of bloody hair. Buggy thought she might have even seen a little piece of flesh dangling off the end of one of the clumps but didn't have time to verify her terrible suspicion. Bennu flung herself towards her again. Buggy dodged and came down hard on several of the scattered cassette tapes, one of them snapping, breaking under her weight.

"Stop moving!" Bennu shrieked, eyes flashing.

"Fuck you!" Buggy shot back.

"Do you not understand," Bennu said, crouching down to be on Buggy's level. The manic anger draining from her face, as fast as water from a spilled glass. For a moment she looked like Loretta again. "Do you not see that I am the only one trying to save us? Can you not see that? Him," Bennu pointed at Theo, who had dropped the piles of hair and was moving to Buggy's side. "Him and those like him, they want to continue the cycle. They want to keep it going. Keep the pain, and hurt, and endless—endless—endless—going—going—going." She sounded like a broken record, with the point stuttering its way across the vinyl. "Me? I want to stop it. I *need* to stop it. For me. For you. For all of us."

"You're out of your mind," Buggy said.

"Of course, I am out of my mind!" Bennu cackled, sharp and humorlessly. "I have lived a thousand lives and died a thousand deaths. We all go crazy after a while. And so will you, if you do not let me. Help *us*."

"Shut up," Buggy barked, but there was a small sickening feeling that skittered up the back of her spine. That feeling that Bennu was telling the truth.

"That is because *I am* telling the truth, Briar dear," Bennu said, face softening as Buggy looked up at her in surprise. "We are the same, my girl. You cannot hide anything from me. Not even your darkest fears."

"We are **not** the same," Buggy said, remembering what Cam had told her. Doing her best to believe, but the words felt limp against her tongue. A script only half memorized, as she stood in front of a crowd, eyes on her.

"But we are, Briar dear. We are," Bennu's expression was one of regret, pain, and Buggy almost felt sorry for her. Because that pain was real. The sorrow in her large eyes was unmistakable. "I was just like you. I was born, and I lived. I had a mother who loved me, loved me more than I knew. But then a group of *monsters*. They took my life from me. They tortured me... *destroyed* me. Then they left me to burn. And I thought that was the end. I thought that at least it would be over. I prayed for it. That is what death is for, is it not? Being over? But no, I opened my eyes, and I had to start over. And over, and over, and over, and that emptiness grew. That one right there," Bennu pointed at Buggy's chest, to the spot where that void had grown so deep. Buggy put a hand there, as if to hide it from Bennu, but Bennu could see it still. Could *feel* it still. "Is that what you want, Briar dear? An eternity of living and dying, and living and dying, while that hollowness in your chest keeps growing? Because you will feel it all, you know. Feel every life and every death. Even if you have no control over it, you will *feel* it. And it will drive you crazy. It drives us **all** *crazy*." Bennu moved towards her slowly, and this time Buggy didn't draw away. "Is that what you want, Briar dear? Do you want this wheel to keep on turning?"

Buggy opened her mouth, closed it, then opened it again. "No," she whispered softly.

"Buggy...." Theo's voice sounded leagues away, across foggy oceans and raging seas.

Bennu smiled, but it was different from the Dream-Cooper smirk it had been before. It was soft, sad, and somehow Buggy knew that this was her *real* smile. The smile that had enchanted so many villagers of a small town long destroyed and turned to dust. A smile belonging to a young girl whose virginity and dignity had been ripped from her. The tired smile of a girl who had been left to die.

"I can stop it all, my dear. The nightmares, the pain, the empty pit in your chest, I can make it all go away. I can save us. Because there are others in here, you know. Others just like you and just like me. Others that want it all to end. Who want to stop feeling this pain. I just want to help us. This was never the way it was meant to be. For others—maybe—but not for *us*. This was never our path. I just want to put us back on the right path. I just want to find us peace. So, let me. Let me find our peace. It is out there, Buggy. The city. The city with the answers we seek. I know it is. I almost reached it before. I can do it again, I promise you. Let me go and get it for us. It is **our right**." Bennu held out her hand towards Buggy. It was a soft hand, palm up, warm, no longer burning hot like an angry flame. Now it was the gentle heat of a fireside seat on a chilly Christmas morning. It was the warmth of a plush blanket, fresh from the dryer being wrapped around your shoulders. It was gentle and inviting, and Buggy felt her mind screaming for her to take it. Take it and let her end it all. Let Bennu take over and find the answers. Let Bennu save her from the darkness in her heart and the future full of too many futures and too many endings. "We deserve rest, Briar. You and me. All of us. We are *so tired*." Bennu closed her eyes briefly, looking as exhausted as Buggy felt. "Everyone else finds rest, why not us? We have suffered enough." Bennu's hand rose a little, closer to Buggy. "It is our right," she said firmly. "It is **our turn**."

Buggy looked at the outstretched hand, then back up at Bennu's eyes—Loretta's eyes. "Only problem is," Buggy answered softly, "your way means killing people. Your way means killing the people I love."

Bennu's eyes sparked with anger at the words, but quickly softened once more.

"What if we made a deal," Bennu said, hunkering down even further, hand still outstretched. "You let me save us, and I will not hurt anyone you hold dear. Cooper, Cam Styger, Theo, Sandra, Andrew, Linny, your parents, not even nice old Mr. Harrison from AP calculus." Bennu's head tilted to the side, soft smile widening. "If I made you a promise—if every hair on the top of their heads would remain sacred—what say you then?"

Buggy could feel Theo beside her. Feel his palpable unease washing over her in crashing waves, but neither she nor Bennu looked at him.

Because right now, he didn't matter. Right now, she and Bennu were talking terms. Her body in exchange for freedom. And no one she loves gets hurt. No one she loves gets hurt. Except, that wasn't true, was it? They would still get hurt. Bennu wanted to call upon a cursed city, one only summoned by great misfortune, despair, and death. And when Bennu used Buggy's body to kill and burn and murder, it *would* hurt them. They would wonder why. They would wonder what went wrong. What they could have done. Why didn't they see it before? What warning signs had they missed? And if Bennu actually found them peace, Buggy would leave them behind, all questions unanswered. Buggy imagined her family at her funeral. Just her family. No one else would come to mourn such a monster's death, for that is all they would remember her as. She saw her mother and father and even Simon all dressed in black, eyes cast down. Mourning, and somehow ashamed of their mourning. She saw Sandra coming back to their empty apartment, walking into her bedroom, and taking hold of the half-drunk bottle on Buggy's dresser. She would sit on the bed, unscrew the top and drink straight from the spout. Sandra would blame herself most of all, because she had seen the signs, she would tell herself. She had seen the signs, the drinking, the isolation, and done nothing. She had failed. And Sandra would tell herself that lie, believing it until the day she died.

Buggy thought of Linny and Andrew and Cooper being berated by newscasters, asking them if they had known Buggy's plans. Had they helped her plan the fires? Had they seen any sign, had any hint what monsters hid under those large brown eyes. They would drink in silence. They would raise no glass to the dead, because the girl who died wasn't the girl they had known.

Buggy could almost see Cooper ordering himself a water and a whiskey sour, placing one to the left and one to the right, the only form of grieving he allowed himself to make. Cooper, who she would leave behind without an answer to the question he had asked before this whole mess started. He deserved better than that. They all deserved better than that.

And what of the others? Those that weren't *her* loved ones? They would be someone's loved ones. They would be someone's mothers, someone's daughters, someone's sons and fathers and lovers and friends. Even if the city *did* exist, and even if Bennu called upon it and it came, and even if she was finally able to stop the curse, stop the wheel from turning, end the cycle... how many would have to die to reach it? Was her peace worth such a price? Worth all those lives that had not yet gotten a chance to live? And Buggy realized, in that moment, that she was one of them. She was one of those lives that had not yet lived. Buggy had been alive for twenty-four years, sure, but she hadn't really tried to *live*. She had been letting life *happen* to her. She had been a passive participant, stumbling through her days, stumbling into friends, friends like Linny who then pushed her towards things, towards people, but Buggy herself was never the one to initiate anything. Her friendships—Cooper and Linny's idea. Dental hygienist school—her father's idea. Therapy—her mother's idea. Her apartment—Sandra's idea. All the active decisions in her life had never been her own. They were all good ideas, they just had never been *hers*, never really *her* decisions. The only decisions she made were the choices *not* to choose. *Not* to adventure out to Alaska with her pen pal. *Not* to take her stepfather up on his offer to pay for college. *Not* to talk to people in the halls at school. *Not* to let that wall down which Sandra had pestered her about so often. *Not* to deal with the emotions and feelings she had, instead trying to drink them down to a white noise background hum, easily tuned out. The choice *not* to answer Cooper's question right away, even though she already knew the answer. Had known since she was twelve years old, when he had plopped down on the bench before her with his brown lunch bag and wide, warm grin.

She had passively meandered through the life she led, closing doors that opened around her because she was too afraid to see where they might go. Too afraid that they would slam closed in her face if she tried to enter. Always putting it off and putting it off. Telling herself that she was broken, that she needed to be fixed before she tried anything new—before she tried anything at all. Not realizing that she was never healing herself. She was just slamming doors.

Buggy looked at Bennu, looked at her and really saw her. Because they were the same, but they were *also* different. Because Bennu had *burned* every door she had passed. She had painted them with blood, then burned them to ash until there was nothing left. Buggy had shut them... but shut doors could be re-opened.

"No," Buggy said the word as if it was an apology. But then she said it again, and it was an iron clad statement. "I say, no." Buggy couldn't see

Theo's face, but she felt him, felt the rush of relieved energy that spilled out from him in ripples of... blue? She wasn't sure why she thought that, but it didn't matter, because Bennu's hand was trembling before her face.

"Excuse me?" Bennu's voice shook in time with her hand, rage building like a volcano, ground shuddering, cracking, ready to explode.

"No," Buggy repeated. "I'm sorry, Bennu. I really am. I'm scared. I'm scared of what may come next. I'm scared of becoming another one of those voices in the dark. I'm scared of becoming just another terrible dream. I'm scared of the death and rebirth that may come later, but right now, it's *my turn*. And I think I'm finally ready to start living it."

"You..." Bennu's expression grew dark, and hate filled her eyes. "You selfish bitch!" Bennu snatched her hand away, then brought it back in a blurred flash that hit Buggy hard across the face. Buggy went sprawling as Theo gave an angry yell and leaped at Bennu. Buggy spat out a mouthful of blood onto the carpet and looked up to see Theo and Bennu struggling, Theo holding Bennu's claw-like fingers at bay, but just barely. Buggy started to her feet and her hand connected with something sharp. She looked down and saw one of the cassettes, but there was something wrong with this one. It was decorated like the rest, but in a way that Buggy had never seen before, and she knew *every* cassette cover. She had memorized every lilt of the font and every sparkly heart, but this one she had never seen. The paper wasn't a cheery blue or pink or green like all the rest. It was black, with plain white words written wide and strait across the front and spine.

Buggy. Play Me Now.

Buggy gave in to utter confusion, staring down at the tape while Theo and Bennu continued to struggle only a few feet away from her. Her mother had planned on naming her Aida. She had never known her as "Buggy." Then why was it written on the tape? Buggy shoved her confusion aside, as if some irritating oaf blocking a much-needed exit. She snagged the tape and the discarded player that had been flung to a far corner of the room while Bennu and Theo continued to struggle. Buggy flipped open the player, shaking out the cassette tape that was already inside and popped in the one from the black case. She snapped the player lid closed and pressed the play button.

"Buggy!" Loretta's voice rang loud in the little hotel room, bouncing off the walls like the echo inside a cave. Unnatural and eerie. "The door! Get to the door!"

Buggy looked around, passed the shrieking Bennu and Theo, toward the hotel door, and noticed with a joy that hit as hard as panic, that the doorknob had reappeared. She flew for it, recorder still in hand. She turned the nob and pushed it open. There was nothing on the other side but darkness. She turned back.

"Theo!" she shouted to him, wanting him to follow, but he shook his head.

"Go!" he yelled, dodging a blow from Bennu. "Get out!"

"No, Theo—" Buggy started towards him.

"Go!" Theo bellowed again. "Finish this. Finish this now!" A second later Bennu got ahold of him. She twisted his arm to an unnatural angle. There was a sickening popping sound and Theo started howling.

"Theo!"

"Go!" Theo was able to bark, just before Bennu grabbed him by the front of his collar and threw him across the room as if he weighed nothing. He tumbled through the air like a surprised rag doll, hitting the opposite wall and slumping to the floor. Bennu turned towards Buggy, chest heaving, eyes flashing with an insane hatred. The hatred of a thousand lives lived, and a thousand more to go.

"Now Buggy!" Loretta's voice shouted from the tape in her hand. Buggy darted into the darkness through the open doorway. Bennu shrieked and lunged for her, but Buggy slammed the door in her face. She could hear Bennu's screams of fury on the other side, and the pounding of her fists against the wood, but it wouldn't open. Buggy took a step back from the rattling hinges, and her feet connected with nothing. Her arms waved wildly, trying to catch hold of something, anything, but there was nothing but the empty space. The sound of Bennu's struggles faded as Buggy fell, down, down... down... down....

16

Theo regained consciousness to the sound of screaming. He moved a little and yelped in pain as his arm sent lightning up to his shoulder. He twisted, looking around the hotel room. Buggy was gone, thank God. She had made it through the door where Bennu was now hitting and kicking and trying to break it down, but to no avail. He could see the back of her head where she had ripped out her own hair. It showed large patches of raw skin still dripping blood, but she didn't seem to notice. All her attention was on the door... until she felt him watching her. She whirled around, wild, hateful eyes finding him.

"You!" she threw herself at him like a crazed tiger, and one hand seized his throat. He felt her fingers digging into his windpipe as she lifted him to his feet. He had a flashback to being in the living room of the cabin with a sleeping Buggy, holding him the same way.

Here we go again. His mind cackled in some insane, shell-shocked humor that stemmed from the very real part of him that wanted to curl up in a little ball calling for his mommy.

"I will find her," Bennu was hissing, spittle flying from her lips and into his face as he struggled against her fingers, which were like metal clamps digging into his skin. "I will find her, and I will *make* her listen. I will save us whether she likes it or not!"

"No, you won't," Theo gasped, grinning down at the demon version of the girl he knew. The girl who had so quickly become one of the most important people in his life and had so easily become his friend. "She doesn't need saving. She's going to win. She's stronger than this day. She's stronger than *you*. And it's her turn."

The guttural snarl that came out of her lips resembled a feral animal more than any human sound. Bennu's fingers dug deeper into his throat, cutting off his air. "Cannot say the same for you, Theo dear," she hissed.

"Perhaps we should just pick up where we left off." She lifted, and Theo's feet came off the ground. He choked as her fingers tightened. He gasped, hopelessly tugging at her hands, willing the air to return. Theo tried to kick at her, but it was like trying to kick a brick wall, solid, immovable. He tried to wriggle in her grip, but Bennu wouldn't budge.

"Stop struggling," Bennu hissed, and all at once flames erupted at the edges of the hotel room. They licked up the walls in reds and gold and blues. The room quickly became an oven, and Bennu's hands were burning his skin. "It will hurt more if you struggle."

Theo stopped trying to kick her, but he was nowhere near finished fighting. He reached out with his mind, trying to push her, distract her, *anything*. But when he touched her, he felt the darkness within. A cold, black and gray slime that was purely Bennu, just as the gold had been purely Buggy. He touched the ruin that was her soul, and he cringed away from it, terrified.

"Oh no, I do not think so," Bennu whispered, that cruel smirk curling her lips as she bared her teeth. "Come now, little Blue. You started this dance. Do not run away now."

A chill ran down Theo's spine and he nearly passed out from the utter terror that came over him. Because he realized what she meant when she called him Blue. She could see what he could see—could *feel* the same way he could feel. She had felt the color in him just as he had in her, the same way he had in Buggy. This twisted, empty creature with teeth like fangs had seen what was *purely him*. He tried to draw back, but the slimy grayness followed him.

"Do not run away," Bennu purred, the sound almost making Theo wet his pants with fear. "Why not stay and play?" The dark gray slime pushed and slithered against the blue, forcing it back out of Bennu and into Theo. He could feel the grayness invading him, seeping into him, crushing the blue to the side, taking up space and reaching out for more.

"No," Theo gasped desperately, struggling harder now.

"You are strong, little Blue, but I have been alive for thousands of years," Bennu laughed. "Dear child, did you really think you could win this fi—" Bennu cut off, blinking in surprise. She looked away from his face and down. Her grip loosened around his neck, just enough so he could take one deep gasp of air and look down himself. She was staring at his left hand which hung heavy and limp in the air to his side. As they watched, the fingers twitched, and wiggled in the air. Despite the flames raging ever higher around them, despite the sweat that had begun to pour buckets down his neck and back, Theodore's blood ran ice cold. Because he wasn't doing that. He wasn't moving his fingers. Bennu was. Bennu was inside him, not a lot, but enough to raise his hand in the air and wiggle his fingers in front of his own face.

"My, my," Bennu said, barely audible over the sound of roaring flames and snapping wood as the cabinets and bed posts caught fire and splintered from the heat. Bennu looked up at Theo's terrified face with a growing triumphant grin. "This is *new*." The grayness pressed deeper.

No! Theo screamed in his own mind, and his eyes slammed shut. He pulled away, pulled the Blue out of the dark grip. Pulled his mind away from that hellish room of fire where cassette tapes melted and the lightbulb on the bedside table burst and sent shards of glass flying everywhere. He pulled away from Bennu, cutting her scream of furious protest short as he wrenched his eyes back open.

Theo was back in the cabin's living room in front of the fireplace. He pushed himself away from it and yelped in pain when he tried to lean on his injured arm. He moved gingerly, hoping his shoulder was just dislocated and not broken, and turned to see Buggy sitting cross-legged on the ground next to him.

"Buggy?" he whispered, but she was still in the "deep dive." Theo heard Cam's voice behind him, and turned, ready to tell him everything. Ready to tell him about Buggy's memories and Bennu and the darkness that had nearly infected him, infected *his own* body, not Buggy's. But the words died upon his lips when he heard the words Cam was saying.

"Who are you? Where is Helena?" Theo's mouth went dry. His heart stuttered, tripped, then took off running in his chest, bolting like a racehorse just out the gate.

"Tell your boy," Theo could just here a strange woman's voice on the other end of the line. "Tell him that if he wants to see his mother again, he should pop in his car and get going. It's probably too late already but, hey, you never know right? Life can surprise you sometimes, can't it Styger?"

"Susanna?" Styger asked, voice even lower now, barely audible.

"Not quite," the strange woman spoke again. "But she says 'hello.'" The line must have gone dead, because Cam lowered the phone Theo recognized as his own, and stared at the empty screen, dumbfounded.

"Cam," Theo said, and Cam nearly jumped out of his skin as he turned to stare at him with wide, startled, eyes. Theo scrambled to his feet, ignoring the pain in his arm. Everything that had just happened a few moments ago, everything which had felt so important, vanished from his mind as fear rose hot and tangy at the back of his throat. "Who was that? What's wrong with my mom?"

17

Buggy was falling. There was nothing but void for miles above and below as she fell, and fell, and fell. There was no ground, no terrible squashing death hurtling her way. It felt like she had been falling for an hour in this endless nothing. Nothing except for her and that little cassette player in her hand. It had been mumbling for a while now, but Buggy was too distracted by the skydive to notice. She noticed now, as the shock of the fall gave way to that oddly human ability to adapt to anything. She held the player closer to her ear.

"Don't be afraid," Loretta's voice spoke softly. "Don't be afraid. We've got you."

Buggy wondered what she meant by "we," seeing as she was the only one in sight. Then she wondered what Loretta could possibly mean by "got you." She was going on—who knows how many—miles of free fall by this point. It didn't really feel like anyone had "got" anything.

"Look down," the voice said, and when Buggy did, her heart flew up to her throat. Ground had appeared and was quickly rising up to meet her. She couldn't make out what type of ground, hard, soft, dirt, pavement, it didn't matter. It was ground, and it was coming for her fast. Buggy closed her eyes, ready for an impact that didn't come. After a moment she opened them again. She was hovering delicately three inches off the floor that Buggy recognized now as polished redwood. She reached out with her toe and touched it. Instantly she tapped down, unharmed. She looked around. The wooden floor spread out all around her and out as far as her eyes could see, only to be swallowed up by darkness past that point.

"Where am I?" Buggy asked no one in particular, but the tape recording answered.

"By now, you're probably wondering where you are," Loretta's voice spoke, and Buggy pulled the player close to her ear again. "Don't worry, you're safe here. She can't get in here. But where *here* is... well it is kinda hard to explain. It's a space—**my** space. Mine and a few others of *us* who found each other in here. The few that know what is going on. Frankly, there are less of us than there should be. Anyway, the point is, we know what you are trying to do, and we want to help you. But first, I want to show you something. Turn around."

Buggy did, and standing a few yards away was a set of double doors. They were large, and made of the same polished redwood as the floor. They donned large horse head door knockers and heavy, curving metal door handles. Buggy reached for them but hesitated.

"How do I know this isn't some sort of trick or game?" Buggy asked, not sure if the tape player could actually hear and understand her. It might. This wasn't exactly the realm of reality they were in, a bunch of strange stuff had already proved that, but it still felt weird talking to a machine. "How can I be sure you're actually Loretta?"

The tape crinkled and she could hear light breathing from the other end of the recording. After a short pause, the voice spoke again. "I don't think you have gone in, so I'm guessing you're doubting whether you can trust me. Unfortunately, the only way I have to convince you that you *can*, is if you step through that door. So, I guess if this *was* a game... it would be your turn."

Buggy twitched a slight smile that disappeared from her lips as quickly as it had arrived. She heard the tape run out and a soft clipping sound as the recording ended, going still and silent in her hand. Buggy gave a heavy, shuddering sigh and reached out with a trembling hand which went still as she gripped the cool metal of the handle as hard as she could. She pushed one of the double doors open. It slid inward without effort, as if the hinges had just been oiled and the ground polished to the point of being slick. Buggy was afraid the door might just bang open on the other side, but it didn't. It simply glided open and hung there, inviting. Buggy peeked inside. The smile returned to her face, and this time, it stayed. The room was vast. It reminded Buggy of the library in *Beauty and the Beast* with high shelves and ladders leading up four stories high. Elegantly carved wooden beams held up the ornate ceiling painted with floral patterns of white and blue daisies. The shelves were long, and they left not a single space open. Every surface, even the small tables and plush armchairs that were scattered around the gray and blue marble floor, were stacked, but not with books. Decoratively colored cassette tapes filled every available space, even spilling off onto the floor in piles and piles that reached up to the second-floor landing.

Buggy stepped into the room, mouth hanging open, too distracted to notice that the door quietly swept closed behind her, shutting off the rest of the world, giving her privacy. It was just her and the tapes. She looked at them all, so many, too many for her to count, and each with their own titles.

First Day of College
First Party
First Drink
Prom Night
Third Day of College
Ninth Birthday
The Day You Met Linny
The Day You Met Cooper
The Day You Started Hiding Your Drinking
Tenth Day of College
The Day You Passed Your Drivers Exam
Graduating Junior College

The tapes were organized without rhyme or reason, the only purpose was to hold as many tapes as possible in the space available. Buggy looked to the side where a small three-legged table had appeared. The only object on the polished wooden surface was a single tape with yellow paper and blue lettering that said:

Play Me.

Buggy picked up the cassette and replaced the tape in the player with the one in the case. With shaking hands, she pressed play.

"Surprise!" the voice said in a happy singsong voice, as if bursting out from behind a sofa at a birthday party.

"What is this?" Buggy asked the tape, still not sure if it would hear her.

"This," Loretta's continued, "is my room of... unsaid things. I only had so much time between knowing I would have you, and when you were born. It was never a certainty that I'd be able to meet you, so I recorded as much as I could, but I had so much more I wanted to say. So, I did. I kept saying it, even though you couldn't hear it anymore. Because I kept *feeling* it, even if you didn't know. I've been keeping an eye on you, hun. Hope you don't mind. I'm not always able to because, well, this is *your turn* and all, but I pop in every so often, just to make sure you're doing okay."

"How?" Buggy looked around at the millions of tapes. The millions of words recorded, but never played.

"I was the first to repress The Daughter," the voice went on, "and I guess that gave me a little more access and control over *this space* then the rest of the reincarnations. I can 'wake up' more often. Not like The Daughter, of course. Please don't worry, I couldn't have 'controlled' anything, even if I wanted to. I'm neither that strong nor that psychotic. I just, kinda, *saw* things, every so often. Little snippets of your life. Check ins to make sure you were doing good. See how my baby girl's life was going. But there was no way to tell you, no way to talk to you. So, I made *this* room, and every time I thought about you, every time I missed you like crazy, I made a new tape."

Buggy looked around at the countless cassettes stacked, scattered, or neatly lined up on every available surface. Her heart ached in her chest. She felt the hot sting coming to her eyes again, but she wiped it away furiously.

"I wanted you to see this, Buggy. I know you don't have time to listen to them, but I just wanted you to know. I needed you to know how much I've missed you. How sorry I am I couldn't be there for all of these moments. All of these moments I missed. I needed you to know that your mama loved you. That she still does. Always have. Always will."

Buggy started to cry, not bothering to wipe away the tears this time. She cried with joy, she cried with pain, she cried over every tape that lined the endless library of her mother's thoughts. Her mother's good wishes. Advice. Love.

"Buggy?" the voice on the player asked. "Buggy? Are you still there?"

"Yes," Buggy hiccupped. "Yeah, Mom, I'm here."

"Buggy? You there?" the voice asked again, and the realization that this tape couldn't hear her either, set another volley of tears gushing down her cheeks. "Buggy, if you can hear me, you got to listen up, okay? The Daughter got out of the hotel memory. She is looking for you. She can't find you here, but we are running out of time." Buggy straightened up and held the recorder close to her ear, still sniffling. "Me and a few of the others—the others that came before us—we made a passageway for you."

"What do you mean?" Buggy frowned, wiping her nose on her sleeve. She could feel that her face was puffy, and probably bright red, but there was nothing she could do about that now.

"I was the first one to carve a path down though all the memories," Loretta continued, as if in answer. "I was the first to... how did your friend Theo put it? 'Deep dive?' Anyway, I was the first to successful 'deep dive' all the way down to where The Daughter's subconscious resides. It left a... mark? Actually, more of a trail. Breadcrumbs guiding the way back. I was able to convince a few of the others to help you. They're not such big fans of The Daughter either," Loretta gave a little laugh that made Buggy smile. "We set up a path for you. So, you can get there quick. But you have to go now, before The Daughter can figure out what we've done and break everything down. We are willing, but she is strong. Stronger than any of us. So, you need to hurry."

"What do I need to do?" Buggy asked.

"What you need to do," Loretta's voice started before Buggy had even finish speaking, "is to go back through the double doors. It will lead to another door, and then another. Just follow them. They will take you where you need to go."

Buggy went back to the double doors but hesitated at the handle. She looked around at the rows and rows of tapes. Every word her mother had for her. Every word left unspoken.

"You can't take them with you," Loretta's voice whispered mournfully from Buggy's hand. "I wish you could, hun. I really do. But they aren't *physically* here. They are *real*, but you can't take them with you when you wake up. I just hope it's enough to know, that they exist."

Buggy nodded, looking around at every colored spine, every word written in that familiar looping hand. A desperate, mournful, joyous, bubbling giggle escaped her. She wiped her eyes and smiled.

"Thanks mom," Buggy said, and then pushed her way through the double doors and out of the library.

18

"Who was that? What's wrong with my mom?"

Cam looked down at Theo, who staggered to his feet. One arm hung awkwardly at his shoulder. Had he dislocated it? Cam wasn't sure how—the boy had just been sitting on the ground and nothing had fallen on him during his meditation—but Cam was less concerned about the boy's arm than he was with the boy's expression. His face was deathly pale, large purple circles dipping under panic-stricken green eyes that had lost their need to blink as they glared Cam down. He could also see fresh, red scratch marks raking up the already bruised and battered skin of his neck.

"Theo," Cam started, slipping the phone easily into his pocket, as if to pretend the call from the mysterious woman had never happened. "God, kid, what happened?"

"What's wrong with my mom?" Theo pressed, ignoring Cam's question. "Who the hell was that on the phone?"

"I don't know," Cam answered, holding up his hands in surrender. "I don't know who she was. Someone just called, and I picked up."

"Whose number?" Theo asked, stepping closer. Cam noticed just how blood shot the boy's eyes were. Green rings floating in twin red lakes.

"What happened in there?" Cam asked. He glanced over at Buggy who remained motionless, eyes closed, jaw loose. "Why did you leave her? What happened?"

"Whose fucking number, Cam!?" Theo yelled. Cam narrowed his eyes.

"Watch your tone, kid," Cam warned, and Theo took a steadying breath. He held out his hand.

"My phone, please, Cam."

"What happened with Buggy?" Cam asked, reaching slowly into his pocket. "Is she alright?"

"Give me my phone, and I'll tell you," Theo answered, wiggling his fingers in the air between them. Cam hesitated, then plopped the phone into his palm.

"We got as far as Loretta's memories," Theo said, closing his fingers possessively over the little device. "Then The Daughter found us again."

"Shit!" Cam said, running a hand over his scruffy face, panicked eyes flashing back to Buggy.

"She's okay, she got away," Theo said, turning on his phone and searching the latest calls. "I—on the other hand—was nearly.... Shit. Cam," Theo's eyes widened at the screen then looked back up at Cam, terror lining every feature. "That was my mom's number. The woman called from my mom's phone!"

"Okay, Theo, calm down. We don't actually know that anything is wrong," Cam insisted, hands raising again.

"Like hell we don't," Theo whacked a palm against his forehead, leaving a bright red angry mark in the center. "Oh, God, Cam, she hasn't been picking up her phone. For days, she hasn't been picking up her phone. Because she hasn't *had* her phone. Who the hell had her phone? Susanna?" Theo looked back to Cam. "You called her Susanna... the crazy bitch from The Fold, Susanna? The one who was hunting Loretta and tried to kill you guys the night that Buggy was born and chased Loretta out into that fucking alley where—"

"It wasn't Susanna," Cam answered.

"But it's someone who knows her," Theo pressed.

"Maybe. What happened with Briar and The Daughter?"

Theo wasn't listening. His thumbs were tapping hastily against his phone's screen, typing in some number Cam didn't recognize. He turned his back on Cam and paced a few feet away, pressing the phone to his ear. Cam knelt beside Buggy, scrutinizing her face. It looked calm enough. The skin was still smooth between her eyes, and she didn't look like she was in pain or frightened. That was never a guarantee, however. Many times, in such trances the body could appear fine while the mind was in agony.

"Hey Peggy!" Theo was saying, words coming so quickly they tripped over one another. "Glad you're in the shop. Is my mom handy, by chance? I've been trying to get ahold of her...." Theo trailed off as the person on the other end of the line started speaking in a rushed, distressed tones that

Cam couldn't make out. Theo gave a great intake of breath. Cam looked up. "Oh God. Oh, God, is she... how long? What happened? I don't...." Theo trailed off once more. Cam got to his feet, with another glance to check that Buggy was okay, and made his way closer to Theo. "No, no, she's not gone to the hospital since she was... so of course they wouldn't have an emergency contact. She hates hospitals and I'm the only... no, Peggy, Mom had my number memorized so she didn't have to write it down anywhere. That isn't your fault, just... no, no, it doesn't matter, I'm on my way. I'll be there as soon as I can. Okay, yeah. Sure, bye." Theo hung up the phone. "Fuck!" he screamed at it, making Cam jump.

"What?"

"My mom," Theo turned back to Cam, his entire body was trembling like a leaf in a storm, seconds away from being torn from its hold and thrown helplessly about. "A couple nights ago Peggy, one of my mom's service technicians, forgot her wallet at work and drove back to get it. Instead, she found my mom. She was beaten half to death in the garage." Theo's voice rose with every word until it was the high-pitched squeak of a bird. He ran his hands through his hair and began tugging on the roots as if to pull his scalp entirely off.

"God," Cam's mouth went dry. "What happened?"

"I don't know!" If Theo's voice grew any higher, soon only bats would be able to understand him. "Peggy doesn't know. She called an ambulance, and my mom is at the hospital. She was going in and out of consciousness for a while, but then last night she slipped into a coma. She's had one surgery already, and she's going in for another one in an hour and—oh shit." Theo dropped his hands from his hair and made a beeline for the door. Cam stepped in front of him, hands going to his shoulders.

"Whoa, where are you going?"

"To the hospital," Theo said, eyes wide, frantic.

Cam blinked. "In Temecula? Back in California?"

"Yes," Theo answered distractedly, trying to step around him. Cam blocked his path again.

"Theo," Cam shook his head. "Temecula is at least a ten-hour drive away, and that is without stopping for sleep or gas."

"Not if I break every speed limit known to man," Theo said defiantly.

"The surgery will be long over before you get there."

"Then I'll be there when she wakes up." Theo tried to pass around Cam again, but Cam stepped in front of him for the third time. This time, Theo shoved him.

"Move, Cam!"

"There is nothing you can do for her right now," Cam persisted, standing his ground.

"I can be there for her when she wakes up!" Theo repeated, anger flaring out of him like a battle flag ready for the charge.

"There is nothing you can do for your mom. But Buggy," Cam watched as Theo's eyes darted towards the girl sitting crossed legged in front of the fire. "*Her*, you can help. And she needs your help, Theo. I can't help her get through this, but *you* can. She needs you." Cam could hear the pleading in his own voice, the begging in it. He had never begged another man for anything in his life, and the macho, toxic masculine part of him—which said he should never show weakness, never show vulnerability—that felt shame, but it was a small part. The rest of him didn't give a shit. The rest of him just wanted his daughter to be alright. A tiny whisper of hope flitted briefly alive as Theo's eyes moved back towards Buggy. That light was snuffed out when Theo turned back.

"So does my mom," he said. "I have to be there for her when she wakes up." He kept repeating the words, reciting it like a mantra. Clinging to it like a lifeline, a last hope.

"*If* she wakes up," Cam said, regretting the words before they had finished forming on his tongue. Theo's eyes narrowed into snake-like slits and his words spat like venom.

"Fuck you, Styger," he hissed shoving the larger man's shoulder, wincing as he only succeeded in hurting his own. "This is your fault. This is *all* your fault. If you had just left us out of it—if you had just left me and my mom alone—we would have been fine!"

"We don't know for sure if Susanna had anything to—"

"Like hell we don't," Theo yelled in his face. "You know it as well as me. Either Susanna, or someone else from the goddamn Fold looking for Buggy, following your tracks. You told me they were. You told me the first day. You promised me this couldn't come back on me or my mom. You fucking promised me and look what happened!"

Cam swallowed, the lump of regret and panic growing heavy in his throat.

"I'm sorry," Cam said. "I wouldn't have come to you if there was any other way. I'm sorry."

"I don't want your apologies," Theo snapped holding out a hand shaking with fury and adrenaline, "I want your keys."

Cam looked into the boy's eyes for three long heartbeats before reaching into his pocket and pulling at a small keychain. The keys jingled delicately as he placed them in Theo's palm. Theo nodded and pushed past Cam, and this time Cam didn't stop him. He went to kneel beside Buggy, the fire heating his back. He reached out and took her hand, unable to do anything other than that, and feeling more useless than he ever had in his entire life. More useless than when he stepped into the ransacked hotel room and found Loretta gone. More useless than when the DNA tests came back negative, and his baby girl disappeared from his grasp. He had never been more utterly worthless.

"Cam." He looked up to see Theo in the open doorway, coat half on and flipping in the sharp wind that whistled into the warm cabin. "She'll be okay. She knows the ropes now, and she will find her way. Buggy's going to be fine. She's stronger than this day."

Cam nodded slowly. Theo nodded back and turned, closing the door behind him. It cut short the wind's whooping wails, and the room filled once more with the fire's warmth, but Cameron Styger had never felt so cold.

19

Buggy stepped across the threshold and heard the double doors swing closed behind her. When she turned to look back, they had already disappeared from existence. There was nothing but ever-expanding darkness. Buggy turned around and wasn't surprised to see another door standing a few yards ahead, waiting for her. She recognized it, but it took her a few seconds to place the wooden panels and smooth metal doorknob. It was the stained glass that finally put it into place. It was the door leading into the cabin. Cam's Cabin. The one where her body currently sat, unmoving in front of the fireplace. She could still vaguely feel her body, her weight pressing against the ground, and the heat of the fire on her skin, but it was far away, more like a half-dreamed memory than an actual feeling.

Buggy stepped up to the door, turned the knob and pushed inside. The place looked exactly the same. Same high roof, same rustic decorations, same lovely windows sending sunlight to scatter across the room in rainbow colors. The living room itself was empty, and the fireplace sat dark and unlit. She could hear birds chattering outside in what felt like a bright spring or summer day. Buggy could also hear a soft humming coming from the kitchen. She followed the sound, walking tentatively towards the door that stood cracked open. She peeked inside and found a girl making breakfast, humming happily. For a brief, forgetful moment, Buggy thought she was looking at herself, but the girl's hair was too short, and Buggy had never actually cooked in the kitchen, whereas this girl seemed quite comfortable flipping pancakes and scrambling eggs. She knew where every utensil was and moved through the room with ease, as if it was her own. Buggy watched her, waiting until she turned around. Loretta moved with the grace of a dancer's step, seeming to flow from movement to movement, in rhythm with the sound of her humming. When she turned, Buggy was able to see her face. Buggy smiled.

"You look so happy," she whispered. And Loretta did. She seemed to glow with a light from the tips of her fingers and ends of her hair. She swept across the room, pulling out plates and forks and setting them on the counter next to coffee cups. There was a creaking sound from another room, and Buggy looked up with surprise to see Styger stepping into the kitchen. He was much younger in this memory, clean shaven, hair at a shaggy length that was half mushed up in the back from sleep. He rubbed his eyes, speaking around a great yawn as he stepped closer to Loretta and planted a soft kiss on her cheek.

"Morning Sunshine," he said, in a voice that was clearer, smooth, not yet gravely from the overuse of cigarettes.

"Morning," Loretta said, leaning across the table to plop a stack of pancakes onto the empty plates. "Eggs?"

"Yes, please," Cam said eagerly, waking up quickly as he plopped himself down on one of the stools at the counter and sipped on his cup of coffee. "You sleep okay last night?"

"Better than I have in months," Loretta answered smiling.

"Good," Cam said, getting up to retrieve a container of syrup from a nearby cupboard. "You still feeling sick at all?"

"Oh, just a little bit now and then. I'm not worried about it," Loretta answered, and Buggy could have sworn she saw a knowing little smirk quirk her lips before she turned back to the eggs.

"Are you sure? I mean I thought I might have heard you puking in the bathroom this m-"

"Eggs!" Loretta interrupted cheerily, and young Cam's attentions were suddenly and wholly focused on his food.

Buggy watched them for a few minutes more. Her parents, young and in love, just having a nice breakfast, sitting, and chatting about nothing. Yet that was everything. Buggy couldn't help but wonder what it would have been like. If her mother hadn't died giving birth to her, if she had grown up sitting at that very counter, her mother making pancakes, her father walking in half asleep with a smile and a, "Good morning, sunshines!" She wondered who she would have been, the version of her that had grown up with Cam as a father and had known her mother as more than just a distant voice on a recording. What path would life have taken her? Would she have grown up in that tiny Utah town, in this very cabin? Would they have made frequent family trips down to The Pizzeria? Would she have taken after her father, been born a psychic? Would she have joined The Fold, getting wrapped up in all their craziness? Or would she, and her father, and mother have stayed under the radar, avoiding The Fold at all costs?

Buggy gave herself just a few minutes to wonder, just a few minutes to daydream about the days that could have been. The life that had died on arrival. Then she turned her back on the memory of her parents' cheerful faces and returned to the living room. There was a door there, standing stoically and out of place in the center of the room, connected to nothing. This door was painted a dark black with a bronze-colored handle, and a long, thin slit that served as a makeshift peephole. A door, Buggy was quite sure, she had never seen before in her life. With a nasty dropping sensation of her stomach, Buggy saw a large padlock that usually barred it closed. For now, it hung unlatched. She slipped the padlock out of its place and set it gently on the floor. Feeling uneasy, she pushed the door open. She half expected it to open on the cabin's living room, but she knew that was a foolish idea. The door opened into a different room altogether, and Buggy stepped through to have a better look. The cabin and the sound of her mother's distant laughter vanished as she stepped across the threshold, and the door swung shut behind her. Buggy looked around.

This new room was plain, low ceilinged, but it expanded a wide distance of around a thousand square feet. Despite the ample space to put them, there were very few items within. There was a small sink connected to a wall on one side, a large, four poster-bed in the corner of the room nearest to the door, a shelf full of books and notebooks beside a square desk covered in stray paper, another notebook, and what looked like a box of crayons. The room was open except for a small added room that Buggy peeked inside and realized was a bathroom. Thick pillars held up the ceiling in several places, giving the space a basement feel. It took Buggy just a moment to take in the ceiling's height, the pillars, and the fact that there were no windows, to decide that it *was* a basement. Just one that had been revamped to hold a person.

Three caged lights hung down from the ceiling, illuminating her way as Buggy stepped deeper into the room. As she did so, Buggy caught sight of the girl. She was sitting on the floor in the far corner, legs drawn up to her chest, hands deep in her long brown hair which flowed and scattered to the ground around her. She was rocking back and forth, and Buggy could hear her whimpering softly. Buggy came closer, kneeling beside the girl.

"Hello?" Buggy asked, knowing it probably wouldn't work, but feeling the need to try all the same. "Hello? Are you—are you one of the ones that came before?" The girl didn't answer, just continued to rock back and forth, muttering to herself. "I—I'd like to help you, if I can," Buggy said, honestly. "I'd like to—" Buggy broke off when she began to make out some of the girl's muttered words. Buggy leaned in to hear better.

"I don't want to," the girl was saying between whimpers and stifled sobs. "I don't want to, I don't want to, I don't want to. No, no, they love me. They love me... they wouldn't hurt me—they *love* me. Susanna said so. They all said so. Shut up, I don't want to. I don't want to. I don't want to."

Buggy drew back, eyes widening, that same sick, dropping, feeling coming back. Like the top of a roller coaster, when the nose of the shuttle teeters at the top, and just begins pointing down. The girl looked up then, and for one terrifying heartbeat Buggy thought the girl saw her, that she was speaking *to Buggy*. The girls face looked like her's, the bone structure, the skin tone, but this version had a thicker scattering of freckles that coated her nose and cheeks, and her large disk-like eyes were not a muddy brown, but a deep ocean blue. Her eyes were red and bloodshot from crying and tear streaks tracked down her entire face. She could have been trying to drown herself in them. For a moment, she seemed to see Buggy, but Buggy realized her unfocused eyes were not looking *at* her, but *through* her.

"No!" the girl whimpered, voice cracking. "No, they won't hurt me. They *love* me. They said so. I won't hurt them, so leave me alone. Leave me alone. Go away. Shut up! Just **shut up**!" She buried her fingers back into her hair as a fresh volley of tears slipped down her cheeks. "Leave me alone. Please just—oh God, hear me—please make her go away." Her face fell back to her legs and Buggy stood watching, helpless as the girl's whimpers turned to full sobs. A knock came to the door.

"Aetheria?" a young, high voice called from the other side of the closed door. "Aetheria? You awake?"

The girl stopped her sobbing abruptly, cleared her throat and called in a surprisingly stable, even cheerful, voice. "Hey Susanna! Yes, I'm awake."

"Okay," the small voice answered. "Mom says that dinner will be ready in ten minutes. Marcus will be down to get you then."

"Okay!" Aetheria called back. Both Aetheria and Buggy waited, listening to the sound of small feet padding away. Aetheria waited until the sound had completely disappeared, before getting to her feet and going to the sink. She turned on the faucet and splashed her face with lukewarm water, washing away the tears and trying to lessen the swelling around her eyes and nose.

"Aetheria, huh?" Buggy mused, leaning on the sink next to the girl, watching her slowly and carefully wind her long hair into a bun at the base of her skull and secure it with a hair clip from the shelf attached to the wall. "You're the one that came before Loretta. You're the one that Bennu took over and killed The Fold members, right?" Aetheria didn't answer. She was staring at her own reflection in the small round glass above the sink. Her dark blue eyes were still a little red, but she had wiped the tears from her cheeks and her freckles masked most of the flush that remained. As Buggy watched, the girl smiled at herself in the mirror, then let her face fall into a blank, hollowed out expression. Then the smile reappeared. Then it fell again. Buggy realized Aetheria was practicing, testing the gesture on her lips like someone might try on clothes. Soon another knock interrupted her. A different voice called this time, a man's voice.

"Aetheria," he said, "you ready for dinner?"

"Yes," Aetheria answered as she turned, practiced smile holding on her lips. Buggy heard the sound of keys in a lock and a great metallic clank of a heavy bolt being drawn away. The door pushed inward, and Buggy had to blink a few times to orient herself. The man standing in the doorway looked like Cam. Same hair color, although this man's allotment was receding back on his skull a bit. They had similar bone structure, skin tone, and eyes of the same gray shade. Not exactly like Cam, but close enough for Buggy to know that this must be his father.

"Good evening, Aetheria," Cam's father said, smiling kindly to the girl who stepped towards him. "Are you hungry?"

"Starving," Aetheria agreed. She took the man's arm as they made their way out the door. Buggy followed them. She looked back and a dark sickening feeling churned deep in her gut as she once again saw the locks that usually bolted the door closed. Locking Aetheria in. Locking *all of them* in. Captives in this basement, a room of caged lights and windowless walls. Buggy turned her back on the room and tried to focus on Aetheria and the man chatting congenially as they made their way up a lengthy flight of stairs. Cam's father, or Marcus, asked Aetheria many questions. How was she doing? How was she feeling? Was she feeling alright? Had she had any nasty dreams recently? Any odd feelings? Aetheria had smiled and answered that she was fine. She felt perfectly well and had been sleeping like a rock.

"Your birthday is coming up very soon," Marcus said, as they reached the top of the landing and pushed open a second door that led up and out of the basement stairs. They entered a large old-fashioned house with wide walls and long polished floors. There were staircases leading off to different wings of the house, with dozens of doors that entered closed rooms. There were no photos on the walls, nothing that made the sizeable house feel homey, but the sound of chattering voices and laughter through a door to their left made Buggy turn her head.

The Fold's headquarters, Buggy realized, looking around. All the skilled psychics and mediums and empaths, all living here under one roof. All here to contain one girl in a basement. Keep her hidden from the world. Keep her *trapped* from the world. Buggy felt like screaming. She wanted to attack Marcus, to attack the house at large, to take a sludge hammer to the banisters and bust down all those closed doors. To burn the entire place down. Burn it until it was nothing but dust and ash.

Buggy reeled in her sudden powerful rage with desperate and terrified mental scrambling. She needed to focus. She could do nothing about what came before, but she had a hand in what would come next. So, she turned her attention back to Aetheria, who was speaking again.

"I know," Aetheria was saying, eyes cast down.

"Twenty-four years old," Marcus smiled at her. "Quite an accomplishment. What sort of cake would you like? To celebrate."

"Oh, I don't know," Aetheria shrugged. "I'm not picky."

"Well, I suggest chocolate," Marcus urged, as they made their way towards the sound of talking and the clanking of utensils against plates. "You can never go wrong with a good old-fashioned chocolate cake."

"Right. Okay," Aetheria stopped short of the half-open door which led, Buggy guessed, into the dining room. She had frozen, eyes on the ground at her feet.

"Aetheria?" Marcus looked at her, giving her hand a gentle tug, but Aetheira didn't move. "Aetheria?" Aetheria looked up at him then, and her eyes were blazing with an intense fear.

"You would never hurt me, right Marcus?" she asked, reaching out and taking his arm again. She leaned in to studying his face, large eyes darting back and forth between his, peering into them, peering into his soul, begging for the truth of her own words.

"Aetheria, I—"

"You wouldn't let anything bad happen to me, right?" she pleaded, hand tightening on his shoulder. "You've cared for me, for so long and... you wouldn't let any harm come to me. Right, Marcus?" Marcus hesitated, then he smiled gently, taking her hand off his shoulder and squeezing it in his.

"Of course not," Marcus Styger lied. And in that moment, Aetheria knew. Her eyes drained of all hope and cast down to the floor in defeat. Her hands fell to her sides, as her shoulders relinquished the last of their strength and sank, wilted, a dying daisy. "Oh come," Marcus tilted her chin up, and Buggy could see actual pain in his expression. "How about some wine with dinner, hmm? A few glasses and everything will be all better." Aetheria just nodded and made no protest as Marcus led her through the dining room door. Buggy didn't follow at first. She just stayed outside the room, fighting the urge to vomit. She breathed slowly in her nose and out her mouth. What kind of monsters could do that to a girl? Keep such a sweet thing trapped in a basement prison. How could you live in such a house, large and beautiful as it may be, knowing that they kept a girl like her captive just below their feet. Knowing that they would kill her every twenty-four years. How did they smile to her face? How did they chat and laugh so happily around the table at dinner like they were doing right now... except, they weren't chatting and laughing anymore. The other side of the door had gone silent. The clinking of plates and scrapping of utensils had ceased. Buggy also noticed that the light in the room had shifted, dimmed. Buggy didn't know why, but her internal clock was telling her that the memory she was in now occurred long after the dinner party Marcus had taken Aetheria. Months had passed, four at least. Buggy reached for the door handle but realized she didn't want to go inside. There was something bad on the other side of that door. Something wrong, something dark, something she never wanted to see. But what else could she do? She needed to go deeper, needed to keep moving. She had one chance to stop The Daughter, and she needed to take it. There was no turning back, so Buggy pushed the door open and entered the dining room. She froze, eyes widening.

"Oh... God...."

Blood was everywhere. It spattered the floral-patterned wallpaper from the ground to the ceiling. It covered the wooden chairs and soaked dark red and brown in the rug, but the worst part, the part that made Buggy lean over and retch, was the dining room table. Bodies lay piled high in a mass of men and women with broken limbs hanging awkwardly, and wide blank eyes held open in expressions of frozen terror. Someone, or something, had ripped limbs from bodies, popping them off like some angry child with a Barbie doll that had disappointed her. The limbs scattered throughout the room, tossed out of the way, some into heaping mounds of bloody flesh. One arm, with a jutting bone and skin that had been torn into jagged, dangling flaps, was propped against the far wall. The blood that still seeped from the arm had been used to write a message on the wallpaper above it. The words were written in large, looping calligraphy letters that dripped red tears down towards the floor.

Happy Birthday To Me.

Buggy heard a child's scream from a doorway to her right and ran towards it. She burst through the door and into a fresh room of horror. The strong acrid smell of burning flesh met her instantly, nearly knocking her back with the force of it. There was no blood smeared on the walls or a mountain of bodies as in the other room, but there were bodies, three of them. They were splayed out on the carpet, and Buggy recoiled as she saw that they had been burned to black hunks of meat shaped like people. There seemed to be no source of the fire, no gasoline cans or lighter fluid, just burnt bodies, like they had spontaneously combusted. There were three other people in the room, these being the only ones still alive. One of them was a young girl, no older than eleven or twelve, wearing a bright blue sundress and scuffed white, sandals. They were both stained with blood. The girl, Susanna, was crumpled in a corner, mouth open as she gave another blood-curdling scream, striking blue eyes focused on the two people struggling in the middle of the room. Buggy tore her eyes away from her and turned to see Aetheria standing, blood-soaked arms outstretched, fingers fastened around the throat of a woman who had the same blond hair and blue eyes as Susanna. The woman was choking.

"No!" Susanna screamed, scrambling to her feet and running to pound her fists against Aetheria's side and arms, trying to make her let go. "Aetheria stop! Please stop! Get off her! Let her go!" Aetheria didn't let go. Instead, she reached out with her free hand, grabbed the girl by the front of her dress, and flung her across the room with the strength that didn't belong on those thin arms. Susanna crumpled to the floor, weeping louder.

"Why are you doing this?" Susanna shirked, on her knees looking up into Aetheria's cold eyes. "Aetheria, please—"

"Oh, my dear little girl," it was Aetheria's mouth that moved, and Aetheria's eyes that blinked down at Susanna, but that wasn't Aetheria's voice, nor her manic glare. "Aetheria is long gone." Susanna's eyes widened, and then she rose shaking to her feet.

"Bennu," Susanna whispered, as if not genuinely believing.

"In the flesh," Bennu grinned and fear shot through Buggy like a bolt of lightning. For a terrifying instant she thought Bennu would turn to her, grinning that terrible fang filled grin. She would see her, dive for her, sink her teeth deep into Buggy's throat. But Bennu didn't even know she was there. It was still just a memory.

"Please," the little girl begged the monster holding her mother's life in her hands. "Please, Bennu, please let her go."

"Why?" Bennu asked, head tilting to the side, that same cruel smirk painting her face, as a trickle of blood dripped from her chin. "Why on Earth would I do such a thing?"

"Because we're friends!" Susanna burst into tears. "Because we are friends! Aetheria and I are friends! Aetheria, if you are in there—"

"Oh, yes, she is here, my dear. But why should she help you, hmm? What did you ever do for her? What did any of you do for her?" Bennu's cruel smile twisted into a satanic leer of a gargoyle, as she turned her attention to the woman struggling in her grip. "You locked her underground, barely let her see the sun. You hid her away, told her she was evil, counting down the days until her twenty-fourth birthday. Tick-tick-ticking down the days until her death, like it was no big deal. Like it was just another day in the life. You did nothing but abuse and mentally torture that sweet girl until she was so scared, she finally gave in. She finally *let* me in," Bennu laughed a high cruel laugh, "You were all so damn busy worrying about what would happen if I woke up, too busy obsessing on how to *contain me*, how to keep me *buried*, that you did not bother even *trying* to *help* her. Just kept her locked away, counting down the days. She was winning too, you know. She held me at bay. That sweet girl was winning, actually winning, **against me**, and you still refused to change your ways. So, she gave up. This," Aetheria raised her free bloody hand and motioned to the dark red stains, already drying to a murky sickening brown, that splattered up and down the front of her shirt and pants. "This is on your head. *All* of your heads. And this dance is over." Aetheria's fingers tightened around the woman's throat. The woman's tongue lolled out the side of her mouth, the gurgling increasing.

"No!" Susanna ran from the room.

"Do not go far, Susanna dear!" Bennu called after her, "Not done with you yet." She turned back to the woman under her hand. "Sweet child you have. Very sweet. Do not worry. Aetheria liked her, so I will kill her quick. No pain. Just a little quick *snap!* And done." The woman struggled harder, and Bennu laughed again. Buggy wanted to help, wanted grab Bennu, tear her off the woman. She wanted to close her eyes and pull herself from this horror show, but she could do neither. She needed to keep going forward—keep moving—end this. Buggy turned away and ran from the room, out the same door that Susanna had vanished. She passed Susanna as she went. The young girl was running back towards Bennu and her mother, a kitchen knife clutched in her tiny hands. Buggy didn't follow, she kept running in the opposite direction as fast as she could. She found herself in a massive entry way with double staircases leading towards upper floors. Buggy ran for the door leading outside, flung it open and threw herself across the threshold, landing hard on her hands and knees breathing heavily, head spinning, adrenaline coursing through her body like three shots and a

Redbull. She looked up. To her desperate relief, the large house had vanished. Buggy was in the middle of a meadow, surrounded by bright yellow flowers. A soft, warm breeze bent the tall grass back and forth as the smell of pollen and flowers filled the air. Buggy got to her feet, looking around, heart beginning to slow. She looked across the meadow and the beautiful blue sky without a cloud in sight. She was alone except for a couple picnicking a few yards away. The girl was in a fluffy white sundress with a wide skirt and matching wide-brimmed hat. Her entire outfit looked like it belonged in some cheap knock-off prequal to "Gone with the Wind." Upon closer inspection, Buggy wasn't surprised to see that the girl looked like her, although a younger version, seventeen or eighteen at most. The boy beside her looked around the same age, wearing old fashioned trousers, button-down shirt, a shock of thick, black hair and a shy smile. They had a woven basket between them, and were chatting happily over bread, cheese, and a bottle of wine. The boy was handing her something. Buggy leaned in and saw that it was a silver cord holding a large, red stone. Buggy recognized it. The woman dressed in black, the one who used her deceased husband's shaving blade to slit her own wrists... she had been wearing that necklace.

Buggy turned numbly away from the happy couple as the girl squealed in delight and threw her arms around the boy she would later marry. The happy couple whose lives would take a tragic turn in just a few short years. Why did that always seem the way? Why was it always a bad ending for these stories? Couldn't there just be one? One story when things didn't go terribly, horribly, irretrievably wrong?

Buggy looked around and saw another wooden door standing in the middle of the thick grass and yellow flowers. She pushed it open, going through without a moment's hesitation. She needed out. Buggy was finished with this hallway of horrors.

She passed by many memories on the way, but she didn't stop to look around. She stepped across years, tiptoed through lives of the ones that came before, going deeper and deeper with every threshold, with every memory. Saw versions of herself living in the seventeen hundreds, the sixteen hundreds, fifteen hundreds, even a medieval era where her reincarnation had been a maid to some great household. The doors kept leading her, back and back to times that history had not bothered teaching her, and further into times that history had forgotten completely. She pushed through, trying to ignore the stories that sped by her, trying to focus on her destination. And soon, she was there. She wasn't sure *why* she knew she had arrived. She had passed through so many strange worlds by this point, they had all started to blur together. But when she stepped out of the door and into the cold, dark, dirt road—she *knew*. She could feel it. Feel it in the chaos. People were running, screaming in every direction. Houses that were little more than thatched huts were burning on all sides. Dark clothed men on horseback rode through the streets, whooping and throwing torches on the few houses that were not yet alight. A man lay to the side of the road, weeping and clutching a young woman's body close to his chest as his entire world burned down around him. Buggy passed by in a daze, walking down the road, through the memory world, following the pull. It was the same feeling that told her this was the right place. A silent cry, calling from the deepest part of the void in her chest. And she followed, one hesitant step in front of the other. It led her to the edge of the village and a small, thatched cottage. Four of the dark clothed men were exiting the little house laughing and joking in a language that Buggy didn't understand. They closed the door behind them and stepped back as one of the men lit a torch and tossed it on the roof. The men hooted with appreciation as the cottage caught fire. They mounted their horses and road off to another section of the village, one of them riding straight through Buggy, noticing nothing. Buggy stepped closer to the house, heart thudding as she watched the building go up in flames. Dark smoke began billowing into the sky like some great demonic bird taking flight, leaping up to attack the heavens. Screams and shouts of men and women faded into the background of Buggy's mind as the sound of the flames enveloped everything. The sound of the flames and something else... a girl's voice. A soft, broken cry of a young woman coming from inside the burning cottage. Buggy felt it. That small desperate scream was the source of the pull in her chest. The one that connected to the deepest part of the void. It called to her, and she followed without thought. Buggy leaped for the door, ready to fling it open and help whoever was inside. Before her hand could so much as touch the door, another hand seized it, stopping her.

"Buggy, don't." Buggy looked up to see Loretta standing beside her, soft eyes watching her sadly.

"M-Mom?" Buggy asked. "What—" She had come out of nowhere. Without a sound, without a whisper, she had just appeared. *Actually* appeared.

"You can't let her out, Buggy," Loretta said, reaching out to stroke Buggy's hair. Her fingers didn't pass through, but brushed strands out of her daughter's face. She was here. She was really, truly *here*. Buggy wanted to cry. She wanted to throw her arms around the woman and hold her. She wanted to feel what it was like to have her mother's arms wrapped around her, protecting her, as she spoke in that voice she knew so well. And yet....

"But, Mom," Buggy turned back to the building, whose roof was bleeding fire, and the walls were quickly going up in red and green flames. "She's going to burn alive in there."

"I know," Loretta looked on the verge of tears. "But inside is the deepest part of Bennu. Her deepest, strongest memory. The part still tethering her, keeping her from taking control. If you let her out, Bennu will be fully free. You will lose your turn."

"Then what should I do?" Buggy asked, desperately.

"Let her burn," came another voice from behind her. Buggy turned to see the woman in black standing on her left side, the red stone glinting against her chest. She stood, hands laced in front of her. Her features were the same as they had been in the dream, tired and aged only by grief. But her eyes were steady, strong, and sure as they met Buggy's gaze. "Let her burn, and she will be trapped until the next reincarnation." Another cry for help came from inside the cottage and Buggy looked desperately between them.

"I can't just—"

"You have to," Loretta rested a hand on Buggy's shoulder. "She's not really dying, Buggy. She's already dead. This already happened. Thousands of years ago. You can't help her."

"But she is in so much pain," Buggy protested.

"I know, hun," Loretta said, pressing her hand firmly against the door, eyes closing. "I know. I've been here before, remember?"

The door rattled under her hand, as if someone on the other side was shaking it, trying to open it. The cries continued, but there was another sound, one that reverberated in the smokey air like some angry god, rising above the screams of the burning village.

"Let me out!" Bennu's wail echoed like thunder, and the door rattled harder. Loretta and Buggy pressed against it, keeping it closed, but it thudded against their weight, shaking the entire wall of the cottage.

"Shit!" Buggy cried, trying to get a better footing, but the softness of the ground and the heat emanating from the door made her hands sweaty. She slipped.

"Hold it!" Loretta shouted over the roar of the flames. "Hold it closed!"

"How the hell did you keep it closed before?" Buggy asked, trying to plant her feet hard, but they kept sliding.

"Your father," Loretta called, also planting her feet and pressing her shoulder into the door. "He used his abilities. The effort to hold the door ended up stripping him of them, but we kept her in."

"Theo," Buggy said, realization striking her hard. "Theo would— But Theo's not here!"

"That's alright," Loretta smiled at her, sweat beading down her face. "We don't need him this time. We've got them."

"Who?" Buggy asked confused. Loretta jerked her head. Buggy looked around to see figures appearing out of smoke and darkness. Women in different clothes from different eras of time, all with the same face, same large eyes. Buggy could see Aetheria, the maid girl from the medieval era, and so many more. Hundreds of them stepped from the darkness. They came, pressing their hands against the door, or holding the shoulders of those that were. Buggy could feel hands against her back and shoulders, supporting her, helping hold her and the door in place. She and all her reincarnations coming together for a common goal. Buggy felt herself stabilize, felt the door stop shuddering under her hands.

"It's working!" Buggy cried, breathing heavily with the effort. "It's working, it's working, its—"

Mama... the soft broken voice called from inside the house, but not with words. When it had spoken, it had been in a language Buggy didn't understand. But the girl inside was no longer speaking with her mouth. She was calling with her mind. Calling with her very soul.

Mama... please help me. Mama, I am scared. Mama, I am so alone... Mama please... please... Buggy stared at the door, blood draining from her face, listening. *Mama it hurts.... Oh, mama it hurts so much. Please I...*

mama I cannot move, help me... someone, anyone... help me... Buggy swallowed hard.

"No," she whispered shaking her head. There was no anger in the silent voice. There was no snarling fury of the thundercloud from before. There was no wind full of hate. This voice was different. There was only fear. Pain. Sorrow—*oh, Mamma please*—despair. There was nothing dangerous in this call, nothing evil—*please, someone help*—there was only broken innocence. She felt it just as surely as the heat of the fire and the hands against her back.

It hurts... it hurts... oh, God it hurts... Buggy felt herself being pulled by the call, drawn to answer. *Please... it hurts, make it stop...please, make it*—

Buggy squeezed her eyes closed and tried to break herself from the voice, but it didn't stop. It just grew louder as the pain—oh God—she could *feel* it. She could feel the pain, the terror, the utter despair, the burning.

"No," Buggy shook her head harder, "this is wrong."

"Buggy, this is the only wa—"

"No, Mom," Buggy turned to Loretta, "the girl in there, the part of Bennu inside there, that's just an innocent girl. That's just a terrified girl calling for her mother. This *can't* be the right way." Buggy pulled away from the door, and the hands fell from her shoulders. She reached to pull the door open, but Loretta put out an arm to block her, eyes wide and panic-stricken.

"Buggy, what are you doing?"

"I'm going inside," Buggy said firmly.

"No!" Loretta said, shaking her head. "No, Buggy. If you go inside, she'll take you. She'll win."

"How do you know that?" Buggy asked. "You've only been here once. Did you go inside?" She could tell from Loretta's thunderstruck expression that she had not. "Have any of you?" She looked around to the others, but they said nothing in reply, just continued watching her with silent fascination. "You don't know what will happen. Letting her burn kept her down before but, you can't say it is the *only* way when you haven't even *tried* another way."

"Even if you go in," Loretta protested, "What are you hoping to accomplish? What will that change?"

"I... don't know yet. I'll figure it out when I get in there."

"Buggy—" Loretta started.

"Close the door behind me," Buggy said. "Just in case."

"What?" Loretta asked, horrified. "No, Buggy—"

"One way or another, we won't let Bennu hurt anyone else."

"Buggy, no. You can't—"

"Mom," she looked furiously into her mother's eyes. "Bennu is evil. Bennu is twisted, but this is before all that. The girl inside that door is the part of Bennu that came *before*. Before everything. Before all of *us*," Buggy said, gesturing to the leagues of lives with familiar faces so like her own. "The girl burning alone in there, that 'deep part,' is just a girl who had no hand in what happened to her. A girl who burns alive over and over again, I know she does, because so have I. I have lived this memory in my dreams, in my *nightmares*. Just like all of us." Loretta's eyes dropped away from her daughter's gaze. Buggy shook her head. "I can't let *that* girl die alone calling for her mother. Not again." Loretta opened her mouth to speak, but Buggy pressed on. "I know what it's like to call out for a mother who is never going to come." Loretta closed her mouth, looking at Buggy with an expression of despair, fear, hurt and overwhelming love. "Mom, you have to let me try. I *have* to try."

Loretta hesitated, then stepped away from the door. As Buggy made to open it, Loretta stopped her long enough to pull her into a firm hug. She whispered brokenly into Buggy's ear.

"I love you, hun," Loretta said, squeezing her painfully. "Always have and always will."

"I love you too, Mom," Buggy said, heart aching in her chest, knowing this was the first and only time she would ever hold her mother in her arms. She wished she could pause it here, simply stop time from spinning forward, the magic to turn this moment to stone. She wished she could live this moment just a little longer... but it was already done. It was already becoming a memory. She pulled away and looked Loretta seriously in the face. "You close that door when I'm inside," she looked around to the hundreds of others. "All of you." They all nodded, getting ready. Buggy nodded back and gave Loretta one last longing look. Her mother smiled to her, and the pride Buggy saw in her face gave her the strength she needed to do what she needed to do.

She turned to the door, taking the handle. To her surprise she found it locked. She frowned, confused. Well, Bennu wanted to come out, not for someone to *come in*. Maybe the door only went one way? Then Theo's voice whispered across her mind like a firefly drifting over a still lake. A quiet hum nearly missed.

The deeper you go, the farther back you go, the closer to The Daughter's original memories, the less ability you have, the less **control**. *The Daughter's memories, she's got complete control over that. You wouldn't be able to get in unless she let you in... and she's probably not going to do that....*

Buggy paused, closed her eyes, and whispered.

"Bennu. May I?"

At first, there was nothing, just the sound of crackling fire. Then Buggy felt the door shift under her hand. Without looking back, Buggy entered the burning cottage. The door swung closed behind her with a heavy thud.

places. The one in her face, the other...

20

It was just as she remembered. Every detail, from the caving roof to the sting of the sparks flying through the air, it was just as it had been in her dream. Although now she knew it had not been dream at all, but a memory. Memories of a death, the first death, but most certainly not the last.

Sweat poured down Buggy's arms, back and neck as she made her way deeper into the room. The cottage was a furnace. Flames licked up the walls, creating a deafening, crackling roar around her. A section of the roof came thudding to a spot a few feet away, and Buggy dodged the flurry of sparks that caught at her clothes and singed her skin. She could smell burnt hair but didn't bother checking, focusing instead on the form in the middle of the room. The girl lay face up, large eyes on the ceiling. A long smear of blood left a dark gruesome trail in the dirt floor where she had dragged herself, attempting to reach the door. It spread out from between her legs. An evil tail, one made from pain and violated virtue. She dragged it behind herself, trying to claw her way to salvation, her broken legs following limply behind. But she had found the door blocked by a heavy fallen beam. Weak, broken, and beaten, Bennu lay in her last moments, eyes on the flames that would soon reach her, soon eat her alive.

Mama... the girl's mind begged, calling outward, bursting from her in silent agony. *Mama, help me.*

Buggy went to her, ignoring the heat of the flames that made sweat pour from her like water. She ignored the smoke that filled her lungs and made her cough and gag. She knelt, legs meeting the floor that was burning hot. She reached out to touch the girl's shoulder. Her fingers met flesh.

"Bennu?" Buggy asked. Her voice trembled and her hands shook. "Bennu?"

Bennu's eyes broke away from the flames. Her face was bruised, smeared with ash and tears. Portions of her cheek were already swelling in places. The entire left side of her face was purpling. She turned to look at Buggy, eyes widening. She had Buggy's face, just a little thinner, a little paler. Although Buggy suspected the paleness was due more to the loss of blood then actual complexion. Bennu's eyes were also brown, but of a deeper shade with flecks of bright green and gold that glinted in the light of the fire. She was twenty-four, Buggy knew, but she looked no older than fourteen as she lay in the mud made from her own blood and dirt. Bennu reached out to her, and for a moment Buggy expected the inhuman strength to crush her wrist, shattering her arm. But it didn't. Bennu's hand was trembling as her fingers wrapped around Buggy's hand in a grip as strong and forceful as a sick child's. The girl opened her mouth to speak, but no words came out, just a low gargling sound. A trickle of blood oozed out of the left corner of her mouth as another burst of sparks rained down around them, dazzling the room with momentary golden stars.

"Don't talk," Buggy said, and then coughed long and hard into her arm. The smoke was getting thicker with every passing second, filling the room with gray and black puffs that pillared into the sky through the hole in the roof. Buggy's head began to swim and her eyes watered.

Mama. Where's mama? Bennu's mind begged, pouring out of her body and mingling with the pulsing heat of the ever-growing flames.

I don't know. Buggy thought back, praying the girl would hear her, like she had heard Theo. It seemed to have worked, because Bennu began to cry. Buggy reached out, pulling the girl's limp body up into her arms with effort, and cradled her in her lap.

They hurt me. Bennu's mind screamed above the crackle of flames. *The men, they hurt me. They hurt me and hurt me. I want my mama. Mama, they hurt me.*

I know. Buggy answered, holding her tighter.

I hurt. Please, make it stop. Bennu begged, eyes searching Buggy's. *Please. Make it stop.*

I can't. Tears began spilling down her face and together the girls wept. Buggy held the girl who looked so much like herself. Rocked her back and forth in her arms as the flames grew closer. She didn't tell her not to be afraid. Buggy knew that was impossible. She didn't tell her everything would be okay, because she knew that was a lie. She just stayed, holding a version of herself who had died thousands of years before. A death she kept reliving with every new life. This part of her forever trapped in a memory. Her worst memory. Always, eternally, ending up here. This was *her space*, just as the library was Loretta's. Always finding herself back here. Forever.

And Buggy understood then more than ever, why Bennu had gone so mad. If this was her space, the deepest part, where Bennu's subconscious truly resided when she wasn't "awake" then...

Out of nowhere, Theo's voice whispered across her mind once more, followed closely by the shrieking voice of a half crazed Aetheria.

The deeper you go, the farther back you go, the closer to The Daughter's original memories, the less ability you have, the less control....

*You were all so damn busy worrying about what would happen if I woke up, too busy obsessing on how to contain me, how to keep me buried, that you didn't bother even **trying** to help her....*

Help....

Control....

Then it clicked.

"Her space. Her memory," Buggy closed her eyes, and a relieved smile spread her lips. "This is your memory—the **worst** memory—but not your *only* memory." Buggy opened her eyes and looked down at Bennu. She didn't know if this would work, but....

Close your eyes. She thought at her. Bennu obeyed without hesitation, large eyes fluttering shut, happy to escape in any way she could. *Breathe with me. In your nose, and out your mouth. In your nose, out your mouth.* Bennu did, the best she could in such thick smoke. *I need you to remember, okay? I need you to remember before this.*

There is nothing other than this. Bennu's mind protested, and fresh tears fell from her eyes, creating dark streaks in the ash powdering her face. Buggy had a flash of her own reflection in the mirror at Elwin Family Dentistry. The horror in her own eyes, her own ashy tears. She shoved the image away violently. She needed to stay focused. *This is all that there is. This is all that is left.*

That's not true. Buggy said, pulling the girl closer. *There is **before**, and there is **after**.*

There is no after. Bennu's mind sobbed. Buggy could feel her despair. Could *feel* the hopelessness of the girl in her arms. She could feel it as clearly as the blood pumping through her veins, and the hope the bloomed in Buggy's own heart—so out of place in this memory of tortured death.

"Yes," Buggy said out loud. "Yes, there is." Buggy thought about her family. She thought about Sandra and Andrew and Linny and Cooper. She thought about all the people she loved, and the feeling of love she had when she was with them. She thought about every time Sandra had made her laugh, or Andrew had nearly knocked her over with a hug. She thought about Linny's sly smile. She thought about the tickling feeling in her stomach, the one she got when Cooper would cast one of those sideways glances in the light of the TV screen. Buggy usually ran from it, but this time she leaned in. She held every feeling, every butterfly, every heart bursting joy of friendship or love and she sent it to Bennu. Sent it like she had sent her thoughts, pouring memory and emotion into her mind. Buggy watched as Bennu's face began to soften.

That is nice. Bennu smiled.

Your turn. Buggy thought. *Think about your times. A memory. Just one will do. Find a moment that makes you smile. Find it and show it to me.*

Bennu hesitated, then breathed. Buggy waited. Nothing happened at first, and for a horrible, heart stopping moment, Buggy was sure the girl had slipped away into death. But then, all at once, the flames disappeared. They didn't fade, nor drizzle away as if in a soft rain. They didn't blur like brush strokes or smear into strange colors as Buggy's memories had done. They were there, and then they were gone. The sparks evaporated from the surrounding air, and a cool breeze filled the room with the smell of spring. Buggy looked around. They were still in the same dirt floored cottage, but there was no fire, no broken beams, and the ceiling was in place above their heads.

Good Bennu. Good. Keep going.

Two windows were opened wide, letting in a bright sunlight and the sound of birds chirping happily in the distance. All sounds of chaos and screaming were gone. The sky outside was a soft blue with little pink streaks of clouds painted haphazardly across the blue canvas. Buggy looked down at the girl. The blood trail vanished. Her arms and legs were no longer broken, her face was clean and clear.

Bennu. Buggy smiled. *Open your eyes.*

Bennu did. She blinked a few times, then looked around her. She smiled at her home, so full of light. Buggy got to her feet and reached down to Bennu. Bennu looked at the hand curiously, and then up at Buggy. Buggy waited, hand outstretched. Bennu hesitated, then reached up and tentatively took it. Buggy pull her to her feet. They gazed at each other, still hand in hand. Bennu looked as if she wanted to say something, but they both turned as the door opened behind them. A pudgy woman in a plain, brown dress made from rough cloth, and fashioned with a rope cord, stepped through the door holding a basket of newly picked vegetables. Bennu made an exclamation, and threw herself at the woman, wrapping her arms around her. The woman laughed, closing large brown eyes as Bennu kissed her mother on both cheeks. Buggy stepped away, completely unnoticed by the mother as she came further into the house, Bennu still holding onto her arm. They were chatting in a language Buggy didn't know, but she understood all the same. This was a memory of Bennu's from before. A memory of a beautiful spring day when her mother came home early to make dinner. It was a memory, just like the one of fire and flame—just as real—but almost forgotten.

Buggy turned towards the door, no longer blocked by a fallen beam. She pressed her palm against it, and it swung easily at her touch. She looked back to see Bennu helping her mother unload the basket onto their wooden table. The mother still didn't see Buggy, but Bennu did. She looked into Buggy eyes, Buggy already halfway through the door. Bennu smiled that sweet, gentle, smile that had belonged to her for so long before it had turned into a snarl. At the sight of it, Buggy was struck by an extraordinarily strong feeling. A feeling that sent her rocking back on her heels. For just a flashing, vertigo-inducing moment, she *was* Bennu. She was standing on the opposite side of the kitchen, facing herself. For that one second, she and Bennu shared the same space in reality. For the same brief millisecond, they mixed, and felt, and were as *one*. Buggy saw it then—saw and felt it—a strange golden light that pulsed like a beating heart around and inside herself, inside Briar Rose Pierce. She saw it through Bennu's eyes, and it was... it was....

Then she blinked, and the world righted itself. Bennu smiled, raised her hand and waved.

Thank you... Buggy.

Buggy smiled back, nodded, turned, and closed the door securely behind her. There was a soft click as some mental lock slid into place. And the entire world went quiet, letting out a long-held breath. And then there was darkness. And Buggy was falling.

21

Cam breathed a deep gasp as Buggy jerked and opened her eyes for the first time in hours.

"Buggy?" he asked, realizing he had no idea what he would do if it wasn't her.

Buggy blinked. "Cam?" she asked as her eyes came into focus.

"Thank God," Cam said, throwing his arms around her without thinking. He pulled away hurriedly, but she was smiling and didn't jerk away. "What happened?" he asked.

"I *helped* her," she said, sounding satisfied. Cam frowned, confused. She proceeded to fill him in on what happened after Theo and she had gone into the "deep dive." She described everything, from Bennu's attack in the hotel room, the library of cassettes, down to the second she and the other reincarnations had closed the door against The Daughter. She had expected him to protest when she told him about going inside the burning cottage, scold her even, but he said nothing. He only nodded and waited for her to finish her story. The only time he interrupted was to step into the kitchen and bring her out a tall glass of water, which she sipped gratefully before telling him the rest. She told him about how she had given Bennu another memory. How she had guided Bennu, like Theo had guided her, to a memory where she could stay without pain. Somewhere she could actually be happy.

"So," Cam said after a long pause. "She's contained?"

"Yeah," Buggy nodded, then shrugged. "She's still in that room. I just gave her a different memory of it. And I don't feel her scratching around anymore. I guess being tethered to a happy memory makes her less inclined to fight for a way out. It's keeping her calm for now, and frankly I'm hoping it will keep her calm for the next reincarnation. Maybe make her think twice before taking over the next girl at twenty-four years old."

Buggy frowned. "But then again, The Daughter might just be thrown back into that evil memory when the next reincarnation is born." she chuckled, "I have no freaking idea, but I hope not."

"Whatever the case," Cam said, patting Buggy on the shoulder, "we now know how to fix it. How to do it *right*."

"I guess so," Buggy mumbled, then looked around with a curious eye, frowning. "Where's Theo?"

Now it was Cam's turn to fill Buggy in. He told her about the ominous call they had received a few hours ago, and about Helena's condition. Buggy listened in silence, eyes widening with every horrible piece of information until they looked like they may pop right out of her head. "Oh God," she said finally, after Cam had told her about Theo peeling out of the driveway in his Jeep.

"She's okay," Cam insisted, only realizing it was a lie after the words were out of his mouth, "I mean, she was alive the last I knew."

"Poor Theo!" Buggy said, closing her eyes and running a hand through her hair, pushing it out of her face, now pale and waxy.

"Yeah," Cam said, knowing he sounded like he didn't care... **knowing** that he *didn't* care. God help him he *didn't*. He didn't care about anything at that moment except for one question, which he asked after a quick pause. "How do you feel?"

Buggy blustered and gave a brief laugh. "Tired," she said, honestly, "tired and hungry."

"Can I get you anything? Anything at all?" Cam asked, leaning towards her.

Buggy thought for a long time, before she parted her lips and asked: "Victory pizza?

Cam laughed out loud. "Really?"

"Yes, actually. I'm starving and I'd just really, really, love some pizza."

Cam chuckled some more but pushed to his feet all the same. "Alright then. I'll be right back."

"What? No," Buggy said, trying to get up. Her body had other plans. Buggy's feet slipped underneath her, and she fell heavily back to the floor. "I can come!" she insisted, looking exhausted, but determined.

Cam smiled, painfully reminded of Loretta's stubbornness.

"No," he said, guiding her to her feet so she could stagger to the armchair. "It's alright. You rest. You look beat. I'll order ahead and be right back. I won't be long, I promise. It's just down the hill. Back in a flash."

"You sure?" Buggy asked, already crumpling onto the cushions, unable to hold back a yawn. Cam smiled, pulled the blanket off the backside of the armchair and laid it gently across her.

"Absolutely," he said, already pulling out his phone, and snagging the extra keys to his second Jeep from the little nob beside the door. "I'll be back in thirty minutes. Tops."

"Okay..." Buggy mumbled, voice already fading into the background of dreams as her eyes slid closed.

Cam watched her breaths slow to a steady rhythm before locking and closing the door behind him. He stepped out onto the porch, where snow had begun to fall anew, drifting down in thick, lazy flakes from the sky. The night was silent, as it always seems to be when it snows. Quiet and peaceful. Cam paused in the chilly air, looking up at the twinkling blanket of stars and bright moon. He closed his eyes, breathing deeply.

"Thank you," he whispered. To God, to the universe at large, he didn't know or care. All he knew was that his daughter was alive, and they had won. They were free. "Just... thank you."

22

A wide, cruel smile slit Waverly's face. It cut like a gash across her bluing lips as she watched Cam Styger step outside the cabin door. He flipped a pair of keys between his fingers, and she swore there was an actual spring in his step as he made his way towards the garage a few short yards from the main building. He pulled up the heavy wooden door with effort and tugged on a string that lit up the garage with a jaundice yellow glow. Inside was a second Jeep, an older model than the one the psychic boy had driven away in a few hours earlier, scattering snow as he went flying like a bat out of hell.

Waverly thought Theodore's leaving would be as *easy* as it was likely to get. One down, two to go. She never dreamed that daddy dearest would leave his precious little monster's side. But there he was, revving up the old Jeep Wrangler with a hesitant sputter that soon turned into a guttural roar of begrudging acceptance. Where he was going, or why he was going, were not questions that crossed Waverly's mind as the headlights pulled out of the garage and disappeared down the winding road below. No, all she thought of was the girl inside. The girl with so many dangerous histories. The girl Waverly had been born to find. Born to kill. The girl that was now completely, and utterly, alone.

Waverly waited until the sound of the Jeep's motor completely disappeared into the dark shadow of the trees before pulling the strap of her binoculars from around her neck and kneeling down to unzip the bag that sat at her feet. Her fingers trembled from the cold, and she could hear her teeth chattering violently, but she ignored them. It would all be over soon. Everything would be over. The years of planning, preparation, everything that had led her to this moment—*all the blood*—this mission, it would all be over. Well, sort of....

Waverly flipped open the bag. She slipped the binoculars inside, where they rested gently against the small pile of baby blankets. They were a light, pastel pink with little ducks donning the edges and white daises scattering the center. Her mother had not told her to bring a blanket, but Waverly knew what would happen after she killed the girl.

"An explosion of ashes," her mother had told her, eyes bloodshot, words slurring at the edges and hands waving wildly through the air. "I stabbed The Daughter, and there was no blood. Just a puff of ashes that fell to the floor. It drifted like snow." Her mother's hands had weaved down through the air, in demonstration. "And there she was... the baby. Just lying there pink and screaming, covered in it." Her mother had taken another long drink straight from the bottle, a little escaping to trickle down her chin and drip onto her night shirt. "Never could figure out why there was so much goddamn ash."

Waverly sifted through her bag of things, double checking to see that she had wet wipes handy. She had also bought a little baby onesie and hat at one of the local stores. Although, when it was all over, it would still be a couple miles walk back down to the Challenger, and the wind was cold. The onesie and blanket probably wouldn't be enough. She could search the house *after* and take a few things for the journey. Maybe a few thicker blankets or a hot water bottle. She could load them all into the bag with the child. It would still be an uncomfortable journey, but what did it matter? Besides, one thing at a time.

Waverly zipped the bag closed, pulling the strap over her shoulder, and made her way towards the cabin. She ran low, out of view of the windows, and pressed her back against the wall. She edged her way, sliding against the cold wooden wall until she was directly under the only normal window looking into the house. Waverly peeked inside. There she was. The girl from the pictures, the stories, the one who set factories alight and tore people limb from limb. The butcher of The Fold. Her grandmother's murderer. The maker of that bloody shirt with its sickening color and stinking stain. She was curled up in a blue armchair, a blanket pulled up to her chin. Her eyes were closed, and Waverly could tell she was in a deep sleep by the rhythmic movement of her chest under the covers. Waverly ducked back down and made her way for the door. She stepped up the stairs, crossed the porch and tried the handle. It was locked, but that was no bother. She pulled the lock pick tools, which she had brought with her for just this sort of scenario, from her pocket and got to work. A few short moments later, the knob turned easily under her touch. Waverly pushed the door open and stepped in on silent feet. The living room was filled with soft flickering light. It spilled both from the half-closed door to the kitchen and the open mouth of the crackling fireplace. The room was warm. Waverly could feel sensation slowly returning to her fingers as they thawed, tingling painfully as they did so. She let the bag slide from her shoulder and set it quietly to the floor. She looked up at the chair, making sure the form under the sheets had not moved. It lay still and silent as before. Waverly reached back without looking, eyes still on the sleeping girl, and closed the door behind her. The lock slid into place with a sharp shushing sound. Waverly unzipped her jacket as she prowled on silent feet towards the sleeping figure. She reached in and unfastened the clip on her shoulder holster, heart thudding wildly in her chest.

Here it was, she thought, the moment she was born for. But as she pulled the revolver from her jacket, flipped the safety off, and pointed the muzzle down between the closed eyes, she hesitated. The sleeping figure looked so calm. So innocent. Waverly had seen Loretta's picture so many times, had it shoved under her face every other night, and this face looked *almost* exactly like it. Waverly had memorized every curve of her cheek, every dip of her earlobe, every line of her eye, but she had never before recognized the pure sweetness of that face. How, even in sleep, a small and sad smile tugged at her lips. Her hands curled under her head as a makeshift pillow, legs scrunched up, just as a child might sleep. Waverly watched as a dream fluttered over the dozing features, eyes darting from side to side beneath closed lids, before coming back to rest. The girl gave a contented sigh.

What is wrong with you? Susanna's voice hissed like a snake in Waverly's imagination, furious at her pause. *Kill it! Kill it now! Why are you waiting? You beat the Helena woman, didn't you? Beat her util her blood ran dark. Without hesitation, my girl. So, do it now! Shoot it! End this!*

Waverly swallowed, pistol trembling in her hand, but not from the cold, not anymore. This was different. Somehow, this was different. She was asleep. She was asleep, helpless, and utterly unaware of what was about to happen to her. The .38 wavered in her hand. Waverly knew it didn't make much sense. Knew that this would be faster, painless compared to Helena, but Helena had been awake. Helena had been aware. Helena had just as much access to the tools in her shop as Waverly did, and she could have avoided the whole nasty ordeal if she had just told Waverly what she wanted to know. If she had just told her straight off and not forced Waverly to pull the information from her. But this—

Shut up. Waverly thought, still in her mother's voice. *Shut up. She's a monster. A murderer. The killer of thousands. Maybe not this life, but her last lives and her future ones too if you don't do what you came to do. If you don't do what you are **good** for.*

Besides, another voice thought in her mind, as she pulled back the hammer with her thumb. This voice was softer, gentler, more negotiating then the other. *It's not like you're actually killing her or anything....*

Waverly raised the barrel of the .38, aligning it between the closed eyes once more, except that they weren't closed. Wide, surprised brown irises stared transfixed at the muzzle hovering above her face. The moment of shock that surged through Waverly's system, temporarily freezing her reaction time, was the only thing that saved Buggy's brains from being splattered across the back of the armchair. Buggy yelped in fear, as her arm shot out. She hit Waverly's outstretched grip, bumping the aim to the left as she dived off the chair to the right. The gunshot vibrated through the air, the bullet missing the girl and lodging into the wall leading into the kitchen. Buggy clutched her left ear, as her knees hit the floor. Waverly could see tears of pain muddying her large, and still so innocent looking, eyes. She re-aimed, tried to fire, but the girl kicked out hard with both legs, hitting her squarely in both ankles. Waverly gasped in pain, falling forward. Her chin and arm hit the hard wood floor, pain jutting up her chin into her skull as the revolver flew out of her hand and skittered across the ground and out of reach.

Waverly snarled and lunged for it, but the girl was closer. She darted, snagging the gun off the ground and turning it to face Waverly. The girl had never held a gun in her life. This was obvious from the rigidity of her arms, and the terrible stance she took which, if she fired, would send her stumbling from the kick. But the gun was loaded, ready to fire, and pointed in Waverly's general direction, although it wavered a little with the terrible trembling of the girl holding it, who looked just about as afraid of the gun in her own hands as she was of the woman who had been pointing it at her.

"*Who*-who the hell are you?" Buggy's voice wavered in time with the gun's muzzle. Waverly winced as the thing swept in and out of range of hitting her. She would have found the wide-eyed girl's reaction to the weapon cute, or even funny, if she hadn't just taken Waverly's weapon like she was some common idiot. Like she hadn't been training for this since the day she could hold a gun. One moment of hesitation. One *stupid* moment of pity, plus a bucket full of dumb luck on this girl's part. Shit. Some things were just not fair.

"Does it matter?" Waverly asked, voice cool, unfazed.

"Seeing as you were about to *shoot* me, yeah it matters," Buggy's voice was half blubbering, half hysterical tumbling of words that Waverly had to fight to understand. She was **really** uncomfortable with guns. Again, under other circumstances, Waverly would have found that funny. Hell, under other circumstances Waverly might have given her some lessons. Starting with her foot placement which was absolute garbage. She almost half hoped the girl would take a shot so she could see her fall flat on her ass with the slap stick humor of a *Three Stooges* episode.

"My name is Waverly," Waverly said, deciding to take as much time as she could to figure a way out of this mess. "My mother's name is Susanna Alastor. I am a member of The Fold."

"Susanna..." Buggy's eyes narrowed, and the grip on the gun became steady. "You mean the crazy chick who hunted my mother down like a dog? The one that sent her running off into the night, barefoot and pregnant?"

"Your mother?" Waverly laughed. The sound was high and cruel and seemed to curl and slither out of her. She could almost see the snake-like form it took, sliding out between her teeth, eyes glinting, slitted pupils glazed and breath thick with the smell of rum and whiskey. Waverly shook her head, as much as to expel the image as to answer Buggy's question. "You have no 'mother' Briar Rose. You haven't had a mother in thousands of years. What you *do* have is a history. A history of blood painted up your arms."

"No," Buggy shook her head defiantly, as if shaking off the words would help her escape their truth. "No, I've never hurt anyone. That wasn't me."

"Yes, Briar. It is you. It is always you," Waverly took a small step forward and Buggy took an equal step back, drawing her closer to the edge of the fireplace behind her. If she backed up just a little bit more, she would be pressed against the thing with no way to escape. Waverly knew that was probably an awful idea, cornering the girl with the gun, but her heart was thudding hard in her ears as anger and hate swept in and extinguished all other feeling. This girl was *not* innocent, had *never been* innocent. She may not remember the deaths, but that didn't make her hands any less bloody. All the reincarnations were the same. They had the same core, were the same girl, no matter what mask of "new" she chose to wear that decade. She was always, at her heart, the same evil bitch who had slaughtered Waverly's family, and driven her mother insane.

"You may be re-born with a different name, build different memories, but at your core you are all the same. The same Bennu."

The girl started at the name, a large shudder furling up and down her back like a wave. The hands around the gun trembled once more.

"No," Buggy said, fresh fear mixing with the anger this time. "Stop talking."

"You want to hurt people, don't you?" Waverly took another step forward, causing Buggy to step back. She was nearly against the stones now, and the fire must be burning the back of her legs, but the girl made no show of pain. Her eyes remained focused on Waverly. "You must. You must enjoy it because you keep doing it. You keep killing. Yes, you fight it for a while. Pretending it will be fine, but eventually your nature takes over. Bennu takes over and—"

"Stop saying her name!" Buggy screamed at her, the gun not just trembling now but violently shaking from side to side in her small hands. Her fingers scuttled over the metal like twin spiders in a fire, unsure where her hold should be. "You need to stop saying—" there was a small click. In her frantic skittering, the girl had accidentally hit the cylinder latch on the revolver, and it fell open. The bullets slid out of the gun and fell like metal rain, but Buggy's reflexes were faster, snagging the handful before they hit the ground. She stared at the six shining bullets in stunned confusion, like they were some strange alien life forms that she had never encountered and didn't quite know what to think of. The gun lowering in her hand, forgotten. Waverly knew the girl might easily replace one of the bullets, press the cylinder back into place and be ready to fire in seconds. But as dumbfounded and confused as the girl looked, bullets in hand, Waverly bet her life that Buggy wouldn't have the chance. And she did bet her life. She bolted forward. Buggy's head jerked up as Waverly moved. She squeaked in panic and did the first thing she could think of. She turned and tossed both the pistol and the handful of bullets into the roaring fire at her side. Both Waverly and Buggy stood there, staring as the flames accepted the offering without hesitation, dark red and blue flames licking every inch of the metal. Waverly turned away from her discarded weapon and back, open mouthed, towards the Buggy.

"Are you out of your goddamn mind?!" Waverly barked at her. The girl flinched a little in surprise.

"I didn't—I just—" she stuttered.

"You just threw live rounds into a fireplace you dumb ass," Waverly snarled with contempt. "Do you know what that might—" But suddenly, Waverly didn't have to explain what that could mean. A great popping bang came from the fireplace, sending sparks flying outward. Waverly and Buggy dived away as another small explosion erupted outward, sending another volley of sparks across the little mat and small stack of firewood to the side of the poker stand.

"Shit, shit, shit," Buggy chanted, covering her ears against the blasts of sound, but Waverly ignored the eardrum busting cacophony. She grabbed a water glass that had been resting on the coffee table and brought it around hard against the side of the girl's face. Buggy's head jolted back, blood flying as small shards of glass buried themselves into her cheek and temple. She flopped to the floor, temporarily dazed, mantra completely forgotten. Waverly took the opportunity. She flipped the girl, straddled her, pinning her legs down. The girl was about the same height as Waverly, but thin, and Waverly was stronger. Much stronger. She seized Buggy's neck with both hands and squeezed with all of that strength. Buggy's eyes bulged from her head, as her finger scrambled at the hands around her throat, trying to loosen them.

"Oh, stop struggling," Waverly hissed, as another volley of mini explosions erupted from behind her. A cascade of red sparks glinted in the air above her, before dying into falling embers. "It's not like you'll *stay* dead. Wouldn't that be nice, hmm?" Buggy gave a small gurgling sound, but that was the only answer she could muster. "You and me," Waverly continued, pressing harder with her thumbs, and Buggy's lips started turning blue. "We are going to get things back to the status quo, hmm? We are going to get The Fold back on its proper footing. Every twenty-four years, little one. Every twenty-four years." The laugh that escaped her now was manic, broken, because she had finally realized—finally *accepted*—the truth. This night wasn't the last. This night ended nothing. Because when this night was over, there would be a baby. Another Bennu re-born. And in twenty-four years, Waverly would be right back here. Right back where she started. There was no escape in Waverly's future. No starting over. No running away and having her own child. No future as a mother in some sleepy New England town, with time to discover what else life had to offer. No. This was it. Every twenty-four goddamn years.

That was what she was born for.

"This is all *your* fault," Waverly screamed in the girl's face, screamed as the face grew red under her grip. Screamed as the fingernails dug deep into her hands, but she wouldn't let go. "All. Your. Fault. If you had not killed The Fold, my mother wouldn't have had to repopulate. She wouldn't have had to go out and find some random drunk at a bar. She wouldn't have had to get knocked up so she could continue on the lineage, continue on the *burden* of stopping your sorry ass from killing. If you hadn't murdered my grandmother," she pressed harder, jerking the neck as if to snap it in half. Buggy's lips were almost entirely blue, and blood vessels had started popping in her eyes, surrounding the large brown irises in a pool of blood. The girl looked satanically up at her, the waxy mask of innocence melting off the evil that lay beneath.

Another explosion from behind Waverly, soon followed by a low crackling sound, told her that the sparks from the fire had launched out and had caught either the mat, the stack of wood, or both, on fire and it was spreading fast. She could feel the temperature in the room rising, the world growing into a hot haze, and she knew the flames were licking towards her ankles. But that was alright. It wouldn't be much longer.

Buggy's struggles had slowed, and her bloodshot eyes were fluttering. "If you hadn't made my mother's life a living hell, she wouldn't have had to make a hell out of mine! Don't blame me, you evil fuck." Waverly jerked the girl's throat again, and her head thudded against the wooden floor. Waverly felt her blond hair falling out of its ponytail, strands cascading down to obstruct her view as sweat slid across her cheeks. Or were those tears? Honestly, she couldn't tell anymore. "You don't get to haunt me after this, you understand? This is your fault, *Bennu*. All your fault!"

Buggy eyes had been sliding slowly closed, but when Waverly spoke those last words, they flew open wide. Her blue lips moved again. No sound escaped them, but they formed around the silent words: "No," and "Stop." But Waverly wouldn't stop, not even as she felt the flames crawling across the wooden floor behind her. Not even as she heard one last explosion that sent sparks scattering even farther across the room or when she smelled her own hair burning.

"If you had just accepted death the first time around," Waverly screamed in the girl's face with all the air in her lungs, teeth flashing, spittle flying. "If you had just died the first time and stayed dead! If you had not been so goddamn selfish, Bennu, none of this would have happened! None of us would be here now!" Buggy was struggling again, furiously mouthing for her to stop, telling her "no," telling her to "shut up."

"Stop struggling, Bennu. Just let me finish, it will be over soon, just—" But suddenly Waverly couldn't finish. The words were stopped halfway up her throat by a hand that moved lightning fast and iron fingers that dug deep into the soft skin of her neck. Waverly's eyes widened as the girl below her changed. It wasn't a physical change. No, she looked the same... but she wasn't. Waverly thought Buggy had devil eyes, but she had been wrong. *These* eyes, the ones that looked up at her out of Buggy's face, made her realize exactly what her mother had been trying to explain to her all these years. Waverly was finally able to understand the half-crazed description that had poured from her mother's drunken lips. She had never truly understood until this instant. Because the eyes looking up at her now, these were the eyes of evil. They bore into Waverly, just as hard as the iron fingers dug into her neck, slicing into flesh. Waverly felt blood starting to stream and could even see a few drops falling and splattering against the girl's shirt below her, darkening it, staining it. Waverly let go of the girl's neck, desperately trying to pull away her hand, but it wouldn't budge, and air was denied her.

"Well, well, well," Buggy spoke in a tone and lilt that was completely different from the voice Waverly had heard only minutes before. "If it is not Susanna's seed." Bennu pushed Waverly up by her throat and rose to her feet without breaking her grip. Waverly was taller but felt so small under Bennu's powerful grip and bloody, entrapping gaze.

"You," Waverly was able to gargle out the single word before Bennu tightened her hold and she lost whatever else she might have said.

"Yes, me. In the flesh," Bennu laughed, doing a half bow with her open hand spread wide to her side. She was a million times stronger than Buggy had been. A million times stronger than any human had a right to be. Susanna had warned Waverly of this, warned her that when Bennu gained control she also gained control over the powers that the Dark Promise and years of rebirth had gained her. But all those years of warning did little good now.

Bennu grinned, seemingly satisfied with the fear in Waverly's eyes. She laughed, blood still trickling down from the glass shards in her face. "Oh, do not act so surprised, little dear. *You* called *me* after all. I was all sound asleep. Buggy dear tucked me in nice and snug, you see? Even sang me a lullaby. I was down for the count. Then I heard *you.* You, calling to me from far, far away. You woke me right back up." The laugh that escaped her lips sent a sickening shiver up Waverly's spine, and if she had any control, she would have doubled over and vomited. "Did not your mother ever teach you, dear?" Bennu went on sweetly, "Did she not tell you, never to call the devil's name? Speak of the devil," Bennu drew Waverly's face closer, so that grinning, manic, bloody face and hot breath were only a few inches away, "and the devil appears." Waverly could smell the blood, smell it as clearly as that shirt shoved up under her nose. It filled her, gagged her, all she wanted was for it to be away. But it didn't go away. It only got stronger.

Bennu held her one handed, continuing to grin that triumphant grin as she looked around appreciatively at the mayhem. The fire had spread quickly through the wooden cabin and had begun to lick hungrily up the surrounding walls. The whole building was starting to burn, filling the room with heat and dark gray smoke that made Waverly's eyes water.

"Made quite a little mess, did we not?" Bennu asked, turning back to Waverly, who hung powerless under her grip, still struggling, although she knew by now it was useless. "Well, do not worry. We are not even close to done. You see," she spoke as if carrying on a conversation they had been having the entire time. Like two coworkers gossiping by a watercooler. A window shattered from the heat somewhere nearby, sending shards of green and blue glass raining down around them. One piece sliced across Bennu's cheek and blood trickled fast from the spot. Bennu didn't so much as flinch, just continued speaking.

"Buggy dear put me in a nice little nap. A nice memory. It was comfy. *Comfy*, you know? No pain, no fear... but you woke me from that slumber, and when you woke me, I remembered. Such a pretty, pretty, nap, cannot last. I will always, inevitably, wake up. It does not matter how pretty the memory. Eventually, I will find my way back to that burning house. I do not want that. No, I will not go back there. Never again. NEVER." Spit flew from Bennu's lips as she shrieked. Waverly closed her eyes briefly, wishing for death. It didn't come, and Bennu continued talking, composure regained. "So, I need to end it, once and for all. But you see, Buggy here," Bennu tapped the side of her temple with her index finger. "She does not like what I have to do to get there. I do not blame her for that. I do not much like it myself. But a girl has to do what a girl has to do, right?" Bennu gave a little sigh, as if coming to the sad climax of a particularly bittersweet tale. "Only trouble is... she was good to me, you know? She was actually *good* to me. First time in a long time anyone has been good to me. I *owe her* one, I guess you would say." Waverly watched as Bennu smiled a gentle smile that was revoltingly out of place on her hellish face. Her blood-vessel-burst eyes sparkled. "So, I am going to try something, you see. Try something for Buggy. Something I have never done before. Something I did not know I *could* do. Something I am still not sure I *can* do. But a little Blue gave me the idea so, shucks, darn it, why not give it the old college try? Huh?" She gave Waverly a shake, as if expecting an answer, although Waverly had barely gotten enough oxygen to her brain to keep herself conscious, let alone form any words of response, even if she *had* the foggiest idea what this insane woman was talking about. "If it does, well then, it will be a brave new world, will it not?" Bennu pulled Waverly close, until their foreheads were touching. The feel of the girl's slick blood pressing against Waverly's skin made her gorge start to rise again. Waverly watched Bennu's horrid eyes slide—thankfully—closed, as the fire crawled higher. Waverly felt sweat start to trickle gently down her face and neck, trying futilely to cool her, soothe her, but Waverly was far past the ability to be soothed. She waited. At first, she felt nothing. Just the heat and the smoke, and the fingers digging into her throat. Waverly had long enough to think about Susanna, and to wonder if her mother would miss her when she was dead, or if she would just go out and make another child to carry on the tradition. Another, born to do what Waverly had failed to accomplish. Just as she had decided that her mother wouldn't shed a single tear at her passing, she felt it. The grayness. Not on her skin. Not in the flames. Not in the ground that was slowly heating up beneath her feet. She felt it in her mind. She felt it crawling in like some disfigured slimy creature. Skulking forward on molten paws of shadow and pain, fangs glinting, eyes wide and bloody—blood thirsty. Waverly started to cry, struggled again. Kicking, clawing, fighting with all the strength she had left. If she had her voice, she would have screamed.

Stop struggling, Waverly dear, Bennu soothed, in a voice that smiled but didn't make a sound. Because it wasn't a voice at all. Her eyes were still closed, and her lips had not moved. *Just let me finish. It will be over soon. All over. That is what you have always wanted, right? For it to be all over? For it to end?*

Congratulations, sweetheart.

You are done.

The End.

23

Cam slammed his foot on the gas, causing the Jeep to toss and rattle across the uneven ground so violently that it felt like it might shatter into a thousand jagged pieces at any minute. He didn't care. The only thing he cared about, the only thing he could think about, was that lonely black Charger sitting half buried in snow down at the end of the driveway. It had taken him a few minutes to recognize it. He had slowed to a crawl as he passed, frowning at the license plate, trying to figure out why such a car might be there, and why it looked so familiar. Cars in the little dirt trail head were not uncommon. The hiking paths that branched out from the parking lot were long and fairly rough terrain, so they weren't the most traversed areas, but they also afforded the most beautiful view of the forest areas in town. People came from time to time, leaving their cars parked while they went on walks with their backpacks and water bottles swinging from their belts. But not this time of year. Not when snow made the paths slick, and sharp rocks hid under soft snowbanks. Spring, summer, fall even, but never in December. So why was there a beautiful, classic Charger sitting alone at the end of the snowy lot? And why did Cam swear he had seen it somewhere before? Such cars were rarely seen and even more rarely forgotten. It only took him a few confused moments for the memory to click in place with jarring finality. A blade that sank deep, paused, then twisted in his gut.

Helena. After Cam had finally tracked her down, she had shown off her new shop, the life she had built, the cars she had fixed up, including the 1966 Charger. Cam made a whistling sound and had asked her if she would ever consider selling it. Helena had laughed out loud.

"'Fraid not!" she said with a grin, running a hand down the sleek paint job. "I fixed her up, and she's my girl now. There ain't no price that would take her from me." Yet, there it was. It had a different license plate, one from Nevada instead of California, and someone had painted on racing stripes, but it was the same car, Cam was sure of it. It had the same original color, same minor scratches on the passenger door and rear-view mirror that Helena had looked at grimly. She had flashed an apologetic smile and promised she was planning to polish out the marks that weekend. She said it as if Cam would judge her terribly if she hadn't made such a clarification. There it sat, all alone at the bottom of the private road leading up to Cam's cabin, while Helena... well, she was back in Temecula, half beaten to death, unable to wake up. So, who had driven her precious possession all the way out of California?

"No," Cam mumbled under his breath, not even realizing he was speaking. "No, no, no, no—" The Jeep gave a hard rattle under him, and he imagined he heard a popping sound. This was trashing the poor transmission and suspension, he knew it. The old Jeep had lasted a long time, and had lived through harsher roads than this, but never at these speeds, and he couldn't slow down. He needed to get back to Buggy. A thick dread had risen in Cam's stomach since he laid eyes on the Charger, because he *knew* who had driven it there.

"Susanna?" he had asked, although half of him had known it wasn't. The voice was too smooth. Susanna's voice had always been rough, low, husky even in her younger years. This voice wasn't harsh at all. It was slippery, like oil floating through water.

"Not quite," the voice had answered. "But she says 'hello.'"

Susanna says hello.

The Fold. It was someone from The Fold. Someone who knew Susanna, someone trained by her. Someone who had hunted Helena down, just as Cam had. Someone who had wanted the same thing as him. Theo. And she wanted Theo for the same reasons Cam had wanted him. Buggy. It was all about finding Buggy. And why had the slippery voice called Theo's phone? Cam had not taken the time, not taken a second to think of why she would have done such a thing. He had been too terrified for Buggy, and then too excited about her victory, to think of why the woman had told Theo what she had done to his mother. Why would she do that? Because she felt guilty and wanted to give a son the chance to say goodbye to his mother before her inevitable passing? No, there was no guilt in that voice. No regret that he could detect. She had done it because she knew what *he* would do. She knew that he would jump in the car and go to his mother's side. And why would she want that? Because she wanted him out of the way. And how could he be *in the way*, unless he had been where she *was going?* Or where she had already been?

She had gotten Helena to talk.

She knew where they were.

She knew where *Buggy* was.

She had gotten Theo far, far away, and unable to protect her.

And what had Cam done? He had jumped into the Jeep and driven off to get some goddamn pizza, leaving Buggy in a cabin surrounded by snow, with no other car or means of escape. He had left his daughter all alone, and that slippery voice was—

Was that smoke Cam smelled?

The Jeep screamed angrily as it reached the top of the hill, and Cam shifted gears just as furiously. The ground leveled, and the Jeep flew down the flat section of road leading up to the cabin, which came into view through the break in the trees. Cam's foot hesitated on the pedal as his eyes widened in horror. The cabin was on burning. Large red and yellow flames licked up the outside of the walls and great pillars of black and gray tumbled into the air, filling the night with demon smoke.

"Briar!" Cam yelled before he had even gotten out of the Jeep. He scrambled with the handle, fingers trembling so hard and adrenaline pulsing so heavy through his veins, he had trouble opening it. He cursed, remembered to unlock the door, tried again, and it opened easily. Cam tumbled out, as he threw his numb body from the car. He managed to catch himself before he could fall face first into the snow and dirt, and ran flat out for the cabin.

"Briar!" he screamed, as the sound of flames grew louder and louder the closer he came. The guttural groan of weakening wood and the roar of the fire was a veritable cacophony as he stepped up onto the porch. Flames ravaged that space which had for so long sat under the stars in peace. The wooden swing where Cam had spent many a dream-like night with Loretta, hung from its metal chains, but the seat was aflame. It swung back and forth in the cold breeze, flickering tongues shifting and swaying with the movement. Cam remembered flashes of the moments spent on that swing, watching the moon drift lazily across the sky, making wishes on shooting stars like children do, for they had just been children back then. Just two kids who had fallen in love and ran from the world that told them they could not be together. He remembered that chilly morning when Loretta had taken his hand and pressed it against her stomach. The moment he knew he would be a father, and his entire world—his entire being—had changed, never to be the same.

"Briar!" Cam pulled his keys from his pocket, sliding it into the slot, only to find that it was already unlocked. He tried the doorknob, hand drawing back as the metal of the handle burnt his fingers. "Briar!" He wrapped his hand in his sleeve and tried the door again. The door handle shifted under his grip, but the door still wouldn't open. Someone had locked the deadbolt from the inside. "Shit! Briar!" he called again, but either she couldn't hear him, or she couldn't answer. Cam stepped back and rammed his shoulder into the door. It shuttered but remained closed. He tried again. It shuddered harder, and the wood gave a little creaking sound. Cam stood back, took a deep breath that burned with smoke. He kicked the door with all his might. The weakened wood finally broke inward. A dark gray cloud of smoke rushed at him, stinging his eyes, and making them water. He pulled the edge of his coat up over his mouth as he entered.

"Briar!" Cam called, pushing inside, coughing. "Briar, where are you? B-Buggy!" Cam caught sight of her. She was laying in the middle of the living room floor, eyes closed, unconscious. The fire burned around her, not yet close enough to touch her, but her skin had grown red, and sweat soaked her clothes. Cam ran to her, lifting her into his arms, trying not to panic. Trying not to think about how hot her skin felt in his arms, the shade of her face, or the blood that ran down the side of her cheek. All that he needed to do now was get her out of this pit of fire. He needed to get her out. So, he did. He ran with her, coughing and choking out the front door as one of the stained-glass windows exploded and rained daggers of color down around them. He got her outside and away from the smoke. He looked down to see the dark smudges that darkened her body, and her skin felt like a fire of its own.

"Briar," he said, coughing. "Briar, please wake up," he shook her lightly in his arms, but her eyes didn't open. He knelt, carefully laying her in a bed of cold snow. As he did, he noticed the dark black and purple bruises blooming on the soft skin under her chin. His stomach clenched at the sight. A sudden, violent rage twisted deep inside his chest, making it hard to breathe.

The snow melted around Buggy's overheated body, and steam rose around them both. To Cam's delight, the red color of her skin soothed. Her eyelids gave a gentle flutter. "Buggy?" For half a heartbeat, he was sure it wouldn't be Buggy at all—certain, when she opened her eyes, it would be Bennu looking out at him. Bennu, who had set the fire. Bennu who had won, just as Buggy said she would.

Then her eyes opened, and he saw the broken vessels staining a portion of her eye a dark bloody red. Buggy blinked again, eyes focusing on him.

"Cam?" she managed in a thick voice before she started coughing. Relief hit Cam so hard that he nearly collapsed right then and there. Instead, he helped Buggy sit up, patting her back until her coughs slowed. She spat into the snow, and looked up at the cabin, blood-stained eyes reflecting the red and yellow flames. "Oh shit, Cam," she said, grimacing and clutching at herself.

"What?" Cam said, relief turning to worry in an instant, flipping like a tossed coin and dropping hard to the pit of his stomach. "What's wrong. Are you hurting? What happened? What is it?"

Buggy coughed, took a deep breath: "I'm so sorry about your cabin."

Cam paused for a single heartbeat before bursting into laughter. He laughed deep and long from relief and spent panic. He reached out and pulled Briar into his arms. He wasn't sure when his laughter turned to tears, but he didn't try to stop them. He knew he wouldn't be able to.

"I don't care about the cabin, Buggy. I have never cared about anything less."

"Oh," Buggy coughed again, returning Cam's hug. She winced as the roof collapsed in a small explosion of sparks and another roar of flames. "Good then, I guess."

"What happened?" Cam said, pulling away enough to see her face, noticing again the blood and glass sunk into her cheek.

"Some bitch named Waverly," Buggy said, noticing Cam's look and reaching up to touch her face. She winced as she did so, and Cam took her hand, pulling it away.

"Waverly?" Cam asked.

"Yep. Think she was Susanna's daughter. Or at least, that's what I *think* I remember her saying. I got a little disoriented and distracted when she started trying to strangle me."

"Oh shit," Cam lifted Buggy's chin gently, to get a better look at the marks on her neck. "We need to get you to the hospital. Get you checked out." It was then Cam realized the obvious question he was missing. He whirled around, looking for the mysterious girl with the voice slick as oil. "What happened to her? Where did she go?"

"I... don't know," Buggy answered, frowning, trying to think. "The fire had just started, and she was on top of me... she was choking me. My vision was going blurry and I was having a hard time thinking. I remember..." her eyes squinted as she spoke, as if trying to recall a dream, one that was slipping away with every passing second awake. "She was saying something, something that she shouldn't have been saying. I told her to stop. I knew something bad would happen if she kept—Oh," her eyes opened wide, and she looked up at Cam. "She was calling me by *her* name. The Daughter's name. That was it. She said it over and over again, and I tried to tell her to stop but she just kept saying it."

Cam's jaw clenched. Buggy had sent Bennu back down in a "better memory," as she had put it. Locked her up for a few more decades. Safely stowed until the next reincarnation turned twenty-four at least. But calling her name... that was always a danger, no matter how deeply Buggy had pushed Bennu down.

"What happened?" Cam asked, trying to keep his voice calm although every muscle in his body was tense, ready for a blow.

"I—I don't know. Guess I passed out," Buggy rubbed her bruising neck. "I don't remember anything else. I was just in the house with Waverly, then I was out here with you."

"And," Cam pressed, looking Buggy in the eyes, looking for any sign, any hesitation or oddity in her answer. Any hint that Buggy wasn't the one in control. "How are you doing? How are you feeling?" She was silent for a time, eyes on the snowy ground around her. Her skin had cooled, and her hands now shook from the cold. Buggy raised one, pressing it against her chest, in that same spot she had done before. She spread her fingers wide over the place she had described as "the void." She waited, seeming to listen.

"I feel..." she looked up to Cam and—to his surprise—a wide smile spread her bloody face, gleaming in the light of the still-raging fire beside them. A smile that was so bright, so clear, so utterly enveloping that Cam could feel his own pains and troubles melt away in the wake of its pure light. "I feel amazing, Cam. I actually feel *good*. For once, I feel *really good*."

24

Theo started, jerking himself from a terrible dream of oppressive darkness. A darkness as thick as molasses and as slippery as oil. It had seeped, spreading until it consumed everything in its touch. The sound of a young girl's screams, and the distant pounding of fists against a closed door, faded fast as he blinked the real world into focus. The bright lights of the hospital room and the white noise beeping of various monitors replaced the dream, and Theo was glad to feel it go. He sat up straighter and stretched, wincing as he tweaked his shoulder. One of the many doctors that floated in and out of his mother's ICU room had noticed his pains and had insisted on checking on it. It had just been a dislocation and had been easily, albeit painful, popped back into place. If only his mother's condition was so easily remedied.

Theo looked over Helena, but she was still asleep. He had arrived at the hospital long after she had already undergone the second surgery. They said she had briefly woken a few hours later, asking for him. But she had soon fallen back asleep before he arrived and remained asleep under her bandages. There were many of those. Large, white strips of tape and cloth wrapped around her arms and covered the left side of her face, half covering her eye. Her right arm was in a splint, and her right pinky, whose tip had been cut off by some dull clippers (the doctors had been reluctant to report to a newly arrived and frantic Theo) had been wound into a large, bundled bandage to heal. Her lower lip was a thick, red and blue bulge puffing out from her face, and bruises that had only now begun to heal splotched her visible skin in yellows, dirt browns, and sickly blues.

Hello, Blue.

Theo reached out and took his mother's hand, careful to avoid her missing pinky as he squeezed.

"Mom..." he started and then trailed off, not sure what more he could say. The first few hours he spent by her side was a litany of apologies and regrets. Regrets that he had not been there when she had woken up. Regrets that there was nothing he could do now that he was here. Anger that he couldn't wake her himself. Begging her forgiveness for this happening, for not being there to protect her. For not feeling her pain, not knowing that she was in trouble. What good was a psychic gift of *feeling* if it didn't tell him when the most important person in his life was being hurt? Almost killed. It had been close for a while. Theo didn't understand most of what the doctors told him when he first arrived. Everything they said faded into warbling background noise in his fuzzy mind as soon as he saw his mother laying, beaten and broken in the hospital bed. He had nodded, as if in understanding, when all he really understood was that his mom had a small trickle of blood drying on the skin below her left nostril.

He had understood eventually. She had apparently not been alone long before Peggy found her and called the ambulance. They had been most concerned by internal bleeding, and she had received emergency surgery. She had shown minor improvement, however, so after she stabilized, they sent her for another. This time, they were pleased with their results, and her stats had leveled out nicely. But she still had severe breaks in her arms, fingers, and her left knee was shattered beyond repair and would affect her ability to walk for the rest of her life. If she ever woke up again, that is. She also had a concussion, but the doctors said that it was surprisingly minor when compared to the extent of the damage done to the rest of her body. The assailant had focused on the limbs and trunk of the body instead, leaving the head more or less alone after one or two hard hits to disorient her. Thank God for small blessings.

Theo barked a bitter laugh and squeezed her hand again.

"Mom, I'm so sorry," Theo said, resting his head against her hand. He bit back the little boy sob that threatened to escape, swallowing it down hard. "I'm so sorry, Mom. Please. Please wake up." She remained asleep. Theo leaned back, wiping his eyes on his sleeve. He stood up, pacing back and forth in the room, wanting to do something, needing to do *anything*, but not knowing what. One of the nurses watched him through the glass doors. He caught her eye, and she gave him a small, sad smile and wave. He tried to smile back, but it was like he had forgotten how. His lips twitched a little, then rested back on neutral. The nurse turned back to the stacks of reports, and Theo turned back to his mother. He watched a strand of her hair blowing up and slowly falling back down over her face in time with her breath. He stepped over and brushed the hair down to rest behind her ear and returned to his seat beside the bed. He was so tired. Theo had barely slept since he had woken up to Buggy sleepwalking back at Cam's cabin, and that felt like it had been at least ten years ago now, although it had been just a little over two days. Every time he tried to close his eyes, he staggered through dark nightmares, and woke to the horrible adrenaline rushing certainty that his mother had just been awake. She had been awake and had called for him but he had not heard her, and she had fallen back asleep, never to wake again. By this point he was running on an endless amount of shitty vending machine coffees, zero food, and a fraying prayer.

He hadn't had much time to think about what had happened to Buggy. No time to wonder if everything had gone well, but he did now. He wondered if Buggy had made it. If she had survived that shitty, shitty day. Had she come out the other end? He felt guilty about just leaving her to fend for herself. He had yelled at Cam, furious for even suggesting that he stay when his mother needed him, but now, sitting here—helpless and utterly useless—he wondered if Buggy was alright. His frayed prayer stretched a little thinner as he extended it across the state lines towards a snarky girl with large eyes. He would have been able to help her. He would have been able to get Buggy through the "deep dive," and help suppress The Daughter, help to save Buggy's life. Even so, Theo knew if he had to do it again, he wouldn't have played it any differently. If it was a choice between his mother and anyone else in the world, he would always choose her. Always. But that didn't stop the guilt from burning his soul until he could feel its essence sloughing off and dripping to the bottom of his stomach. If something went wrong, if Buggy had needed him and he wasn't there... he would never forgive himself for that. He would live with it. He would have to, but he would never forgive himself. For that, or for the lives of the others. The lives lost if The Daughter took control. If she re-started the killings in a panicked attempt to find a city of dancers and moonlight... well, that would be his fault too.

Helena gave a gargling noise and Theo shook himself out of those dark thoughts. He waited, hoping, but his mother's eyelashes only flitted slightly, before going still. Theo squeezed her hand gently and let out a lengthy sigh. He looked down at her hand. It had never before seemed so small. So tiny a thing in his own, even with the large, white bandage that cut her pinky finger off short. A million memories crossed his mind. A million times that she had waved at him as he was going off to school, off to work, or just going out. She always waved, fingers dancing slightly with the movement. That thought lead to a more recent, and far less pleasant memory. He remembered his own hand rising from his side, fingers wiggling in the air without his permission, feeling the darkness seeping into him after he had... he had....

Theo sat up straighter, looking at his mother's sleeping face.

"Hey, Mom. I'm gonna try something okay? Just... hold on a sec." Theo closed his eyes. He breathed deeply, in his nose and out his mouth. In his nose, and out his mouth. Blue. She had said he was blue, so that was what he tried to picture, a blue light glowing inside him. A light that he now tried to harness. He imagined that light moving through him, down his arm, into his fingertips. He imagined it touching his mother's skin, the light raising up her arm and to her bruised and battered face.

This was different from trying to connect with Buggy. By the end, Buggy had been open to it. She had been working towards the same goal Theo had been. They had both been trying to connect, but even then it had been difficult. His mother was completely unaware her son was sitting in the room, let alone trying to connect with her. He just hoped that, somehow, she would hear him. That somehow it would work, even just a little.

His mind reached out, stretching towards his mother, gently touching the edges of her mind, just as delicately as he held her hand. He could sense something, a glow of color, a mixture of green and yellow that he had never seen before but was now all that he *could* see. Theo took a deep breath.

Mom. He thought silently.

Theo waited for the color to react. Waited for anything to happen, anything at all. But as the seconds stretched on into minutes, and those minutes began to pile on top of one another, he concluded that it had not worked. Disappointed, he pulled away, opening his eyes. He froze, shocked. His mother's eyes were open, watching him, waiting for him to open his.

"Mom?" Theo bolted to his feet, relief flooding his body so fast and so hard his knees nearly buckled.

"Theo," she answered, smiling. She reached out for him, and he took her hand back with a force that made her wince in pain.

"Shit. Mom, I'm sorry."

She shook her head, brushing away the apology. "No, Theo, no. I'm sorry."

"What?" Theo frowned, confused. "Mom what are you talking about."

"I told her." Tears began to well up, bringing a gleam to her eyes that struck Theo like a serrated knife to the soul. "I didn't at first. I told her nothing. I swear to God, I wasn't going to tell her anything. Even when she started hitting me, I didn't. But then," her hand trembled hard in his, and the tears began to tumble down her face. "Then she said she would kill you. She said if I didn't tell her, she would *kill* you, slow and painful. She would make what she did to me look like child's play and I... oh, Theo, I told her. I told her where the cabin was."

"Shh, Mom, shh," Theo tried desperately to soothe her, rubbing a hand up and down her arm.

"She could have lied. She could have just killed you anyway! I didn't know, but I couldn't think I... I thought she would kill you if I didn't and—"

"'She' who, Mom? Who are you talking about? Do you mean Susanna?" Theo asked, but his mother kept going without pause.

"Theo, I should have never sent you with Cam. I should never have let him talk me into letting you—"

"No, Mom, shh, please stop, it's okay. I'm okay," Theo insisted. "I needed to go. They needed my help."

"You're really okay though?" Helena asked from her bed of broken bones and yellowing bruises. "You're alright?"

Theo gave a shaky laugh and knew he had never loved his mother as much as he did in that very moment. "Yeah, Mom, I'm fine. I'm just fine."

"Good," Helena said, relaxing back down into her sheets. "Good." Her eyes began to drift slowly back to closed, sleep not yet done with her.

"Mom?" Theo asked.

"Hmm?" she mumbled. One of the many humming machines had sent another round of morphine through her IV, and she was fading fast.

"I love you."

She gave him a sleepy smile. "I love you too, honey."

"I'll be here when you wake up."

"Good," she said, voice drifting. "That's good." She was asleep, but it was different from before. It was softer, and Theo knew, when he called her name, she would open her eyes. Theo sat back into his chair and ran his hands through his hair, relief and the aftermath of panic slowly dulling to a sickening hum in his chest. He only got a few minutes to watch his mother sleeping peacefully before his phone rang in his pocket. He picked it up, looked at the caller ID and quickly accepted the call.

"Buggy?" Theo had bolted back to his feet. His reserves of adrenaline had been run pretty much dry, but there was still enough for a quick jolt through his heart as he waited to hear the voice on the other end of the line. Would it be Buggy? Or would the voice laugh, sneering into his ear that he had failed her. That he had left when she had needed him most and that Buggy wasn't Buggy anymore.

"Hey," Buggy's voice answered. "Yeah, it's me."

Theo slumped back down into his chair, completely spent now. "Really?" Buggy laughed. If the tone of her voice had not been proof enough that Buggy was still "Buggy," then that sweet laugh confirmed it.

"Yep! Absolutely no pyro-psycho inclinations on this end."

Theo ran a hand over his face, rubbing his closed eyes. He was so very tired.

"I am so sorry, Buggy."

"What for?" Buggy actually sounded confused.

"I just left you to go through all that shit on your own."

"Oh, God, Theo please," Buggy said, "I completely understand. Cam told me about the weird call and what happened to your mom. How is she doing?"

Theo glancing over to Helena, who was still sleeping soundly. "It was rough for a while but she's on the mend now. Just needs time to heal up. Maybe a new kneecap, but she'll be okay."

"I'm so glad," Buggy's voice was soft and genuine, and it made Theo smile.

"How are you?" Theo asked. "What happened with everything? Did you get her?"

"Yeah," Buggy said, "We got her."

"We?" Theo asked, confused.

"Yeah. I mean, you may have left but, you didn't exactly leave me all alone in there." Buggy proceeded to fill Theo in on all the events that had gone on during the "deep dive." How she had escaped the burning hotel room, finding the library full of cassette tapes, and how she and the other reincarnations had stopped Bennu from breaking out. Theo had nearly lost his shit when she had told him about going inside the room with Bennu but had let the story play out.

"The fire was everywhere. Then it was over."

"And she's just... locked down there?" Theo asked, unsure. He knew it must have all been terribly exciting in the moment, but having the tale of the long-dreaded event told to him in such a matter-of-fact way of which only Buggy was capable, it felt downright anticlimactic. "And it's just done?"

"For me, yeah," Buggy laughed. Her laughter came easily. There was no hesitation, and it sounded like it came from deep down in her belly, instead of the high chested sound it had been before. Theo tried to tell himself that it wasn't strange. After all, she had just fought a thousands of years old being and won. But he couldn't shake the feeling that it was all too *easy*. That there must be something they were missing. Then again, it hadn't been *that* easy. Theo glanced back towards his mother as Buggy kept speaking. "I did my part. But I guess you guys may have to deal with it again after I kick it though, right? Twenty-four years after the next reincarnation is born."

Theo winced at Buggy's off-handed comment about "kicking it," but decided not to comment. Instead, he answered, "Oh, hell no. I did my part. Let some other member of The Fold deal with the next one, I'm out."

"Fair enough," Buggy said. "Although, the last remaining members of The Fold don't seem like they'd be eager to *help* any time in the near future. Unless, of course, the *helping* involves sticking me in a body bag."

"True," Theo shrugged. "Susanna does sound crazy. And whoever the hell she is working with," he squeezed his mother's hand, "they are fucking psychotic."

"Waverly."

"Hu?" Theo frowned.

"Waverly," Buggy repeated. "The woman who Susanna's been working with. The woman who called your cell phone and who, I'm pretty sure, did this to your mother. That was Susanna's daughter. Waverly."

"How do you know this?" Theo asked, leaning forward in his seat. His tired adrenal glands started gearing up for another volley of fight-or-flight mode.

"Oh, just because..." Buggy said in that nonchalant tone of voice that Theo had grown so accustomed. They had only known each other for a short time, but with everything that they had gone through together, everything they had experienced.... They had walked the vast abyss of the mind together. They had traveled the darkest corners of human consciousness and had battled an ancient monster, wrestling her back into her cage. They had trusted each other, seen *into* each other in ways that were not usually humanly possible. Some friendships that had lasted an entire lifetime had less basis. It felt like they had known each other for years. At least, that's how it felt to Theo. He was tempted to ask the girl her thoughts on the matter, but miss "feelings are gross" would probably just have laughed it off and called him a name. Besides, what she said next flushed every other thought out of his head in one swift whooshing of emotion, leaving him frozen in his seat. "She told me right before she tried to strangle me to death."

"I'm sorry..." Theo said after a long pause. His voice sounded robotic, some sort of metallic mimicry of Buggy's natural nonchalance. "What?"

Buggy proceeded to fill Theo in on the events of her evening *after* coming out of the "deep dive." How she had woken to the strange blond girl holding a gun to her face. How they had fought. When she recounted how she had thrown the gun and bullets in the fireplace, Theo had groaned out loud and smacked his forehead with the palm of his hand. Buggy had shushed him and continued, only stopping when she had woken up outside on the snowy ground with Cam by her side.

"And you're okay?" Theo clarified.

"Oh, I'm great!" Buggy answered emphatically. "I mean, my neck makes me look like the living dead of some horror movie and my eyes make me look like a goddamn demon, but other than that, I'm good."

"What happened to Waverly?"

"Don't know," Buggy said. "When I got up, she was gone. No idea where. I guess she just thought the fire would finish the job and left?"

That doesn't make any sense, Theo thought, lips turned downward, head cocked to the side. She's a member of The Fold. She should know that the fire, if it had burned Buggy alive, would initiate the re-birth, causing the next re-incarnation to appear.

Then again, as a member of The Fold, she should have known better than to speak Bennu's name anywhere near Buggy. She hadn't seemed to realize how dangerous that might be. Or, at least, too stupid to take the danger seriously. Still....

"And you were both sure she was gone," Theo asked dubiously.

"Yep," Buggy said. "Cam went to check after I got the 'okay' from the docs at the hospital, but it had started raining at some point and the ground was all mush. He took a look around the cabin, but any tracks that might have been there were washed away. And the Charger was gone too, so I guess she just split."

"The Charger?" Theo asked, confused.

"Oh! Right, so it looks like after she attacked your mom... she then stole her car."

Theo gaped. "Bitch."

"The words that came to my mind were 'heinous monster,' but yeah, pretty sure they both apply," Buggy said. "We told the authorities that the house burned down because of an issue with the fireplace or... honestly I wasn't paying much attention at the time, I mostly just nodded along with what Cam was saying. But the moral of the story is, we lied through our teeth and they think it was an accident. Which it kind of was. So, not entirely a lie, but we weren't able to throw any sort of suspicion on Waverly. She's driving in your mom's 1966 Charger, though. Oh, and she's going by the last name of Alastor. In case you guys wanted to start filing formal charges."

Theo glanced at his mother's sleeping figure, debating. How exactly would that go? Theo had already talked to Peggy, who had been front and center on this whole thing since it started, and she had told him that the cameras on the nearby shops had not caught a single glimpse of an intruder entering or exiting the area. None of the alarm systems had gone off or been tampered with, and there had been no trace of physical evidence of the assailant left behind in the shop. No fingerprints. No tracks in the blood, nothing. Waverly had been careful. Even if she *had* left trace amounts of evidence, a hair, a scuffed shoe mark, anything like that, they had clients coming in and out all the time. They frequently checked on their precious car's progress or even just came into the shop to decide whether it was the right fit for them. Helena was very welcoming of visitors in one form or another. She felt like it gained a level of trust between her and her clients that was sorely lacking in many auto shops these days.

"Transparency," his mother often said, "Transparency and respect. None of this, 'drop it off and three weeks later we'll have a price tag for you,' or 'ripping um off just cuz ya can,' bullshit. Nah. Let um see the work you're doing. Let um engage a little. It will keep them happy and keep us honest. Transparency and respect."

Well, transparency and respect led to trace evidence of thousands of people being scattered across that shop, making any left by Waverly weakly circumstantial.

But she's awake now, a different voice in Theo's head piped in. This one spoke softer than the other, but he could feel the thunderous rage building behind it. Like a great furious beast in a bull fight, shoulders shifting, loosening, ready for the attack. *Mom's awake now, and she can testify to the attack. Testify to* **who** *attacked her.*

And the motive? The other voice answered, equally quiet, but with a practical, almost cold-hearted air of defeat. *What would you say the motive was? She beat her to get information about a girl named Briar Rose, who seemingly has* **no** *connection to either Waverly or Helena herself? Unless, of course, you go about explaining The Fold and their affinity for psychics and ritual murder. Oh, and by the way, Briar Rose, she is a reincarnation, so, no big deal. They'd believe all that, right?*

The car! The bull-voice snorted, pawing angrily, eyes narrowing, refusing to be cowed. *We could say her motive was the car! It's a classic. Expensive. And she had my mom's phone! The call is on the phone records and would have come in long after my mom was... unconscious. Cam could even testify to the call and—* But the other voice didn't let the idea finish.

A car she probably got rid of in Utah long ago? The other voice interrupted, weary in its own surety. *Besides, even if you were able to make that angle work—even if you were able to make a case with no real evidence, or motive—even if she had been stupid enough to keep the car and cell phone—even if they found Waverly, dragged her back to California, and you got Cam to testify to the call—even if you were somehow able to explain away all the strange circumstances revolving around how you all know each other and why you were at Cam's cabin without bringing up The Fold... there's just one problem...*

Buggy, the bull-voice lost steam in one exhale of breath, the name hitting like a well thrown spear.

If you brought Cam in to testify, there is already a record of his cabin burning down on the same day the call came in. How likely would it be that such a massive event, only an hour or so after the call, wouldn't be brought up? In what likelihood would Buggy's name not be mentioned? Even if she wasn't part of the proceedings, her name was on the report, and she had been there at the time of the call. One way or another, Waverly would probably find out that Buggy had survived the fire. And Buggy would once again be in danger.

But if you contacted the authorities and informed them of the situation. If you tell them the truth—

They would never believe our story. That Waverly wants to kill Buggy because she is a reincarnation of a murderer? Seriously?

*We can **make** them believe,* the voice added weakly, not even believing its own words anymore.

How? The other voice asked, coolly. *And even if we do, how do you think that's gonna work? Think they will put her in witness protection? Say "oh, here mam, don't worry, we will keep you and your next reincarnation safe, no problem"? No, anyone finds out what Buggy is, they'll throw her in a padded lab. They will dissect her, take her apart piece by piece until they found out what makes her tick. Until they figured out how to emulate it themselves. Because if she can reincarnate—well—who wouldn't want eternal lives? People have done horrible, **horrible** things for far, **far** less.*

"Theo?" Buggy's voice chirped in his ear, pulling him roughly out of his thoughts like someone yanking on his collar.

"Yeah, sorry," Theo said, casting another glance at his mother. He would ask her. That's what he'd do. When she woke up again, he would ask what she thought they should do.

"Why would she just leave?" Theo still mused.

"I honestly don't know, but I'm not complaining, that chick was bat shit."

"And The Daughter?" Theo pressed.

"I guess she's locked down deep this time," Buggy said, cheerily. "Shit, I feel fantastic! I fell asleep a couple hours ago and slept like a rock. A *dreamless* rock. And I feel—well—I just feel good. I guess it feels like I'm in control again. I'm just *me* again. It's really nice."

"I'm glad, Bug," Theo said, and he really meant it.

"I couldn't have done it without you," Buggy said, voice growing serious. "You saved my ass, Theo. I don't know how I could ever repay you, but if you ever think of anything, I'm one phone call away."

"I'll keep that in mind," Theo said.

"Well, I guess... that's it then?" Buggy's voice sounded a little sad, and Theo thought he understood. They were both glad this ordeal was over, but like any grand adventure, letting go was bittersweet.

"I guess so," Theo replied.

"I hope your mom is back up and about soon."

"Thanks."

"And, you know, feel free to call me when she does. Updates are nice."

Theo grinned. "Would you *like* me to call to give you updates?"

There was a pause on the other end and then Buggy answered. "Yes, please."

"Okay then, I will."

"Hey, Theo?"

"Yeah?"

Another pause.

"I hope you guys have a merry Christmas."

"You too, Buggy," Theo said, smile never leaving. "And good luck to you." They finished their goodbyes, and Theo hung up the phone.

"Was that the girl?" He turned to see Helena sitting up in her bed watching him with a smile of her own.

"Yeah," Theo said, taking his seat by her bed.

"Sounds like a sweetheart."

"She kinda is," Theo agreed. "In her own quirky way. I'm glad you sent me to help her. She's one of those people worth helping, you know?"

Helena nodded and then smiled wider. "I really do know. It's why I didn't blow the whistle when I caught Loretta and Cam sneaking out of the safe house."

"You saw them?" Theo asked, thunderstruck.

"Yep. I was still very young at the time. I had just gotten pregnant and was having my 'morning' sickness around twelve thirty at night. I had gotten out to use the restroom when I saw them sneaking out the front door."

"And you didn't say anything?"

"Nope."

"Why not?"

"Because, like you said," Helena reached out and patted his hand. "Some people are just worth helping." Theo nodded. For the first time since stepping into the ICU room, he noticed the Christmas decorations hanging on the walls and around the window, which looked out onto a second story view of the parking lot. Snow had started falling outside, drifting through the air in soft, white tufts. Theo reached into his pocket and pulled out his phone. He tapped into the hospital Wi-Fi and pulled up a Christmas playlist. Bing Crosby's soothing voice began serenading the hospital with the sounds of "White Christmas." They sat back and listened in silence for a long time, until Theo noticed the TV propped up in the corner of the room, with a long cord connecting to a DVD player on a sterile white dresser below.

"Hey, Mom?"

"Yeah, hun?"

"Do we still have those old seasons of *Friends* in the house somewhere?"

25

Sandra had been over the moon when Buggy had called to say that she was coming home. She had been so excited, in fact, that she didn't pester Buggy with questions about the events of the last week at all. Which was good, because Buggy still had no idea what the hell she would tell her.

"The truth?" Cam had shrugged, flipping over a half-cooked egg and cursing as he accidentally cracked the yoke. After calling the police, making their statements (which ended up being half-baked, bull shit, lies), they left the cabin in the hands of the fire department and the rainstorm which had unexpectedly swept across the sky, turning the snowy ground to ice and sludge. They had driven directly to the hospital, where an ER doctor gave her a quick look over, informing them that, other than the bruising and broken blood vessels in her eyes, Buggy was perfectly fine. They had run a few tests, and to everyone's surprise other than Buggy's, her lungs were perfect. They showed absolutely no signs of damage or even discomfort from smoke inhalation. Cam fretted and fussed and pointed out the same old bruises until Buggy nearly shoved him out the hospital door. She had already seen the looks of suspicion in both the doctors and nurse's eyes as they flitted back and forth between Buggy's neck and Cam. She felt no need to feed their suspicions any more than they already were. Besides, she felt fine. She felt good. Hell, she felt damn great!

Having no place to stay in town, they had headed back for Marshall County. They decided to break up the long drive with a night stay at an Airbnb. Buggy was delighted to be heading home, but they weren't in any rush. The place turned out to be a converted pool house with its own kitchen, a bathroom and two bedrooms. It was small, but just what they needed. Cam had taken a walk down to a nearby grocery store before Buggy had even woken up and had started making breakfast before she was halfway through her first cup of coffee. It was then that she had called Sandra and told her the news. Well, some of the news.

"The truth? So, she can think I'm a nut job?" Buggy answered Cam, sipping her orange juice and cutting at her syrup-soaked pancakes with the side of her fork.

"Show her the marks on your neck?" Cam asked helpfully.

Buggy laughed. "So she can blame you, and think I'm just making up crazy stories so as not to admit to myself that the father I have been wondering about for so long is actually an abusive asshole?"

"Oh... right, that is how that would go down, isn't it?" Cam frowned, sliding the eggs out of the pan and onto his plate. He took a stool across from Buggy and began to dig in. "I don't know, Buggy. Everyone I knew, my father, The Fold, Loretta, everyone important to me already knew about all of this stuff. I've never really had to explain this situation to anyone before. I didn't even have to explain to Theo. His mother did that."

"What about me?" Buggy pointed out. "You explained to me."

"Yeah, and that went just dandy, didn't it?" Cam said, rolling his eyes.

"True," Buggy shrugged. "I thought you were out of your mind until I literally melted the *handcuffs* you put on me."

"Again," Cam bowed his head in utter shame. "I am so, so, sorry about that."

"Maybe it's just best to go with the 'hanging with my bio dad' story," Buggy said, turning back to her pancakes. Cam watched her a while.

"No," he said. "No, you should tell her."

"Yeah?" Buggy asked, looking up at him.

"I mean, I don't think you should go spread the story around, because it *is* pretty incredible, but I think you should tell your sister."

"Why?" Buggy asked.

"With this stuff, this insane thing that you and I call reality, we *need* people we care about to know."

"You know," Buggy protested. "Theo knows."

Cam smiled and shook his head. "Nah, Buggy, you just met us. You need someone you *love* to know. It makes things... just trust me. If Sandra loves you the way that it sounds like she does, she'll hear you out."

"Yeah," Buggy nodded. "I guess so."

"Eat up," Cam said. "We got to get back on the road. Get you home in time for dinner." Cam was smiling when he said this, but Buggy could detect a tight strain behind it, the force it took to keep it in place. It only grew more and more artificial as they clambered back into the Jeep Cam had rented after his own broke down in the hospital parking lot. As the miles ticked by on the odometer and the road signs zipped past, drawing them ever closer to Marshall County, the tighter the edges of his smile became and the more lines that appeared around his eyes. Buggy watched his slow descent into despair with confusion as she rattled off directions from her phone and he in turn grew more and more quiet. It wasn't until they pulled up to the apartment that Sandra and she shared, that she finally realized what was wrong. It snapped into place like the last piece of a convoluted puzzle, as Cam put the car in park.

"Well," Cam said, turning his smile—which was now little more than a tortured mask of false cheer—towards her. "I guess this is—"

"I don't want that," Buggy blurted, interrupting him.

"What?" Cam blinked, thrown off his axis.

"Back before, when you said you would help me, then take me home, and I'd never see you again—I don't want that." Cam seemed frozen in his seat, hands still on the wheel, terrified that if he moved, he would break whatever spell she was under.

"Really?" he asked after a few tortured seconds and a million different emotions had flown across his face, spanning confusion, shock, and finally landing on hesitant elation.

Buggy smiled. "Do you have anywhere to go? I mean I did, you know, burn your cabin down."

"Yes," Cam nodded. "The cabin was just a family vacation spot. I've also got a house a few cities over. I'm good."

"Okay, well," Buggy bit her lip, nervously. "I've got your number. Maybe, um, maybe sometime I could call you? Maybe come for a visit? We could grab some lunch and you could tell me all about Loretta." Cam took a deep, slightly shaky breath. Buggy caught a slight sheen in his eye.

"I would love that," Cam answered.

"And about you, too. I mean, I know all about your involvement with The Fold, but I don't even know what your actual job is."

"Financial advisor."

"What?" Buggy asked, taken aback.

"I am, or at least, I *was*, a personal financial advisor for a private corporation in Utah. Although, I was on thin ice before my two-week sabbatical turned into seven months. I was finally able to find Helena through that old neighbor I was telling you about. Maggie. She became a client and at one informal dinner meeting she was telling us about how she had recently beaten cancer, and she had sworn that it was all because of a little boy. Long story short, I found out about Theo, realized I had a chance of finding you, and dropped everything. Pretty sure they replaced me by this point."

Buggy just stared at him. *What the hell are the chances?* Buggy wasn't one to put much stock in "fate," but then again, she had not given much thought to reincarnations until recently. Then she grinned. "A psychic by night and a corporate financial advisor by day? How on Earth did that happen?"

Cam shrugged. "Well, being a member of The Fold didn't really take up much time. We had monthly check up meetings and discussions of The Daughter's status, but mostly it just involved daily care of the captive reincarnations, waiting for her to turn twenty-four and The Daughter to go ballistic. In the meantime, I went to a good college and found out I have a mind for numbers. My father had been working at that corporation for years. Friends with several of the CEO's, so that helped a great deal in getting the job."

"But weren't you on the run with Loretta?" Buggy asked confused.

"For a couple years, yes. But after she died, and you disappeared... well I was still a kid. I had nowhere else to go."

"So, you went back home," Buggy nodded.

"My father considered disowning me on the spot, but decided it was better that I was close by so he could keep his eye on me. I went to work for the corporation and my father cut me off from all Fold business, which by this point consisted of looking for you. Didn't stop me, obviously, I still kept looking, but there was very little I could do. The only solid information I was able to glean, was that you were adopted out to a family shortly after leaving the hospital."

"That was it?"

"Well, Social Services isn't big on handing out information to random people. And as far as they were concerned, I *was* a random person. I had no way of proving I was your father, so I had no legal precedent to gain any more information on your whereabouts."

"You and your private corporation money couldn't buy your way into an answer through less legal means?"

Cam laughed. "You're thinking established operations. The one my father and I worked at was fairly new. Lucrative, but not rolling in it. I'm not going to be buying any yachts, skyscrapers, or illegal favors any time soon."

"Just fancy cabins," Buggy said.

"Nah, actually, that's been in the family for years. Well, my mom's side of the family at least. Hell, my father didn't even know about the place." Cam shot a grin at Buggy. "Your grandparents weren't exactly on speaking terms."

"No?" Buggy asked, leaning in. Grandparents? She had been too wrapped up in the events of the past week to even think about the consequences of finding her biological father. She hadn't even considered the possibility—the *actuality*—of biological grandparents. She had never had grandparents, not really. Both grandparents on her mother's side had died before her mother had even met her father, while her father's dad died two months after Buggy was adopted, and his mother following less than a year later. Unfortunately, it seemed Buggy's bad luck didn't end there.

"Not really. They met through the company. She was the cousin of one of the founding members. They hit it off rather quickly, but they were never married. Your grandmother didn't believe in it. Rosa Clarice Eisten. Hard core feminist, let me tell you. She also had a hefty amount of family money, and her own position in a sister company, so she never felt the need for someone to 'support' her. I was about three months old when she stopped seeing him."

"How come?" Buggy asked.

"Why?" Cam barked a laugh. "Because my father told her he was a psychic. He was a fairly powerful clairvoyant, actually. Not foolproof, otherwise he would have been able to stop Loretta and I from escaping, but he was talented. He made the mistake of trying to prove his ability to my mother out of the blue. It worked... and freaked her the hell out. She left him but continued to allow partial custody because she still believed a son needed a father."

"I take it he didn't tell her about the whole mass murdering, suicidal-psycho, or the psychic cult that he had you involved with instead of boy scouts?" Buggy grinned.

"Nah, conveniently left that out of the itinerary," Cam grinned back. "Anyway, she had bought the cabin after she and my father had split. She died when I was nineteen. Lung cancer. Smoked like a chimney since she was fourteen."

"I'm sorry," Buggy said.

Cam shrugged. "That's how those things go, I guess. But she left me a decent stipend of money and the cabin in her will. I never felt the need to tell my father about it."

"Gave you a safe haven," Buggy nodded.

"And somewhere for Loretta and me to hide when I finally broke her out of there," Cam agreed. "It was after that, when I actually had somewhere safe for us to go, that I finally started planning."

"But if the cabin was yours and your father didn't know about it, why did you leave?"

"Well, because your mother got pregnant," Cam smiled.

"I don't understand."

"We weren't sure what would happen when she finally gave birth. We weren't sure if she would have you and then you would just be our little girl, or if you would be another reincarnation, meaning—"

"That she would die," Buggy finished, voice hollow.

"I was ready to do whatever she decided," Cam said. "It was her life on the line and I just.... Anyway, she decided, no matter what the consequences, she wanted to have you."

"But that gave you an expiration date on your time together," Buggy realized, and tried to imagine that position. That uncertainty, as time suddenly wasn't just ticking by but counting down.

"So, we decided to live it to its fullest, just in case. The money my mother left me had gotten us through the few years, and there was enough for at least nine months of adventure. We traveled around the country. We saw the Grand Canyon, Yellow Stone, Yosemite, Mount Rushmore, the list goes on and on. We had to start slowing down the more pregnant she became, but we didn't stop, just took more time, spent more time relaxing in hotel rooms. Soon enough we *had* to stop, but we couldn't exactly hole up back in the cabin either."

"Why not?" Buggy asked.

"Hospitals," Cam said. "I mean, the local hospital is good for a little broken finger here and a flu shot there, but there was no way I was going to trust them with the birth of my baby. Besides, you saw that private road. Can you imagine screaming down that thing with a woman in labor?"

"Hell no," Buggy laughed.

"Me neither. So instead of going back, we looked around the bigger cities where we already were. That just happened to be in California at the time. We looked into the quality of their birthing centers, found a nice hotel nearby and holed up to wait. Didn't take more than a few weeks, but a few weeks was long enough for Susanna to catch our scent."

"You had been hiding out in Amberhill for years," Buggy said, thinking it through. "And when you weren't in the cabin you were bouncing around from state to state."

"We were finally holding still," Cam agreed. "And me? I left to get tacos."

"And the rest is history," Buggy added in a mock newscaster voice. Cam grinned.

"For me at least. Your mother... well, she's a story all of her own."

Buggy smiled. "I'd like to hear it sometime."

"I mean, I've got all the time in the world," Cam said, perking up. "Including right now. I'm sure there's a place in town we could grab some lunch. You could show me around."

Buggy's smile widened but she shook her head, glancing down at her watch. "I should really get inside. Sandra is probably waiting for me. And I'm kinda looking forward to getting back to a familiar rhythm for a while... check and see if I still have a job. But another time, okay?" Cam looked disappointed but nodded in understanding. Buggy turned to look at her apartment, and the smile slid from her face.

"What if she doesn't understand?" Buggy muttered. "What if she thinks I'm crazy? What if she leaves me like your mother left your dad?"

"She won't," Cam said firmly.

"How on Earth can you know that?" Buggy asked, turning to look at him.

Cam laughed. "Because this is the girl who called you eight times a day, called everyone you know, and was about to call the police when she thought something *might* be wrong. This is the girl who then backed off when you said you needed space. This is the girl that was so happy you were coming home that I could hear her squealing from the phone while I was standing on the other side of the kitchen. Because that is a sister who loves you so much, she can't even contain herself. She will understand. She will at the very least try. Either way, she's not going anywhere."

Buggy smiled at the apartment and nodded once. She opened the door and slipped out into the chilly afternoon air. She turned back to Cam, who was watching her with a soft smile on his face.

"See you soon, Cam," Buggy said, truly unsure what else to say.

"See you soon, Briar," he answered. She turned to leave when he called her back. "Briar!" She looked back at him, and he was holding out the chunky cell phone, the one with her mother's last message. "I thought you might..." he trailed off. Buggy looked at the phone, considered, then shook her head.

"No. You keep that one."

"You sure?" he asked.

"Yeah," she said. "Half of that message is for you, anyway. She'd want you to have that one. I know she would." Cam curled his fingers around the phone, pulling it to his chest. He smiled at it, and Buggy saw the love there, the devotion that never ended, not even with death. Without another word Buggy closed the door, padded up to her apartment, slipped the extra key out from under the only potted plant on the porch and turned to give Cam one last wave as he pulled away from the drive. She watched him go until his taillights disappeared around the bend. Buggy felt both relieved, and a little sad at the sight.

She took a deep breath and turned the key in the lock, giving the door a hard shove to push it open. She braced herself to be bulldozed by Sandra the instant her feet met carpet, but she entered the house unmolested. But then again, that wasn't too surprising. Buggy had erred on the side of overestimating how long they would take to get back into town and was home a day earlier than planned. Sandra didn't know she would be back yet.

"Lucy, I'm home!" Buggy called, closing the door behind her. Surveying the familiar apartment, Buggy was swept up in the overwhelming feeling of "coming home." She had not been gone long, but as the weight of everything, of every insane event of the past week melted from her shoulders like thawing ice, she would have sworn it had been centuries. Thank God, she was home. Buggy rode the wave of relief past the pale sky-blue wallpaper that she recognized for the first time in years. She ran her hand over the broken cup they used to hold keys. Buggy stepped into the living room and looked around, but there was no sign of Sandra anywhere. She took a peek into the kitchen and saw the slip of bright pink paper tacked onto the fridge by a round magnet. She smiled, recognizing Sandra's slanted handwriting.

Buggy!
I know you said you'd be home tomorrow morning... buuuut I'll leave this just in case you come back early. First off, Welcome home!
I'll be back a little late tonight. Christina and I are having dinner after work. If you are reading this... don't you dare fall asleep till I get back! Or I swear, I will wake you up with a blow horn to the ear. I mean it. You need to tell me everything! I've been on pins and needles all week. Oh, and I've missed you.
See you soon!
Love you girl!
—Sandra

Buggy plucked the note off the fridge and carried it back to her room. Her door gave a little creek as she pushed it open. Her smile widened at the sight of her familiar neat room, with its perfectly organized makeup, smoothly made bed and hanging blue dream catcher. The smile faded a little as her gaze fell on the half-drunk bottle of whiskey that sat patiently on her dresser. Buggy stepped slowly towards it, as if expecting the bottle to jump at her, furious at her neglect. She stood, dropping Sandra's note next to it. Buggy stared down at the liquid and waited. Waited for it to call her name the way it always had. Waited for the pull, the urge that had followed her for months. The one born out of the void in her chest, that hollow place that begged to be forgotten and yet refused to be unfelt... except... she didn't feel it. Not anymore. No pull, no call, no need. The void, for the first time in a long time, lay silent. Dormant.

Buggy reached out, carried the bottle to the bathroom, unscrewed the top, and drained it. The dark liquid swirled in the sink's bowl, disappearing down the drain, and she didn't feel even a hint of regret as she watched it go. She discarded the bottle in the recycle bin under the kitchen sink and went to take a hot shower. Buggy took her time, letting the water burn down her back and steam up the room, turning it into a homemade sauna. She stepped from the shower feeling refreshed, cleansed even. She wrapped a towel around herself and padded back down the hallway to her room, humming as she went. Buggy riffled through her clothes, hair dripping on the floor, leaving a wet dotted trail behind her as she moved. She pulled on a pair of jeans, some fuzzy blue socks and a long-sleeved blue turtleneck sweater that covered the bruises on her neck. She was going to have a hard enough time explaining away the busted blood vessel in her eye. The ER nurses had picked out the little shards of glass from her cheek, and the cuts being so shallow, had nearly healed up entirely. With a little foundation the marks would be entirely invisible. But her eye still looked awful. No need to add obvious finger bruising on her neck to the explanation she would inevitably have to give everyone she knew. Buggy wound up her hair in the towel and stood in the middle of her room, hands on her hips, suddenly unsure what to do. She had spent most of the drive amping herself up to tell Sandra everything, but with this unexpected time in between, she felt antsy, and needed something to distract herself. Buggy looked around, and her eyes landed on the photo beside her bed. She stepped over, and picked it up, inspecting the photo of herself, Linny, Andrew and Cooper when Andrew had dragged them to some concert by some esoteric rock artist that Buggy couldn't remember the name of. She didn't even remember any of the songs. She just remembered having the time of her life. Remembered getting a little too drunk, dancing in a crowd of strangers with her friends. Remembered falling asleep in the taxi ride home and waking up to Cooper carrying her into Andrew's house. Remembered him handing her a glass of water and aspirin before pulling the blankets up to her chin. They had stayed up chatting long after Andrew and Linny had fallen asleep, and she remembered the feel of his hand against her cheek, brushing away a strand of hair when he thought she had drifted off. Then there was that bolt of emotion, the feeling that struck her deep in her chest and belly at his touch. Buggy had shrunk from it, pretending to be fast asleep, knowing that if she had opened her eyes, he would have been watching her. She would have seen the sleepy half-drunk smile tilting the left side of his mouth upward. And she couldn't do that, because she knew it would make her feel something. That fluttering sensation in her belly that was completely out of her control. So, she had kept her eyes shut. Just another door she had slammed closed.

Buggy set the picture back and dropped to her knees, reaching under her bed and pulling out the bag full of tapes from her mother. Placing them on the bed, she started sifting through them. Buggy had listened to every tape, every word she had memorized, except for two. It didn't take her long to find the one she was looking for. She held up the tape with soft gray paper and bright pastel pink calligraphy lettering that said: "First Love."

Buggy cleared her throat, opened the cassette tape, and slid it into the empty player cartridge. She closed it, sinking down onto the bed, and pressed the play button before she could change her mind.

"Hey, honey," Loretta's voice spoke sweetly from the player. "Whoa... I guess some stuff has been going on in your life, huh? I wonder how old you are now. Fourteen? Seventeen? In your twenties? When did you know you first fell in love, my love, hmm?" Buggy closed her eyes and laid back on the bed, listening to the new words, the new lilt of her voice. A tape she had been waiting years to hear. "Well, I was about..." her mother's voice paused to think. "I was about twenty-one when I knew I was in love with your father. Cam was always a sweetheart. I had known him since we were both kids... but it was a complicated relationship we had... he'll explain everything to you, I'm sure. It took me time to know that I loved him... but when I did, oh, that was it. I was lucky. My first love was the only one it took, the only one I ever needed. But I know it doesn't always work that way. Sometimes it takes multiple loves, multiple people, loving and being let down, and loving again until you find the right one for you. But you never know, right? You never know if the one you love is the *right* one until you try. Until you give it a shot." Buggy could hear the smile in her mother's voice as she continued. "What was it that caught you? Was it his sense of humor? His eyes? His smile?" Buggy smiled, shrugging to herself. "Yeah, I bet," her mother said as if in answer. "Well, I just have a few questions, okay? Is he good to you? Does he care about you? Does he treat you well and respect you? If the answer to any of these are no, dump him immediately. I mean it, my girl. Right now." Buggy laughed as her mother's voice took on a very Sandra-like tone with a dash of Linny attitude. "But," her mother continued, "if the answer to these questions are all 'yes's... then hun, I am so happy for you. And I wish I was there to giggle incessantly with you or help calm any nerves you might have... because I know feelings can be hard, especially feelings like love. They are strong and sometimes wild and many times run away with you, and that can be really scary." Buggy was leaning forward now, eyes still closed, focusing on her mother's words. "They can be scary, and they can be hard and even a little messy. Sure, things might not work out the way you want them to. Sure, shit might get complicated, but darling, life is goddamn complicated." Buggy laughed out loud. That was the first time, on any of the hours and hours of recorded tapes, that Loretta had ever sworn. "I guess what I'm saying is, trust your heart, don't run from it. Running does not make you strong, it just takes you further and further away from those same people that you love. Be stronger than that, hun. I know you are. It's your turn now. Make sure you play the game to its fullest, okay?" Buggy smiled and opened her eye. She could almost feel her heart glowing inside her chest, and she felt no hint of that void now. "As always, hun... I love you. Always have, and always will."

"I love you too, Mom," Buggy said, and then the tape clicked to a stop in her hand. Buggy lowered the player and wiped her eyes with the back of her hand. She sat there for a few minutes, letting her mother's words sink in. Letting her mind run wild until she slid off the bed and padded over to her cell phone, which she had left on the dresser in place of the bottle. It had been the only thing, other than the clothes on her back, that had made it out of the cabin fire. She had fallen asleep with it in her pocket before Waverly had interrupted her dreaming. It had gotten a little wet in the melting snow outside when Cam laid her on the ground, but it had dried out well enough after she had bought a bag of rice and set it inside overnight at the Air B&B.

She picked it up, skimmed through her contacts, tapped on the screen, and held the phone up to her ear. It rang only twice before he picked up.

"Hey, you," a voice answered, with that cheery tone that belonged to no one else.

Buggy smiled. "Hey, Cooper."

26

She had made plans with Cooper first, setting times and places to meet up before she called the others. It wasn't Friday, but since she had missed the last one, the group was more than happy to have an impromptu night at The Lookout to catch up, but only if she promised to fill them in on where she had been for all that time. Buggy, her excuses and lies already prepped, accepted the condition without hesitation.

Buggy had organized the time, which wasn't her usual style. She usually just went along with whatever everyone else wanted, easier that way, but this time she had taken the lead. First, she made plans with Cooper. Next, she called Andrew, Linny, and left a message for Sandra, telling them to meet a half hour later. Buggy wanted a little time alone with Cooper before the rest arrived and assumed a half hour would be long enough. Well, she hoped it was enough. She worried about that as she stepped out of the Uber who dropped her out front of her favorite bar in the city. She tipped the guy, closed the door behind her and stepped into the familiar dim lighting and lively country music that was The Lookout. The place was decked out in preparation for Christmas, with Santa posters, Rudolph statues, tinsel and mistletoe hanging from every doorway. It was a mellow night and still a little early for the bar hop crowd, so there was only a half-dozen people mulling around the tables, and only one person sitting at the bar. His back was to her, but there was no mistaking those sangria highlights. His shirt pulled snug over his broad shoulders as he leaned in to hear what the bartender was saying. A male bartender this time, Buggy noted, with mild relief. Last thing she needed right now was to watch Cooper taking another glance at a pretty bartender's skirt.

Cooper answered a question and the bartender nodded and turned to make his drink. Buggy took a deep breath, instantly regretting every choice that she had made in her life that had led up to this moment. Fear flooded her and her belly gave that butterfly sensation that she had hated for so long. She paused, took another deep breath, stepped up, took the stool next to him, and tapped Cooper on the shoulder. He turned, and that wide smile spread from cheek to cheek.

"Bug—" he started but broke off as his eyes focused on her face. His smile withered into a look of surprise and gut-wrenching worry. "Oh, shit Buggy, what the hell happened?" Buggy blinked, confused, before she remembered her bloodshot eye.

"Oh this!" Buggy laughed, waiving a hand as if to brush away his worry like a mosquito. "Just scratched my eye a little too hard in the night I guess."

"You're fucking with me, right?" Cooper asked, leaning in and gently tilting her face to the side with his thumb and forefinger. "You're telling me you did this in your sleep?"

"It's not as bad as it looks," Buggy said, thinking about the bruises around her neck.

"If you say so," Cooper looked unconvinced as he pulled his hand away, but his smile brightened once more. "Good to see you."

"Yeah," Buggy said, nervously. "Good to see you, too."

"Where have you been all this time?" Cooper asked, turning to wave at the bartender.

"I wasn't gone that long," Buggy insisted.

"Sure, but you were hella cryptic about wherever you were. The message I got from Linny sounded downright frantic. Got a follow up call from Sandra, saying everything was alright, but she wouldn't give any details other than that."

"That's because I asked her to keep it under wraps," Buggy nodded.

"Why's that?"

"Oh, because I was in the process of getting to know my biological father," Buggy said, turning to face the bartender to order a bottled water and can of diet Coke. When she turned, Cooper was leaning back on his stool, eyes wide and mouth hanging open.

"What?" he said finally. "Sorry. Repeat?"

"My biological father," Buggy spoke slowly, drawing every syllable out three times as long as it needed to be.

"Well..." Cooper said, processing. "Damn."

"Right? Met him last week. I was walking home from work on Monday and he just..." Buggy remembered Theo stepping out from the night, hearing the word "Bennu," and then darkness. "He just randomly popped out of nowhere."

"Just stepped out of some creepy ass alley like 'hey, I'm your father'," Cooper asked, thanking the bartender as he slid his drink towards him and Buggy's water and soda towards her.

"Sort of," Buggy laughed and shrugged.

"What 'sort of'? Come on woman!" Cooper protested, exasperated. "Details."

"I'll give um," Buggy said, knowing she would be giving no such thing. Or at least, not all the details. "But do you mind waiting until everyone else gets here? I'd rather just tell it all at once. Besides, I wanted to talk about something else before they get here."

"Oh, yeah?" Cooper asked. Then he noticed the drinks in front of her and pointed. "No whiskey sour?"

"Nah," Buggy shrugged. "Not tonight."

"Different," Cooper observed, but not as an insult or a complement. As he had said, he was just along for the ride. Whatever ride that ended up being was up to Buggy. Buggy shrugged again, and automatically placed the water glass to her right and her drink to her left, flipping one of the little paper napkins that came with the glasses open into her lap.

Well, she thought, looking down at her handy work. *Not totally different.*

"So, what did you want to talk about?" Cooper asked.

"Well... things," Buggy said, eyes still on her glass of water, watching the condensation gather and roll slowly down the side to pool on the bar.

"Ah, yes, **things**," Cooper laughed. Buggy went quiet, her tongue suddenly feeling heavy in her mouth as her cheeks grew warm. Maybe she should have planned for more than half an hour. "Buggy?" Cooper asked, leaning a little to get a better look at her down-turned face. "Oh my God," his voice rose, and a barely held back chuckle trilled his words to the breaking point. "Briar Rose Pierce are you blushing?"

"You, *shush*," Buggy said, glaring up at him and pointing an accusatory finger in his face. "You know I'm not good at this shit."

"You're right," Cooper admitted, hands up in surrender. "You're absolutely right. I'm sorry."

Buggy turned back to her water glass, hoping it would be easier to speak to that instead of the guy at her side. "So, I've been thinking."

"Okay," Cooper said, but he sounded serious now. She could almost feel his body tensing next to her, prepping himself for bad news. It was incredibly cute.

"I've been thinking about what you said. What you asked. Considering. A lot."

"Okay."

"And I, uh, I've been thinking... I... I...." she took a deep breath and blurted the words without thinking how they might sound. "I don't want to leave a library full of moments missed and things I never said."

"Okay?" Cooper sounded confused now but didn't interrupt as she started over.

"I've been thinking and..." her voice was trembling now, and that pissed her off. She clenched her teeth and tried again. "I have been *thinking that...*" but the right words wouldn't come. Suddenly she was back in school, standing in front of her class about to give her presentation when her mind goes blank. Any words that did come flitted by gossamer thin, so quickly that Buggy couldn't catch or see them clearly. They spun dizzyingly, then disappeared, and she was left frozen to her seat. Then her mother's words filled her ears, drowning out her fear, drowning out that rising, bubbling panic in her stomach. The words came and quieted the entire world, narrowing everything down into two simple sentences.

Running does not make you strong.

Be stronger than that, hun.

Buggy turned, grabbing fistfuls of Cooper's shirt collar, and kissed him. He froze for a second under her lips, completely caught off guard. Quickly he regained his mind, and one hand cradled her cheek while the other wound around her waist, pulling her in closer, pressing her against him. After a few moments, Buggy pulled back, just enough for them to breathe.

"So, that's what I've been thinking," Buggy said, slightly breathier than she would have liked, but she was a little too excited to care.

Cooper swallowed; eyes wide, looking down at her. He barked in surprised laughter. "Gotta say, I'm really liking how you think." It was her turn to laugh now.

"Good," she said. She leaned in and kissed him again, this time he kissed her back eagerly and without hesitation.

"Holy crap," said a voice from a few feet away. Cooper and Buggy broke apart just far enough to look around and see Linny and Andrew standing, staring at them, both mouths open. There was a long, awkward silence as the playlist switched songs and none of the group said anything. Cooper and Buggy just sat frozen like a pair of foxes caught in the crosshairs, arms still wrapped around each other. Linny and Andrew seemed to vibrate with held back emotion. They didn't hold it back for long.

"FINALLY!" they both shouted in unison, their arms thrown up in the air. Cooper and Buggy burst out laughing. Buggy pulled away so she could catch Linny as she threw herself into Buggy's arms. Buggy was still very aware of Cooper's warm hand resting against her lower back.

"Oh, my freaking Lord, girl," Linny said, pulling away from the hug and cupping Buggy's cheeks in her hands, squeezing her lips into a duck face. "Where have you been? And you come back and start making out with Cooper? Who *are you?* And where have *you been?* And what on Earth happened to your eye?!"

"Linny," Buggy mumbled through smooshed lips, "Can I have my face back please?"

"Why? So, you can use it to make out with him some more?" Linny asked but let her go all the same. Buggy was saved from having to answer as a voice spoke from behind them.

"Who's Buggy making out with?" Buggy turned around to see Sandra had just walked in hand-in-hand with Christina.

"Sandra! Christina!" Buggy called, slipping off the stool and reaching out her hand.

"Hey, Buggy," Christina smiled taking her hand and shaking it. Buggy had only met Christina a few times, but every time she was struck by how beautiful she was. With short blond hair that cut off just above her shoulders, long legs that made her a little taller than Sandra, and a phoenix tattoo that peeked out from under her collar and climbed halfway up her neck—she looked like something that might have stepped out of a sexy lingerie ad. That wasn't true, of course. Christina owned a coffee shop in downtown Sacramento, one that was quite popular and on the way to becoming a chain of coffee shops, if she played her cards right.

"Who is Buggy making out with?" Sandra repeated, stepping forward, completely ignoring everything else that was happening.

"Cooper, apparently," Andrew piped in, beaming with satisfaction so bright it was nearly blinding.

Sandra rounded on Buggy and started jumping up and down in her excitement, hands clapping together like a child. "I KNEW IT!"

"Sandra... please... so loud," Buggy winced, looking around at all the people turning their heads towards the sound of Sandra's shrieking.

"Sorry," Sandra said, dropping her voice to a breathy, almost inaudible whisper. She raised her hands in the air and shook them as if she was holding invisible pom-poms, "yay!"

Buggy grimaced at Cooper, but he was laughing, and her grimace quickly melted into a smile. She took the stool next to him again, and she soon felt his hand return to her lower back. She decided she rather liked it there.

"Well, now that these two have finally fulfilled the prediction that I made four minutes after meeting them both," Andrew said, holding up his hand as if to toast, although he lacked alcohol or even a glass to hold it. Cooper and Buggy chuckled, but held up their actual glasses in toast, his a rum and Coke, hers just a Coke. They all drank, or fake drank, then Linny rounded on Buggy once more.

"Okay, I'm going to be pestering you for details about this 'you and Cooper thing' for the next year and a half so—"

"The 'me and Cooper thing' literally just started three minutes ago," Buggy laughed. Linny waved her hand dismissively as Andrew and Sandra took turns hugging Buggy and snagged their own places at the bar.

"So first, you got to fill us in on where the hell you've been the past week and a half." Buggy and Sandra exchanged a look, and she felt Cooper's hand reach out and take hers. She gripped it tightly for support.

"Well... I've been spending time with my biological father."

"What now?" Andrew sputtered over his newly arrived drink as Linny blanched. Buggy proceeded to tell the story, or at least, bits and pieces of it. Okay, seventy percent of it was complete bullshit, but it had to be. None of them would believe the actual story. Not even Cooper. So, she rattled off half truths about spending time with her father at the pizza parlor, and him telling her all about her mother and giving her the last recording that she had sent her. She even gave the vague excuse of Styger having a medical condition that convinced her to stay with him until things were finalized. She explained away her eye, and everything else they had questions for. It sounded terribly false to her, but the rest of them seemed to buy it easily enough. Everyone... except for Sandra.

About halfway through the story she caught Sandra's eye. Her sister was watching her with a peculiar suspicious and questioning look. Buggy blinked at her, gave her the slightest of nods, trying to telepathically convey that she would explain the rest of the story, the *real* story, when they were home alone. To her surprise, Sandra gave a little nod in return, and dropped the subject, allowing her to finish her tall tale.

"Well, holy crap," Linny said, shaking her head. "No wonder you've been weird the past week."

"Sorry to leave you in the lurch like that though," Buggy grimaced. "You think Elwin will hold it against me?"

"Oh," Linny rolled her eyes. "Dr. Elwin absolutely adores you. Besides Sandra called him up and told him you were having medical family issues. You're also one of the best technicians around so he's basically just been sitting, fingers crossed, hoping you'll come back." Buggy let out a breath she didn't know she had been holding.

"Thank you for picking up my slack," Buggy said, reaching out and squeezing her hand.

"Any time!" Linny said, "But I am super glad you're back."

"We all are," Andrew said, and they all nodded in agreement.

Buggy looked at them all, all her friends, her family, and her soon to be family, all sitting around her as they chatted and exchanged stories. Exchanged memories. Some of them she was a part of, some of them she wasn't, but she enjoyed them all equally. And she realized, in that moment, as Andrew took a shot with Christina and Linny went arm and arm to the bathrooms with Sandra, and John Lennon began to sing "Happy Xmas (War is Over)" on the radio, that *this* was a memory of its own. This moment, here at The Lookout, with the ones she loved. This was one of those memories that she would hold on to for a long time. Sure, the future scared her. She had no idea what waited for her in that distant, unknowable fog. She didn't know if The Daughter would remain content in that happy memory or, after the re-birth, she would be awoken once again. What would happen when it all started over? Because it would start over. Buggy had contained Bennu—for this lifetime—but the curse was still in play. Buggy just bought herself control over *this* life. What would happen when this life, well, ended? Would Bennu remain in that happy memory? Or, after twenty-four years of the next reincarnation's life, would she be woken once more by her home burning around her. Would she once more try to take over? Escape?

And what would happen to Buggy when death slowed its carriage for her? What would happen to Buggy when it was time for her life to be exchanged for another? Would she be thrown into a darkness, just like Bennu had been, or would she find herself a happy memory? A memory like this one. *Or,* Buggy wondered, smiling at Cooper as he slid another diet Coke towards her, *would I be able to see Loretta again?*

So many questions that she couldn't even begin to answer. She had no way of knowing what would happen when her turn was over. This was utterly uncharted territory. All she knew was that it was her turn now. And she wasn't going to waste it. It was time to start opening those doors she had closed. Time to think about what she wanted to do with whatever strange life she had. A four-year college? Travel? Finally find that dream job? She didn't really know yet, but she had decided she could be open to the possibilities at least. Enough distancing. Enough passive participation. She was still terrified, and that nervous feeling bubbled unhindered in her belly and chest, and she hated it... but she kind of liked it, too. Because Bennu had been wrong. It did *not* mean Buggy was out of control. It meant she was *doing* something. Something that made her feel more than just being *numb*. More than just that empty void. And that, Buggy decided, was a good start.

"You two took a while," Andrew said, as Linny and Sandra finally pushed their way back through the crowd that had built up over the past forty or so minutes they had been at the bar.

"Long line!" Sandra said, huffing a little as she took the stool next to Christina, who ran a hand up and down her back.

"Yeah, and one of the bathrooms is still out of order!" Linny grumbled, leaning against the counter.

"Oh?" Buggy asked, innocently.

"Someone broke the sink a while back. They still haven't had time to fix it yet, I guess."

"Really?" Buggy asked, hoping the frown on her face looked as confused as she was trying to make it. Without thinking about it, she turned her palm, the one which sported a jagged scar, face down on the table and out of view. "Accident?"

"Doubt it. Looked like someone had taken a baseball bat to it or something," Linny shook her head.

"Weird," Buggy picked up her glass and took long drink of soda, but made no further inquiry. As the conversations started up again, Buggy felt a little tug on her hand. Cooper motioned for her to lean in, away from the rest of their chattering friends.

"Uh, here," he said unceremoniously, turning her hand in his and dropping something into her palm. "I brought you something." He had already turned towards the bartender, signaling for another drink, when Buggy lifted the little thing into the air, getting a better look. She squinted at it in the multicolored lights from behind the bar. It was a necklace. It had a thin, silver chain with a small, silver pendent in the shape of a detailed cassette tape. Tiny little blue stones glinted in the light, forming the letter "B" with the rest of her nickname "uggy" carved in loopy cursive behind it.

"What on Earth is this?" Buggy asked when he turned back around, a drink in his hand.

"A necklace," he said with a shrug.

"I can see that, smart ass," Buggy laughed. "But why? Where did you get it?"

"Oh, I found it in a pawn shop."

"A pawn shop?" Buggy asked, cocking her eyebrow.

"Yep," Cooper said, clearing his throat and taking a sip of his soda. "Dannielle and Brian were trying to get rid of some stuff that they didn't want to move into their new apartment, and while I was helping up out, I saw it at the checkout counter."

"At the checkout counter, you say?" Buggy smirked.

"Yep. On one of those little tree necklace holder, things." Cooper said, trying and failing to demonstrate such a stand with his hands. Buggy snorted.

"You're telling me," she said, swinging the little necklace through the air back and front in front of Cooper's eyes like some hypnotist's talisman. "Out of all the pawn shops you and your sister might have gone to, you just happened to choose the one that just *happened* to have a silver necklace, in the shape of a cassette tape, with the words 'Buggy' written on it?" Cooper widened his eyes and shrugged his shoulders, a mockery of innocence.

"Crazy, right?"

"Uh, hmm," Buggy nodded, holding back laughter, but just barely. "And why are you lying?"

"Well," Cooper started, blowing out a little puff of air, and shrugging again. "Because I thought, if I told you that I had gone to a jeweler a few weeks back and had it specially made, that you might 'Buggy out' about the whole thing."

"What do you mean 'Buggy out' about the whole thing?" Buggy frowned, necklace stopping its swing.

"You know," Cooper gestured in a circular motion with his free hand. "Feel there were too many feelings happening, over analyze the gesture, freak out, panic, and then bolt."

"Oh," Buggy thought, then shrugged. "That's fair."

"You like it?" he asked, looking a little nervous. Buggy smiled and closed her fingers around the little cassette tape. She held it to her chest, where the empty void no longer emanated darkness. All she felt was light. "I love it," she said.

"Hoped you might." Cooper beamed.

"You brought it with you."

"Yeah."

"So sure I would say 'yes' to this?" she asked.

Cooper shook his head vehemently. "Hell no. Not at all... but again, I was kinda hoping you might." He shot her one of those sideways smiles.

Buggy turned back to the necklace and unclipped the silver chain. "Here," Cooper said, reaching out and twisting her hair into a gentle cord in his hands so she could clip it around her neck without the latch catching. He let her hair down as the silver cassette came to rest, shining against her sweater.

"I'm glad you like it," Cooper said. "It sounded like a good idea at the time, but when I got it back, I was a worried you might find it... I don't know, cheese or tacky."

"Eh, maybe a little bit," Buggy shrugged looking away from the necklace and up at him, grinning. "But that's what makes it timeless, right?"

His grin widened, white teeth flashing. "Right." He leaned in. It didn't take long for Andrew, Linny, Sandra and Christina to notice them.

"Awah!" they all sang in unison. Both Cooper and Buggy flipped them off without breaking their kiss.

"You guys are just so darn cute," Andrew said, planting his elbows on the bar and his face in his hands, watching them like some sappy rom-com movie ending as the two finally broke apart. "You're so cute in fact," he started, a mischievous glint in his eye, "You could be the next Ross and—"

"Don't you *dare*!" Buggy snarled at him.

Everyone laughed, including Buggy.

It was a fantastic memory.

EPILOGUE
WAVERLY

The blond yawned and rubbed her eyes. She had been driving for a solid day and was worn out. She thought she might take a quick nap before hitting the road again but found herself unable to sleep. That happened a lot these days. Frankly, she was worried about falling sleep. Whenever she slipped into dreams, off into the darkness, she was always afraid she would never find her way back out. It was a ridiculous notion—she knew she would wake, but it was unnerving all the same. Despite how exhausted her body was, she was tired of sleeping. So, she occupied herself with her messages, hoping the sound of Susanna's poorly disguised pretense at caring would lull her to sleep. Waverly had called yesterday, left a message that the job was done. She had burned the girl to the ground and saved everyone. She had done what she had been born to do. Susanna had called back and left a warm, relieved message that dripped with insincere pride for her daughter. She had played it several times now, checking to see if that dulcet falsity could bore her to dream land. It had not worked. On to plan B.

She sat up and looked through the window at the night sky above. The moon was half hidden, but the light lost from the moon was made up by the spattering of stars across the billowing darkness. The blond crawled into the driver's seat of the stolen 1966 Charger, started up the engine, and headed back down the road to a hotel she had passed a short way back. There had also been a bar next door. She decided it was well past time for a little self-medication.

She made it back to the hotel, checked into a room, left the car in the hotel parking lot and was soon pushing through the bar door. It was a small place, quaint even. The lights were low, and the music was a soft mixture of classic rock and country. There were only ten or fifteen other people in there, most of whom gathered around a pool table which seemed to be sporting a rather hefty bet. A few guys looked around as she stepped in the door wearing her old blue jeans, thick black boots, and snug leather jacket. She made zero eye contact as she made her way to the bar. Eye contact led to conversation, and she was not here to socialize with strangers.

"ID," the bartender asked automatically. She fished it out of her pocket and placed it on the table with a little snap. The bartender picked it up, gave Waverly's face a little once over, before handing it back to her. "What do ya want?"

"Whiskey," she answered. The bartender looked at her a minute, as if about to suggest something a little more "girly" for her to drink, probably something with fruit slices and a pink umbrella poking from its lip.

"What kind?" he asked, instead.

"I do not care."

The bartender nodded and turned to fix her drink. She slipped her phone out of her pocket as she waited. She pressed replay on the messages and held the phone to her ear, trying to hear over the disappointed cry of pool players as someone missed a shot.

"Waverly, it's your mother. I got your message. Just wanted to say that I am so proud of you. I know it must have been hard. But you did it. I'm sure you need some time alone. Your mission... it was a lot to ask of anyone. But it was necessary... you did it. And I am so proud." Waverly's eyes rolled. *Lying bitch.* "Now on to more pressing matters. I assume you have the child with you. Bring it here and we will—" Halfway through the message, one player peeled himself from the pool table and sidled over to take the stool next to her.

"Talking to your boyfriend?" the man-child asked, not bothering with being subtle. Apparently, subtlety is overrated when you are several beers, and what smelled like at least two tequila shots, into an evening.

"No," she answered, eyes fixed on the bottles of alcohol lined up behind the bar.

"Who then?"

"Mother. A message."

"You two get along?"

A smile flickered across Waverly's lips. "Not really."

"But she called recently."

The blond just grunted in reply. The bitch wanted to meet up with her, huh? Ha. Well, that could be arranged. It had been a while. Another smile twitched across her face, like a spider scuttling across a counter. There, and then gone.

"No boyfriend then?" the stranger asked, drunk and jovial.

"Leave the girl alone, Tucker," the bartender said, stepping back into view and sliding the whiskey over to her.

"I'm not here to bug her!" Tucker insisted, words slurring a little. "I'm just sayin hi's all!"

"Looks like you've succeeded at both," the bartender answered. The blond looked at the bartender for the first time. He seemed to be in his thirties with a short, brown beard and light brown eyes. They held the type of gruffness that was merely skin deep. She could tell. It was all in the eyes. Always was. She glanced away when the bartender felt her watching, looking down to sip her drink instead.

The gruffness seemed to fool Tucker though because he shut up for a few minutes. Soon enough however, his drunken courage returned.

"Potent drink for a small girl," he said.

"It is really not," she answered flatly, downing the drink and motioning for another. The bartender quickly refilled her glass.

"Oh, tough little one, huh?"

She did not say a word, only watched the dim lights reflect off the bottles in rainbow shades. Her eyes traveled to the dirty plate a short way down the bar, discarded by the last visitor. A long-pronged fork rested innocently on its edge.

"Well, you know," Tucker said leaning in a little and resting a hand on Waverly's knee. "The tough girls are really th—"

"Get your hand off of me," she said.

"Huh?" Tucker sounded bemused, as if he did not realize he was touching her at all.

Waverly's face turned slowly to look into the man's watery, red-rimmed, blue eyes. Pale eyes. Ignorant eyes. Idiot eyes. As she turned, she got a face full of his breath. It was salty, sour, and thick enough to choke on.

Instantly she was back in that evil place. It was the evil that pressed in on you from all sides, suffocating, breaking. The air was humid, sticky, hot. Hot like fire. Hot like hell, but she was shivering like it was winter. She felt that fear, the desperation, the fight, the tearing sensation that reverberated through her throat like a scream. She screamed for help, screamed for salvation. Help did not come, and salvation did not listen. Then came the taste at the back of her tongue. A tangy sensation, and she knew what came next. The hands. The pain. Pain. Fear. Emptiness... and the enjoyment of it all. It was all in those eyes. Those eyes and their hands that had touched her. Touched her and hurt her. Hurt her and then left her to die. Left her to burn.

Waverly's piercing blue eyes looked into Tucker's foggy, bloodshot ones. She smiled.

"If you do not get your hand off of my leg," she said in a soft, sweet voice. "I am going to stab you through the eye with that fork."

Tucker seemed to take a second to process this information, leaning back slightly in his stool, one leg lifting off the ground. But he did not remove his hand.

"Well, there's no need to be rude," Tucker said after a pause, moving his thumb back and forth in a comforting motion that made Waverly's skin crawl. "I was just trying to—"

She made a move for the fork. Tucker yanked back, hands leaving both her and the bar all together. Which was exactly what she wanted. Without his hands stabilizing his already disoriented state, all she had to do was give his stool a good hard kick and guide his head downward with her empty hand. Tucker's face met the bar, and then his ass met the floor. Tucker howled and clutched his nose as blood streamed down his lips and chin.

When the bartender looked back around, Tucker was rolling in little circles while the blond finished her second drink and set the empty glass on the counter. The other players just watched Tucker wriggle and moan with a mixture of mild concern and amusement. The bartender took the empty glass.

"I thought I heard you say you were going to stab him with a fork?"

She looked down at Tucker, then back up at the bartender and shrugged.

"Changed my mind."

The bartender nodded, a minuscule smile quirking his lips.

"Want another?"

She considered, looking around the room. Fifteen. Sixteen including the bartender. Small... but every journey must start somewhere, right? Every success starts with one step. "Perhaps just one," Waverly lips pulled into a grin, "Make it a double. And... sorry about the mess."

"No trouble," the bartender said with a shrug, sliding her drink back to her. Tucker's friends had already helped him to his feet and walked him, wailing, towards the bathroom. "He honestly needs that sometimes. I've known him for years and... well, yeah."

She grunted and downed the drink in two quick gulps.

"Bad day?" the bartender asked, watching her, that small smile curling higher on his face.

"No, actually," Waverly's lips split into another wide grin, as her tongue slipped out to catch the few drops of runaway whiskey. "It is a good day. I am awake, and that makes it a good, *good* day." She pulled some bills from her pocket and dropped them on the table, not bothering to count them. In a few minutes, it wouldn't matter.

"Thanks," the bartender said, pleased with the pieces of paper. "Have a good evening, Miss...?"

She stopped by the exit, one hand pressing against the closed door. Waverly's head turned to peer over her shoulder at the bartender. "Oh, this evening is not quite over."

"No?" the bartender asked, still grinning. He thought she was flirting with him. *Oh, poor dear boy. Poor dear, stupid, stupid boy.*

"No, dear," she said, pressing her hand harder against the door, and she felt it grow hot under her palm. She flashed the bartender a wink. "We are just getting started." The metal door jamb and the doorknob immediately began to glow red. The smile on the bartender's face melted away and dropped in drips to the floor like the doorknob under Waverly's hand.

"What the hell?" the glass that he had been cleaning slipped from his fingers and shattered behind the bar, but he did not seem to notice or care. He was watching the door to his bar as it melted into itself, solidifying door to door frame, sealing closed. No way out.

"Is this the only door?" the blond asked, knowing by his expression that it was. "Well, that is a fire hazard. Naughty, naughty."

"What the hell did... how did you—" the bartender blubbered while the players around the pool table gave another shout as someone lost another game.

"Bennu," she said, cutting him off.

"What?" he asked, as she moved on silent feet to the edge of the bar and placed her hand flat against its polished wooden surface.

"My name," The Daughter smiled with Waverly's full lips. She flashed the cool blue eyes as if they were her own, their usual chilly nature overwhelmed by the manic glee of anticipation. "You asked my name. It is Bennu. My mother gave it to me. A long, long... *long* time ago. I haven't seen her in a while... but I really need to have a chat with her. And I think you can help with that."

"We have a phone," the bartender gestures dazedly toward a door leading to a back room, but his eyes were still on the door she had just seared shut.

Bennu laughed with Waverly's voice. "No, no dear. That will not work... but this might." She pressed both hands firmly against the wooden bar. It burst into flame under her fingers.

"Fuck!" The bartender grabbed the bucket of ice from behind the bar, usually meant for drinks, and dunked it over the flames. It did nothing. The fire only roared higher, reaching for the wooden ceiling. The players jerked around and started shouting. Two thirds of the men ran for the door, but found it sealed shut. The other third went to help the bartender put out the flames, but that worked even less. The bartender ran into the other room and grabbed a fire extinguisher, spraying the entire can empty against the flames, but they only grew hotter, climbed higher, unfazed by any attempts to tame it. They weren't any normal flame. They were *hers*. They had killed her, eaten her alive. She and they had become one and now they burned with the intensity of her anger, her rage, her despair, and her desires. They were *hers*. And they were ravenous.

She grabbed a stool, pulled it to the side of the room and took a seat. She smiled as she watched the ceiling catch, and the rainbow bottles of booze exploded behind the bar. The bar's occupants tugged helplessly at the door, or scrambled through the room like rats, ducking from flying shards of glass, desperately looking for another exit. They broke windows, trying to crawl out, but they were too narrow, too small for any of them to fit. A child maybe, but no grown man. They scattered desperately searching for a way out of the flames that would soon consume every inch of their flesh. She knew what that was like, poor dears. And she knew there was no escape.

"I am coming, mother." Bennu whispered. She would find it. She would find the city of moonlight and the woman who cursed her to this eternal cycle. The city... it *heard* only one thing, *cared* about only one thing, *came* to only one thing... blood. Sacrifice. And Bennu would provide, oh yes. This time it would hear her. She would *make* it hear her. She would call to it, call with the sound of their screams. *All* of their screams. As many as it took for it to hear. As many as it took for it to appear. For her to enter. For her to *end it*.

"It is time to end this dance." Bennu's words faded, unheard over the growing roar of flames and the yells and shrieks of the men about to die. The first of many. The first of thousands. The first of millions, if that is what it took to open a passage into the city. If that was what it took to end this hellish cycle and quiet the screaming gray voices inside her heart. If that was what it took to find peace. Final, blissful peace.

It was her right.
And this time, she would not fail.

About the Author

Lydia R. Outland graduated from California State University, Sacramento with a bachelor's degree in Philosophy. Because she struggled with significant dyslexia, it was not until high school that the endless universe of books opened up to her. Her dream is to open that world to another person, even just one other.

Lydia's debut novel *The Strangest Woman*, was published by Black Rose Writing in July of 2020.

Lydia is active in animal disaster rescue and lives in Amador County, California with her family and numerous animals.

Note from the Author

Word-of-mouth is crucial for any author to succeed. If you enjoyed *Ash and Gold*, please leave a review online—anywhere you are able. Even if it's just a sentence or two. It would make all the difference and would be very much appreciated.

Thanks!
Lydia R. Outland

We hope you enjoyed reading this title from:

Subscribe to our mailing list – *The Rosevine* – and receive **FREE** books, daily deals, and stay current with news about upcoming releases and our hottest authors.
Scan the QR code below to sign up.

Already a subscriber? Please accept a sincere thank you for being a fan of Black Rose Writing authors.

www.ingramcontent.com/pod-product-compliance
Lightning Source LLC
Chambersburg PA
CBHW010725100726
47899CB00009B/2930